UNMASKED

EM Kaplan

Cover design by Elizabeth Snively

Copyright © 2014 EM Kaplan

All rights reserved.

ISBN-10: 1499593945
ISBN-13: 978-1499593945

For Jeremy

CONTENTS

	Acknowledgments	i
Part 1	Keep	3
Part 2	Return	61
Part 3	Mask	115
Part 4	Reveal	163
Part 5	Oppose	219
Part 6	Ascend	267
Part 7	Unmask	323

MANY THANKS TO

Amy Bland
Amy Bush
Esther Kaplan
John Kolman
Elizabeth Snively
Eric Streem
Derrick Wise

Part 1

Keep

CHAPTER 1

The beast grabbed Mel with a gray-skinned hand and dragged her across the rutted dirt road. He wrenched her away from her wooden carriage, from those who might have saved her, the coarse dirt and stones shredding the soles of her feet. She fought him, scratching the thick arm around her waist and the inhumanly strong fingers clamping her ribs like a vise. His other hand covered her mouth, muffling her screams. Her attacker—no kind of creature she had ever encountered before—lumbered toward the trees where she knew they'd be swallowed up from sight with no chance for rescue.

She tried to push strength to her arms, to redirect it into her shoulders so she could twist and strike him in his neck or groin, but he had immobilized her body and her mind. She had none of her Mask-trained abilities left. A strange mental cloudiness crippled her, destroying her ability to focus; it rendered her dizzy and nauseated. She was at half of her strength, if that. He crushed her against his dirt-caked side, dragging her off the road into the trees.

You will not die this way. You will find a way out of this mess. Think.

She forced herself to calm down. She was a scholar despite her current appearance—the filmy white dress, the matching silk ribbon now torn from her hair, the useless paper-thin shoes that had fallen off. She needed to tamp down the fright, but she was not used to dealing with her emotions. She needed to fight through the foreign haziness of her thoughts and try to observe him, to gather information, and to figure out a solution to this problem.

The staccato gasps of air she could take through her nose weren't enough to identify him by scent. She could hardly breathe. She knew he smelled like the worst kind of offal only from the first moments of the attack—his powerful odor had filled her nose in the seconds before he pulled her from the carriage, but now she couldn't smell anything.

She focused instead on what little she could see. The hand covering the lower half of her face was larger than a man's. He wasn't human? His fingers were gray, caked with brown dirt, and locked together, effectively forming a muzzle. She couldn't bite him, though she tried to. One side of her face and an ear were smashed against his chest, so she listened to his breathing. His breathing was uneven and rasping with obstruction, but telling of an enormous capacity under his ribs. He was very large; the entire length of her body traversed his ribs and dangled just a hand or two above the ground. She was a mere doll in his grip, small prey easily overcome.

She paid attention to his gait, which was uneven, possibly from a deformity or injury. He wore a coarse tunic and breeches made from animal skins and a thick belt that secured a large, wooden-handled tool or weapon, an axe maybe. While the clothes were rough, they seemed expertly made. Under her questing fingertips, the stitching on the band of leather around his wrist was fine and well-done. He lurched unevenly down a slippery incline, jarring her limbs, momentarily knocking the breath out of her.

She steadied her rapid breathing but could not control the shakiness of her inhalations. Her eyes burned as a fever overtook her, and her head swam. She struggled to rein in her thoughts. Whatever he was, he had rendered her a normal person, just like any other helpless human. Where were her usual abilities? Gone. She felt as if she had been blindfolded, gagged, and then pitched into a whirlwind.

What kind of creature is he? Think, think, think . . . This is not working. If I could remember any prayers, I would say them now.

He was not natural, she suddenly thought, her widening eyes barely registering the blur of passing blue-hued leaves—the very same leaves that had been the focus of her study these past months at the Keep. A branch whipped her forehead, and she slammed her lids down trying to retreat into the comfort of darkness. Her mind was battering down from fear, seeking to huddle far inside herself to escape from the horror of her circumstances. She fought against it, forcing herself to sift through the details that she could gather to try to deduce what he was.

But what if he were a troll? What if he were not from the realm of scientific fact and concrete evidence, but a bad dream drudged up from childhood? Her mother used to tell her to clean her teeth well or the trolls would come down from the mountains and eat her up. Had she scrubbed her teeth this morning?

This will not be my last thought. If I am going to die, I will die calm and observant. I will die a Mask. But preferably, I will not die at all.

How far had they run? And how fast? He covered a lot of ground very quickly, maybe half again as much as she would have at a full running pace for her if she had proper shoes. The forest was darker here. Thorns and branches whipped her skin, leaving dotted lines of blood across her face and arms. He was unaffected, like a maddened bull crashing through fence after fence, though he had a far thicker hide than a bull. She might be broken by the time they arrived wherever they were going, and she thought maybe that would be best.

Go on. Continue. Analyze the situation.

She forced her mind to categorize the facts and process the information, as she had been trained to do her entire life. He was not a human, but he was a male. Why would a male attack her? She was young and dressed enticingly, virginally, purely. To stay at the Keep, she had to wear their garments instead of her sturdy boots and leather leggings. She looked like a normal, young human woman. The creature wore man's garments, although larger sized. He was a male, so perhaps he intended to violate her. Her unchecked pulse sped again with a burst of fresh terror. She would try to run at first opportunity. But what if he had captured her for another reason altogether? Her mind sought out other avenues and stumbled on the terrible possibility that he might have taken her *to eat her.*

Oh God, I'm going to die.

She allowed herself a measure of self-pity. She wished she could see her mother one more time. She hadn't seen her father in years. He was away on an assignment, but surely he'd hear of her death and feel loss over what she might have been. Both of her parents had high hopes for her. They wanted her to be a Mask of renowned talent—one who would be celebrated in the lengthy history of Masks. They hoped that she would solve crises, bring peace where there was strife, and gather knowledge where there were gaps in their vast library. Her people had always wanted her to be a noteworthy mediator and a scholar, the two most revered occupations of their kind. They had wanted her to go on to great accomplishments, not to have her flesh ripped from her bones by the teeth of this creature.

Her neck and spine ached as her adrenaline spent itself. Her captor's uneven stride caused her head to bang against his chest. Her rapid breaths finally evened out, but now exhaustion threatened to overcome her. Her eyelids drooped as she, at last, let herself retreat and fade into unconsciousness.

A series of crashes came down through the forest canopy. Three crashes descending, getting closer, growing louder. Then Mel felt, more than heard, a dull thud that jolted through her attacker's body from his head down. Her eyes snapped open. Her captor paused and wobbled on his feet. He stood still for a breath or two, and then fell to his knees. When his grip on her loosened, she jumped away from him. He dropped, stunned, and sprawled on the forest floor. A stone, bigger than a normal man's head, rolled away from the creature and stopped against a fallen tree. Without bothering to look where the rock had come from, Mel found her footing and pushed off the ground in a dead sprint. As she ran through the underbrush, her breathing cleared a little. Then, her captor's horrible odor flooded back into her nose making her shudder and try to blow the smell out, chuffing like a horse.

She ran blindly with only the vaguest sense of where the carriage was. The ground cut her feet, and branches caught and tore at the hem of her dress. She breathed deeply. Only sweet, blessed luck had saved her from being pinned under his body when he fell. Red dripped into her eye. Somehow, she had hit her head when he fell, maybe on his weapon. Her bare feet bled, too, leaving a blood trail on the ground and on leaves that brushed her. If the creature had a good sense of smell, he would find her again easily. He'd be back on his feet soon, if his head was as thick as his hide. Without slowing her pace, she focused on her feet, *pushing* into them, and thickened the soles, bringing the small fissures together so that the bleeding stopped. Putting distance between herself and the creature made it easier for her to concentrate. Maybe her handicap was caused by his hideous odor. A little of the malaise cleared from her head.

A second later she heard thrashing from the underbrush behind her. Her heart pounded so forcefully she was sure she'd be able to see it beating through the bodice of her dress if she could stop to look. How had the beast caught up with her so quickly? He was moving faster than she was. It had to be him; she could smell him now. As he got within range, she became disoriented and muddled again. It irritated her to the point of anger, something she rarely felt. Emotions, on the whole, were frowned on and to be avoided for her kind.

At first, she was certain the road was ahead of her to the south. With her acute hearing, she had been able to pick out the cacophony of her friends' voices as they discovered she was missing from their wooden day carriage. Three hundred paces west a doe had been poised to flee, and from the east came an unusual and intriguing savory spice traveling on the wind, a strange air current bringing it over her head. The very next minute, her senses spun and her eyes blurred. The ground rippled under her feet in a confusion of swirling leaves. Her pace slowed as her vision became foggy, and the headache came hammering back. She hesitated for a second, crouching behind a tree, her dress ruched up around her knees, as she blinked and tried to regain her sense of direction. A breath later, she was tackled from the side and sent sprawling down the slope, rolling, entangled with a new person altogether.

She gasped for air as she tried to determine whether the new assailant was an evil worse than the first. He was a man, not a creature. He was much broader and taller than she was, yet a human man, without a doubt. He was dressed in brown patterned clothes meant for concealment in the brush, but clearly out of place in this strange blue forest. They rolled to a stop covered in leaves, she on her back, and he lying next to her on his side, his heavily muscled arm draped over her as he scanned the forest for signs of the other creature. The man's chin was above her face, and she realized that the strange savory smell was coming from him.

Delicious.

The aroma made her mouth water with something shockingly close to hunger. She blinked and shook her head to clear it. She was truly out of her mind. She had completely lost control of her senses. She was close enough to see the pulse racing under his deeply browned skin. The warm, heady smell of him rose up from his shirt with every gulping breath he took. The weight of his arm across her stomach did peculiar things to the rhythm of her heart. Though she felt safe momentarily, she was far from calm.

He felt her move and looked down, putting a finger to his

mouth. *Quiet.* His chin shot back up, and she froze as her former captor crashed through the woods close by them, passing them, on to another scent. They stayed frozen until the noise of his footsteps faded in the distance.

The underside of his chin had a thin white scar, like one he might have gotten from a tumble as a child. The white line ran through the golden brown stubble across his face. His jaw was broad and angular, and his skin well-weathered from his forehead down his neck inside the collar of his shirt, which gaped open as he leaned over her. Her nose was nearly tucked into the indentation at the base of his neck, and her clearing sense of smell came back in a rush that was full of him, so intense that when she opened her mouth, it came through her lips and onto her tongue, lingering in the back of her throat as if she could swallow it.

She was a half-breath from pressing her mouth against his skin and licking the hollow in his neck when he lifted his head. As he scanned the woods, he turned his head, and she saw the soft skin behind his ear under his hairline. Tiny flecks of dark forest loam dotted the side of his cheek. From his look, his clothes, and his scent, he was most likely an outdoorsman. What was that scent? After the sensory deprivation the other creature had caused her, she was overwhelmed with the sensation this man caused. She didn't realize she'd taken a large, gasping inhalation until he looked down at her again. His eyes were the color of agamite, the dark green stone ribboned with brown and gold. His hair was light brown with yellow streaks caused by the sun. He couldn't have been more than twenty-five years old, but she wasn't certain, confused by the laughing lines at the corners of his eyes. And that scent.

Oh, my God. Now, she offered a prayer.

She must have made another sound as she stared into his green eyes because they widened slightly. His mouth parted a little and his breath feathered across her face. She blinked slowly, feeling the blood rush around her body, toward her head, her toes, and the part of her that would have readily accepted him at that very moment. She shivered and lost control of herself.

Violent. There wasn't any other way to describe her reaction. She launched herself at him, wrapped her arms around his neck, twined her fingers in his hair, and pressed her mouth against his. Matching her lips to his. Tasting him. A smothered sound of surprise came from his throat as they rolled onto his back, and she kissed him harder, feeling the stubble of his cheek against hers. Her long hair, bedraggled and undone from its ribbon, made a curtain around their faces as she inhaled his scent, pushing herself into him. She couldn't get close enough. She wanted to rip his clothes, to feel and see all of him, but she couldn't let go of him long enough to move her hands elsewhere.

Oh, the taste of him.

He pulled back slightly, his lips parted, and she pressed into him, slipping the tip of her tongue into his larger mouth, seeking his warmth and wetness. Her skin grew sensitive. Her thin dress chafed her as she moved against him. Her knees fell to either side of his legs. Uncontrollably, she began to glow.

Rampant, golden joy. Overwhelming sensation of all kinds, all at once. A release of all that she sought to contain every moment, every day of her adult life. Every fact, every minute detail of data that she stored contained a certain amount of energy. And now it was exploding from her, radiating from her skin, her hair, eyes, lips, from her pores.

His eyes shot open, and he broke away from her with a fierce push, shoving himself back against a tree. He scrambled to sit up. His hands grasped at the branches alongside him. His boots pushed the leaves between them as he kicked himself backward away from her.

Stunned at first, her eyes widened. Then she quickly dimmed to her normal color, her gilded shine fading, though her cheeks and mouth were swollen and raw from his beard stubble and the violence of the kiss—*her kiss*, not his. They were both out of breath, him against a tree, her on her knees, mortification quickly taking over. She hugged her hands to her chest. Her fingers still tingled from the feel of his hair and the skin of his neck. She smelled him all over her face, her skin, and her mouth.

"What the hell manner of creature are you?" he managed to say, his voice deep and hoarse, his chest heaving. His expression was obscured by shadow.

She looked down at her hands and her muddied, torn dress. Her heart pounded. She couldn't steady herself, never mind even look at him. Her loss of control over her senses was horrifying and now humiliating; he scrambled farther away from her. It was one thing for loss of control to happen to a child, but she was a Mask among outsiders. She was absolutely a danger to the sanctity of her people, the time-honored tradition of anonymity and impartiality. Masks did not entangle themselves with outsiders; they studied them. Masks were not overcome with irrational passions or fits of emotion of any kind. She'd never experienced anything like it, not even when she was a child having a tantrum. Control, study, and control. Those were her constant companions. Not recklessness and . . . and worse, sitting just a few feet from him hardly lessened her desire to go at him again.

"I'm just a Cillary girl," she mumbled, a shot of panic suddenly going through her. She sprang to her feet, took a last hesitant step backward, and sprinted away through the trees toward the road.

CHAPTER 2

Just one day earlier, Mel had been playing a game of flutterby on the lawn under the leafy blue trees at Cillary Keep, the centuries-old stone turrets standing tall and proud above them. At one time, scribes had lauded the natural phenomenon of the "golden trees at Cillary," but now the leaves were blue. Azure as water, as the sky, as nightfall—and no one knew why. Across the flutterby net, the tall woman called Rav served up the fly. The small netted ball left Rav's long brown fingers and traveled straight up an arm's length over her head. It hung mid-air for a heartbeat, maybe two, and then began to fall toward the ground. Rav swung her racket and tapped the fly into an arc toward Mel. A small part of Mel's mind patiently watched the fly.

Mel was playing a mental game to amuse herself. The other women at the Keep worried constantly about their beauty, their mastery of courtly manners, and their individual futures—a mundane occupation bred by their present and unremitting leisure. In other words, they had nothing better to do. Set apart as she was by her training and breeding as a Mask, Mel only partly focused on the immediate activities at hand. She was, after all, required to socialize and to set aside her collecting of leaf specimens for the moment. The rest of her mind flexed in mental gymnastics: constant, invisible acrobatics, a juggling of sensations and a gathering of minutiae to be sorted and stored away for later, for whatever future Mask mediation might require it.

Her mind exercises weren't magic, just genetics and highly developed skill. Most Masks could make themselves marginally stronger through focused concentration. Some could help heal themselves and others, though it was mostly through a careful application of herbs and observation of the body's symptoms. Prognostication? Foretelling the future was merely the result of carefully studying the records of the past. The most skilled "seers" among the Masks were simply experts at spotting patterns in history. Stories for children told of Masks who could change their appearances entirely, but that was ridiculous. Fantastical. And Mel didn't believe in magic.

The irony of her present situation, however, was not lost on her. She was more of a Mask here than she was among her own kind. At home, she was fidgety, nervous, and, as she had been told numerous times, a general nuisance to others. The fact that she had been sent away from home weighed on her heavily; she needed to do well on this remedial assignment.

She watched her new friend—she saw the slight hesitation in Rav's swing and the flicker of her eye to the figures in the walkway above them. She noted how Rav's pulse quickened at her throat and how she took a shorter inhalation of breath than normal during her flutterby service. Mel saw increased heat come from the skin on Rav's wrists and on the slender brown forearms emerging from her white eyelet sleeves. Rav's eyes dilated, the pupils nearly lost in the inky darkness surrounding them.

Mel, with her eyes on the game but her focus on the periphery, searched through the shaded figures above them. The Keep ladies lingered in the walkway above. Some were instructors in etiquette and courtly behavior—the head of the Keep, Lady Skance, for instance, who was wearing her customary black plumed hair ornament. Young men were up there also, ostensibly as messengers, but actually scanning the field for potential wives. Such activity was hardly a secret, but was never overtly acknowledged.

Mel had to force herself to distinguish among the young men, just as she had found it a challenge at first to separate the women into distinct persons on her arrival at the Keep. At the beginning of the season, she had developed memory keeps to remember their names until she'd gotten every detail of each person down. Now she was matching women to their potential mates because, despite being an outsider, she had gotten caught up in their contests. This was how she passed the time and amused herself.

The young women here at the Keep represented thirty-two regions all across the country. Although no one had come from the frozen north—no one ever came from that sparsely-populated, harsh region. Being selected for the Keep was an honor that no one ever turned down. Rav—Ravita, actually—from the southern state, was fiercely competitive in all things, but placid on the surface. Pei, tall, sleek, and golden, from the east, had a habit of touching her thumbnail to her smallest finger of the same hand when she was uncertain. Liz, from teeming Tooran city, never thought a thing without saying it and had learned many difficult lessons this summer.

Women from both near and far away assembled here at this court. They were all shuffled together and reduced to monosyllabic, nondescript nicknames. Rav. Pei. Liz. And, of course, Mel.

The flock of thirty-two young women in their white cotton afternoon dresses decorated the rolling green lawn, lounging in chairs, reading, strolling, Mel among them. All thirty-two behaved casually on the surface, but were acutely aware of the observers above them. Mel listened to the asynchronous quickening of thirty-one heart rhythms. Snippets of conversation drifted toward her.

"I like him, but he has a strange laugh . . . One more week . . . Mastered the steps . . . I think she's pretty, but not very bright . . . "

The final assembly of the session would be at the end of the week. Part promenade, part ball. Mel suppressed the urge to cringe. The Art of Movement had been one of their courses during the season, along with other household arts such as attending to accounts, and supervising the work of others—encouraging them without appearing to shame them. Useful skills for women who intended to rule great households or states. The women were talking about each other. They rarely talked about her. She strove to be average. Not unpleasant, but not memorable.

From reading historical accounts prior to her arrival, Mel had learned that for hundreds of years, Cillary Keep had stood high on the hills in the largely uninhabited northwest state. Nestled in the rocks above the Cillary Forest, it had been a place of respite for one of the first rulers of the realm before falling into disrepair for nearly half a century. Largely forgotten while the rest of the world developed bustling cities and thriving ports and other modernizations, such as the powering of machines by steam and compressed agamite, Cillary Keep lay in ruins until a singularly-minded wealthy family depleted their entire fortune refurbishing it nearly three centuries earlier. Since that time, it had served, among other purposes, as a religious encampment, an exile for diseased patrons of brothels, and now, finally, a retreat for young, privileged women.

Mel's people, the Masks, had two interests in the Keep. First, she was supposed to observe first-hand some of the mannerisms and motivations of the representatives there. In no other place in the world would she have the opportunity to interact with so many cultures, and here at the Keep they were gathered together all in one place. No other person in Mel's settlement met the age and gender requirement to attend the vernal gathering—the Mask settlement rarely produced children. And although the compulsory activities seemed frivolous to Mel, she could not deny the number of observations she had made so far.

Foremost, however, Mel had been dispatched to the Keep because of the matter of the leaves. The normally golden-leaved forest surrounding the Keep had, over the course of the last few decades, been turning slowly blue. The earliest mention of this phenomenon that the Masks had been able to corroborate had been in a personal letter from a surprisingly poetic local shopkeeper some forty years ago to his sister in Port Navio. In the letter, he mentioned observing a "distinct indigo sheen to the woods" one evening as the sun struck the top of the forest canopy that reminded him of their coastal childhood and subsequent upbringing.

In her trunk in the chilly dormitory of the Keep, Mel had carefully collected and pressed leaf specimens of all types. She had a notebook of fastidiously made drawings and careful observations. At summer's end, she would distribute her findings when she returned to the settlement. Although it was not her place to draw conclusions about her observations, she felt well-equipped to present her research.

For now, on the lawn of the Keep by the flutterby courts, Mel's mind worked at pushing back the oddity of her surroundings. Although her home was not more than an hour away by carriage, the lands surrounding the Keep felt very foreign to her. The blue-veined bark and leaves distracted her. Their strangeness was pervasive, invading her senses, and she had to exert herself to remember that they were now normal here. The leaves cast a cool light over everything, the grass, the stone walls of the keep, the fluttering white dresses of the women displayed across the yard. The other young women did not seem troubled by them. Sometimes she cursed her own sensitivity and forgot it was a privilege to be born this way. Or so she had been told on numerous occasions.

Mel sought out the voices of her instructors above. They were too soft for even her to hear, but she felt their momentary attention on her as they, too, surveyed the women and judged their qualities and their potential. Instinctively, Mel dulled the shine on her hair. She turned slightly from direct sun and used the shadow to turn her hair to a grayish brown. To an observer, even Mel's white dress took a grayish cast. Eyes passed from her to others, and she relaxed her manipulation somewhat. She merely blended.

"Cover!" shouted Mel's flutterby partner. No, it was not a shout. The voice was more melodic and much softer.

"Return," Mel said, tapping the fly back over the net to Rav.

Rav returned the fly skillfully, Mel's partner let it drop to the ground, and the game was quickly lost. The women returned their bats and fly to the storage casement, and Rav took Mel's arm for a walk around the garden. To Mel's eye alone, the dark woman's face was flushed with pleasure at her victory.

"Well, Mel," she said, "The season's almost over. Just a week left." Mel nodded. Rav was not expecting an answer. She had several younger sisters at home and was not used to the luxury of soliloquizing, so she enjoyed it when she was with Mel. "I am growing tired of all these trees. And the blue. It makes me feel cold although I am not. It gets through my skin. At home, I'm used to red, orange, and brown—brilliant yellow of the hot, hot sky. No trees like this." Rav fingered a silvery blue leaf as they made their way into the walled garden where there was a tall hedge maze.

The far south where Rav was from was mostly high plateaus made of red dirt. In a way, Rav herself smelled like heat and sand, a dusty mix of dry cleanliness that Mel could detect even after a whole season at the Keep. The people in Rav's homeland raised a highly valued breed of lean meat herd animals. They mined gemstones. They warred with each other without end. Women could be wives or warriors, or both. Their people didn't have the choice of confining their women to any one occupation, and after generations of such freedom, would not have been able to confine them. Mel had seen pictures of the southern lands in books in the massive Mask archives in her home. She'd read some of the older writings of Rav's people, the stories from their oral traditions transcribed and collected by Masks over generations.

Mel liked Rav very much. The tall woman had a cap of tight black curls and a wide, though seldom-shown, smile. Rav spoke her mind and seemed to sense that Mel was not a threat to her. The other women were Rav's competitors.

Very few people anywhere required women to become wives, but as the saying went, "No woman ever went to Cillary Keep who wasn't looking for a husband." Except Mel. The Cillary Keep season was famous for assembling beautiful and ambitious young women. Most of the women were in their early twenties. Mel was twenty-five, but her smooth face and other appearance-shifting abilities allowed her to pass among them. She stood five feet and eight inches tall, the average height of both men and women of her kind, which allowed them to be nearly indistinguishable from each other when cloaked. She had other interests than catching a spouse, but that hadn't prevented her from enjoying herself at the Keep.

Mel's people, the Masks, were public servants, born and bred arbiters, and the source of simultaneous awe and fear. Masks rarely married, although some partnered to raise offspring. Children like Mel were brought up in an atmosphere of intense scholarship. They made it their mission to study the people and customs of any place known, anywhere. Masks lived in seclusion. A message arrived by roundabout means, passed from one hand to another, when a Mask was required for arbitration, or a *task*. A Mask could be requested to mediate a small-scale problem, such as a wealthy family's feud or divorcing nobility, or for a larger one, such as a land dispute or war. And although they lived apart in their own settlement, no one ever put much effort in trying to find them. Their hypersensitivity to others' thoughts, feelings, and motivations generally made people uncomfortable. When they traveled on tasks, their full cloaks, covered faces, and official medallions granted them safe passage in their duties.

Mel's full name was Ley'Amelan, the prefix *Ley* meaning "of the mask" in the old language of her people. The second half of her name signified a type of wild forest rose that smelled like cinnamon. It embarrassed her. She called herself Mel, for short, even at home. The rose was a pink and orange color that matched its aroma and obstinately grew at the base of trees where very little sunlight reached it. Her mother insisted it suited.

"What do you miss about your home?" Rav suddenly asked her.

"A decent pair of shoes," said Mel, deflecting the question. Rav was her first real friend outside of the Mask community. Most people feared Masks, so Mel preferred to let Rav think she was like any other woman at the Keep. While Mel clearly didn't fit in here, she didn't exactly fit at home either, so she was enjoying this new friendship while it lasted.

"These clothes are very confining," agreed Rav. In their first night in the dormitory, Rav's simple, flimsy undergarments and nightclothes had shocked the other women. They whispered uncharitably about the poverty of Rav's homeland, but Rav was proud and reminded them of the simple fact that it was much hotter there. Mel had stood apart, inwardly amused.

"But always, you joke," Rav chastised.

"Joke? It's no joke. These are ridiculous things," Mel said. She stuck out her foot for emphasis. The thin cotton slippers, meant to be worn for one day only and then disposed of, were stained with grass and nearly worn through after one afternoon of flutterby. And the formal shoes were worse, tall platforms on which they were required to balance and yet move with grace. Walking took concentration, and dancing? . . . Nearly impossible.

"Me, I miss the sky," Rav said, gesturing upward dismissively at the bluish leaves with her lean brown arm. "The great big, orange sky in the morning. I wake up, lift the door to my *ya'tuvah*, and walk right out into the open under the sun." Rav said it as if it were a simple stepping out of a tent on an overnight campout, but Mel knew the elaborate shelters could house as many as three hundred people, especially for a prominent family like Rav's. They might have begun as nomadic tribes, but as their wealth increased over time, so had their possessions and everyday conveniences.

"Isn't this enough sky for you?" Mel said mildly.

Rav rolled her dark eyes, the whites standing out starkly against her dark skin. "A sky isn't a thing over you like a roof." She searched for words. "A sky is like the inside of your mind. It should never be too low." Her hands gestured expansively, long brown fingers and smooth skin stretching wide.

"Well, you'll be home soon," Mel said, trying to lighten the mood, trying to retreat ever so slightly from the ebb and flow of interaction. Of all the people at the Keep, she was most at ease with Rav. Now, Mel was thinking about her own home, a small stone cottage also in a forest like here, but green and warm, with the clearing near her house where she could run from one side to the other at a full sprint in fifteen minutes of full sunshine. Mel's kind didn't need to run, but it was one of her greater pleasures. The flex of muscles, the impact of feet on dirt, the rush of blood under her skin. She loved it. If a Mask could be said to love anything.

The two reached an opening in the hedge maze where there were benches and a vine-covered arbor. Mel had caught and held in her hand the blue leaf that Rav picked walking into the maze. While the leaf was outwardly blue, its veins were, in fact, a dark puce color, the purplish-brown of blood, almost. Life, moisture, and air still circulated through the veins as she held it in her hand.

"So which one is it?" Mel asked her friend. She arched an eyebrow up at the walkway behind them and the observing young men. "Rally, I'd bet. He's quite interesting, isn't he?"

Rav's teeth flashed in a wide smile. "I can't hide anything from you, can I? He's got a lot of qualities that I . . . admire."

"Lean. Good teeth. Fine stock," Mel goaded playfully, dropping the leaf. She watched it twirl its way to the ground. She walked a few steps to better catch the scent of a fruit blossom in the breeze. The fruit arbor was on the other side of the Keep, but the air currents swirled clockwise from the west and into the hedge maze. Outside the maze, Mel could feel the boredom settle Rally's pulse on the upper walkway. He'd been watching the entrance to the hedge long after she and Rav had disappeared from sight. She was tempted to tell Rav the feeling was mutual, that Rally returned Rav's interest, but it wasn't her place to intervene regardless of their friendship, even as a gift.

Rav smiled again. "All this waiting around. This fine-tuning of the manners. I understand its purpose, especially if I want my family to get along in the world. Things change. Herds die out." She shrugged her shoulders, dark brown against the white dress. "But it's very indirect. It makes me impatient."

"You'd rather buy your bull at the market and go home." Rav's pulse quickened somewhat, and Mel laughed because she'd finally been able to embarrass her friend.

"You yourself have not made a selection? No one pleases you, Mel?"

Mel shrugged. "There are plenty of pleasing ones." And there were. She'd spent many afternoons with some of them, always arranged in strategic groups with other women. She loved observing them. Who made the other flush with pleasure or trip over her words? She was entirely entertained by it, but felt very little compulsion to participate other than to *appear* to participate, to hide her true disinterest, to blend in.

"But not one for you?" Rav looked puzzled. The slight narrowing in the corner of Rav's eye told Mel she was treading on fragile ground with her friend. With some regret, Mel retreated from the truth and smiled.

"I do like the tall one." She randomly settled on a young man who matched her height and coloring, dark brown hair and fair skin. She'd already marked several times how tall, golden Pei looked at this man.

And instantly, Rav relaxed and nodded. "Then I will see you dance with him on the final night."

Mel arranged her face to show complicit pleasure, thereby closing the matter. Though, in the end, it was uncomfortable to be duplicitous with a friend.

"Meanwhile," Rav continued, "we'll keep ourselves very busy until we are released into the world again. We'll take a carriage to town. I need to buy gifts for my little sisters or they will be very angry with me. I've been away from them for months. For the first time in their lives, they haven't had me there."

"I'm sure you left a large gaping hole in their lives."

"Yes. Very vast," Rav agreed.

"As big as the sky."

"Without me, they've probably had no discipline. No order. So, I'd better bribe them with good enough gifts into respecting me again. Will it suit you to go with me?"

"Certainly. I'd be glad to go," Mel said. "Should we gather a small group together, perhaps include Rally?" Under her dark skin, Rav blushed again and Mel laughed.

CHAPTER 3

At the appointed hour the next day, the intimate group gathered at the horse-drawn carriage that would take them into the sleepy local town, which was nestled in the forest further down the hill. Rav and Mel joined Liz and two young men, Rally and Jack. Rally was the tall, broad-shouldered one in whom Rav had expressed interest the previous day. Jack, a freckled young man, perpetually cheerful and pleasant to be around, had arranged for the carriage, which drew up to them at the front gates of the Keep.

Liz, always talkative, said, "I don't think you have heard the news, so I'll tell you. The dance is going to be a pageant." Usually, she was fun-loving and full of energy, but today seemed to be one of the days when she was slightly anxious and therefore more assertive and abrasive, more likely to offend others. Her cheeks were flushed. Her dark, curly hair looked moist in the humidity. She had a way of flashing her eyes from one side to the other, an artifice practiced so long that she now did it unconsciously.

Mel could see that Rav was unfamiliar with the term, but Liz was already explaining. "Costumes. It's going to be a costumed dance, like a masquerade. The girls are already crowding into the sewing room, looking at fabrics and digging through the feathers and whatnot. Beads. Fringe. I don't know what in the world I might be." She climbed up into the carriage and arranged herself opposite Rav and Mel so that she'd have the opportunity of sitting close to at least one, if not both, young men. She was placing herself at an advantage—another Cillary lesson learned. Jack obliged by lowering himself next to Liz. Rally sat between Rav and the window, forcing Mel to press against the window on the other side of the bench. He gave her an apologetic smile and shut the door, securing the handle with a firm twist. Then they were off.

Liz feigned exasperation, gesturing too broadly in the small space of the carriage. She had pretty hands, smooth and plump. Mel doubted either of the young men noticed her hands. The effort was lost on them. They watched her mouth, her animated eyes, and flicked their eyes at her bust line, even Rally, who was not interested. A whole season of training, strictly attended to, when really, the simplest and oldest attractions still held true between the sexes. Liz was saying, "What do you think? It's such a dilemma to choose a costume. I just don't know what I'm going to do. I've been thinking about it for hours. Maybe I'll just go as a Mask."

Mel's eyebrow shot up in astonishment, and then she wondered at her own unchecked reaction. The scent of the bodies all together in the warm carriage was very strong, almost stifling, and might have accounted for her lapse of control. Because it was a warm day, none of them wore wraps or jackets. Mel was acutely aware of Rav's and Rally's arms touching. The heat between their skin shimmered to Mel, though the two of them were studiously not looking at each other. She was aware of each half-thwarted movement of their fingertips toward each other.

She reached beside her and began to crank the glass window down. She rolled it all the way down so she could rest her elbow on the sill. The dappled blue light strobed down through the trees onto her lap. The wheels of the carriage scraped noisily along the worn road through the woods. Her eyes stung. The light seemed too bright, and she hoped she would recover as soon as they reached the little village.

Jack laughed, his hand catching the sill of the carriage window as they were jostled. "A Mask? Then no one will even be able to tell whether you're a male or female. That big heavy robe scratching you like a punishment. Cloak over your head. Face covered. What good is that? The whole purpose of the dance is to show yourself off. It's your last night at the Keep. Better to go as a *farharini* dancer. Two diaphanous scarves and you're done." He waggled his eyebrows salaciously. Liz turned pink. Mel doubted she would have blushed before training at the Keep.

When Liz first arrived, she'd regaled them with tales of her exploits in the large city that she was from. Nothing serious, just risky, like having drinks with traveling strangers, passing the time with an older gentleman in a public park so that he could be prevailed upon to buy her a pretty bauble. Then she would turn on her heel and leave him after acquiring what she desired. She told other stories like this. Not deadly, although malicious and with an element of mild danger. Nevertheless, her blush was honest now. In fact, her neck was reddish, too. Like a mild heat irritation or rash.

"I really feel like we should choose something that reflects where we're from since we're from all over the place," Jack continued, more earnestly. "You know. Warriors. Contributors of agriculture. Nomads. *Grrrr*." He gestured at Rav. "Or like myself, disgustingly wealthy, charming, attractive, witty. Though that's more of my nature than my culture. Still, there's no help for it. I'll just have to come as myself. Fabulous though I am."

Mel suppressed a smiled though her head was really starting to ache. There was something odd in the air; she wasn't able to suppress her perception of things around her. Jack could be sweet. He was easy to read. He wanted no specific girl at the Keep and yet, he wanted all of them. He'd happily accept any girl who returned his affection, though it wouldn't be Mel by any stretch of the imagination. "What about you, Mel?" he turned to her, intruding on her thoughts as if asking her if *she* could be that girl.

She blinked. Even in a small group of people such as this one, she should have been able to divert attention from herself. He was staring at her intently, leaning forward, his hand nearly on her dress-clad knee. Liz fumed. Mel looked back and forth between them and around the carriage. Details flooded her senses. The window sill was made of dark wood, a strip of it molded to the shape of the window and painted blue. Gold, actually, but colored blue by the light. Jack's foot was pressing against hers. She fumbled for the window handle to get some air, though her window was already down.

Mel was grateful when the others turned the other windows down, too. Maybe she *was* sick, she thought, though she had no recollection of what it was like to feel sick. Usually, her kind fought illness off quickly once they detected it. It was just a matter of diverting energy. Energy followed thought, coaxed it into the right paths to heal the body. Fresh air swirled into the cabin, although it did little to alleviate her strange discomfort. "Oh, I suppose a Mask would do for me, too," she said.

Liz made a face. "How original, I'm sure."

"Sorry," Mel offered lamely. There was a gust of air through her window with a peculiar odor, almost like rancid meat, maybe a dead animal on the road. She was starting to feel a little dizzy, and wished she could get out of the carriage.

Rav squeezed her hand, "Are you feeling unwell?"

But Liz lashed out, "You're a terminal tease and you know it, Mel. The less you say, the more interesting you become and I hate you for it." Mel blinked. Liz's face was flushed all over. The curls on her forehead were clinging to her face with perspiration. Mel was gasping for air, trying to get as far away from the others as she could, physically and emotionally, but it wasn't working. Just the reverse, actually. She felt herself expanding out over the others, affecting them in a way beyond her control, like watching a cup of wine spill and not being able to stop it. She tried to gather herself in, but Liz was going on, disrupting her concentration.

"Go easy, Liz," Rav said sharply.

"No, I will not," Liz said. "You slobs can take it, but I won't. She has spent this entire season laughing at us. To our faces. Let her try to deny it." Mel frowned. Liz was standing up in the tiny carriage now, yelling into Mel's face. She was so close that Mel, with her distorted perception, felt as if she were going to fall into the pores of Liz's skin. A sheen of sweat broke out across Mel's forehead. She was unable to even regulate her own temperature, as if she had a fever. She couldn't breathe properly through her nose. She panicked, not able to smell anything.

"Liz, you're making her cry," Jack shouted, grabbing Liz's arm to pull her away from Mel. Was she crying? Mel stared up at Liz, who shot out a hand to brace herself as the carriage rocked violently. Liz sensed weakness and attacked more viciously with harsher words, words that didn't even fit. Nothing fit. Nothing made sense. Mel's vision blurred.

"Thinks she's smarter than us. Better than us. Stronger. Bigger than all of us. I could just bite you. Rip that smug look right off your skin." Liz's jaw jutted out, the veins at her temples standing out, too, bluish under her fair skin.

The carriage hit another rut in the road, and all five of them were jostled. A hand was flung up and struck the underside of Mel's chin. Someone's fist struck a dark brown cheekbone. Skirt fabric billowed. Jack was thrown backward at first, his boot suddenly level with Mel's eye. Despite her impaired senses, she saw it all happen slowly in fragmented pictures. Surprise and confusion on Jack's face. Rav seeming to fall away from her as the carriage car buckled for an instant at the diagonal pressure from being tipped on its corner. Then Liz was flung backward so violently that she lost her balance. Her feet came up, she bowed at the waist as if performing an elaborate exit from a stage, and then she tipped backward out the window. Jack lunged after her disappearing feet.

"Stop the carriage!" Rally stood and pounded the carriage ceiling. The road sped by as they dived toward the window calling for Liz. The carriage, at last, slowed, shaking in a drunken wobble as it lost the last of its lopsided cant. They were all focused on the opposite side of the carriage, reaching for the door, getting their own bearings.

No one saw the arm grab Mel. It reached through the window behind her and clamped around her waist, sucking her out. Her ankles scraped against the sill, and her cotton shoes were torn right off her feet and left behind.

CHAPTER 4

"What do you mean, an attack?" Vanese Skance's fan twitched in her hand, the back of which had a slight sheen from the rare, imported cream she applied daily. A carriage attacked on the road? She was personally insulted. The lands around Cillary Keep were entirely neutral for miles, with only that piddling town of former Keep servants in the immediate vicinity, which was why families chose without hesitation to send their daughters there. Generations of daughters, as she personally could attest to. This protected forest was not for bandits and thieves. It was not for marauders. The driver of the carriage and the young man Jack stood in her receiving room relaying the events. "How many attackers? More than one?" she demanded. She was careful to keep her face smooth, though it took great effort.

"At least one," the young man Jack said, standing on the thick woven rug in her antechamber. "We were very involved in rescuing Liz when she fell out of the cabin, you see. We didn't exactly see what happened to Mel. Not at first." He was only a little distressed, mostly excited. Less than twenty years old, she thought. Very far from home for maybe the first time. She evaluated his clothing and accent, and decided he was only moderately wealthy, but well-schooled. A very pleasant demeanor, respectful toward women as well as toward the driver standing next to him. Not a stunning match for any of her top students, but a very good one for one of the middle ranking young women. Very good, indeed.

Lady Skance smacked her fan against the arm of her chair, slightly harder than was decorous. She would get to the bottom of this . . . this *vandalism*. "And you, driver? What did you see?" The driver was an elderly man who'd been at the Keep for years. Lady Skance knew he was called John Teaves, that he had a daughter and granddaughter who both had positions in the Keep, that he suffered from pain of joints during the colder months and often complained about it to the stablemen. It was her duty to know many useful things about him, but she chose not to use his name. It simply wasn't done.

"A big fellow," he said. "A man . . . sort of . . . with a great axe in his belt. He came running out of the woods and ran into the carriage."

"Ran into it?"

"Smack into it," he reiterated, hitting his hands against each other. "I thought we hit a rut at first, for we nearly tipped right over. Never seen such a man before. He hit the carriage like he was an angry bull. I was tossed right out of my seat. I didn't even see when he took Miss Mel. But that was the thing, when she came running out of the woods some time later, she was fine, thank the Lord. Don't know how she got away from him. He was a big fellow."

Interesting, Lady Skance noted, momentarily distracted, noting his thanks to a sole deity. Teaves was a monotheist, a rarity among the Keep staff. Locals and polytheists, most of them, praying to this god or that. Colorful and quaint, was how she viewed it when she'd first arrived at the Keep herself many, many decades ago, long before the trees had started turning blue. More than she cared to mention. The locals were an interesting people to reckon with, friendly, loyal, and stubborn. She'd have to learn more about Teaves. Clearly, there were some things in her Keep that she did not yet know.

"And he was carrying an axe?" When she turned away from the man speculatively, she caught a glance of herself in the gilded mirror on the opposite wall. She was pleased to note that her posture did not need correction. She faced Teaves again and met his eyes firmly, demanding respect, yet coaxing his trust. Always manipulating, encouraging, no matter how insignificant the encounter might be. She'd spent decades honing her skills, so long, in fact, that she could not *stop* using them; it was ingrained behavior now.

"Yes, a big one maybe half again the size of a regular one," said Teaves, "It was a big one, like a woodsman might have, maybe."

"Maybe not like a woodsman," Jack suggested unhelpfully.

Lady Skance turned to Jack, "And the girl is fine?"

He nodded enthusiastically, "She was very well. She looked . . . " He seemed like he was about to say more. His face went lax in the attitude of one who was entirely smitten. Lady Skance watched him closely. Though he didn't say it, she could tell he had thought Mel beautiful, stunning, and absolutely gorgeous. And he was wondering why he'd never noticed it before. "She was barefoot. Her hair was full of leaves, and her dress a bit muddy, but she was fine," he said out loud. If he had the facility of a poet, Lady Skance imagined he might have spoken volumes about the way her eyes shined, the tendrils of her tawny hair, and the gentle flush of her cheeks, obviously from running away from the fellow that had gotten her.

He might have said, *Really good of her to have run away from the lout like that. It said she could look after herself a little. Her dress kind of flowing around her with the sunlight shining through it. Angelic, maybe. Heavenly. He'd hardly left her side since they'd gotten back to the Keep, which made Liz a bit put out, but she was hardly one to be jealous. When they'd rescued Liz from the middle of the road, she was a bit bruised and angry and feeling clumsy. Nowhere near as angry as she'd been the moment before she'd fallen out of the window. And then after they'd all gotten back in the carriage, Liz had sicked up out the window and that had shut her up for the rest of the drive home. But she was a big girl from a big city after all. She'd get over it.*

All these pretend thoughts, Lady Skance manufactured, imagined, concocted from the dreamy expression on the young man's face. But Mel . . . for some reason, she could not recall the young woman's face at the moment. That rarely happened to Lady Skance. Usually she had an excellent memory for placing a name with a face for every woman currently at the Keep.

Lady Skance dismissed the two men from her antechamber and immediately rose to visit the two women. They were confined to the sick room, which distressingly had been used long ago to house the very worst of the socially diseased—although that was never spoken of now—where they were being watched over by physicians. It was better to be safe than sorry. She had made it to the end of the season with no great illnesses or injuries to any of the participants only to have this happen during the last week. She felt greatly irritated and ill-used by the bandit, whoever it was.

"Lady Skance?" Jack said, turning back, suddenly pink around the ears, "You won't cancel the end of the season promenade, will you?"

She drew herself up to her full height as she exited the room. "Certainly not."

She walked with measured steps down the chilly corridor to the sick room, smooth faced and composed. The Keep's stone walls locked the cool air in no matter what modernizations had been made—indoor water pumped by heated agamite, the best adornments money could procure—but still, the chill persisted. After all this time, Lady Skance was accustomed to it. And no matter what situation she encountered with these young women, she would meet it as usual, absolutely proper, never flustered, always assured. She certainly remembered who Liz was. The girl was a plump, mouthy little thing at the start of the season, but she could not call to mind any face to match the name Mel.

It was that ridiculous shortening of their given names that they did without fail every season. Lovely names turned curt and masculine. Marinda became "Mar." Patriana became "Pat." Perhaps Mel was one of five or six of those nondescript brown-haired women that she so desperately tried to encourage to shine, to stand out, and to distinguish herself. Every season she had a few girls like this, and some moderate successes. The boy Jack seemed taken with her. Perhaps she had made something of the woman well enough.

Lady Skance decided not to announce anything to the families of her students. This season—yet another successful one—would be over within a few days, and the women would be released either to their families or other appointed escorts. There was no time to send messengers, and she had not the means—neither horses nor additional riders—to notify all of the families in such short time.

Without a doubt, the young women were already well aware of the events, chattering about it in the dormitory. One could change the behavior of the women, but not their very nature. She could treat the whole thing as if the attack were by a wandering vagrant, an *anomaly*. And then hope that nothing would happen in the next handful of days to prove her theory otherwise. And perhaps, hold her breath and pray.

Lady Skance did not have much on hand in the way of security. It might have seemed an obvious thing to require with such a nest full of highly valuable fledglings. Thoughts of kidnap and ransom used to cross her mind frequently when she was a younger headmistress, but time had faded those worries. She had gamekeepers and stablemen. And the young men, of course. For the first time in nearly forty years, she was uncertain and felt ill-prepared. She could artfully bully and coerce statesmen and courtesans, but she could not prepare a strategic defense. She set her back straight and continued her measured steps toward the sick room.

CHAPTER 5

Mel was embarrassed, an unusual predicament to find herself in, for sure. The attendants in the sick room were forcing her to stay overnight so they could observe her. They had bandaged her head up in tissue like a stuffed pastry. Lying in the sick room would have been a good opportunity for her to regulate her mind and smooth out the erratic beating of her heart, but Jack insisted on staying with her for a long time. Rav and Rally had visited, too, and now Liz was across the room shooting her apologetic glances.

Mel's further embarrassment stemmed from waking up from a dream in the sick room and calling out for her mother. The sick room attendants had tried to comfort her, murmuring that she'd be home in no time. Liz had stared across the room at her with wild eyes. When the attendants left them to rest, Liz, who seemed genuinely ill, queasy with bouts of disorientation, climbed out of her bed and crept across the room to Mel to whisper and tell her how sorry she was, how she had no idea what had come over her in the carriage before the accident.

Mel was puzzled as to why the creature had affected Liz, too. Mel was fairly certain Liz's outburst and Mel's muddled head were connected in some way to the attack. Maybe the traits that she'd come to think of as her people's alone were not merely theirs. The acute sensitivity and awareness. The control. Certainly, Liz's explosive anger had been greater than Mel's own emotional upheaval. Maybe Liz had distant connections to the Masks? Mel had heard of people leaving the settlement . . . once every century or so. Liz was from Tooran, a busy metropolis to the southeast where an outcast could certainly hide in anonymity. So perhaps there were people outside the settlement with varying degrees of the Mask skills. If so, what had the creature done to them?

Despite the bad dream, Mel *had* wanted her mother, but it was more on a matter of research. Her mother was a thorough scholar, and Mel brimmed with questions for her. Although she'd heard of trolls only in stories, maybe they did exist. Stranger things had proven real over time.

Rumors of noisy, horseless carriages that ran on compressed vaporized agamite came from the east. The greenish stone melted under extreme temperature and, if rumor was true, produced greenish-blue clouds of steam where the carriages ran.

And truly, she needed some explanation for her own behavior, particularly her rampant lust for a complete stranger. Even sitting in her sick room cot now with the thin sheet over her knees, she flushed hot, her skin warming with slow heat from inside. If that man was a hunter, which his appearance suggested, he was most likely stalking the thing that had gotten Mel. And if that thing had a keen sense of smell, maybe the man was wearing some kind of scent camouflage. She didn't know much about hunting, but she had heard of the use of the hunted animal's musk to disguise oneself from detection.

Every time she closed her eyes, she saw him again and the remembered smell of him—the addictive smell of him—filled her nose and made her heart pound. *Olfactory hallucination.* She heard his voice, too, the scant six or seven words he'd spoken. She felt the touch of his mouth. She replayed every tiny detail over and over in her mind and she was convinced it had something to do with that troll or whatever he was. Maybe the scent the man was wearing—the one that affected her—was for repelling the creature. She started to laugh out loud sitting in her cot and had to disguise it by clearing her throat. If she'd been overcome by some kind of trollsbane . . .

She turned over in her sickroom bed and sat up, smoothing her hair, adjusting her bed covers, having detected a new visitor. Not much later, the sound of footsteps clicked down the stone hallway. Lady Skance was coming. Mel gathered from Lady Skance's footsteps—the pace and force with which she placed her shoes down—that she was concerned and also angry, but not at Mel or Liz. There was a small, unlikely trip in Lady Skance's tread once—the headmistress was upset. A minute later, she entered the room with small, even steps, floating effortlessly on her glossy stilted shoes. Lady Skance spoke briefly with the head physician and went to Liz's bed first. Liz was solemn and scared, which Mel could feel through the waves of nausea coming from her and the extra swallowing of her throat. It dawned on Mel that Liz was suffering as if she'd been poisoned, though Liz's symptoms were more severe than Mel's. Lady Skance spoke in a low, calm voice asking general question about her health. How did her head feel? Had she gotten some rest? And so on. Then she turned to Mel.

The anger that radiated from Lady Skance was unwavering and intense. Mel searched the older woman for other signs. The headmistress felt her school had been compromised. Her face had several layers of paint and powder, smoothed to look like natural skin, but she had been the head of the school for several generations. Her expressions were carefully controlled. Other than her obvious anger which anyone could see, she was very difficult to read. Startled, Mel realized that perhaps she'd had more to learn from her this season than she'd realized or taken advantage of. Lady Skance leaned toward Mel and said, "I hear, young lady, that you have been asking for your mother."

Inwardly, Mel grimaced, "Yes. I . . . had a bad dream." She searched for the skill to pull herself out of the situation. The last thing she wanted was to be under this woman's scrutiny. Especially now, so close to the end of the season. Mel's people had gotten her into the Keep without detection or notice. Just a simple manufacturing of credentials, an added recommendation from a past satisfied recipient of Mask mediation, and the right clothing had gotten Mel into the Keep. All that artifice could crumble if she made a mistake. She soothed herself, gathered her senses, and was relieved to find her body cooperating, at an almost normal level again for the first time since the carriage attack.

"Understandable, given the circumstances. Hopefully, you'll have no lasting effects," Lady Skance replied. "And your people are from where?"

"Port Navio," Mel said, naming the largest and wealthiest port city near her home. The easiest non-truth was always the one closest to the truth. None of the other women at Cillary were from there, so none could confirm or deny it. She sought through the things in her mind that she'd read about the place.

"Ah, yes. That is a very populous city. And not altogether safe for a young lady."

"It has its undesirable areas," Mel said. "My family is well-aware of certain . . . incidents there. For instance, I'm not allowed to traverse the riverwalk on my own."

Lady Skance considered this and then said abruptly with a distinct pursing of her painted lips, "In all my years as headmistress of this school, I have never experienced an affront such as this. This . . . this trespass in our pristine arena, our sanctuary. It is absolutely unheard of." She looked distracted for a minute. "You have been checked by the physicians here. And you are well?" It was less a question than a pronouncement or demand. Lady Skance would never outright ask if Mel had been injured or . . . physically compromised.

Lady Skance waited for Mel to nod. "Very good." She rose to leave and pronounced, "When you ladies are well enough, you should prepare your dresses for the end of the season festivities. We will proceed as planned. You will join us when you are fit."

Mel listened to her fading footsteps, whisper-quiet, all the way down the hallway until they disappeared. She glanced over at Liz and crossed her eyes at Liz who gave a short burst of laughter. Then she slid her feet over the edge of her cot and tested how she felt standing up. She made her way over to Liz.

"Are you all right?" Mel asked her, though she knew she wasn't.

"No, I'm not," said Liz. "I'm sick as a dog. What do you think?"

"Think it was something you ate this morning?"

Liz looked at her like she was a moron. She felt like one with the huge bandage on her head. "Yeah. Black tea and toasted bread made me crazy as a hornet? And then sick as a dog? I'm not a complete idiot."

"I don't know. Have you run out of animal comparisons?" Mel asked casually, though she found herself snappish and short-tempered, at least for her.

Liz laughed and then groaned. "I think I'm going to vomit."

"Use the pan. Not on me," said Mel, but Liz just grimaced. Probably thinking about her outburst in the carriage. Not very elegant or attractive. Various other emotions crossed Liz's face, and then it steadied in more or less simple anxiety. Mel was relieved to find Liz had dropped her concerns to more mundane problems. Though she would have liked to mull over the attack more herself, she certainly didn't want to discuss it with Liz.

Mel read her and said, "Don't even think about it. I've got a plan."

Liz looked startled then recovered her sarcasm. "You're a very talented mentalist as well? What was I thinking just then?"

"You're worried about your costume for the dance."

Liz squinted. "OK. I was, but I changed my mind. You're not talented. I'm just very obvious in what I'm thinking. Always have been. Always will be, despite the teachings of *her ladyship*." Mel considered quizzing Liz about her family. Maybe she wasn't the only naturally combatant one in her family. Maybe that was a genetic gift as well. Mel glanced toward the door a couple seconds before two women entered.

Rav said, "I have brought Pei like you asked me to, Mel. She is the best seamstress among us. I am pretty sure she can make even you look beautiful, with that which is on your head." Pei, the slim golden girl, always elegant, looked them over, assessing them. Her eyes flicked toward Mel's bandaged head.

"Don't worry," Mel said. "This thing is coming off."

Pei nodded. "Good then. My headdress idea will work better. You and two other ladies will be wearing costumes modeled after the exotic *fratuka* birds, wildly colorful birds with impressive plumage. Each lady will choose a different color to most complement her complexion. Together, you'll be a dazzling flock."

"Thank God," Liz said, leaning back on her pillow, her black curls making a halo around her face. "I was making myself sick with worry. I just want to look decent, you know."

Mel noted with some amusement that Rav declined to be included in the flock. Mel herself was glad to be rid of the decision. She didn't mind participating. But in truth, she would have preferred being alone elsewhere, thinking about a certain encounter with a certain huntsman, and why it had been completely out of her control. Completely out of control. Like the man was magnetic. She gave a little shiver as her senses were flooded again by the memory.

"Are you all right, Mel?" Rav placed a hand on her shoulder.

"I'm fine," she said gesturing to her head bandage. "Just being an idiot."

CHAPTER 6

Mattieus Ottick, sometimes known as "the Ott" but more often called just Ott, sat across the fire from the hulking form of his good friend Rob in their makeshift camp. He'd finally gotten up the nerve to ask Rob to change their plans to chase this thing, this *idea* hovering over him that had been torturing him the last couple of days. An obsession with a stranglehold on him, actually. The roasted bone that Rob had been gnawing on clanked down into his metal plate. The big man stared at him.

"So let me get this straight, Ott, because *only you* could find a girl deep in the forest. We went into the woods chasing a beast and you found a girl. A girl. Who kissed you. I can't quite get this into my head. Let me . . . let me just sort it all out again, if you don't mind. You're saying you locked your lips with those of some girl out in the woods and that is why we gave up the hunt and strayed two days off course out of our way so that we could get into costume and be dressed like fools? For a dance?"

Ott didn't know how to explain it. How she wasn't just a girl. How she might have been some kind of witch or fairy, elf or enchantress, if those things existed. How *she'd* kissed *him*. How he was sure it hadn't been a dream or some kind of beast-induced hallucination because something as coarse as the beast they were chasing could never conjure up something like her. How he'd been thinking about the whole thing endlessly. And yet . . . he was confused and ashamed to admit to himself he couldn't remember what she looked like. He was a hunter and tracker, but yet he couldn't exactly remember if her hair was brown or fair. Was her skin fair or golden? Were her eyes brown or green? All these details were completely hazy in his mind. He did, however, remember her words, that she was "a Cillary girl." But even if they found her at the Keep, how would he recognize her? That damn beast they'd been chasing must have muddled him. That, and six weeks of tracking with only trail food to eat and hard ground to sleep on.

Rob chewed thoughtfully. He shrugged. "Well, I've been an idiot for far less."

Ott slumped with relief. He hadn't realized he'd been holding his breath. A lot rode on the opinion of his friend. It had always been like that, the whole two dozen years of his life. Rob had been there from the beginning. Ott would be the first to admit that his friend was cut from nobler cloth than he was. One day, Rob would be lord of the northern region, and Ott . . . well, he'd just keep relying on his luck and good looks as he always did. They had never failed him in the past.

"Thanks," he said. Rob was a true friend. Not just friend, he realized with a little chagrin, but his employer also. Well, indirectly. Rob's powerful father had hired him to track this *thing* that was running through the hills on his land and messing with his mining endeavors. They'd chased it for days this far south. So far, only to lose it after it had attacked the girl and her friends in their carriage. Disappointing for sure, but Ott was so befuddled by the girl and the kiss that he'd lost the momentum of the chase. Or transferred momentum to her, he realized sheepishly. He was like a dog thrown off the scent.

But still, he owed a lot to Rob. While they were down here fooling around in these temperate Cillary forests, Rob's entire future was on hold. He should have been at home in his father's palatial manor learning stratagem and how to order people about or whatnot. Though, to Ott, traipsing around in the forest was a thousand times better; he'd rather be strung up feet first than have to deal with those self-important windbags who called themselves advisors and dignitaries. Dignity? What kind of dignity was there in wandering the halls of that frozen place in a dress and slippers like an old biddy?

Across the flickering campfire, Rob mused, "So, what costumes should we use? What do you see yourself as? A prince, bandit, or perhaps a ghostly Mask?"

Ott looked down at himself. "We'll go as hunters, I guess. Easy enough, right?"

"Well, at least you could bathe if we're going to be rubbing elbows with the ladies. You're a bit gamey, as they say. Plus, what's that additional delightful new perfume you have on?" He took an exaggerated sniff and wrinkled his nose.

"Don't you like it? It keeps off the bugs," Ott said. "I made it myself from some of that *citronus* plant. Seemed to work this time, too."

"Stinks," Rob said bluntly. "And while you're bathing, give yourself a shave."

Ott scratched his bristly chin. "If I'm all cleaned up, I won't look very authentic. Not a true man of the outdoors." He postured with exaggerated bravado, though he was filled with misgivings about the whole excursion. He *was* being an idiot. Following his urges instead of his head. It wasn't the first time he'd been distracted by a pretty face chasing after a kiss. A stolen kiss here or there, but Lord alive what a kiss this one had been, he thought, pulse speeding. He rubbed a hand over his face. He *was* a complete idiot. She was probably just a regular girl. And he'd realize that for sure as soon as they found her. But now he had to go through with it; he had asked Rob to give up the hunt and wait it out while he chased after . . . what? He wasn't sure what they were going to tell Rob's father. The old man was as hard as the stone he mined and equally tough on Rob.

"Don't look so grumpy," said Rob. "You don't want to be outshined by me, do you? In all of my masculine glory." He mocked Ott and batted his eyelashes, foppish gesture in ridiculous contrast with his dark features. "Not sure what she'd see in a runt like you anyway."

Ott pitched an empty tin cup at him over the fire, which Rob batted away with the back of his hand, giving Ott an amused grin. Ott stalked off to the river frowning. Well, he guessed he deserved it. He owed Rob a lot for this possibly pointless chase. Scratch that, he owed Rob for his income, his way of life, and most of his training and experience, too. Ott's own family had crumbled apart. Mother dead, sadly. Father dead, thank heavens. Family home in ruins. He sighed again as he stripped off his clothes and waded out into the river. Sand gave way to river rock. He was forever in debt to his friend, but there were far worse people to be beholden to. Ott's own father had been one of them. Ott pressed that thought to the back of his mind as he pushed off the slippery rocks and treaded out to the center of the water.

The water was very warm. Not far upstream were hot springs they had found a day earlier. Almost too hot for a bath up there. Even this far downstream, the rocks were colored blue-yellow from some of the mineral deposits, and the plants along the banks were warmer weather plants than the surrounding areas. Whatever it was, it made for good bathing. Ott unwrapped a chunk of milk soap and a small, soft bristled brush for scrubbing, for which he had bartered a pheasant in the last town.

He sniffed the soap suspiciously. Some kind of herb mixture. Mint, for sure, plus something else he was unfamiliar with. That was both the benefit and shortcoming of moving around to new places. There was always something to experience that was novel, strange, or both. The soap was not bad. At least it wasn't flowery, not that he minded the smell of roses by themselves.

He froze mid-scrub. The smell of roses came back to him for a second as he remembered lying on his back in the grips of that girl, her hair brushing his face, her mouth bruising his, her small hands in his hair. He hadn't remembered the rose smell before now. Fresh, not cloying. More like it had blown in and cleared away the stink from that beast they hunted. Before that, it had been hard to notice anything but the taint in the air. They had probably rolled through some flowers going down that hill together.

As pleasant a memory as it was, remembering the location where he met her didn't help him remember anything about her other than the way her mouth felt on his, how her waist felt under his hands. He couldn't very well ask for a kiss and a squeeze from every girl he met from now on. It was maddening, the lack of details. What else? He lathered up his hair and rubbed his scalp. *Think. Think. Think.* Brown hair or fair? The memory just slipped away from him, kind of like the way she had just run off. Barefoot, he suddenly thought.

She'd been barefoot. That compounded his image of her as a fairy, Lady Lutra's handmaiden, or some kind of woodland sprite running around the woods without any shoes. No shoes, that was odd. But she said she was from Cillary, which was some distance away, which meant carriage or horse. Maybe they didn't require shoes at Cillary. All right, that was plain idiotic. Most likely, she'd lost her shoes being dragged around by the beast. Ott grimaced, his chest tightening with worry. How had she gotten back to Cillary without any shoes?

He attacked his nails with the brush. It had been a while since he'd cleaned up. He and Rob had followed the beast for days. They tracked its erratic path south from Rob's father's land, sometimes losing the trail entirely, though Ott still was not sure how that was possible. Outwardly, the beast had little cunning and no subtlety, crashing through the underbrush, bellowing at them in rage. And then, for a half day or so, it was completely gone, only to reappear somewhere else entirely. More than once, finding the new trail had come down to nothing but absolute luck on their part. He didn't want to admit it, but he suspected there could be something magical going on here. Some kind of disappearing and reappearing of the sort in children's tales. He and Rob were skilled trackers, and it irked him to have lost the beast so many times. It irked him further that he was grasping at ridiculous excuses for having lost his trail.

Really, Ott, magical beasties?

They had had two previous confrontations with the beast, not including the time Rob had dropped that enormous stone on its head from above and caused it to let go of her. His *her*, Ott thought—he wished he had a name for her. Another lucky instance with that stone. Good timing all around. Lady Lutra had kissed him with her usual benevolence again, it seemed. Ott had been attempting to chase the beast under the spot where Rob was hiding in the tree above, but it wouldn't be herded the first time through and they missed completely. The second time with the girl tucked under its arm, it ran right under Rob, who was usually a good shot, and wham, he got him directly on the head. Lucky again that he hadn't managed to hit the girl though her head had some blood on it from something.

There, he'd remembered another detail. She had a wound on her temple. Why hadn't he offered to clean it up for her? She'd been hurt, and he'd been too much of a dunce to offer assistance. Then, at least he would have prolonged the conversation; he would have had the wherewithal to ask for her name. He groaned in remembrance at his brusque words to her. *What kind of creature was she?* Accusing her of being some kind of fairy when it was his own body he hadn't been able to control. No wonder she had run away from him. He stank and he had no manners. The only thing he was good for was torturing himself with regret.

"If you're quite done moaning out there, I'd like a chance at a bath," Rob said appearing from behind the trees. He had a shaving blade and a leather strop over his arm. He tossed Ott a coarse towel. "At least I can't accuse you of letting the water run cold."

"All right. All right," Ott protested. "I'm getting out."

"Right. And don't worry yourself. No amount of scrubbing and scraping will make you as pretty as me." Ott took the proffered shaving tools and made his way back to the camp. He intended to shave, and then go back for their clothes to wash them. Thanks to Ott's bartering skills, they each had one change of clothes for emergencies like tangling with the sharp end of the beast's axe, washing . . . or masquerade balls.

Ott propped up a little piece of reflective glass and set to work on his face before his skin cooled off from bathing. Rob was a decent guy, although a bit prickly right now. Ott always thought of himself as a lucky, right time right place kind of guy, while his friend had had a rougher course to go. Rob's father, Col Rob, made life tough for him. Rob was his father's only child, and he was expected to be his father's physical self now that the man was older, not in the best of health, and not able to go beyond his own property. Even his entourage, the cadre of aged bowers and scrapers who surrounded him, was getting old and crumbly, a bunch of crusty old men, the lot of them. It made Ott cringe. Although Col Rob was stooped by the years and much shorter than Rob, he was still able to snap Rob to his command by a mere look. It was a crying shame to see his friend bow to anyone, let alone a man of questionable ethics and character. Ott wasn't positive if his friend had endured physical discipline at the hand of his father, but he suspected it was so. And now this.

Ott nicked his chin with the blade in exactly the place he already had a scar. He cursed under his breath and looked for something to press on the bloody cut. He took the collar of his dirty shirt and held it to his face.

Rob's lord father expected them to come back bearing the head of the beast that had been systematically sabotaging their mines and terrifying the workers. At first, the miners had not reported anything. Long hours and grueling work made them jumpy and apt to doubt what they saw. Equipment went missing. Trolleys were broken. Superstitious, the old man called them. He treated them like unruly children. Then they came to him as a group at the end of a shift one day to report that they had all seen the creature. A troll, they called him. Taller than any of them, including the tallest of them. Broad as an ox. Skin dirty, gray, and thick as hide. Reeking like the worst decayed refuse they'd ever smelled. Three-week old chum out in the sun, a rotten *beezil* carcass—this was much worse than any of that. They were terrified that the beast would destroy the mine entrance and trap them, condemning them to a miner's perpetual fear: to be buried alive.

The old man, ensconced in his pomp and finery like a feudal lord, set

Rob and Ott on its trail, imparting the message that they had better not return until they brought back irrefutable proof that the thing was dead. He wanted the head in order to display it to his miners so that they would return to work and continue mining the agamite obediently. Displaying the head was rather gruesome. Definitely not the route Ott would have taken on that one. He was not sure how much loyalty it would inspire. More likely, fear and disgust. But that was Rob's old man through and through.

Ott finished up his face and dressed himself. He tossed the looking glass to Rob, who was coming back from the river. "Your turn, beautiful."

CHAPTER 7

On her last night at the Keep, Mel lingered in the steam-warmed dormitory. Despite the rich furnishings—the heavy carved beds and fine, embroidered linens for which the local townspeople were famous—she had not grown fond of the place over the summer. The dorm was cavernous and over-crowded with young women. She had, however, developed a strong attachment to some of the girls, and she also regretted that she had not figured out until her final meeting with Lady Skance exactly how much she could have learned at the Keep. The headmistress had shielded entire layers of behavior and intent from Mel, who had no idea how to deconstruct or even interpret the defenses. She was probably alone among all of the girls in her sentiments, but she wished she had had more time alone to talk with Lady Skance.

There was going to be some kind of final benediction the next morning, but Mel would not be staying for it. Instead, she would take a covert route home. She intended to take a carriage all the way south, several hours to Port Navio and then backtrack and travel north to the Mask settlement on foot—wearing the shoes in which she'd arrived at the Keep. She had already finished packing her trunk. It was just a ruse, really. The trunk contained all her dresses and mementos that she'd collected during the season, but she was going to abandon it on the dock when she reached Port Navio, where it most likely would be quickly broken down and dispersed by the thieves and pickpockets there. Her real belongings, the leaf specimens and written notes of her observations of the blue-leaved trees, were in a bag that she would wear across her shoulders. Not that she had stumbled across any startling conclusions in that respect—but that wasn't her responsibility. She would leave the theorizing and postulating to the elders in her settlement.

For that reason, she packed her trunk of clothes carefully, removing her name or anything that would identify her, fingering each item in it for the last time. She had to confess that more than once she'd had the fleeting thought of how simple it might be to descend the stairs into the ballroom and be given the firm hand of a young man with agamite-colored eyes, to be courted, and to accept the attentions. To return them without hesitation, fully. But perhaps it was better not to begin an attachment that could not be wholly fulfilled. She was to have no love for a specific person, only *people as a whole*. No marriage. No home outside the settlement. No role in refined society. No costume other than her Mask. Clearly, her time among the young women was making her even more sentimental than she normally was. She would have to depart them to shed their influence if she were ever going to be a true Mask.

When dusk fell, Mel and the others adorned themselves for the evening. In just a few days, Pei's talent with needle and thread had produced five lavish outfits that were beaded, feathered, and that fit each girl. She assigned them each bits to sew and embellish, but she did all the planning, coordination, and final fitting, all with a cool, orderly detachment that Mel found fascinating. Clearly, she was an artist. She made each modification without effort, her nimble fingers flying over silk and fine netting without so much as a ripple in either fabric or her countenance. Each girl wore a silky, thin shift of a slightly different color that best suited each of them, slit to the thigh on either side so they could walk without impediment . . . as well as for display. Over the shoulders, an elaborate, ornate drape beaded with light metallics that would shimmer and flow under candlelight. On each head, an equally elaborate headdress with beaded mask over the eyes.

As was required, each girl applied traditional, ceremonial face paint, the dark dye around the eyes, the rouged mouth, although each was given rein to modify the colors and designs as they desired; Mel had self-mockingly painted an ornate gold mask under her beaded one. And of course, though it chafed Mel, they were all required to wear the formal shoes, the high lacquered platforms with thin ribbon straps that made every movement, by necessity, deliberate unless she wanted to lose her balance and fall on her head. She would not regret leaving the shoes tomorrow in her trunk at Port Navio.

That night, together, the girls were a bright flock, and Pei smiled at the collective gasp in the ballroom when eyes turned to look at them as they entered. Slowly, they paused as planned in the entryway, then slowly fanned out and joined the other masked revelers. Several young men had dressed as hunters, and it made Mel's heart speed in her chest each time she spied one . . . until she had identified each as just another of the

Keep's young men. The hunter in the green was Jonat, who always held his arms slightly bent at his sides; his posture was an easy marker. A hunter in brown was obviously Mackwan, who could not ever remove his signet ring from a swollen, previously broken knuckle.

Mel quickly located Rav and Rally and picked her way across the floor to them. Rav was easy enough to identify. She had adopted the *farharini* dancer suggestion after all. Although not transparent as was traditional, her costume was two artfully tied scarves—and that was it. Her dark brown skin had been dusted with cosmetics to a glossy sheen, and she balanced naturally and easily in her formal shoes. Despite the perfumed bodies and aroma of a banquet in the next hall over, Mel could still catch the smell of the desert that was distinctly her friend's as she stood next to her. Rally, nearby, had dressed as a soldier, trying not to be overly proud of his companion. Mel observed a sweet contentment between them.

"Gorgeous, Rav," Mel couldn't help saying, in pronouncement of the obvious.

"Of course I am," said her friend smiling broadly, her white teeth flashing. Rav touched the edge of one of her scarves. "At home, this would be a winter outfit, I think."

Mel laughed. "I'll be sure to visit you in the winter then, when it's snowing at my home."

"Do," said Rav seriously. Mel nodded, not promising anything, and her friend accepted her silence. Most likely, they would never meet again. Rav glanced up and gestured. "Your flock is waiting for you. By the mother hen."

Mel saw Lady Skance perched stiffly on an elevated chair at the head of the ballroom. The headmistress was wearing complete formal attire with her face painted stark white, usually reserved for royalty. Mel wondered suddenly if Lady Skance was a distant member of the royal family. Another question to research. Lady Skance sat with her knees and feet together, in proper posture, as each girl presented herself for inspection. The other four members of Mel's costumed flock were beckoning her to join them for their presentation. Mel excused herself to her friends and made her way carefully, attempting to glide across to Lady Skance now that all eyes were on her as the others waited.

Just as she reached Liz and Pei, she caught a faint strand of a familiar savory scent. Startled, she hesitated, wondering if she had imagined it. Maybe it was her overactive desire to see him again manifesting itself. Another olfactory hallucination. She wished—with a kind of unwilling desperation—that the man from the woods were here, that he could see her in her last evening at the Keep in finery instead of muddied and barefoot. Liz caught her by the elbow and gave her a little pinch. Mel blinked, and Liz smiled pointedly at Lady Skance. *Right.* There was a task at hand. The five young women arranged themselves in a group, a semi-circle in front of the headmistress, Liz and the other shorter girl forward, Mel and the taller girls at the curve. They perform a synchronized low curtsy that they had practiced, and rose to face Lady Skance's scrutiny, their final evaluation of the season.

The headmistress examined them as a group, and then asked each one to approach individually wherein she critiqued their bearing, artistry in face paint, and costume workmanship. Then she had them reassemble as a group. She gave them a final nod. "Very fine indeed," she said, and with a rare smile, she dismissed them. Officially, their time at the Keep was over and they were free to do as they pleased. As they walked away from the headmistress, chatty Liz offered her hand to Mel.

"I'm sorry again about those things I said that day in the carriage."

"Consider it forgotten. It's long over," said Mel. They clasped hands formally, Liz's small, fine hand squeezing hers for a second or two. Then Mel watched her move away, sliding away in her plumage and high shoes. Jack intercepted Liz before she made it across the room. He spoke to her very quietly, and Mel saw Liz's face go pink with pleasure. Perhaps they would start something long-lasting after all.

Behind her beaded mask, her gaze drifted, drawn to yet more young men dressed as hunters. Two of them stood together, one very tall with dark hair that she didn't recognize. The other behind him made Mel's heart pound and her mouth suddenly go dry. She froze in her precariously tall shoes, not sure if he was the one she was looking for, but unwilling to decide that he wasn't. She detected no intoxicating aroma, but the room was already filled with perfume, taper smoke, and food. She had to get closer, realizing belatedly it was hard to be subtle when dressed as an exotically plumed bird. She edged around the room, her attention fixed on him. Dozens of masked faces blocked the pathway between them.

She circled the gallery, moving nearer and nearer, closing in. Just as she had maneuvered around the room to stand behind him, he abruptly turned and walked toward an open door where a breeze from the garden blew in. She nearly growled in frustration. She followed him with small steps, balancing gingerly, unable to hurry, unable to run, to sprint, and to capture. The smell of him suddenly wafted toward her, riding on a cool burst of air from the garden, filling her nose, instantly dizzying her. The same savory smell—although much fainter than before—mixed with something else like mint and herbs, a clean smell. He was standing in the doorway, staring out the door indecisively, balanced on the balls of his feet as if he were going to take flight and escape her forever.

When she drew close enough, she suddenly wasn't sure what to do. If she had been in her sturdy leather boots from home, she may have lunged at him again. Her tall lacquered shoes forced her into self-restraint for which she was somewhat grateful. After another hesitation, she put her hand on his sleeve and said, "Hello."

He turned, startled, and stared at her without recognition. They were standing very close and were nearly eye to eye because of her tall shoes. For one horrible instant, she thought she imagined the whole thing, all the way from the color of his eyes, green marbled with brown and gold to the warm smell of him coming up from the collar of his shirt. Then he tipped his chin up, looking at her headdress and she saw the scar on the underside of his chin, and realized that he didn't recognize her because of her costume. She felt like she had no choice, so she balanced higher on her shoes, leaned in and, gently this time, put her lips on his and kissed him, her mask brushing his close-cropped hair. Some pressure, painted skin on skin painted by the sun, breath inhaled. When she pulled away some seconds later, her head was swimming, and his mouth was reddened by the paint from her lips.

"You do exist," he said, his mouth widening into a smile.

"I could say the same," she said, a little less elegantly than she'd hoped. Her heart was pounding uncomfortably, but she couldn't calm herself. And it seemed unimportant to do so at the moment. She didn't want to ask him why he had come to the keep. She wanted to remain ignorant and hope that he had come back to find her.

At first he looked like he was afraid to touch her, but then he took her hand and said, "Come with me a little way. Just outside." She went with him out to the garden in a daze from just the contact of his roughened hand, but when he stopped at some wooden chairs by the lawn, she shook her head and led him to the seclusion of the garden maze. They stopped at the first clearing where there were benches, and he sat down looking up at her. It took some skill for her not to lose her balance on the uneven turf, so she first kicked off her shoes.

"Stupid things," she said lifting off her mask and headdress as well. "Although I kind of like the mask. It's nice to hide sometimes. And feathers are not bad. I don't have anything against feathers. Birds are strange things though. Flapping all the time. All scaly and beaky." She stopped to gasp for a breath. Somehow talking and breathing were mutually exclusive, though she'd been doing it with success her whole life. She was nervous almost to the point of wanting to run away. She still hadn't decided not to.

He slipped an arm around her waist, to her surprise, and guided her onto his lap. "The bird hunting the hunter this time." He laughed about that.

"You smell good," she said, relaxing when she realized that he wasn't going to push her away, feeling like she'd had too much wine though she hadn't had any. He smelled so very good, just the same as she remembered. Except, now she didn't have to think about it because he was right here. The real man, not the memory.

She slid her arms around his neck and drew his face close to hers. She stared intently into his eyes, then leaned in, dipped her head slightly, and pressed her cheek against his, smooth, freshly shaven face. She nuzzled him behind the ear with her nose and delicately took his earlobe between her lips. His breath came in short gasps on the side of her neck. She felt his hand sliding up from her waist along her back. Her silken dress felt like skin under the heat of his hand. Then she took his face in her hands and kissed him gently, small soft kisses on his lips until it seemed he couldn't stand it. With his hand cradling the back of her head, he kissed her back until she lost her breath.

He broke away to breathe as well, but when she leaned toward him again and lifted the bottom of his shirt to sneak her hand against his skin, he shied away and stopped her. "Wait."

"What is it?"

He smiled, still out of breath, panting warm puffs of air, the corners of his mouth curling upward. "Your name. I want to know your name."

She gave a smile, too, though with a twinge of anxiety. "My name is Mel," she said, stopping there. No further explanation.

"I'm Ott." His voice was low, roughed by the moment, and it won her over again. She liked its deep timbre, his northern accent with its gently slurred sounds. He seemed oddly shy and formal for someone she had just kissed so feverishly.

"I'm very pleased to meet you, Ott," she said, kissing him again. She was lost again for some moments. Gradually, for the first time since she arrived at the Keep, even the sounds of all others faded away. The trees vanished. The Keep itself blurred. Only the two of them existed, and the blood pounded throughout her body, flooding her head and chest and in her ears, drumming against every part of her, her fingers, her neck, her toes, up the insides of her legs to where she sat on his lap. Every last part of him seemed to be for her, his mouth, his eyes, his mind, and his skin.

He broke away, looking dazed. She leaned closer, or maybe fell toward him, gravitating toward him.

"What kind of name is Ott?" she asked. "It's a nickname? Is it short for something?"

He smiled. "I have to know you at least five minutes more before I tell you how I got my nickname."

"Perhaps you're related to the infamous Otter family?" When had she learned to joke, to tease? When had she ever wanted to?

"Weasely water-dwellers, the lot of them," he said. She liked the creases at the corners of his eyes. He had sun freckles across his nose. She strove to memorize every detail of his face in the dim garden light. Not much of a moon. The night was testing what little ability she could master with her poor concentration.

"Or maybe it's just an imperative. I 'ought' to learn more about a young man before I kiss him." She dipped her head down as she said the last part, embarrassed suddenly. But he lowered his head as well and met her mouth with his own. He was very gentle at first, but his urgency escalated until her mouth felt bruised. His tongue laved hers until the blood roared in her ears.

When he pulled away again, his face was flushed, as she was sure hers was as well. He traced his thumb from her earlobe to chin. "I'm glad you told me where to find you."

"I'm glad you found me," she said. "I thought maybe I had . . ." She didn't want to say scared him. Repulsed him.

"Intrigued me?" he asked. "Infiltrated my very thoughts 'til I couldn't get you out of my mind?" She blushed wholeheartedly then. "I still don't know what you are. Or rather, who you are. But I knew I had to find you before I lost my chance. Tomorrow you leave the Keep?" he affirmed, having learned so from a local townsman. When she nodded, he asked, "And you'll go where . . . ?"

After a moment's pause, she said simply, "Home." She knew he could sense her evasiveness, but she couldn't tell him more. She had to concentrate to keep herself separate from him even for simple conversation. She felt like she could easily lose sense of time, of herself.

"And will you let me know where that is?" he asked, which she answered with silence, not able to meet his eyes. His breath still came rapidly, now with his own anxiety. "Are you promised to another?"

She couldn't lie to him to say either yes or no. In a sense, she was promised to the Mask, much like believers took to their religious cloaks. More so, in fact. Her very nature determined her course. Zealots of all types often said they felt a calling or a compulsion. Mel was obligated by genetics, by the very cells and composition of her body, her earthly shell. If she did not comply, wasn't she, in fact, denying her usefulness as person, her existence as human? Yes, she was human. But not human like this man, like Ott. Her future was with her people and was not hers to choose. She wasn't the owner of her destiny or her future. And at that very moment, she was incapable of acting.

She sat mutely, miserable, as she struggled. It would be easy to stop his questions by covering his mouth, by distracting him. But that kind of a kiss was as good as a lie; it was not a kiss out of love's sake. And to kiss him again would be telling him that she belonged to him. To turn away would be lying as well, because she *was his, forever* as she saw it. No matter where she was from here on, till the day she died, till the day he died, she would always be his. Together or apart. The pounding of the blood in her head was terrible. The weight of an entire world was hammering her skull from both inside and out, combatants in a battle to win her will. What should she tell him? How could she have him but not keep him?

The first screams that came from the Keep made them both jump to their feet. They stood, poised, eyes open wide, staring at each other, but straining to hear and to understand what was happening. The ground under them shook and rumbled, as if the very hill under them were coming loose and falling down. She was trying to grasp the cause and effect. At first, she thought that her own horrible indecision had caused the Keep to shake. She shook her head at her own self-absorption. Ridiculous to think that their soft, protected bubble of warmth had anything to do with the rest of the world. The rest of the world moved on, with or without them.

CHAPTER 8

"The earth quakes," Ott said. He held his arms out for balance as another tremor rippled under the lawn.

"No. Something else," Mel said. She had caught an acrid smell in a gust of air coming across the lawn. Fear, fire, and something else terrible from under the earth that was very, very old. Mud, decay, and anger. Noise of an explosion, of rocks and fire, came from the ballroom. They were showered with debris, a curtain of rocks and dust.

Together they ran toward the Keep across the lawn that now was dotted with chunks of smoldering rock. Mel was barefoot; she had left her shoes in the hedge maze. She lost Ott in the rubble as she broke through the outer wave of smoke, but she forged ahead, pushing moisture to her eyes. Tears ran down her face, but she could open her eyes without having to fight the dust.

She first saw Ott's big friend, a gash on his forehead, carrying a limp, bloodied body, a girl still masked and in costume, someone so covered in soot Mel didn't recognize her. He couldn't see Mel in the smoke though she could see him, she realized. She was hidden in shadows and clouds of soot. He knelt and put the person roughly on the grass. The girl's arm fell away from her body almost bonelessly. Mel could not see a pulse on her neck, could not detect a heartbeat from where she stood. Ott's friend was limping, and blood ran from his shoulder. He turned to go back into the Keep, raising his good arm to shield himself from another spray of flying rock and dust. The Keep tower swayed dangerously above them, its singed flags snapping in the wind.

Mel found a girl lying on the floor, unconscious, partly crushed by a fallen stone. Certain that no one could see her, Mel focused, diverting all her strength, pushing it up the backs of her legs, into her back, through her arms, and into her fingers. The stone gave a little and moved off, and Mel saw it was Liz. The girl gave a faint moan, blood streaming down her face from under the dust-covered curls on her forehead. A quick assessment with gentle fingertips revealed broken ribs, but worse, a crushed hip that hid catastrophic injuries behind it. Liz's silken shift was in shreds. A gray sheen of dust covered her, though it ran in black rivulets where her eyes, nose, and mouth streamed with tears and blood.

Mel carried her outside and gently laid her on the grass under the sky where a breeze blew in cleaner air. There was less shouting here. Mel held Liz's hand and stroked her sooty forehead until she calmed. Pain, terror, and fear: all of it, Mel drew out of Liz's body through her skin, through the hand that she clasped, soothing her. The pain came like a tendril of smoke at first, uncoiling into Mel's body, spreading through it. Mel took it all, ate it, digested it with heaving gasps until she had all of it. Liz's jaw unclenched. Then her breathing stopped. Mel sat for a minute longer listening for another sound, a heartbeat, a gasp, a sigh, some small sign of life, until she knew for sure there was nothing. Shouts still rang out around her. Smaller explosions still shook the ground. Then Mel let her go.

Numbly, Mel re-entered the wreckage with little more than a dim hope of finding Rav or any of the others. The sulfurous smell choked her. It was much worse now, but she couldn't determine its composition or source. People, still costumed but covered with gray powder like ghosts of the revelers they had been, stumbled blindly into her. She guided them toward the door, linking them hand to hand, their desperate fingers grasping one another's, so they would not be alone when she left them. She had lost Ott, but heard his voice calling to his friend Rob outside, which shored up her courage.

Another explosion shook the foundation under her bare and bloody feet. She bent her knees to ride out the tremors as a shower of dust and rocks pelted her head and shoulders. A wall of putrid odor blasted over her. She squinted. An enormous hole had opened up in the ballroom floor. The ground had disappeared right out from under the room. Her heart pounded as she stared at it. And then, hulking, dark forms swarmed out of a hole toward her and in all directions. It was the beast from the forest *in multiple*, and then more of them than she could count, pouring out of the hole in the ballroom floor. Gray, leathery skin and that nauseating smell. They carried weapons, hammers, picks, and axes like the one she'd seen before. They snarled, teeth exposed, the whites of their eyes bright and shocking in the gloom. Cries and moans of the wounded turned into screams as the creatures began dragging bodies toward the hole, *taking the wounded and the dead underground.*

Mel blinked, her head swimming as she lost her bearings. The same dizziness overtook her, the same as when she'd been attacked in the carriage and dragged into the woods. Only now, the sickness felt magnified, even stronger than before. Her eyes darted around the room for Rav, for Ott, *for anyone*, but now the moisture in her eyes had dried up. She blinked, hardly able to breathe, and the rocks under her feet cut into her skin. All of her abilities were gone, swept away in a gust of foul air. Another explosion rocked the Keep, and shrill screams sounded from somewhere beyond the ballroom. Blasts of sulfurous gas and smoke stung her eyes. Flames licked up the curtains and the murals that hung on the walls. More of the beasts were coming, spilling out across the lawn, hacking with their enormous axes and broad swords at bodies, wood, and whatever was in their path. Mel could do nothing but cough weakly and stumble in the haze.

Would-be rescuers fled. All the humans, the ones who were still mobile, ran from the Keep. She was alone except for the creatures. She backed away and ran, leaving bloody footprints on the floor as the hallway collapsed behind her.

Then, the stone walls crumbled on her.

Part 2

Return

CHAPTER 9

"What's your name?" the townspeople kept asking Mel. Faces, one after another, appeared in her line of vision and faded out. She forced her mind to focus, her vision to clear, and she looked around. She was weak, very weak, caught in a malaise left behind by the creatures that specifically affected her. They had poisoned her with their presence. Now they were gone, yet she still felt ill. The townspeople were writing names down on a list. They had three lists—one for people like her, another for the dead, and a third for the missing, which was the longest of the lists. She shook her head mutely, and they pinned a piece of colored cloth to her sleeve so that they would remember to ask her again later.

They were efficient at categorizing. Born collectors of data. They might have made good librarians. They had red cloth for the hurt, white for gravely injured, and blue, like hers, for minor wounds. No serious wounds, but God, she was weak. Something was wrong inside her, in her head. They had brought her to the village inn. For the first day, she could do nothing but lie on a cot and stare at the knotted beams of the ceiling. She was a tiny thought rattling around inside her head, inside a body that was as vast as a world. She was too small to inhabit her body. She was too shaken even to take comfort in sleep.

Mel had been carried away from the destruction with the other victims down to the local town where the people took them in, washed them, and cared for them. The quiet little town had become a makeshift hospital that continued from building to building; pub flowing into home into market into bakery. Doors were thrown open. People stopped at the thresholds only to scrape their feet before entering. She didn't remember being pulled from the wreckage. She came back to consciousness while they were carrying her, while being gently jostled in someone's arms. She couldn't remember the face of the person who had held her. She had been taken to the triage at the local inn where they sorted the survivors.

She received warm food, drink, and anonymous kindness that she could not comprehend, only accept. People she didn't know touched her hands and her face. A bandage circled the top of her head again, but she didn't remember having been hurt. The names of her friends swirled around in her head—Liz, Rav, and . . . Ott. Even now, thinking about him brought back the phantom of his unique scent. The memory made her chest tighten and the blood rush to her aching head. But she heard nothing more of her friends and the others who were missing. *Poor Liz*, Mel despaired, with a clenching in her belly that she did not try to control. She curled up on her narrow cot. Had Liz's body been dragged away by those beasts, those killers? After a day's time, the last few survivors straggled in, but none of them were those for whom she waited. Like her, they sat on the pub benches and cots in a stupor, bandaged and bleeding, numbly taking what was handed to them.

Her fingernails were dirty and broken. One nail on her left hand was gone. She looked at it with detachment, as if it weren't her hand on her wrist at the end of her own arm. She was swimming around in someone else's loose, ill-fitting skin. She was not the only one of the survivors who could or would not give her name. Unlike the other victims, however, she unwound the bandage from her head, unpinned the fabric from her sleeve, and, when no one was looking, she got up from her cot. She stumbled away, marginally steadier with each step. She was clean, and they had given her clothes to wear. She looked like anyone.

She began to ask people what had happened. Did they know what had happened? She wanted their stories. She soaked them up. Each person had a little bit to add, another embellishment that made her frown. She asked another, then another. Slowly, they pieced together the events for her. They filled in some of the blank spots, the things she couldn't remember. Beautiful girls, beautiful young men, and a steady, age-old tradition—all were torn apart. As swiftly as the beasts had invaded, crawling up from the bowels of the earth through their hole, they had retreated back into the ground, leaving destruction behind them.

"But what did they want? Does anyone know?" Mel asked, just as others were asking. But no one had an answer. They shook their heads, shrugged their shoulders with a mixture of sorrow and apology. Plenty offered speculation.

An older man, stout and still strong of spine, told her, "They took the women alive. That can mean only one thing. And it's no good for the ones they took." He shook his head, no doubt thinking about the girls, the lovely ones who had spent all summer floating in white cotton dresses and learning court etiquette only to be taken by savages to be raped and worse. Mel felt sick, too. Even the petty gossips among the Cillary women she knew didn't deserve the agony, the terror, the abysmal ending to their short lives. And the good ones among them, the sweet ones, the strong ones like Rav . . . It wasn't fair, and Mel wondered if anyone could be called into account. Could the missing be rescued? Could they be saved?

The man continued, "If I live a thousand years, I'll never forget the sight of all those beautiful Keep girls burned up in their fancy dresses." He passed an unsteady, speckled hand over his eyes.

Another man standing in the muddy street, his cap askew, said, "I don't know what those creatures were, but they're nothing but animals. They took the bodies of the dead, too, as well as the living. The dead we found had teeth marks on them. They use them as food, the young men and the old ones. The ones they don't use for food . . . " and Mel stopped listening, as the locals talked on, milking their own fears and their undeniable relief at having been far away from the Keep at the time. She didn't have that comfort, though she was alive. She wondered how she had been spared. A vague memory of a wall crumbling at her came, and then drifted back into the depths of her mind. No, there it was again. She had been crushed by the falling stones of the Keep. She hadn't been saved; she had merely been overlooked.

Mel heard more narratives from men in the village who had gone up to the Keep with weapons, hoping to capture some of the creatures and kill them, but that none of the beasts were left. The only ones left were a few human dead, whose names were added to the list after they were identified. No Rav, no Ott. Neither was Ott's big friend on any list.

When she came back to herself, when her mind finally cleared, Mel began to feel frantic. "What about a search party? We need to find the others. Surely, there are others still up there," she asked them, trying to keep the desperation out of her voice, trying not to cling to their shirt fronts and shake complicity from them. They had to go back, she kept thinking. She had to find her friends and Ott—especially him. She didn't feel right in her own skin. She wanted the warmth of his hands and the shine of his green eyes looking back at her.

"It's no use," they told her, shaking their heads. She listened to them talking, everywhere, describing the great, gaping fissure in the floor of the Keep, a strange hole that was so deep and noxious that no light would penetrate it and no person could breathe there. They had thrown ropes down into it, intending to lower themselves down, but the best any of them could do was one or two arm lengths down the rope before the fumes were too much.

She wandered around the now overcrowded village thinking maybe she could go into the hole, that great scar in the center of the Keep. She could slow her breathing, hold her breath for minutes. A quarter of an hour at the most, but that was without other physical exertion. She'd have to climb and adjust her eyes to see in almost absolute darkness. Protect her skin from noxious gas. Her weakness nearly made her cry. She was only one mostly ineffective person. They would need an army. An army of her kind. She shivered remembering how large the creatures were. Tufts of coarse hair sprouting above their foreheads. Gray, glaucous eyes and always that labored, raspy breathing. She leaned against the rough stone wall outside the inn, and in bright sunlight, allowed herself to be afraid. Bone-wrenchingly, mind-numbingly terror-stricken.

Mel couldn't go back to the Keep and search for the dead. She did not want to see Rav's burnished, bronze skin dulled by char and dust and lack of life. She did not want to see the Keep in ruins, flags never to fly again, crumbled piles of rubble that were once beautiful stone walls. Mud, soot, and blood churning through the soft grass on the lawn. And where was Lady Skance? Had her ceremonial facepaint and fastidious posture been destroyed forever?

Even now in the village, Mel could hardly determine the identities of the survivors; their gray slack faces all looked alike. Did she not know anyone because of her own diminished ability to sense anything? Her persistent numbness? Or did they actually look all alike, transfigured by grief, shock, and bodily injury? She stumbled around for days, taking what she was offered: clothing, shoes, food, and a place to sleep. The villagers were very, very kind. They were not wealthy by any means, but they gave what they had. Some offered prayer, mostly to gods that were not hers. Falcun of the sky. Pesca of water. She shook her head no. Would they have taken such good care of her if they had known she was a Mask? Without the cloak, was she even a Mask at all or just another wounded body to tend to?

For days, she drifted in and out of her mind and her body, always startled to come back to herself and always relieved to retreat again into numbness. After a couple of blurrily indistinct weeks, they put her on a carriage out of town that would take her to Port Navio.

CHAPTER 10

Ott could not be dead.

She told herself this again and again as the large carriage jostled her down a deeply rutted road to the distant port city. In fact, she knew he wasn't dead. He couldn't be, or else she knew something in her would sense it, would cry out, would protest. They had bonded, had they not? Made an emotional and spiritual connection. She refused to believe it had been physical attraction only. If he had been slain in the assault on the Keep, something inside her would have ripped apart. She would bleed, not feel this terrible numbness.

Wouldn't I feel something?

Doubt, fear, and dread. Hope. And then guilt—Ott was alive out there somewhere and probably thought she were dead. She trembled like a coward for another reason. It was easier to let him think her dead than to tell him she was a Mask . . . but letting him think she was dead was a lie. She would have to find a way to make that right. If she ever found him again. Outside the carriage window, trees turned from blue to green. She could smell the water of the river miles before they reached it—the brine and far-traveled wind from distant lands. It was not until then that the sulfurous smell of the creatures truly cleared out of her nose and her mind.

News traveled with her to Port Navio, and the whole countryside was alive with talk of the attack on Cillary Keep. She heard about it at every stop they made, at every small town and inn. People clamored for more information, but they would take whatever rumor or half-truth was available. From the port, news would travel across the lands to others. That was how it always worked. Port Navio was the hub, the gateway to more than one direction. Up the Uptdon River or down or across to the far eastern states. The great river was the conduit to the southern sea, and from there, on to worlds hardly known, even by Masks.

On the teeming docks of Port Navio, Mel perched, exhausted, on a lumpy, donated bag of cast-off clothes that she had neither wanted nor been able to turn down. She might have seemed out of place in the crowd, sitting numbly in the middle of the pedestrian thoroughfare, if it weren't for the collective preoccupation of the crowd, which was alive with uncertainty and gossip. At any other time, her behavior might have struck an observer as odd. Instead, people passed her by without notice, intent on news from the west. Survivors had made it to Navio before her with their fear-ridden tales of the beasts and carnage. The people were ready to believe the hearsay of baby-eating trolls come to life from stories of childhood. Yet, these were no made-up stories.

Parents' voices were a little too shrill in calling to their children. Others kept their heads entirely down, eyes averted in fear or suspicion of strangers. The only safe thing to do was to keep to themselves and go on as before.

There was comfort in the familiar patterns of life, but sometimes you had to adhere to them despite all evidence telling you things were not normal and perhaps, would never be again.

Threads of conversation filtered down to her between passing groups. The crowd swirled around her, bodies creating eddies as they stopped to greet loved ones, listen to news bearers, or, like her, to rest wearily.

"They say there are ogres, but there are no such things. That's the stuff of fairy tales, things to scare children into behaving. But these eat human flesh. And they are probably cannibals, too . . . They're bluer and taller than those blue Cillary trees . . . And then they left the very next day, back down to the hell they came from. Such a terrible waste, all those dead, beautiful girls and their young men . . . We wanted to get out of there as fast as we could carry ourselves . . . Well, you're safe now."

A hand fell on Mel's shoulder, radiating warmth and comfort, and she turned to look up its owner. Jenks. Sunburned skin, deep lines, blue eyes, and a simpleness that harbored no duplicity. Could never. He was an outsider who ran errands for the Mask settlement. He lived with them, but apart, on his own, in a hermit-like cabin that he'd constructed himself.

"Go on home," he said, slight pressure from his fingertips. "I'll take care of your things."

She nodded because Jenks would know what to do with her second-hand bag. That was the type of thing he did. Erase traces of each Mask when they had to go out in the general population. He delivered messages to them from the world outside. He was the one who had set up her passage to the Keep. She stood, feeling his warm hand slip off her shoulder. Fifteen paces into the crowd and he was gone completely. Then she slipped away from the river, away from the dock, away from the crowded streets, and into the woods unnoticed.

She had been away from home for only a few months. As she jogged northward through the woods in the underbrush and things began to be familiar to her, she didn't feel as relieved and comforted to be there as she'd hoped, even though these were the familiar green woods she'd grown up in. While she ran, she worked on healing the minor injuries on her skin, her broken or missing fingernails and the scratches on her face. She was grateful for the high-ankled and thick soled shoes on her feet, which were slightly too big. Wearing them through puddles and mud had helped to mold them to her feet over the past days since they had been given to her.

She smelled the clearing near her mother's house before she reached it: a sweet, warm scent with clover, grass, and a sunshine dryness. She stopped at the edge, gazing at the open field, which was home, but not entirely so. She started to walk, trying to shake the feeling that a small piece of what she called home now moved around somewhere on two legs, clad in hunter's garb. Her fingers tingled thinking about him, wanting to touch him again, to feel the roughness of his unshaven face under her hands. She shook her head to clear it and walked to her house.

"Mother," Mel said.

And as Ley'Ana embraced her, growing softer and velvety around Mel, a flicker of confusion crossed her mother's placid face as she scanned and categorized the changes in her daughter. Her mother hugged her tightly. Mel inhaled, taking in the familiar scent of her mother's soap. Otherwise, her mother had no natural aroma of her own. Every regular human outside of the settlement had a distinct aroma, like Ott or Rav. Within the settlement, occupation determined a person's scent: bakers smelled like yeast and sometimes sugar; woodcrafters smelled like wood chips and sawdust; and everyone smelled of book dust and ink. Otherwise, Masks purposely concealed themselves; it was part of taking the Mask, depersonalization so as to be the blank, unwritten face of impartiality. Even at the most basic level of scent.

Her mother held her at arm's length and said with an owlish blink of her eyes, "We have trouble. We must study this problem." No tsking, no mindless chatter or need for pointless details of her trip: the bumpiness of her carriage, the sogginess of the weather, the makeshift meals she had eaten. Mel had a sudden, wistful yearning for Liz and her need to speak the obvious, sometimes over and over. *Poor Liz*. Mel mourned her for a minute, and then silently berated herself for her sentimentality, her weakness—her *feelings*—and followed her mother into to the library. She couldn't allow herself to be compromised by emotion. *But, poor Liz.*

A library was a loose definition for the endless rows of shelves that made up the majority of their small and tidy, bricked home. Mel had hung her muddied cloak by the wooden door and dropped her borrowed shoes outside on the front porch near the box where Jenks normally left their traded vegetables. She had washed her hands in a sink in the kitchen where water could be pumped into the house, and taken a piece of cheese on bread. They went into the largest room of the house where they kept their journals and books. They each had a desk, but Mel sank into a chair near a pile of books and papers. Light washed in from the window. To protect the older books, there were no windows in the back of the room where the shelves reached up to the ceiling.

Mel's mother with her always even, always moderate heartbeat, exactly Mel's own height and build, except with threads of gray woven in her auburn hair, perched on the desktop next to Mel. Her eyes tightened with a hint of worry as she studied Mel's face again. "You've been crying." Mel gave a minuscule nod of her head. "You lost friends. But there's something more. You have an entirely different color about you." Her mother spoke as she always did, the way all Masks did, carefully considering each word before she spoke.

There was no point in concealing any of what happened to Mel from her mother, even if Mel wanted to. It would take more energy to hide the truth than to reveal the whole of it. Nothing could come of her feelings for Ott now. She would have to take up the Mask very soon and become as impartial an arbitrator as she could, as she was supposed to. So, as simply as she could, she described her final days at the Keep, culminating in the attack and siege.

Her mother sighed. "Your father and I did not mean for it to unfold in this manner. You've always been so much more given to action than the rest of us."

"I don't understand." Mel had leaned back in the chair, trying to feel at home, but there was a net of anxiety pulling tightly across her face and eyes that she couldn't unweave. She rubbed at her forehead. She was sure her mother saw her always as a bundle of nerves, a jangling, pulsating ridiculous person. When her mother didn't answer, Mel looked at her. Her mother wore a small, bittersweet smile that spoke volumes. It reminded Mel of how she always ran, while other Masks always walked, even the children among them. It told her gently that though she was one of them, she would always be something else besides. Other.

She saw herself now, sprawled across the chair while her mother gazed at her mildly, seriously, and calmly, her hands folded in front of her, gathering her fine-woven tunic at the waist. Mel gave her mother a helpless half-shrug, and the older woman did not try to suppress the wider smile that spread across her smooth features.

"We sent you to the Keep to see if you would become more or less like the others, the outsiders. We wondered if you would find yourself at home amongst them or see yourself as separate." Her mother did not continue; she did not ask Mel what she had discovered.

"And you think I've changed in just these few short months?"

"Go to the mirror and see for yourself," her mother said. Mel blinked, trying to decide if her mother were speaking metaphorically. She got up and walked to the wall where she peered into the same circular mirror that she used to make faces into when she was little. The looking glass had a plain wood frame that was dark and had been rubbed with oil until it shined. Mel looked at her reflection and was surprised to find it difficult to meet her own eyes. When she did, she saw a lot of her mother's features.

She had the same, straight auburn hair, high cheekbones, and thin nose with a smattering of freckles across it, though more freckles than her book-loving mother. That was where the similarities ended, however. Although she had not seen her father in almost four years now, she knew she shared his dark eyes and wide, full-lipped mouth. She thought she looked the same as she always had, and as she turned to her mother to say so, she stopped. From out of the corner of her eye, she caught something, a strange yellow shimmer. Her mother was right. Something about her color was not the same. Her skin was different. It looked more elastic, almost, and it had a strange glow, a shine to it. She frowned.

"Step into the light more," her mother suggested. With an eye on her reflection, Mel took a step backward into the direct sunlight and froze, startled. Her color wasn't yellow, but golden. Her normal skin tone was there, but there was a distinct golden glow. She touched it, rubbed a spot on her arm, and found it was permanent. Had she wandered around the wounded and dying survivors of the Keep looking like this? Had she sat in the middle of the bustling port city glowing like a golden idol?

"What is this? I'm not doing this." She looked questioningly at her mother, although something tickled her min. The memory of kissing Ott in the forest, of turning inexplicably golden, floated into her mind. Warmth crept into her neck and face thinking about it. Looking at herself in the mirror, she tried to control the color, to dull it in shadow, but it didn't change. It was still there, faint to anyone out in the world, like a touch too much sun perhaps, but highly noticeable to her mother.

"I don't know what it is. I'll have to look through my books and see what I can read about it." Mel fought unsuccessfully to hide the desire to roll her eyes. She pretended to contemplate the ceiling. Her mother's response was laughable: always, the impulse to check the books. And her mother read her look and laughed outright, a rare sound.

To distract herself and to avert embarrassment Mel said, "What do you know about these things, these creatures? Those beings that attacked the Keep?" As soon as she brought it up, her stomach twisted in a tight, painful knot, uncomfortable nearly to the point of making her sink back into her chair. Her mother crossed the room purposefully, gathering up a book and her shawl as well.

"That certainly is the question of the moment. We've been calling them 'troglodytes' so far, but we shall wait to see how they refer to themselves before we set on it. It might be preferable to some of the other terms Jenks has reported hearing in the city. They are certainly not ogres, though the people will want to resort to their childhood stories and fears when confronted with the unknown. But 'troglodytes' is not too demeaning, I think. After all, they deserve representation as much as you or I. But in any case, we're discussing it right now in the hall. We should join them."

Mel was shocked, yet kept her mouth shut. It should not have come as a surprise that her people viewed the attackers as people entitled to the same rights as everyone else. As for herself, she wasn't entirely sure they were people. She followed her mother out the door into the smooth unpaved road of the street. And for another thing, although her mother accused the general populace of resorting to their fairy tales and bedtime stories, her mother herself clung to research and scholarship. Turning academic was as comforting and as cloistering as any fiction.

"Will we send someone among them to learn their language?" Mel speculated aloud, wondering where exactly that would be and if, for another thing, the trogs wouldn't slaughter them on sight. And possibly eat them.

"That's something that will have to be determined."

"Do we have anyone among us who knows anything about these . . . people?" Mel asked, walking alongside her mother, matching her methodically even pace as they made their way down the road to the rest of the settlement. A cluster of larger buildings, similarly bricked as their own house, lay ahead of them. They approached the largest of them. Its heavy wood doors were open, but the meeting was already in progress. Mel thought she heard a small catch in her mother's breath, a small hiccup in her pulse.

"We do, in fact, have someone who knows a little," Mel's mother said casting a sidelong glance at Mel. "Your father. He returned from his task while you were away."

CHAPTER 11

The meeting hall, in which Mel had often been left as a child to amuse herself for long hours, was a remarkably quiet place for having almost two hundred people in it. Mel could hear just a faint murmur of voices and the sound of shuffling papers, a dulcet ensemble of whispers. The hall had amphitheater style seating with descending rows of tables around a central open floor. Books and papers covered most of the tables, and Mel could see clusters of two or three downturned heads at each. She spied her father descending the stone steps to the center of the hall.

She slid into the empty wooden chair next to her mother at their family table. Their neighbor, an older woman named Magla who used to tend to Mel when her mother was away on tasks, looked up at Mel with a seemingly blank stare. Mel saw a minuscule creasing of lines around Malga's eyes and a tightening in the corners of her mouth that indicated her pleasure at seeing Mel. Mel gave Magla her sweetest, most courtly smile that she'd practiced at the Keep. The light caught Magla's eye, and Mel saw a twinkle of amusement, a returned warmth. Then Mel looked back at her father.

Ley'Albaer was exactly as Mel remembered him. Steel gray hair, fair skin with a deeply wrinkled forehead—what her mother called a permanent scholar's scowl—the same unsmiling countenance that was not an expression of anger, but one of intense concentration. He had the same leanness, the same rigid posture as always. In four years, he had not changed at all, yet she herself had changed quite a lot. Would he notice? She repressed the urge to tap her foot under the table. She was a ball of nerves, and she knew that she was broadcasting all her emotions to everyone in the vicinity. They were all adults, all trained and practiced Masks. No one else her age. She flicked her eyes at her mother, who was watching Ley'Albaer approach the center of the room.

Her mother and her father were not married. They had not *chosen* each other. In fact, they had not even joined together in the traditional, witnessed bonding ceremony meant to publicly record an agreement between a man and a woman, or likewise, business partners. Her parents did not live in the same house when they were both home from tasks. They didn't show any particular affection for each other, even in the hardly discernible fashion of Masks who did.

The only thing they had truly agreed on, without reservation, was to raise a child together. They consulted each other in everything about her upbringing and offered equal guidance when each was available. Although it wasn't unheard of for men and women to produce a child without a formal relationship, Mel knew of no other such arrangements in her immediate acquaintances in the settlement. Although the truth was, there weren't many people within ten years of her age here at all. For that, she missed Cillary Keep.

Without any particular introduction or greeting, Ley'Albaer addressed the gathering, "We believe," he said, in his carefully measured speech, "That the creatures or 'trogs,' as some call them—although that carries a negative connotation—might require representation by us to determine their demands. From their actions, their entrance into the Cillary Keep, it appears that they consider themselves to have some sort of claim over those particular lands and its occupants. They gained entrance to the Keep by subterranean means and seem to have detained some of the Keep residents. It appears, in fact, that they might have obtained hostages, we think, to lend weight to their demands."

Murmuring in the amphitheater increased almost imperceptibly. He held up a hand to halt what was barely more than silence itself, and he addressed an inquiry that he had heard from somewhere in the voices.

"No, we do not know their language, although we have some ideas about what it might be and from where it may have been derived. They have been observed to have a certain guttural quality to their vocalizations. Possibly their throat structure has not developed in the same manner as ours. Certainly, it will make a fascinating thesis for any scholar among us looking for a particular specialization. We have not observed enough to make phonetic transcriptions, but we feel that there will be ample opportunity, doubtless in the near future. We have certain texts among us that refer to ancient cave dwellers, although we have not given enough attention to these texts, as those before us have categorized them as being the stuff of fairy tales and legends, if you will. Needless to say, we will need to locate and revisit these particular tomes as, undoubtedly, they have a certain pertinence as of late."

Mel fidgeted and made a small twitch of her head to try to loosen the tension in her neck. The slow cadence of her father's speech was irritating as he detachedly described her attackers. Her mother's eyebrow rose just a hint, a sign of her surprise at Mel's lack of self-control. Others around them turned their bodies away from her, trying to shield themselves from her disruptive behavior, though she had not made a sound.

"We are not certain," her father continued, "if they are, in fact, a peaceable people merely driven to violence by circumstance, by provocation. We do not know, for example, if they house a substantial population or even, perhaps, a militia underground or in another land, which they merely transport themselves from in a subterranean manner. We have heard accounts, for instance, of the weaponry that they carry. There's been some discussion as to whether these are, in fact, tools of industry and not originally intended as means of violence."

He then launched into a discussion, including line drawings and detailed diagrams that he and others had redrawn by hand on a large scale for the express purpose of presenting them to others now in the amphitheater. He proceeded in this manner for the better part of the day into the late afternoon—detailed discussion of a trog axe. Hours and hours to discuss the dimensions of the haft—the belly to the grip—the composite of the bit and the butt. Were they made of a common wood or an agamite-treated compressed material? Did the dimensions and materials of which they were made implicate the material which they intended to hew? Finally, Mel could not take it any longer.

The legs of her chair grated on the stone tiles as she pushed her chair back. She stood, and all eyes turned toward her. Watery, blank stares. Her father, too, silenced by the violence of her motion, looked up at her.

"What difference does it make whether the axes they carry were meant for mining stones or chopping wood?" she shouted, shaking. "What difference does it make when I have seen these blades sink into the flesh and bone of men and women?" She looked around, wide-eyed, and breathing hard. "My friends are *in that pit*."

"Mel," her mother said quietly. Mel looked down at her. Mortification hit her like a wave. She had disregarded her entire upbringing without any consideration for their methods, their conventions. Her self-control at this moment was that of an infant. She was livid, flushed, her heart beating like a doe's. Yet, all she could see in her mind's eye was Liz's body, lying inert on the soot-littered lawn of the burning Keep.

"I—I'm sorry for the interruption. Excuse me. I have to leave," she said and walked quickly out of the assembly hall and then sprinted across the clearing.

CHAPTER 12

Under the forest canopy, Rob stared across the burned-out campfire at Ott's back. The last embers had stopped smoking hours earlier, but he hadn't bothered to relight it because he had hoped they would head north today. The day wasn't warming up, and his feet were cold. The eerie blue leaves would be falling from the trees soon, and this forest would be bare like almost any other in winter, blue or not. He and Ott would need to trade large game for heavier coats within the week. For that matter, he wished he had woolen socks now—even badly-knitted ones would do. He suppressed a shiver. He would trade his firstborn for a scarf.

In any case, it wasn't good weather for sitting on the ground around a dead campfire. Ott had been lying on a bedroll all afternoon. Though it was still light, they had wasted hours when they were both better off at home. It was their fifth day in the same camp. Before the massacre at the Keep happened, they'd rarely made camp in the same place for even a single night. Rob was all right with letting his friend grieve, but figured he could still mourn on his feet, if it was all the same to him.

"Ott," he said. Then, not gruffly, gentler, "Mattieus." Ott turned his lanky body onto his belly, nose down on his blanket, but his ear was toward Rob. "We can't stay here, Ott. She's not here, man. The girl isn't here anymore, and we need to leave." It would take them weeks to get home. First, they would trek back through the forest. After that, there was the hike up the mountain roads, which could be treacherous if they iced over. There, the roads were little more than well-worn trails. And if the cold came before they made it home, they might as well be "taking a walk in winter," as the saying went. It would be the equivalent of suicide.

He knew what Ott was seeing in his mind, probably running it over and over till he wanted to scream or cry or kill something. Even Rob saw the images in his own dreams. The gigantic plumes of dust and choking smoke, the raining ash. Falling rock scattering underfoot. Wailing and moans of the wounded. Those damned, filthy, reeking animals swarming out of the hole in the ground with their rough-hewn axes, their blades going sinking into the skin of those girls. Beautiful girls in their costumes and masks, feathers and silk covered with blood and soot. Long legs, in high-soled shoes, bleeding from the knees, ankles twisted unnaturally—they hadn't been able to run away in those shoes. A smooth, brown, bare arm mostly severed from its shoulder. Those animals had come up from hell it seemed. Skin as tough and gray as animal hide. And they weren't more than animals, grunting at each other.

And then Ott saw his girl dash back into the dance hall just at its worst. A pretty girl prettily dressed, lithe like a deer. Barefoot, and surprisingly fast on her feet. Rob didn't know what she was thinking, rushing back into the fray, the horrible chaos too much even for a full-grown man. That she could save some of her friends? Maybe she had just panicked. Poor, dumb thing, crushed in a collapse of rubble now. Mel, she had been called. Hopefully, she had died quickly and had not suffered.

Rob had had his own share of losses. His mother's heart had stopped young, leaving him and his sisters with his vindictive snake of a father and just the house staff to raise them. He didn't remember what his mother looked like, although when he looked in the mirror, he knew his blue eyes must have been hers because they were not the coal black ones of his father. Then Rob had lost the girl he loved for lack of speaking up, for lack of courage. Saw her married off to another, now with kids to rear while he still pined for her like a fool. He had never been able to hold another woman up to her in comparison, even now.

And she would never know what he felt, even if he could put it into words now, nearly a decade later. He sighed, rubbing his eyes and forehead harshly with his own big, dumb, rough paw, as if he could wipe entire years out of his relentless memory.

"Ott," he said, this time with irritation. "Get up. Go home to Jenny and the kids. Do your duty. What the hell are we doing out here anyway?" With more noise and force than was necessary, he began to pack up the camp. Ott didn't move from his bedroll as Rob stomped away, kicking at the campfire stones.

At least they wouldn't go home empty-handed despite giving up that initial chase through the woods for Ott's girl. Rob had thought his old man would humiliate him if they arrived home without the troll's head. "Bring me its head or don't bother to bring yourself back," the old man had said.

His wheezing rants and rages could still make Rob's stomach twist into greasy knots, though the old bastard now was stooped and gnarled—as much from anger as old age, it seemed.

As it turned out, Rob and Ott had had several heads to choose from. Rob would never have thought that likely to happen when they arrived at the ball and saw all the young girls in their finery, the hall with its twinkling candle light and smell of rich foods. Yet, here was one of the blasted beast's heads in his hands. He hefted the large glass jar with the pickling solution. Double the size of a cooked cabbage and just as gray. The eyes were shut, thank Dovay, the bear-god of perseverance. Rob had screwed the metal lid on tightly, but couldn't help checking it several times a day as if the thing could come back to life and get them in their sleep. Rather grotesque, but a head was what the old man wanted. And what he wanted, he got. Always.

And here Rob was, holding it up to the light, contemplating his own life. All he knew was, it was better outside the jar. At least marginally.

After the first explosion at the Keep, Ott had followed the girl Mel back inside to help, to . . . do whatever had to be done. And when the hallway collapsed on her with its crushing stones, no possibility of her escape, Ott screamed and bellowed in such a rage as Rob had never witnessed in his life, in man or animal, not even in his father during the worst of times. The scream had been followed by a foolhardy attack on the trolls in which Ott launched himself directly at the nearest one, knocking it to the ground and stunning it. He grabbed its axe, and in one swing, beheaded it. It had been a true berserker's rage—Rob read about those once. They were the stuff of fairy tales, just as much as these ogres. Ott had stood there, panting and wild-eyed, and Rob had run at him and knocked off balance the troll who was at Ott's back. When the beast was down, Rob grabbed the axe out of its leathery, hide-covered fingers and hacked its head cleanly off. After that, they managed to kill seven, maybe eight, of the creatures. Which had been futile, as they became a swarm of hundreds. He and Ott would have died had the monsters not retreated back into their lair.

In the end, Ott dropped his blood-soaked axe and stumbled out of the Keep across the lawn and into the woods. He sank to his knees at the base of a tree. Rob found him there later, after collecting the requisite head for old Col Rob. The creatures had retreated, taking their dead, taking some of the human dead back into the pit from which they had exploded.

When Rob took Ott's arm to lead him back to camp, Ott broke away and ran back to the black hole. He was at the point of throwing himself into it when Rob caught him around the waist. "Just let me go," Ott had said, causing a part of Rob to crack open inside. Some stones from underfoot fell down the abyss, and stinging fumes rose up. He was not sure either of them could survive down there or even if there was breathable air. Ott went limp then, and Rob lifted him up and carried him over his shoulder back to camp, the monster's head still gripped in his other hand.

Now finished packing up their modest camp, Rob went to check on Ott. He was sitting up now. His face had a gray look to it, and his eyes were dull, but he set his jaw, got up from his bedroll, and began to tie it up. They had a long journey north ahead of them, and Rob hoped a little life might come back to his friend before they reached home.

CHAPTER 13

For his part, Ott found himself on his feet one day, upright and walking alongside Rob. They had been traveling north toward home, but he wasn't sure for how many days. He saw the road stretched out in front of them, blue woods disappearing to the south. He found himself slamming down walls inside his mind, jailing the thoughts that would otherwise make it impossible for him to put one foot in front of the other.

Rob was right—Ott had Jenny to look after. She was at home with the three little ones who looked nothing like her, but like him instead. How was that for motivation? It was hard not to feel a little lighter just thinking about their soft, perfect faces and their small hands on his cheeks and around his neck. Poor Jenny had it tough. She was always there at the house with them, unable to move about as she liked, as Ott did. He loved and fiercely protected her as if she were his younger sister instead of his elder. She and her children lived in his crumbling family home not far from Rob's father's land. Rob was right. God only knew how she was managing. They had been away far too long, and now Ott picked up his pace. And Rob, relieved, picked up his as well.

CHAPTER 14

In her modest low-ceilinged room Mel was not asleep. She didn't like to dream anymore because when she slept, her dreams weren't the comforting, escapist forays they had been in the past. Now, they were filled with suffocating smoke and severed limbs or else the empty promises of a green-eyed person she would never see again. Lying awake in her bed, she thought her breathing was shallow and even enough to fool her parents, had they been paying attention to her. However, they were in the library, both of their pulses running high. She lay in her bed watching the movement of their shadows under the crack of her door.

"Would you rather she stay here and be considered sub-par and deficient like Jenks?" her father was saying in a low, cool voice. "Or would you let her leave and be considered more than average out in the world at large?"

Like Jenks? Why would I be like him?

"She is talented. She would not be a failure here," her mother said. The unspoken like Jenks, trailed her words. "And she might be ostracized and viewed with suspicion out in world. What would she do, be a fortune teller, a healer, or a courtesan? You of all people know how difficult it is to live among them. And she is not deficient. Not in any way."

"She lived among them all this past season successfully, did she not? She had a whole season to make friends and connections."

"Who are all dead or missing. Use your heart, Ley'Albaer, if you have one. It must be somewhere still beating inside of you." Then her mother said, "I will not send her away. And that is my final word."

"I have never known you not to compromise, Ana," her father said calmly. He was surprised, but his pulse was slowing. He was beginning to detach from the conversation, Mel realized. Her mother realized it, too and ceased pressing her point, knowing that the discussion was over.

He doesn't care what happens to me?

Mel heard the sound of shuffling papers, the whisper of books being removed from a stack. Without any bidding of goodnight or farewell, her father left silently, closing the front door behind him. His restraint was far worse than any outburst may have been. Mel heard a faint gasp, an intake of breath, and she realized with alarm that her mother was crying. She sat up in bed, but before she could get up, the door opened and her mother came in.

"I'm sorry you had to hear that," she said sitting on the edge of Mel's bed. Mel wasn't sure if her mother meant the argument or her gasping sob. She'd never heard her mother cry before. *Never*. As she examined her mother's face in the near-darkness, she didn't find any trace of tears or discomfiture. Her mother was still upset. The air in her room was chilly, but Mel preferred to hug herself under the blanket instead of going to the trouble of warming her skin by concentration. She liked the feel of the warm weight against her, its familiar smell of herbs and rainwater that they used for wash.

"I've never thought disparagingly of Jenks," Mel said. But she had never considered Jenks one of them, that was for certain. He was not a Mask. He was just a quiet man with kind blue eyes, a solitary outsider, who ran messages and errands between them and the outside world. She thought he lived apart from all people by choice.

"Jenks was born here," her mother said. "He's a relation, in fact. Related to you by blood."

That news stunned Mel. "You grew up with him? Trained with him?"

"Yes."

"But he doesn't live here in the settlement. Was he made to leave?"

"Made to?" Her mother shook her head. "No, he was allowed to stay here if he liked. He chose to leave." Mel struggled to comprehend. Her mother was being purposefully cautious with details.

"But he was asked not to wear the Mask?"

"We all thought it a wise decision, but it was his to make. However, it's true, he would not have made an adequate Mask. He was too . . . impulsive. Unable to remain neutral, which is essential to our role when we're on the outside. If we cannot remain impartial, we are all but useless to others."

"And you think I am like him?" Mel steadied herself. If she let herself, she could burn with shame at her earlier outburst in the meeting hall.

"No, Mel, I do not."

"You don't think I need to leave, too?"

"No, Mel." Her mother took her hand. Her mother's fingers were cool and smooth. She had calmed herself as well.

"But my father does."

Her mother was silent for a minute. "I'm afraid you do not know your father as well as you might. He has been away these four years during some of your most formative times. He's very highly valued as a Mask. And further, he cares about you very deeply. Never doubt that for an instant."

"He may care for me, but he doesn't think I belong here," Mel said.

"He merely wants what is best for you."

"Does he?" Mel wondered aloud.

Instead of answering, her mother said, "Maybe you should talk with Jenks about his decision, if he's willing to discuss it. He might talk with you." She sounded doubtful. "In any case, I intend for you to take the Mask and to accompany me on my task."

Mel was stunned yet again.

Her mother explained further, "I have received a summons. We have an assignment. I'm preparing to attend a labor dispute in the north. I mean for you to travel as my second."

Mel had a thousand questions. She was going to wear the Mask? So soon? Was it the right thing for her to do? Though frequent travel was in the cards for a Mask, did she want to leave home again? Was she ready? She could manage only one word. "When?"

"The dispute is quite heated. And although I need time to prepare, we have been solicited with some urgency. I have past experience with these types of negotiations and a great deal of scholarship in the behavioral patterns of workers. We are hoping to curtail any violent actions, so we hope to be in place fairly quickly. I believe we can prepare ourselves and leave before winter. We will not want to encounter their winter while we are traveling. It could make for quite a treacherous passage. Also, that will give you time for study and memorization until then, and I can gather a few provisions." She stood and smoothed the blanket where she'd been sitting. "We travel very lightly, you know."

"I know," said Mel.

"You are satisfied with this plan?" her mother asked her.

In the dark, Mel nodded, knowing her mother could see her.

"Good night then, Mel." They did not embrace—it wasn't their custom other than following a long separation—and although her mother's presence soothed her, Mel wished for a moment that they could be like any human mother and daughter that she'd read about, that she'd heard about first-hand at the Keep. She would have liked to have been wrapped inside her mother's velvety caress.

Sometime later, Mel still could not sleep. She draped her blanket around her shoulders. Pausing by her mother's room, she could feel, finally, the relaxed mind of her mother as she slept deeply, the even exchange of breaths in and out. Mel pushed open their heavy wooden front door and slipped outside, stopping on the porch to slide on her shoes before she stepped out onto the road. Her father's house was a few hundred paces down. Though it was the middle of the night now, she saw light in the windows. Her breath came in ghostly clouds in the chilled air. The sky was clear, but she was sure they would have their first snow before too much longer.

At ten paces away, she saw the front door of his house open. He stood waiting for her. How great a distance did his sense radius encompass, she wondered. Did he know she was awake even as she lay in her room tossing and turning? She climbed the steps of the porch. His face was calm, unreadable. He stepped aside to allow her to enter. The inside of his house was the same cool temperature as outside despite its cozy light.

"Do you feel the cold?" Ley'Albaer asked her immediately, not concerned but curious. His steel gray eyebrows flickered upward.

"Yes," she said. "But I like the comfort of a blanket."

"You can control your temperature, but you choose not to do so," he said, summarizing carefully.

"Yes."

"Why?" He surprised her.

She struggled to find words. Then she said, "I like to feel."

"It's our ability to control our emotions that makes us valuable to others."

She felt chastened and pulled the blanket tighter around herself.

"I'm sorry," he said, though she wasn't sure if she believed he was. "I don't mean to antagonize you or to lecture you. I would just like to understand." She was silent, so he continued. "You have twenty-five years. I have sixty-four. I forget that I cannot always treat you as my equal. You look full grown now, so it is easy for me to forget."

She frowned. "So in four years away, you have forgotten me?"

He allowed himself a smile, faintly amused. "I begin to remember." He lifted his arms, the most infinitesimal gesture, but it was enough encouragement for her. She threw her arms around him and hugged him tightly. He stiffened, but accepted her embrace.

"I missed you," she said.

"Ah, our little rose, so like your mother." He clucked his tongue like a grandmother and awkwardly patted her hair. "Perhaps what makes you superior to us is your ability to feel so much more. And to make us envy you for it. What are we going to do when you leave us?"

"You were gone for four years. My mother and I won't be gone as long as that," she said stepping back from him. He nodded thoughtfully. She searched his face, but his features were as fixed as iron, as smooth as glass. She swept over his face again looking for a crack in the façade, any movement or tick. Then, she simply realized what his silence meant. "You're coming with us? On the task?"

He nodded. "It might be a bit more than the labor dispute that your mother thinks it is. Yet, she insists on taking you for training." He gave a little shrug. "Trial by fire?"

"Now *I* don't understand," she said.

He flicked his hand. "I don't want to presume anything prematurely. We must collect the evidence before attempting to administer opinion."

Mel looked at him with exaggerated skepticism, which caused him to laugh, a strange sound coming from him, as strange as from her mother. Rare and warm. It transfigured his face, and she saw something of herself reflected. "Such broad humor. And from my own child. I believe your mother has given birth to a comedienne. I know you're giving me that ridiculous look because you think *I'm* ridiculous." He held up his hand when she started to protest. "I think I might be out of touch with you, as they say."

"No, Ley'Albaer, you're above ridicule. I grimaced at you because you, of all people, are gifted enough to be called a seer. You must know that people think of you this way." Of course Mel didn't believe in magic. Masks disavowed its existence. Seeing the future was really just a matter of reading the signs and making educated predictions.

He shrugged noncommittally. Humble acknowledgment, she wondered. Well, she would be like him then. She would wait and see before she decided who he was. She would have their entire journey to figure him out.

CHAPTER 15

One afternoon, Mel headed away from the settlement to see Jenks. When she thought she was far enough from the settlement's collective range of sensation, she broke into a run through the forest. A sleeping owl awoke momentarily as she passed underneath, and then shut its eyes. Her furtiveness was not about her desire to run, but rather, her failure of communal expectation—definitely a broader concern than her wanting a little exercise but entwined inextricably with her love of motion, her inability to always sit still, her failure to become one of *them* and further their knowledge base.

Since coming back from the Keep, her lapses in control were becoming more and more frequent. She hoped a run would help alleviate some of her excess . . . she didn't know what it was. Energy. Spirit. Restlessness. Heart-break. She leaped over a fallen tree, skidding slightly on a carpet of fallen leaves. More evidence of encroaching winter. That and the snapping chill in the air. She caught her balance easily and accelerated. Her arms pumped, and a light sheen of perspiration beaded on her skin. Instead of stilling her breath and matching it to her pace, she let her heartbeat escalate, the blood flowing into her skin to cool.

Let it move. Let the heart pound. By pumping, it tells me I am alive. I am here. Beat away the numbness.

And then tears welled up in her eyes. For Liz, Rav. For Ott. For herself. She could hardly see, but pushed her pace further, not caring if her footsteps rang out, not caring who she startled or what walls within her suddenly came down out here in the open with no one to hear her. She pounded on. By the time she reached Jenks' low-roofed clapboard cabin, her face was wet. She was soaked to the skin, panting, and winded.

"Well, that's interesting," he said, observing her as she braced her hand against a tree and tried to catch her breath. He was sitting in a rocking chair on his porch reading a book. She straightened as soon as she heard him, but he gestured with his hand, a peculiar, dismissive move, a tired wave mingled with the half-hearted brushing away of an inattentive fly. "Don't trouble yourself on my account," he said. "But if you'd like to sit while you rest, I have a hard and uncomfortable porch step you can help yourself to."

She concentrated, dried her skin, and slowed her heart. She left her legs to cool and ache on their own. "Did you know I was coming to see you?" she asked him, throwing herself down on the step inelegantly, almost defiantly, waiting for him to chastise her.

"Expected it. Didn't know it for sure," he said. "Thought it might have been sooner."

"I meant to come," she said. "Every day, I meant to come talk with you." She plucked at the sole of her shoe where it was separating from the rest.

He flicked his bright blue eyes at her and set his book aside, spine split open at his place on the dusty porch floor. It was an old book. She glanced at the spine and corrected herself. Not an old book, just a beat up book. It was a recent publication, a *novel*, a story written for the sake of entertainment. He saw her looking at it.

"You can borrow it when I'm done. It's a little romantic though. Don't know how you'd feel about that. Heroes and heroines. *People running around in a big hurry.*" Right. Just as she had been doing.

She looked at him. Dark, weathered skin. White hair, cut short so it bristled. He was looking at her wryly, a faint glimmer of a smile around his mouth. She said, "Why didn't you ever tell me we're related? All those times we said hello. All those times you delivered things to our house? Messages. Vegetables. Family connection thrown in along with the delivery?"

"It's true. We didn't say much more than 'hello,'" he said.

"We don't even look alike. You don't look like my mother, but you're related to her? Are you cousins?" She ran a hand through her own auburn hair, thinking of her mother's. Her mother had the same color hair as Mel, but light brown eyes and ultra-fair skin. Librarian skin. Jenks was ruddy with silver hair. Bright blue eyes—he was looking at her with amusement, slight crinkling in the corners. Pure, unadulterated amusement, emotion on display. Being with him was like being with outsider humans. Except, he knew everything about her. Somehow, he managed to live in both worlds. On the other hand, he lived in neither world.

"Don't look like her at all, do I?"

"What's so funny? This is all amusing to you?" Mel asked mildly. He was teasing her. Not that she minded. She'd just forgotten what it was like, casual banter, conversation at cross-purposes. Plenty at stake, though, at least for her. She was reminded of the verbal give and take they practiced at the Keep.

"Of course it's funny to me." His eyes met hers directly. As she looked into them, they changed from bright, crystalline blue to black. The outlines of his face blurred for an instant, and she realized his appearance as she knew it was a façade, a disguise. For just an instant, she saw pale skin. Eyes as dark as her own. Hair as dark as her father's. She stared, slightly open-mouthed. She caught just a glimpse before the Jenks that she had always known wavered back into focus, his bristled white hair and sun-weathered skin. She gasped, not sure what she was seeing. Because there was no such thing as magic.

"It's always entertaining," he said again, ignoring her shock, smiling again with the face she knew as his, bright blue eyes twinkling. "That's my job. My role as village idiot. To react inappropriately to things." He stood up and opened the door to his cabin. "That's why I live over here. And the rest of them live over there." He gestured vaguely in the direction of the settlement. "Are you coming?" She scrambled up and followed him inside the cabin.

"You're a shifter?" she asked, breathlessly. "I didn't know they existed outside of children's stories. You have a truly rare talent. I can change the shade of my hair for about a minute and then I'm exhausted. Do they know about this? You have this talent and you're hiding out here? Doing . . . " she searched for words that wouldn't be insulting, but ended up just waving dumbly at the furnishings of his modest cabin. Comfortable chair. A warm fireplace. Piped water. Indoor kitchen. Wooden carvings littering the floor. Door to another room off the side. Strong smell of herbs and something mineral, but not unpleasant.

Standing in the middle of the small room, he shrugged. "Shifter. Seer. Healer. Scholar. Your mother is a natural healer when she chooses to let herself be. We all have our talents. Who better than I to walk among them?" Did he mean the settlement or the outside world? He shifted again. A little man, hunched with arthritis and dotted with age spots, stood in his sitting room. Dressed in a stained, wrinkled holiday-best suit, he shrugged, his voice weak and cracking, "Who better than I?"

"That's really disconcerting," she said with a sharp intake of breath.

His blue eyes twinkled and he shrugged again, back to his former appearance. "A lot of people think so," he said cryptically and looked away from her.

"Is that why you were asked to live out here? Were you ostracized?"

He chuckled. "Me? No. They didn't ask me to leave. I chose to."

She thought about it. "And this is as far as you went? You can just about see the settlement from here."

He laughed outright. "Can't have it both ways, can I? Too near. Too far." He abruptly turned and left the room through the only door. She stood, uncertain of whether he meant her to follow. Then, she went to the doorway and looked in.

The room was as big as all of the other parts of the house put together. Part workshop, part laboratory, part artist studio, but utterly cluttered. She identified the source of the herbal smell—dried bunches hanging from the ceiling. Not just dried herbs though. He also had live cuttings that he seemed to be rooting in glass jars. And dyeing. Jars of colors, swatches of paint lined the table. Those were the sources of the mineral smells. Yellow dyed flowers which should have been white naturally stood in brilliant yellow water. And blue ones, sitting in what looked like crushed agamite, *turning blue like the trees near the Keep*. Mel froze at that thought. Was there a large quantity of agamite underneath the Keep? Did the agamite bring the beasts? She stared at Jenks.

"What else are you?" she said with an uncontrollable edge in her voice, aware that she might be overstepping the boundary of polite manners. She lightened her tone, tried to match his playfulness. "Herbalist? Alchemist? Are you trying to turn things into gold?"

He smiled ruefully. "I'm what you might call a 'dabbler,'" he said, the little old man's voice coming out with the last word. "Not enough focus to do any real harm. Or good. Just curious about the ways of the world. Not enough to see anything coming."

See things coming. A seer. She felt the jab at her father. "Have something against my father, do you?"

"Hmmm?" He willfully misunderstood her meaning. "Your father is as close to a seer as we have seen in many, many generations. We would do well to encourage him."

"That sounds like a line, something you say by rote," she said. "Have you said that one before?"

"A few times." He smiled and let his facade shift briefly, his eyes changing to coal black for a flicker. It could have been menacing, but it wasn't.

"How long have you known that you were a shifter?" she asked, wondering if she had latent talents that would someday surface, especially if Jenks were a blood relation of hers.

"Since I was old enough to focus my eyes," he said. She gave him a quizzical look. "I was a baby lying in my bassinet. First thing I saw was our household cat. World's first and most adorable cat-baby. At least for a minute. Couldn't hold it very long then. That came with practice."

She leaned against the counter. "During the attack on the Keep, I lifted a stone that was five times my weight, but I was exhausted for, I don't know, days, maybe weeks." She didn't mention the other factors that had incapacitated her as well. Namely, a heart and mind that were ripped open. And, well, nightmarish ogres.

He looked at her appraisingly. "Probably not your forte then, even though you can do it."

"Then how did I lift the stone at all?"

He shrugged. "Natural anxiety in the heat of the situation. Unusual circumstances. We don't always know what we can do until we're pushed." He paused. "Look. Masks can all do the simple things. Heal ourselves to some extent. Manipulate the light immediately around us by reflecting it or absorbing it. You're wondering if you're a shifter, a healer, or a seer. You're not going to know till it happens. It is what it is. There's no pushing it. And there may never be an *it*." He resumed gathering some tools together on the table surface. "It takes the right circumstance and the right person in it to awaken a talent." He said the word without bothering to hide the bitterness in his tone.

She realized, then, why he lived apart from the settlement. His ability to shift was so strong, how could they trust him to be who he said he was? He was built for subterfuge, not impartial observation and scholarship.

He was still talking. "Take Malga, your nanny. She didn't know she was a natural nursemaid till she was in her seventy-fifth year and met you. Didn't know that, did you?" He smiled at her surprise. "She can soothe babies of all kinds. Didn't know it until her own womb was long dried up. Might not have ever realized it at all. Destiny is a very unsympathetic mistress sometimes."

She watched him pour a white powder into a small stone mortar and begin grinding it with a pestle, his dry-skinned fingers wrapped around the stone tool. He reached up and broke a sprig of plant off a hanging bunch above him. He dropped it into the mix and ground it some more. It released a sharp smell that was both fresh and sweet. The whole mixture abruptly turned green, then lightened as the white mixed with it.

"Go ahead and ask me," he said.

She watched him grind the mixture until it became smooth. She couldn't contain her curiosity. "All right. What is that?"

He shrugged. "Toothpaste." He scraped the creamy mix into a jar and screwed the lid on tightly. "But that's not what you want to ask me."

"Are you a mentalist—a mind reader—too?"

He laid his hands flat on the smooth wooden work table, and said again, "*Ask me*. Speak your question. You've had plenty of time to work up to it. What are you waiting for? Just ask me."

She came out with it. "When you see a path in front of you, how do you know if you should choose it and not some other path? How do I know if I'm supposed to take the Mask? What if it's not for me? What if I fail? Am I like you? Am I destined for something else? Or nothing at all? Am I . . . am I better off leaving the settlement and finding my own way? What if I do that and I just end up hurting everyone and failing anyway?"

"Kind of one question, but kind of a lot of questions," he said.

She rephrased it. "How did you know *you* didn't want to take the Mask?"

"Hm," he said. "But I did."

"You did? You did what?"

"I *was* a Mask. For a while." While she stared at him in surprise, he continued. "I went on only two tasks before I put it down. Very simple tasks, generally speaking. No nations at stake. No people being tried for their lives. A divorce, in the first case. An estate dispute in the second. The first lasted four months, and the second only seven weeks."

"How did you know that you couldn't do it?"

"Too much anger," he said with a half-smile. All she had seen of him was wry playfulness. It was hard to imagine him with a scowl. The corners of his eyes creased as he watched her try to digest what he'd said. "I have what was deemed 'an excess of emotion.' I couldn't help people. I couldn't listen to their problems objectively when I cared too much about them. These people I was supposed to judge—they were complete strangers at first. Then suddenly, I was invested in their lives. I knew them. Cared for them. Loved them. And, as you know, anything but absolute objectivity is . . . "

"Useless in a Mask," she finished for him. He shrugged, and she wondered, "But how do you tell them? How were you able just to tell all of them?" She didn't gesture toward the settlement, but they both knew who she meant.

He wiped his hands on a towel and stood for a moment. "It was better to hurt them for a short while than all of the people out there, possibly forever. If I had continued as a Mask, I would have failed many people, many times over. I can't even comprehend the harm I could have done."

"But how do I figure out what I'm supposed to do?" she said. "I'm leaving on my first task in just a few days. And it's not an insignificant one, as far as things go. And I'm not the primary. Both of my parents will be there. But I'll be there. As a Mask. Don't I owe it to these people to be the best we have? To be objective and cool-minded, scholarly, and rational?"

"And compassionate?" He looked at her with a tilt to his head, his blue eyes twinkling though his expression was somber.

"Compassion? That's the very thing I need to hide."

"Maybe," he said, though it didn't sound like a maybe.

"So there is a place for compassion in all of this confusion? How do I judge?" She looked at him, not bothering to control what she knew were wild eyes and flat-out fear written on her face. "What do I do?" she asked finally. She had no idea what to do. She needed guidance. She needed advice. She needed someone to tell her, specifically, word-for-word, what to do.

He gave that simple half-smile, blue eyes glinting black. "Just try not to foul it up."

CHAPTER 16

Ott and Rob had been traveling for days. No, it had been weeks, Ott realized, slowly coming back to himself a little more, hour by hour. The ground here was frozen, he noticed, making their path slippery as they ascended north into higher elevation. Gasgun Lake off to their left was solid, most likely for duration of the winter. He couldn't see the cold letting up now that it had started its icy sweep over the area. The lake was always the first one in the area to freeze. Probably had an iceberg at its core from the way it felt, even in summer. No fishing there for a while, not even in an ice house. Ice crystals formed on his scarf under his nose.

The sky threatened snow at any minute, but they were only a long day's walk from home, and it wasn't windy, thank Lutra. And just as he thought that, the wind picked up, as if to taunt him. *Home*, he thought ambivalently, squinting against the sting of the air. He would be glad to see his sister and her children, to feel their small arms around his neck, and to sit in front of a warm fire with dry, unfrozen toes. But he wasn't sure he had a place there anymore. He had a room. Yes, it was his room and had always been his, but he'd been gone for so long . . . Never mind the urge to turn his feet back south toward that oppressive blue forest, not just in footsteps, but to turn back in time to where *she* was. His chest tightened like it was gripped by very real bands, instead of ones made of misery.

"Looks like it's going to snow," Rob said from under his fur-lined hat for about the fifth time. Ott grunted. He tucked his chin in and returned to his thoughts. They were loaded down by their packs. Ott eyed Rob's where it was distorted by the large jar with its ghastly contents. The head. Thankfully, the thing's eyes were closed in there or Ott would not have been able to sleep in the same camp. It made him feel queasy. A lot of things made him feel sick right about now—things he couldn't get out of his mind for the life of him.

The worst part of it wasn't thinking about one of those creatures dragging Mel through the blue-tinted underbrush—although that was an awful memory. The beast had been ponderously crashing below them with her tucked under into the thick hide of its side, rough hands clamping her down like she was a rag doll. They had saved her that time. The worst part was not having been able to save her a second time. He couldn't even remember what happened at the Keep after the stones crushed her. After the hallway collapsed and she was . . . killed. Everything leading up to that, he remembered in sickening detail. How the smoke filled his nose and eyes. A scream behind him. Stones crashing down all around. The sting of debris. The hallway disintegrating. Then nothing. Rob said later he saw Ott kill one of them, but Ott didn't remember any of it. A part of him had been sliced out. He felt its absence, but suspected it was a festering wound that his mind had wanted to quarantine for good reason.

What price would he pay to have her back? Anything. He would give anything he had. Or was he elevating the memory of her to impossible perfection now that he would never have her? He'd had only one conversation with her, an interrupted one at that. How could he know, especially from such a short time together, that she was perfect—perfect for him, as flawed as he was?

Stupid line of thought. It served only to make him feel the loss more, to stab at an open wound with a hot poker. He blinked his stinging eyes as the wind picked up. They might have to find shelter soon. The first tiny, biting grains of snow began to blow. He raised a gloved hand to scrub across his eyes and crashed into the back of Rob, who had stopped. Rob grabbed Ott's arm trying to steady him on the icy path as their feet attempted to slip out from under them.

"What is it?" Ott shouted irritably over the growing wind.

Rob pointed. The road split ahead. From the mines westward, a steady stream of people flowed, heading east toward home. Not just people but all kinds of creatures—children, animals on leads, and people carrying or dragging their belongings. Not moving slowly either. They were traveling at a fairly steady clip, with the smaller children being carried. Now that they were closer, Ott could hear the clank of mining tools strapped to the pack animals, children crying, and the occasional dog bark. Ahead of them at the fork in the road, there was a wagon upended in the ditch, one set of its gray wooden wheels pointing toward them. Two people—adults—with other smaller figures huddled nearby were staring at the wreckage, no one stopping to help them, their pots, pans, and other belongings strewn on the frosted ground. Yet, the stream of bodies flowed on.

CHAPTER 17

"Mass exodus," Rob said, his voice breaking with shock. He had more reason than Ott to be concerned. These people worked for Rob's family mines. They were his father's people. One day, they would be *Rob's* people.

"Where are they going?" Ott asked as they drew closer. Rob laid a hand on the arm of a man passing by and repeated Ott's question.

"We're getting away from the cursed trolls. What d'you think? The bastards took over the mines. They slaughtered us. We can't stay there," the man told him, his manner suggesting he had clearly not recognized Rob. Otherwise, there would have been deference or at least a hint of respect in his tone. The man moved on with the others, his head ducked down in the wind, and soon disappeared in the dark, shuffling crowd of huddled shoulders.

"Do you need help with your wagon?" Rob shouted at the man standing in the ditch. The man looked up with a sour expression. He was middle-aged with thin wisps of gray hair blowing out of his blue woolen cap, his bony wrists dangling beyond too-short sleeves.

"It's a lost cause," he said. "Damn thing broke an axle. It'll be covered in the snow by tomorrow. Me and the young ones were just picking up what we can carry."

"We'll help you," Rob said, gesturing at Ott to come with him as he slid down the side of the incline.

"Get them pots over there," the man barked at his blue-lipped children, who scrambled to collect the scattered cookware on the cold ground. Not a gloved hand among them, Ott noticed.

When they were moving again, back among the crowd, the man pointed to his own chest. "Jonas. And my eldest daughter Treyna," he said pointing to the other adult with him. Ott was surprised when she lifted her eyes to meet his and then looked at him from under her snow-laced lashes. She was not put off at all by Ott's scowl. He had thought she was the man's wife from the way she had care of the younger kids, but she was young, too, maybe younger than Ott by a couple years even. Her eyes were gray-blue and clear. She smiled at him and then lowered her face again. She was gloveless like her siblings, and her knuckles were raw and cracked from the cold where she grasped the edges of her shawl together. Jonas didn't bother introducing the younger children, of which there were three, the eldest only thigh-high to Ott, maybe five years old at the most. Rob gave Ott a look and hoisted the nearest child up in his arms as they walked.

"Where are you headed?" Rob tried again. His fur-lined hat was pulled low over his eyes, so he was able to remain unrecognized.

Jonas was willing to talk. "To the big house. There's a camp and they're taking us in. There will be food and a roof and strength in numbers. There will be warm fires and safety." Over the head of the child in his arms, Rob's eyes widened at Ott. The big house meant Rob's father's house, and was somewhat of a misnomer. The structure had rooms for well over 100 families, meeting chambers, and private antechambers. It housed the remaining members of Rob's family along with the elder council members and their kin. Building it had taken Rob's ancestors more than a generation using the sweat off the backs of their servants.

"What happened to the mine?" Rob asked.

"Attacked," Jonas said simply, with a shrug that seemed inappropriately casual. It seemed the presence of the creatures, the beasts, was common knowledge now.

"Where are you coming from?" Treyna got up the nerve to ask, risking a glare from Jonas. She fell in step with Ott, the mud darkening the hem of her skirts.

"Farther south," Ott told her shortly.

"And were the trolls there, too?" she asked. Her voice was low and didn't carry well in the wind.

He nodded, a curt jerk of his head, a twinge of loss hitting him hard.

She read his face easily, but, not knowing his exact ailment, simply said, "We've lost everything, too. A lot of people have. We don't know where else to go. Wandering here and there at the mercy of strangers. It's hard on the little ones." She looked away, then down. Then, her eyes flicked back to him. It was a strange and telling look. A hardness in the set of her mouth caught him by surprise. Then it cleared as she twisted her mouth into a small, forlorn smile. Her tiny body was small and needed protection—he could feel her trying to draw him in with her eyes as surely as a honey trap. The wind picked up then and snow fell harder. Treyna hefted up her smallest sibling, so Ott picked up the other, a girl with gray eyes like her sister's who buried her face too trustingly into his neck, away from the stinging snow.

They walked through nightfall, trampling the snow in the road with their hundreds of footprints, though it collected to either side of the road. Miners were not nomads. They dug in by nature, perhaps by instinct. They set their shoulders to the task and worked in rhythm until the day was done. Walking was no different for them. There was no point in stopping. It was too uncomfortable to rest and real comfort was close enough to keep them on their feet.

Ott and Rob walked on with them. The little girl in Ott's arms fell asleep despite him shifting her from arm to arm when he ached. He imagined Treyna had it worse. She was slim and poorly dressed. Her face was wind-whipped and her eyes were drooping from exhaustion, but somehow her feet moved along with the crowd. Jonas walked ahead of them. Ott knew they were headed in the right direction, but he wondered how many others in the crowd besides himself and Rob knew that for certain. How many of them were frozen and filled with despair?

A few hours after dark, they heard a shout from ahead of them. Someone had spotted lights in the distance, and spurred on, they were soon walking into the camp city. The outer tents were cold and nearly deserted—wind blocks, really. The inner tents were warmer and filled with people sleeping on rugs surrounded by the mishmash of their belongings. Ott heard Rob swear under his breath, quietly enough not to wake the sleeping children, but loud enough that Treyna heard him, too. They found a place to spread their blankets and put down the children who instinctively rolled together, sharing warmth like sleeping puppies.

Ott pulled Rob aside, "They can't sleep out here much longer. When winter truly arrives, they'll freeze to death, every last one of them." He was looking at the sleeping children. Treyna, sitting tiredly next to them, caught his eye, but looked away quickly. She gathered her shirts around her legs, tucking them in, shivering. Rob rubbed the back of his neck, which probably ached as much as Ott's did. A small child was not a heavy load to carry, but even a light load became a burden after so many miles.

"I know that as well as you," Rob whispered back fiercely. "But there are hundreds of people. Where would we put them?" Ott knew well enough that *we* meant Rob's family, not necessarily himself included. Part of him was thankful for that. Part of him wanted to duck out and go home to Jenny and her kids, to sit by their warm fire and to be grateful for it.

Jonas saw them standing apart, getting ready to take their leave. "Stay and make camp with us," he said, a little too forcefully, a little too demandingly. "Treyna!" he hissed at her. Her head, which had been resting on her skirted knees, snapped up at his command. She started to get up, to try to play hostess in their makeshift camp without anything to offer them. Dutiful daughter, Ott thought. Jonas glared at her, and she hastily stood up, shaking out her skirts, smoothing them. She placed a tentative hand on Ott's sleeve.

"Please stay with us," she said in a low, compelling plea. She lifted her eyes to his. Dark gray eyes that turned sapphire in the camp light. Her cloak had fallen open at the neck, exposing a beaded string. Lutra, Ott's family's goddess. Ease. Sociability. Family. Treyna was very beautiful, but Ott felt nothing for her. Did Jonas think they owed him something? He seemed to expect that they would join his camp, to be entertained by his daughter. These people's future was uncertain in the camp, Ott realized. Three small children, a young woman, and an old man. Someone would take advantage of them, as cold as it was, as desperate as they all were. Rob pulled Ott's other sleeve, a short jerk that made him frown. Treyna's coaxing smile faltered.

"We'll go look for food," Ott said to her haltingly, his lie sounding flat. His exhaustion made him weave on his feet. He couldn't remember the last time he'd eaten and the frozen air robbed their bodies of moisture—the thirst alone should have made him restless. Yet it didn't. Perhaps he should have worried about his lack of appetite and thirst, but he couldn't muster up more than a passing notice of it.

"Bring some to share at our fire," said Jonas, not quite disguising his frustrated scowl. They had no fire. They hardly had space to call their own in the communal tent.

"We'll let you know if we find any," Ott told Treyna, as he backed away, though it was not much of a promise. The sooner he was away from them, the better. Her sad, desperate eyes made him want to run. He cast a parting glance at the little ones. Light from other people's fires cast shadows on their faces, relaxed in slumber, lips red and stung by wind and frost. They could be cast in ice and never know to wake up, the three of them together frozen in one piece, held together by one thin blanket. They were probably too tired to eat, but perhaps they could be coaxed to wake for some warm milk.

Rob was waiting for him already some distance ahead talking softly with a man, one of the ones who had arrived at the tent city with them. Ott caught up to him. He gave a final glance behind him to find Treyna watching them. Rob cuffed Ott on the shoulder. "Idiot," he said gruffly. He walked on without waiting.

"What do you think happened to their mother?" Ott asked him, catching up. "All those children without a mother." They walked shoulder to shoulder through the tents toward some fires and a communal eating area around which others gathered.

Rob squinted at him and said somewhat harshly, "*She's* their mother."

"What? Do you really think so?" Ott stopped in his tracks. He blinked, not comprehending. The edges of his mind had already shut down from exhaustion. Only the very core of his brain—the only part still warm—propelled him, with the single driving instinct that at the end of all these footsteps would be a warm bed, somewhere dry and out of the wind.

Rob, a couple steps ahead, stopped walking. "Who knows? Perhaps Treyna is their mother, whether natural or by foster, if they are foundlings. Didn't you see the markings on their wagon? She deals in the potions and salves, the manipulation of aches and pains. She puts her hands on the limbs and bodies of others for medicinal reasons, or even, perhaps for pleasure as well."

Ott stared at him, not sure which stunned him more, that he had been taken in by her act of innocence or his next thought. "And Jonas allows her to make a wage this way? That's no way to treat a daughter." She was just a girl, younger than him. He could feel his eyes narrowing, his jaw tightening up.

Rob shrugged. "Or common-law wife. Not sure what she is to him."

They resumed walking, though Ott was silent in thought. He shook his head. He had been away from civilization too long when something like this could take him by surprise. Every village had a manipulator or two . . . or more. He wasn't a complete innocent about their business, often touted as medicinal, though he preferred touch given and exchanged freely, and usually had luck in procuring it. But he never thought about it so close to home. And in a setup like that. A traveling wagon with children packed along for the ride.

What kind of life was that? What would happen to those children? Would they, too, become part of the trade when they were old enough? Then he said, "You knew this when you stopped for them, but you still helped them?"

Rob looked at him. "What would you have done if you had known? Ott, they're my people." Rob looked at him for a second longer, and then shrugged it off tiredly when Ott didn't answer. Ott didn't honestly know what he would have done. At this level of exhaustion and absolute road weariness, he was amazed at his friend's capacity for considering himself responsible for these people who lived off his father's land.

Would Ott have stopped to help? He wasn't sure. And the uncertainty made him wonder what kind of person he was. Was he worthy of his luck, not to have grown up in a traveling wagon, not to have frozen to death in a frigid land outside the gates of a richer man? Was he worthy of finding a woman who loved him and of discovering exactly what his capacity was? Was he deserving of a life, the winding together of threads of luck, opportunity, and whatever fiber in him that might make him a better man than Jonas?

Rob broke into his scattered, exhaustion-riddled anxiety and said, less gruffly, "You need to go home to Jenny before the snow piles on." Ott nodded, tiredness numbing him more. Above them, the snow was swirling, falling between the gaps in the massive tent city. It would weigh down the roofs soon. The refugees would need more than their body warmth to keep themselves alive out here. Just a few hundred more steps and he would be home. Across the farm lands, through a small wooded area, and then onto his family land, a small, secluded plot, barely enough to be bothered with. His land now, nonetheless, not that he would ever take it from Jenny.

"Where are you going?" Ott asked Rob though he knew. Rob's pack came into his line of vision again, the shape of the jar that had the head floating inside of it. Rob was going to have to go through the gates to the house and present the head to his father. That seemed like a harder journey home than Ott's. He did not envy Rob, having to face that hardened old tyrant, especially now that a tent city of people had sprung up at his gates as if he were a feudal lord.

Rob ran a hand across his bearded, travel-worn face. Truth be known, Ott had put his friend through more than was necessary. It should have been easier than Ott had made it. They'd traveled together for months, every day waking up across a campfire from this man, his best friend—Ott felt strange parting with him now. But the big man was pulled by higher duties, more pressing responsibility than coming home with Ott to Jenny and putting off his troubles till the morning.

"Food first," Rob said gesturing tiredly to a cluster of cooking fires behind him. "To take to Jonas."

CHAPTER 18

Ott knocked softly on the front door of his childhood home. Everything looked the same to him. Worn, but well-cared for. His sister Jenny hadn't let a thing go by the wayside while he was gone. Gate hung straight and locked tightly. Wood stacked on the front porch. Windows tightly shuttered. Roof snug-looking and intact. A little bit of smoke snaking up from the chimney. He took a cursory inventory and relaxed. In the morning, he would reassess properly if there was a break in the weather. The house was dark and quiet as far as he could tell in the wind, so he knocked again softly, wrapping his scarf a little tighter when a gust breathed wet flakes down the back of his neck. The door was suddenly thrown open, and the muzzle of a pipe gun connected his nose down in a straight line to the wide eyes of his younger sister.

Jenny stared at him, taking him in. Her gaze passed over his face, her eyes narrowing then widening as recognition set it. She leaped on him, grabbing the back of his neck with her hand, pulling him inside the house in a tight embrace, her thin arms locked around him. He shut the door behind him.

"You stupid mutt," she said fiercely, pulling away and glaring at him. "I nearly killed you." Then she hugged him again. He held her tightly, and she suddenly burst into tears, hiding her face in his shoulder.

"It's OK now," he said gently, patting her on the back. She cried for a minute longer, then stepped back and wiped her tears on the back of her sleeve, her black hair escaping in strands from the tight tail she kept it in.

"As a matter of fact, it has not been OK," she said. She balled her left hand into a fist and punched him on the shoulder once, hard enough to sting. "It's been somewhat horrible. Is Rob with you?" Her eyes, black as coal, flicked to the door behind him.

"He's at the house," said Ott. She would know what he meant. There was only one house that counted in this country above the snowline. And it was near palatial.

"Then you've seen the masses of people, I take it."

"Hard to miss them," he acknowledged as he moved farther into the house and began unwrapping his layers. The room was warm and dry. It was small and worn, but crowded with soft, padded chairs. And it smelled like home: years of indoor cooking, a little bit of dust, and the sweat of kids, himself included, who had played hard, confined to the indoors by harsh weather. "How long have they been here?"

Jenny sighed and leaned her gun against the wall by the door. It was a homemade gun that he'd made from hammered metal water piping. It had a valve and worked with pump action and a pocket of compressed air. Big enough to blast a root vegetable at an intruder. Strong enough to bruise but not kill. Unless she had shot him at close range in the nose as she'd been aiming to. They'd used to shoot hard packed snow balls at each other when they were kids. She was a better shot than he. He took too many risks and didn't take as much time to aim as she did.

"The attacks on the mines started maybe a few weeks ago," she said. "Lots of lives lost. We don't know how many except to count the missing." She glanced at him. "They don't leave the dead. We don't know what they do with them."

The news that they'd been attacked at the Keep suddenly seemed stale and useless. Ott imagined that Rob's father probably had a row of gruesome souvenirs on the mantle above his fireplace already. Ott did not envy his friend having to face his father. Their long absence, it seemed, had resulted in a gain of exactly nothing against these creatures.

"Have you been hurt at all, Jenny? Are you and the kids all right?" he said, frozen in place until she answered. Then he sank into a chair limply at her curt nod. He'd been carrying the weight of worry since he'd come out of his haze of grief for his lost girl. He pulled off his boots and started to roll down the slush-soaked stockings that had molded to his feet, sticking between his toes, which were frozen and painfully regaining some warmth.

"Someone ran off with one of the goats and broke into the root cellar," she said ruefully. "We've had to trade some things for our winter stash. But we'll do OK. The kids didn't know about it," she added quickly. The fire was dying, but she didn't make a move to build it up again. He wasn't sure if he should offer to do it, but then, he wasn't sure if his legs would obey him if he tried to move.

"The kids are all right?" he asked again, needing to be reassured though he'd heard her the first time.

"They're fine. Jack has grown about three inches since you've been gone." Then she saw his face. "You look terrible yourself. You're a hair shy of filthy and I near didn't recognize you with that scruff on your face." She examined him. He didn't hide from her, just lay back in his favorite chair and closed his eyes. He'd had dreams about this chair. He heard her moving around.

"It's good to be home," he murmured.

"Will you eat something or are you too tired? You're very thin. Too thin," she said, nearing him again, but his eyelids refused to open when he thought about looking at her. He felt her finger on the underside of his chin. "Have you been ill?" she asked.

He wasn't sure how to answer, so he shook his head, feeling himself drifting. He felt the small gust of air from a blanket brushing over him. He was home. Then he was asleep.

And when he slept, he dreamed about Mel. In his dream, she was alive. She wasn't lost. She was in his arms telling him it was all right.

Were they in heaven? "Is this the *cealo*?" he asked her.

She hushed him with fingers to his lips. Small, soft, velvety fingertips. They were lying together in a field of grass and sweet clover, green-leaved trees around them with the warm sun shining around her. A halo. A heavenly presence. So much warmth.

Surely this was the afterlife.

Though he wasn't certain what he had done to deserve the reward. She rose above him and as she smiled down at him, she looked golden.

Part 3

Mask

CHAPTER 19

The day Mel took the Mask, she thought about Ott. She indulged in her memories, for perhaps the last time, bringing out the images of him and laying them in the front parts of her mind. The speckled green of his eyes. The creases in the corners of his eyes when he smiled at her. His hands skimming along the second skin of her silken costume that night. The scar under his chin. His voice, low and melodic.

She spent that last morning alone, sitting at her desk in the library at her mother's house. She traced her finger on the wood grain of her desktop. It had been only a few months and now the smell of him was gone, faded from her memory. She tried and failed to conjure it up again from the two short times that they had met. She could only play mental alchemy and imagine the lost scent as some combination of cinnamon, pine, earth, sweat, and something else warm. It had been so intense those few weeks after losing him that she thought it would never stop ambushing her at unexpected times and in her dreams. She had woken up many nights clutching at the sheets gasping, as much for air as for trying to breathe in more of the smell before it faded completely.

She traced her finger over a knot in the wood, around and around, a swirling eddy. He was lost, or he had moved on. How long had she been in the village by the Keep recovering from shock? Wouldn't he have come if he were alive? Wouldn't he have looked for her? The silence in her soul told her the answer that she had been denying. She felt nothing. There was no connection. No thread of connection to him in the living world.

She dropped her chin on the desk and closed her eyes. The truth hurt.

And the truth was that she was a woman who had met a man. They met each other twice. A horrific event separated them, a rift that was completely external to whatever short time they'd had together, and they had not had a chance to part naturally. Any other summer couple would have broken apart amicably, gone their separate ways after realizing that the summer was over. But the truth was, she felt more than that.

It didn't matter that she didn't know anything about him, where he was from, how old he was, who his people were. It didn't matter whether he ate meat, worshipped one god or many or none at all. In her lowest self, she didn't care whether he was cruel to animals or other people. Whether he lived in a house or slept on the bare ground. Whether he had a wife and children already—her chest tightened with that admission. He could be home, wherever that was. Happy, in front of a warm hearth, his children playing on the rug at his feet. If he were alive. It didn't matter. None of it mattered. Not even whether he thought about her, if he were even alive or not.

Then, in a burst, the scent came back to her in a rush so dizzying that she pressed her cheek against the desk and splayed her fingers out, fingertips pressed white. She gasped and struggled for air, for control of herself and the rush of panic at the loss of him. It washed over her like a tidal wave, spinning her head, filling her nose and throat. She was drowning. Unable to fight, to resist, to push it away, tears rolled sideways across the bridge of her nose and onto the desk. She let go of herself. She was lost to grief.

Sometime later, Mel stood up from her desk. The worst of it was over. She could move on now, so she moved sedately. She was ready to take her oath.

Impartiality. Diligence. Fair-mindedness.

She was ready to slide the thick woven cloak over her head, adjust the cowl and netting over her face, more comfortable than rumor had it. More than comforting in its anonymity. The hammered metal medallion that both identified and protected her would slip over her head and lock with the clasp around her neck. She would stand coolly, emptied and alert, between her parents aboard the riverboat headed north, ready for her task.

Her task was the labor dispute that she had been studying for weeks— land owner versus laborers. The only viable option was dispute resolution to avoid loss of time and loss of life. She had absorbed the facts, the history of the land and people. The climate. Their lack of alternatives. She could recite dates of area settlement. Major edifices in the area. Religious preferences of the people. But she could not muster any feeling for them. She patently did not care a whiff about any of it. And now, she was ready to help them.

Without having to look at the mirror on the wall as she passed it, she knew that the gold was gone, and her skin had returned to its normal color.

At mid-afternoon, the Masks gathered once again in the meeting hall. Mel spoke her oath in front of rows of cloaked witnesses. Her mother and father were among them somewhere, she knew. The oath was one she'd heard many times since childhood and had no need of memorizing now. It was very short. Its brevity spoke of infallible single-mindedness, the lack of room for interpretation. The disdain for alternative meaning. Her spoken words were the only ones in the room.

I am the faceless arbitrator who gives myself up so that I may be of use to others.

Then the procession.

Hands helped her remove her clothes. Her loose-fitting pants were untied at the waist and they fell from her hips to the floor around her ankles. She walked down the steps of the amphitheater, her bare feet on the cold floor. At the center of the meeting hall, on the platform, she stepped into a metal tub. Hands poured warm water on her from pitchers. Water, always water, the medium of birth, rebirth, cleansing, and baptism, here the same as the world all over. This rite was each of those. She was divested of her identity, and when she stepped from the tub still dripping, hands held out and swathed her in the cloak and cowl, the Mask.

She stood feet set apart in resting stance, weight distributed for the next part of the ceremony, balanced and relaxed. The medallion slid around her neck, locking into place. The hands slid away from her and became still. Everybody in the room stopped. Heartbeats melded into one rhythm. One mind. She drew a deep breath and stilled herself. Then there was silence. Absolute silence. They stood in meditation—one body, one mind, one purpose—until the sun went down.

CHAPTER 20

"Daybreak. Three days from now," the wounded man managed to say through cracked lips so dry they no longer bled, his voice quavering with terror. He was a miner who had been captured during a fresh attack—any more of them and they would lose the mines completely. Rob had ordered they give the man warm broth, but he could not take it.

The beasts had released him to crawl on his hands and knees to the big house, painting a red path through the snow with his own blood. He was a dying creature barely recognizable as one of their own. He was human, but beaten to a pulp and nearly mute from fear. They learned from the man, with the assistance of the biteweed, a powerful sedative, that his missing hand had been removed from his arm and eaten in front of him with great relish, bones of his fingers picked clean of meat and sinew and tossed at his feet. Rob sat near the man, leaning closely toward his battered face, murmuring nonsense words of comfort. He sat with the man until he died.

Later, much later, Rob sat staring at his father—yet another dying man. The old man's rotting eyes were closed, his paper-thin eyelids run through with blue-gray veins. He coughed wetly and brushed his mouth with a stained cloth, eyelids still closed, then drifted back into sleep easily like a contented cat in the morning sun. The snow had let up briefly. The old tyrant had a considerable stockpile of anguish he had inflicted on other people. Rob thought sourly that the tyrant ought to be proud of himself. His spoils were the rich misery of others. He traded in the blood and toil earned on the backs of other men and women, the calluses and ripped skin of other people's hands. Rob stared down at his own hands, folded into each other so tightly his fingertips were devoid of blood.

Just as Rob had predicted standing outside in the tent city looking up the frozen lawn at his father's mansion, his presentation of the troll's head to his father had gone over like another snow flurry in a blizzard. Unwanted and barely acknowledged. Now the jarred head, the gray-haired back of the dead beast's head turned toward Rob, sat on the floor next to the old man's chipped chamber pot.

"What are you looking at?"

Rob had not noticed that his father had awoken. Finished with his nap, apparently. The old man stretched in an abbreviated fashion, displaying a frailty that Rob didn't believe. Rob got to his feet out of habit, long ago drilled into the habit of standing at attention for the old man. Beaten into it in the past. Memories of himself passed briefly through Rob's mind—twenty years seeming only a breath ago—gripping the arms of a chair as his father punctuated each lesson of subservience with the whip of a lash. They were never far under the surface of his thoughts. Though the switch marks across the backs of his legs had faded into silver scars, he expected them to break open and start weeping again at any moment. The joke was, he himself would never cry, but the scars were free to do as they wished.

He shifted his eyes briefly to the window beyond his father's bed. If Rob himself were free to do what he wished, he would have been across that snow-covered field knocking on Jenny's door, standing awkwardly with his hat in his hands in the corner of her low-ceilinged kitchen, just to hear her voice and see her face, flushed with the effort of whatever she was doing. Always moving. Whatever she did seemed far more important that what was happening around him. Always busy with her hands and her quick eyes, her dark, silken hair which she punished by pulling back with a tight band, so she could chase after her little ones. He would gladly stand in the corner and serve as a hat rack collecting dust if it meant he could stay close to her, serve her, if only just by adding a body to her house to keep it warm. But he didn't know how to serve her, how to throw himself at her feet.

"Wake up, you idiot," his father rasped at him. The old man had shoved back his furs and had thrown his stringy, naked legs over the side of the bed. Angrily, he gestured Rob away as he stood and gathered his robe together. He gripped his cane and stood on shaky legs, then gathered his strength with a spiteful narrowing of his deep-sunken eyes at Rob. The old man was all tendon and sinew through his neck and skull, incongruous fuzz on his bony pate. Though the years had curved his back and forced him to stoop so that his eyes met with Rob's chest, he could still make the boy cower before him.

"We need to assemble the workers into platoons," his father said, working his way from his bed chamber to his sitting room where there was a high fire. The heavy gold chain and agamite-encrusted pendant of Colubrid, the snake god on their family crest, dangled over his collarbones. "I have given them industry—working in my mines has grown the muscles in their arms and strengthened their backs. They are not spoiled calves fattened for slaughter. Now they can use their axes to fight the trolls."

Rob cleared his throat. "These creatures are strong. Our people are not trained. We will be massacred."

"The workers have strength. They are obedient. They will fight."

Oh God. How many generations had their family lived off the sweat of others?

"There are children out there," Rob said, wanting to run a hand across his face, wanting to lash out at the old man, who now paused in front of Rob's chair.

"Why? Why do they have their children with them?"

"They have fled their homes. They brought the children with them."

"What? Perfectly good homes I gave them. Strong, made of good wood and stone," he said, turning slowly to guide his old body into the chair. He waved away Rob, who had found himself unconsciously taking a step forward to assist him. "Strong against the winter, the way I had them made. Those houses have plenty enough room for their families, but not enough for them to over breed." He arranged his robes around his legs and now gestured for a blanket to be spread over them. Rob complied, though he kept his back away from the fire. It was over-hot and made him feel febrile. As his hands placed the blanket in his father's lap, he imagined them snaking up to grip the gristle of the old man's neck to choke the life out of him.

"The creatures attacked their homes, sir. They were forced to abandon them and come here."

The old man looked at him suspiciously. "Well. What do they want from me? Haven't I provided enough for them? Given them a good living?"

"As they expect us to continue to do," Rob said. Maybe the house physician could prescribe the old bastard a sleeping drought. A lot of it.

"And where am I supposed to come up with the food and shelter for the lot of them? What am I, a magician? A conjurer?"

Rob sighed. It took every ounce of his self-control not to rub a hand over his face, which was a gesture of weakness that he'd been trained to hide. His time away from the old man had been a gift. Pure luxury. Wandering in the woods with Ott, topped off by that ridiculous costume party and ending in smoke, destruction, and death. A bubble of a dream punctured by reality. He wondered if Ott would ever be the same. He'd been a wily devil their whole lives, always a favorite with women. Good looking and lucky as a sprite. Rob gravitated toward him, full of envy. It hurt to see his friend turn taciturn and hollow, a ghost of his former self. When the girl died, she'd taken most of Ott with her, Rob realized. The best part of his friend. What would Rob be if something ever happened to Jenny? He quailed to think of it. Having nothing left to hope for in this life would take away any fear of dying. Perhaps it would spur him to kill his father finally, after all these years of fantasizing about it, he thought ruefully.

"It's settled then," the old man said. Rob snapped back to attention.

"Sir?" Rob said, clenching his jaw.

"*Sir?*" the old man mocked him, screwing up his face. He rasped, "Use the damned balls dangling between your legs unless, as I suspect, they never descended. I did my best with you, but I can't make you a man yet if you weren't born with a snake between your legs like the rest of us. You'll never further my house nor add to my riches. Always suspected your mother was weak. Damned Insectoj worshippers like her. All of them weak." He named the god of insects as if he were referring to a pile of animal dung. Rob didn't flinch. He'd long ago given up faith in any god. They were the idols of his childhood. Silent and abandoning just as he had later come to abandon them. His father grunted. *"I said take care of it."*

"The people?"

The old man let loose another string of obscenities that ended with a wet cough. "I don't care what you do with them. Just make sure they protect my mines. Without that agamite, what are we? Do you think I built this house with borrowed treasure? No." He slammed his bony fist on the worn arm of the chair. "I earned it. Every rug. Every cup. Every last stone. Every thread on your back. Paid for with agamite. Protect my mines. At any cost. Without them, I am lost. And you have no future."

CHAPTER 21

The heels of Rob's boots pounded on stone as he stormed down the hallway. He worked his empty fists, opening and shutting them. By the time he reached the dining hall, he had regained control of his anger. The smells of meals past and smoke-stained walls were as familiar to Rob as his own skin. The pounding of fury from his conversation with his father receded. Harro, Rob's ad hoc adviser, was sitting over the remnants of a midday meal, waiting for him.

The man wasn't meant to be an adviser. He wasn't a scholar trained in warfare or stratagems. Harro was a stableman, rough around the edges, though he'd been inside the house for a couple years now. Surprisingly verbose when given enough drink—and only then, come to think of it. He was dark, with a full, neatly trimmed beard, and also unwaveringly loyal to Rob, who knew it and valued it beyond measure. Rough-hewn though he was, Harro's mind was sharp as a faceting tool for honing gems. His eyes glittered like black ice, the whites of his eyes clear as new snow, the kind of early snow fall called *haut* by the locals. Crystalline and pure.

Harro said, "Well?"

Rob sat. "No problem a little patricide couldn't fix." His remark was met with uncomfortable silence and the clearing of Harro's throat, which he took for acknowledgment of fact.

"Do we wait for the Masks?" Harro asked him. They were both grasping at straws. They were racked with indecision. *Rob's indecision.* The entire house was waiting for him to do something, to take command. Again, he felt like scrubbing his hand over his face but refused to let himself.

"We don't have time. The creatures have given us till daybreak three days from now."

"What are our options?" Harro asked again. They had been over their situation a thousand times, but each time, Rob was as willing to rake over them again hoping a new solution would present itself. Harro fingered the carved bear that hung from a braided leather cord around his neck. Dovay the bear, god of perseverance, a popular deity in these parts—god of hunkering down and waiting out the winter.

"We could try to prepare ourselves to fight. We have no weapons, no training, or even food. If we attack them, we leave most of our families unprotected. We squander what meager defenses we have. However, if we defend against attack, we have more time to prepare, to protect the families, but we still do not have enough resources to shelter and feed all of them when winter truly arrives. Or," Rob continued, "we can send a delegation to negotiate a truce."

"We need the Masks for that," Harro said with a shudder—they could make even a hardened outdoorsman tremble just thinking of them, their wraith-like facelessness. The stableman nervously picked at his nails, an incongruously tidy gesture for a man who had been accustomed to working with his hands in the stables his whole life, but he'd had the nervous habit as long as Rob had known him. Self-conscious of dirt perhaps, and low beginnings, though at the moment Rob would have traded places with a stableman in a heartbeat. Their inability to find a viable solution to their present situation was torturing Rob.

"We need the agamite," Rob said sitting down at the table. Without the agamite, they might as well abandon the entire northern country. A small part of him flinched and wondered if he were merely parroting his father's commands. While he could easily picture himself living as a faceless citizen in a city far to the east or even in the southern desert, he could not abandon his people.

His place at the table was set with a loaded plate. Someone was looking after him. Rob began to eat methodically and without feeling, without tasting anything. Roasted roots, roasted meat, well-prepared and well-laid out, but they could have been clods of dirt for all he cared. However, the people outside were eating worse and much less of it, so he forced himself to continue chewing and swallowing. After months on the trail dreaming of a soft bed and well-prepared food, he was now unable to appreciate so much as a bite of it.

As if reading his mind, Harro stood and paced toward the window. Down the snow-covered slope of land in front of the house, through the barren branches of trees, and above the stone wall that lined the property, they could see smoke from the campfires, as well as the tops of the taller peaked tents. There had to be upwards of six hundred people squatting there in the camp town.

Rob swallowed, washing a bite down with a swig of bitter tea. "And defense? We needed to defend the mines when we were still there, not now that we've fled from them. It's too late for that. We've lost the mines. We're defending our people against the winter now."

"So bring the people in," Harro said. "We'll figure out how to feed them. Bring them inside the walls. We'll build temporary shelter that we'll try to heat. Under the trees and away from the worst of the wind. Let the most feeble and youngest come into the stables now."

Rob thought briefly about the shriveled old tyrant lying in his silken sheets and woven blankets by his over-warm fire on the other side of the house while children were losing their toes to the cold. He slowly lay his fork down on his plate and looked at Harro. "Bring the people in then. Inside the walls. Build roofs. Whatever walls we can. Before the weather arrives."

Harro turned and looked at him. Slowly, he straightened his back, stood fully at attention as a sign of respect. He nodded at Rob. "Yes. Consider it done."

CHAPTER 22

Jenny took advantage of the calm weather to beat dirt from a rug out on the front porch. She chewed a tiny wad of mint gum, an indulgence, switching it to the other cheek. Her stash would be gone soon, but she was celebrating a moment to herself. Though it was frigid enough to make clouds out of her breath and require her to wear her badly knitted wool mittens—she had always been terrible at knitting, probably because she was frequently distracted—the sun was out and the wind was gone for now. The heavy rug hung over the side rail of the porch—the one that her middle son had recently broken and she'd struggled to replace. A carpenter, she was not. The repaired section of the rail was not entirely in line with the rest it, but it was sturdy, in there for good, which she found when she'd gone back and tried to square it up. Wasn't that always the case? The most crooked things were the hardest to budge. Her mind flew back and forth. Where was that boy anyway? She wrapped her fingers around the end of his flatball bat and took a hard swing at the rug, sending up a cloud of dust—a half-year's worth, at least.

The sun on the snow made her squint, and she heard the boys' laughter coming from inside the house. They ought to be outside tiring themselves out before the storms started rolling in. She usually set them to doing their letters and reading on bad mornings. Afternoons were for wearing themselves out and destroying the house. But her brother was home. She paused for a minute, hearing the low cadence of Ott's voice, but not making out the words. Their mother should have named him Lutros, the male variation of Lutra, after their otter goddess. He was clever and sleek and stinking with luck. Most of the time. When she didn't want to kill him. She sighed, not sure if it were her brother or her sons she was thinking about. Sometimes, at her most tired, they all blended together into one troublesome boy.

She had bread dough rising in the kitchen and wanted to make a special meal for her brother. He and Rob sometimes traded game for fresh food on the trail, she knew. But it had to have been a while since they hit the snowline coming north, and supplies and people to trade with would have become scarce. She tried not thinking about Rob though she hadn't seen him in weeks. She wondered if he were as thin as her brother, though that was hard to imagine. That man was a mountain, as solid as one and just about as quiet. He wouldn't be like her brother. Ott had returned with a strange and forlorn gauntness about him that she'd never seen before. A tightness around his eyes. He was lackluster with the kids, though she saw he pushed himself to be cheerful for them. He looked like he'd rather curl up in a corner somewhere and pull a blanket over his head the way he used to when they were little. *Worrisome.* Something had happened out there on the trail this time. Maybe something to do with those underground animals coming up. They brought something into the air with them, an underlying menace, the feeling that the very ground she and the rest of the people walked on, herded animals on, and built their houses on was unstable and riddled with holes like an ant colony.

She pushed the frenetic pace of her thoughts toward what she could straighten and clean next now that she had a chance. She wanted to sweep out the house, but great lady above, though her hands were busy, her thoughts were traitorous and turned back to Rob. Her throat closed up thinking about him. She wished he could forgive her. One terrible mistake after another. Marrying, having three children so closely spaced together, not that any of them had been conceived in joy. Eight, seven, and five years old now. The birth of the youngest one had almost killed her, tearing her, nearly bleeding her out, making it so she'd never have children again. Three children—good, rambunctious boys like hers—were a bounty, especially in a place like this where a person had to be hearty to make it to adulthood, and either lucky or stubborn to live much beyond that.

She would never wish them undone. They were sweet and healthy boys, who thankfully got their looks from her family, each one of them. She would not have to watch them grow up to be copies of her terrible husband. At least they didn't look like him. But, she sighed and allowed herself a good two minutes of wallowing in self-pity, if she were herself again from a few years earlier, before any of it was promised or conceived, she would have no qualms about throwing herself at Rob, and forcefully. She didn't care that he lived in the great house across the field, while she lived in an ancient, patched-up shack that passed for a cabin. Because she wanted him, loved him—so much that she didn't *want to think about him*—and that was the truth. But rivers ran their same paths as soon as the ice melted.

She understood why her brother admired him, why they were close friends, and if she were a male, she would have had the good fortune of going with them often when they hunted. Rob was so silent, so attentive to her—a respectful, distant awareness in honor of the friendship he felt for her brother. But that was all, she was certain. She was the idiot who allowed herself to crave a man she could never have. If only she had known herself better before she went to her husband, the cruel man who used her badly and deserted her for another woman. If only she had known herself better while her husband was still around to feel the effects of her skills with a paring knife. She huffed at herself, bringing another rug outside on the porch to beat it to death. The floors would never get clean if the rugs held onto their dirt.

With each swing of the bat, she enumerated her faults as Rob would see them. Mother to another man's children. Not able to bear any others for a better man. No money. House falling down around her ears. No family lineage or wealth to speak of. No fine manners. And not even the good grace to give up. One more harsh winter and she'd lose whatever feminine features she had left. She would be nothing but ropey muscle and bones, truly a glorious vision. Her washed-out dresses were already hanging off her shoulders. Her winter-dried skin, once as soft as buttermilk, cracked during the worst times of the year. Even her hair was a frizzy, brittle mess. And add to that, now a split knuckle.

She pulled off her mitten despite the cold and sucked her knuckle between her lips. Worst thing to do for it, she knew, but it felt good for now. No tears. She never allowed herself to cry. Two minutes of self-pity was a healthy serving, but it was never good to overindulge. She pushed her hair back under her knit cap and took a deep breath, starting to slam back into place the walls of self-control. And the upside was, now she had clean rugs.

Why hadn't Rob come?—to look in on Ott, she quickly added. Her brother was clearly not well. He had that hollow look around his face that had nothing to do with food. Maybe Rob knew why. Obviously, something had happened to her brother out there. Her mind spun from thought to thought, like the swirling dust motes she had beaten from the rug. Rob was occupied, she knew. Hundreds of people camped outside the wall looking for shelter, food, and protection from the underground animals. *Trogs*, people were calling the creatures. Or trolls, though that was ridiculous. Trolls were the monsters of old tales. They didn't exist in real life except to scare her children into staying in their beds at night.

Rob had more than his share of people to look after, and the crazy old bastard who called himself Rob's father wasn't going to do it. He'd more than likely set dogs on his own people. On Rob himself, that was for sure. She got steamed just thinking about the old man. Maybe there was someone who could watch her kids while she crept up there and wrung the old man's neck. Blasted him back under the rock from which he had crawled. She snorted because that was hardly a new thought.

Someone cleared his throat behind her.

She didn't bother turning around. Embarrassed, yes, but her brother knew her well enough. "Yes, I know. Say whatever you want. I'm reduced to talking to myself and laughing at my own riddles. I make good company for myself. It's a long winter."

He didn't respond, and an odd prickly feeling ran up the back of her neck. She felt as if she'd been touched. Stroked by a feather of warmth. Something blooming out of season. She whipped around.

"Hello, Jenny," Rob said, standing on the porch steps. His deep voice sent a tingle of heat down her spine all the way down to the backs of her knees.

He was one step down, but still a good half-foot taller than her, all bundled up in fur-lined leathers, pants brushed to the knees in snow dust. He stood still, broad across the shoulders, and solid. Not imaginary. He was standing here, real and true. She didn't stop to look at his face. Threads of regret and fantasy still clung to her, swirling around her mind, eddies of desire and memories of long, dark nights alone. And fear, too, hearing noises outside the house in the dead of night. And again with her brain addled with terror—not for herself but for her three sleeping boys—when she opened the front door to confront whatever creature might be outside savaging their goats or stealing their pathetic stash of winter food.

And panic, too, when she thought she might not have enough to make it through winter when it finally, inevitably arrived, thinning her boys' faces and dulling their eyes. *Please*, she prayed fervently at night to her one lady god while alone in her bed, *please don't let them starve or freeze or be the spoils of others.* Now, when she saw Rob standing on her step, she didn't stop herself, but flung her arms around his neck, still clutching one mitten in her hand, the other hand bleeding. He was here and safe. She pressed her face into the shoulder of his cold coat. He froze, and then slowly put his heavy arms around her.

"I should leave often," he said finally. She felt a tentative pat on her back as his hand gently came down, and he embraced her.

She laughed, truly embarrassed, "Please don't." Then she pulled her face away to look at his. Yes, thinner, but not as bad as her brother. Cheeks flushed from the walk over. Dark eyes almost unreadable. He looked unsure, though his hands were still around her waist.

He was hesitant, but she was not. She leaned closer, closing her eyes, and kissed him firmly on the mouth, then softening and lingering as a flush crept over her body despite the cold. She was in his embrace, lips pressed against his at last, just as she'd imagined it again and again, countless times since . . . before her children, before her husband, as far back as she could remember him. Except her eyes flashed open, her uncertainty reared up, ugly and nauseating, when he failed to respond.

She froze, horrified, waiting for anything that might save her from absolute mortification, a laugh, a chuckle, a brotherly squeeze, which she would gladly accept though she could still taste him on her lips. She would take anything to relieve the crushing mortification. She stepped back and knew she was flushed to the ears, probably red and splotchy under her ridiculous snow hat, made from scraps of yarn salvaged from old sweaters. *Stupid, stupid.* She gestured toward the door, not able to meet his eyes, to face whatever shock or pity might be in them. "Come inside. My brother is awake." Then she retreated in haste, tripping at the threshold she'd been passing over without trouble her entire life, leaving him to follow her or not.

CHAPTER 23

Mel stood on the deck of the great wooden riverboat that chugged up the Uptdon River, staring at the choppy water from behind her Mask. Every other tributary river she knew of flowed south and emptied into the gaping maw of the Great Sea. Every river *except* the Uptdon mixed its waters with the ocean. The water that Mel's boat churned through took an obstinate path northward, where it eventually froze in the harsh, frigid mountains, and where, if legend were true, a great white beast sat at the top of the river chewing chunks of frozen water with enormous glass teeth. The beast would crush the river into icy shards, swallow them so they passed from its stomach back through its underground bowels into the rivers that flowed south. A lifecycle explained through local lore.

Mel felt as if she were traveling to the end of the world. She stood in her cloak and Mask on the wind-whipped deck and watched the choppy whitecaps. She diverted her energy toward quelling motion sickness and warming her skin. For the sake of propriety, she could not enjoy the heaviness of a warmer coat or wraps. All she was permitted to wear were her regular daily garments—loose pants tied at the waist, tunic shirt with straps over her shoulders—and Mask cloak, veil, and medallion. The garments of her uniform would identify and protect her. The boat's passengers and crew certainly walked wide circles around them. They knew the Masks, knew what they were, and gave them wide berth. The few on the outside deck peered at her from behind fur-lined hoods, what skin they showed chapped red from the unrelenting wind. Her inability to get a chill bothered them more than her facelessness. If she had any courage, she would dress as one of them and walk among the passengers and crew anonymously, so she could be at ease.

It will get easier. She tried to use the thought as a balm.

At any rate, it was much better up on deck than in their stuffy, cramped cabin. She felt stifled by the proximity of her parents and Guyse, the guard who accompanied them. In their windowless cabin, two sets of bunk beds lined the walls. They also had two small desks provided upon their request and a small washroom. She had the top of one bunk, her mother had the other. Her father and Guyse slept below them. While her parents spent their time resting or reading, Mel was restless and knew her unease bothered the others. The small cabin amplified her nervous energy, so she took herself to the deck as often as she could. It was the only place she could breathe.

The river was broad, a mile across at its widest. They had traveled for days upon days. The sandy banks had turned to craggy, forbidding cliffs, and now, in the distance, she could finally see the shore again as they approached the northernmost port. After nearly two weeks on the water, only a few hours separated them from land. She wanted to lean toward it, to balance on her toes to see it more clearly. She couldn't wait to feel the ground under her feet once again. She wanted to run. After they arrived at the port, they would journey on by sled. Mel scanned the horizon, giving reign to her anxiety, a final full burst before she would have to take the wooden steps below deck to inform her parents and Guyse of their imminent arrival.

She didn't know Guyse well at all—she had seen him maybe a few times a year in the settlement, but never spoken to him. He was big and imposing, a scowling man who didn't wear the Mask. He often accompanied other Masks on their journeys—part guard, part servant. Her parents addressed him as an equal though he never seemed to acknowledge it. He brought them their food in the cabin, ran errands for them, and carried their belongings—not that they needed physical help, but arriving any place with an established hierarchy helped in travel. Often, people preferred to deal with a servant rather than directly approach a Mask, though Guyse was imposing in his own right. He stood a full head taller than her father, with dark weathered skin and thick brows on a protruding forehead that hid intelligent eyes. He radiated menace barely in check, and Mel had to make herself relax at night when she knew he was sleeping only feet away in the bunk under hers. After meals, she had to force herself not to vacate their cabin immediately. It sometimes felt as if the other three people in it seemed to use more than their share, filling it, spilling over into each other's space. It was a little like a coffin housing four scentless bodies, but not for much longer. They were nearly there.

Still lingering on deck, Mel stepped closer to the rail and focused her eyes for far, far distant sight as the northernmost port city came into view. Squat, dark buildings. A gray seawall. The dismal, windy day evidently did not deter the port traffic, either in the water or on foot. Wooden boats, all smaller than their vessel, bobbed at their moors. Metal bells rang out. Sea birds screamed overhead. She gathered her cloak and went below for the last time.

When, at last, they disembarked, Mel followed her parents down the narrow, planked ramp that led from boat to solid shore. Guyse came behind them supervising the unloading of their trunks. Mel kept her head steady and forward-gazing, but behind her Mask, her eyes flew from left to right. From the water, she hadn't seen the magnificent carved statues of the gods. Six of them stood in a phalanx—bear, otter, snake, falcon, fish, and insect—fifteen feet each of pure, glorious green agamite, a show of wealth and dominance to all visitors who came ashore. Here was where civilization ended. North of here, they would meet ice and the end of the world. Though Mel stared, the townspeople and travelers milling around the statues hardly seemed to notice them.

The port's activity belied the frigid air temperature. The passengers disembarking from their wooden riverboat gasped collectively when the first gust of frosty air raced up the ramp to their legs and passed through their clothing as if they wore nothing. Mel forced the blood within her legs to circulate somewhat quicker. The port was busier than Navio, if that were even possible, yet there were no outdoor merchants here. No musicians panhandled. Pickpockets still did a decent business, she noticed, seeing the bare hand of one slip from a furred muff into an unsuspecting man's bag.

Aggressive, white-winged and heavily-feathered birds swooped overhead, wavering in the strong gusts that chilled their ears and necks. People shuffled and jostled from boat to shore, from carriage house to inn. Not carriages, she corrected herself, *sleds*. A grimy layer of packed snow covered the streets, even the most heavily traveled ones. Passage on foot was treacherous, yet the people persisted, sometimes slipping against each other, braced upright by the crowd, saved from tumbling by the sheer mass of bodies. Rather than give the impression of crossed threads, crossed paths, the bodies of people seemed to undulate as a population. Gray and brown waves of sturdy leathers were dotted by dyed wool color here and there. Harsh voices called out in the local accent and drew her eyes, but nothing seemed amiss, just travelers greeting familiar faces. She tried to absorb it, the patterns, the stoicism about the climate, the human adjustment for the sake of survival.

A shout brought Mel out of her reverie. The voice, hoarse and angry, cried, "We're not bargaining with those fecking monsters. We don't need your kind here."

Just as Mel stepped off the ramp onto solid ground, the crowd surged toward her. Her eyes wide under her Mask, she felt a wave of anxiety crest off Guyse from where he stood behind her. His hand gripped her shoulder and pulled her against his body as an object flew from the crowd at them. She watched it flying toward her as it spiraled, a stone falling through the gray sky. Guyse's fingers dug into the muscle of her shoulder.

A hoarse voice shouted, "You're not welcome here, Masks."

Then the object, an unrefined hunk of stone mottled with dark green agamite, struck Mel's forehead above her eye and shattered, dust and green sparkles erupting in a cloud against her skin, and she reeled. Voices in the crowd shouted in dismay. Hands guided her quickly to a sled, where she was placed in the center of the bench, her back to the driver. In minutes, the others were in place with the trunks secured on top. Guyse commanded the driver to speed the horses, and the sled was jerked away, horses' hooves muffled by densely packed snow, skimming away over slippery cobblestones north further from the port city.

"Damnation," Guyse cursed, throwing out string after string of escalating violent curses, drawing the curtains of their covered sled. Such anger from Guyse, Mel mused, muzzy-headed and helpless as she lay back on the leather bench in the sled, gently rocking. She could hear the whisk of the runners on the dense-packed snow. The sled was much warmer than the outside air. It smelled of leather, the breath of past travelers, and her mother's herbal soap. She adjusted her eyes to darkness as hands—her mother's—undid Mel's medallion and gently lifted her cowl.

"It's a deep gash," her mother said calmly from behind her own Mask. "Do you need assistance healing yourself?"

A dribble of blood was flowing into Mel's eye, making her blink repeatedly. She stilled herself and was about to divert her energy to her wound when her father stayed her with a raised hand. He shook his head, his eyes hidden from her.

"Leave it. We will show it as a sign of how we have been greeted."

Guyse grumbled, his voice escalating. "There has been violence all along the coast. Yet we were not prepared. You should have heeded my warning. Why did you not take my counsel?" He slammed a meaty fist into the cushion of the bench. His heavy brow creased in further scowl.

Mel's mother froze, but only Mel spoke, arrested by her father's words. "I will show my face?" Even in this short time, she had grown used to hiding behind her Mask. Her father didn't answer, merely leaned against the seat submerged again in his thoughts, no explanation to share. Her mother gathered herself together and, also seemingly lost in thought, blotted at the inside of Mel's Mask where blood darkened it. What kind of show of power required them to arrive with one who was wounded? *And unmasked?*

Mel frowned and dug a cloth out of her pocket. She flicked her eyes at her father's Mask. Surely he would allow that she at least could see clearly. She blotted hesitantly at her eye, cleaning away the blood and dust that obscured her vision. Then she pressed the cloth firmly to the gash, where swelling gathered. She wanted to stop the flow of blood and prevent any accompanying dizziness. She hazarded a glance at Guyse, but the man wore his usual scowl, low forehead obscured by heavy brows.

What was her father thinking? She shook her head inwardly. Arrive wounded? Why would it matter in the least? She was a Mask. They should plan to arrive at the house as a trinity of black cloaked and Masked figures. Ominous and inhuman. She knew how it was supposed to appear. She shot a glare at her father. Perhaps he should have been the one to receive the blow to the head.

"Control yourself, Mel," her mother said behind her Mask without a single movement. Sound from a statue. Mel could have screamed, but she was suddenly overcome with a wave of shame. It crested over her as she forcibly drew breath and fought for control. Her mother hadn't had to speak a warning aloud to her since she was a child. This should be getting easier, not worse. Her control should be improving, not slipping more and more. She wanted to strike out, to rant, to break things under her feet. Shouldn't it be getting easier?

She closed her eyes and lay back against the bench. To calm herself, she took deep breaths in time with the gentle rocking of the sled. She drew a breath in. The whisper of sled runners on the hard-packed snow. She pushed the breath out. The draw of the reins in the driver's leather-covered fingers. She stretched her mind, careful to avoid healing the gash on her head though it tingled and throbbed. She unknit her anger, her irrational outburst that had never come out, though it hovered below the surface like a bubble waiting to break through a layer of oil on the surface of a pot of boiling water.

She traveled with the emotion through the cotton cloth at her head, head to cloth, through blood to her fingertips. She radiated out from her fingers in coils of heat, floated up into the ceiling of the covered sleigh. Through grains of wood, hewn by hands just years ago. She traveled the tree from which the sled was carved, through its felling, through the moisture in its roots, deep into the earth, into the green pockets embedded deep in the stone, watery rivulets, veins that led out from the core. It was green underground. Green like Ott's eyes. Mel's eyes shot open.

CHAPTER 24

Ott watched his sister stomp into the house. She cursed under her breath, which was something she never did in front of the boys. The littlest one, Jamie, the one who looked most of all like Ott, took a running start and catapulted himself onto Ott's lap for the fourth time in as many minutes. All three boys had identical, closely-shaven heads. He knew their hair was like his, thick, sandy brown, and unruly if left long. His sister kept their heads shaved out of convenience. She could examine them for bumps, gashes, head bugs, or dirt at a glance, and with three of them, who could blame her. She had the house and grounds set up for self-sufficiency, like a blind man able to count the steps from door to bed with how many paces to the coat track between. Tidy and tight for the winter.

Jenny banged pots around the kitchen, making enough noise to ward off whatever evil spirits might be in the immediate area. Or, at this noise level, possibly anything above ground. An instant later, the door opened again, and Rob came in looking flushed from the cold. Ott caught Jamie before the boy hit his lap again, narrowly avoiding injury to any future progeny of his own, and stood to greet his friend. It had been less than a day since he'd seen Rob, but he'd missed him more than he liked to admit. Staying in the house was stifling. Though it had soft chairs, warmth, and small faces with eyes like his, who had screamed in pleasure to find him sleeping in their sitting room that morning when they awoke, Ott felt like he didn't belong there anymore. Frankly, he was starting to feel that he didn't belong anywhere.

He glanced at his big friend as his sister continued her assault on the crockery. Rob looked distinctly uncomfortable, stock still in full coat and boots, now dripping melted snow on Jenny's floor. Ott looked back at Jenny, who pointedly refused to meet either of their eyes. Ott wondered if one of them had at last made a declaration to the other. They'd been mincing around each other since childhood. As usual there were always obstacles and complications, like Jenny's bastard of a husband.

It had killed Ott, later, to learn of the abuse his sister had suffered at the hands of the man who had vowed to love and care for her till the end of his days. Ott had witnessed their exchange of vows. That day, his sister had looked young and happy, and plump with hope. She could have been a tradeswoman, a cook, or . . . . well, not a seamstress, but near about anything she'd wanted. She was a good deal smarter than he was, Ott knew, and a much harder worker. Where he had lucked into most of the fortune that smiled on him, Jenny had earned everything she had now by the sweat of her brow and plain perseverance. She had found the man whom she had thought would stand up beside her all her livelong days, for whom she had thrown away so many chances in her life.

And for what? For false promises. And for worse, harsh beatings and infidelity. Ott cursed himself for his long absences and for failing her as a brother. He had never known she suffered so much at the hands of the man who should have cherished her. She had hidden her bruises well, even from him. Well, good riddance to her long-gone husband, and best of luck to his new fool wife, who had lain with an adulterer and who would be paying for her mistake with the currency of flesh and skin.

The boys were getting on their boots and wrappings. Ott had promised them a romp in the snow to look for winter hare and to get them out of Jenny's hair. He stood, clearing his throat, which set Rob back in motion, if only an awkward shuffling to the side and a tentative loosening of the scarf at his neck. Ott reached for his own coat and without a word, followed the boys out into the snow.

CHAPTER 25

Rob heard the door close behind him. He removed his coat and slowly shucked his wet boots at the door by Jenny's tiny boots. Even without his, he towered over her as he approached. The kitchen was steamy and smelled like yeast. She was kneading dough, rolling it into ropes, and braiding it. Her dark eyes were cast down, thick lashes hiding them. A wisp of dark, silky hair curled down from her forehead—a forehead that was wrinkled in consternation. What he wouldn't give to smooth that worry from it. Flushed cheeks smoothed down her face to her soft, gently pointed, obstinate chin. He moved closer and then closer, but still she refused to look at him, pressing her lips together tightly. She finished her doughy braids and covered them with a limp white cloth, then wiped her hands on her apron, having to tuck her elbows into her sides because he stood that close.

All of his thoughts, everything that usually weighed his shoulders down—his father, the mines, the people suffering in tents in front of the gates of the house, the monsters underground, Ott's beautiful dead girl—all of it fled in the presence of this woman. Jenny. His Jenny. All roads pointed to her. Even when he was home, lying in his bed in the dark, at the dining table across from Harro or the others, everything inside of him pointed across the field to this low wooden house, to this dark-haired woman with the small, strong hands that she now held limply to her sides, hidden in the folds of her gray, worn skirts. She looked the same as always to him.

Gently, very gently, he cupped her flushed cheek, engulfing her face with his clumsy hand, his fingers coming up behind her ear. Then he leaned down and, gentler still, brushed her warm mouth with his lips. Only when he broke away and stood straight did she raise her eyes to his, piercing him with their sword edge sharpness. A flicker of disbelief crossed her face. She tried to speak and had to work her throat before she could.

She said, "Still? Even now, you would want me?"

He rubbed his thumb across her lips, not as gently this time. "Would, yes. And do."

Jenny stared at him, looking at the lines of his sun-darkened skin that she had long since stopped memorizing again and again, and listened to the rumbling words issued deep in his throat. She would not let herself cry. Not then, not now, and not ever, for whatever reason. Instead, she put her hand in the center of his chest and pushed. She pushed him—but not away, because she went with him. She walked him backwards till the back of his legs hit the wood of a kitchen bench. He sat down heavily, though the sturdy chair didn't so much as creak under his considerable weight. She let him gather her between his knees, his hands on her hips. Now, nearly eye to eye, she took his face between her palms, stroking his dark, smoothly shaven skin with her thumbs. He had a straight mouth, given neither to smiles nor grimaces, just neutral normally, but now, the lips were parted slightly, anticipating hers.

The flush of warmth that traveled from her neck into her cheeks now traveled downward into her chest, then to her belly. She touched her lips to his, gentle suction on his wind-burned lower lip. His breath came in rapid pants, mingling with hers, mint-flavored from her gum, which she realized had slipped down her throat. She closed her eyes and leaned toward him, bringing their mouths together again. Her hands traveled through his dark hair. It was smooth, untangled, carefully groomed since he'd returned from traveling. He could give her brother a lesson or two about tidying up. With a start, she realized that Rob had taken special pains for her. The idea that he had dressed for her, cleaned his teeth for her, and thought about her while moving around his bedchamber, shut down all anxieties, the banal worries in her mind. She parted his lips with her tongue, and a low sound of arousal came from his throat. His hands tightened around her waist, lifting her.

Her skirts frustrated her, bunching between them. When he broke their kiss to slide his mouth down to her neck, she gathered her skirts up and straddled his lap, pressing herself against him. He buried his face into the loose neckline of her dress, voicing a hoarse groan. His head tipped back for a moment, eyes closed, as he sought air. Her hair escaping her band and falling into her eyes, she watched him, and his eyes flashed open, locking on hers. She said his name, more like an oath or a vow, and he answered in a wordless ascent.

CHAPTER 26

Foolish hope, Treyna thought, as she stood in the tent city. The people were restless, but still thought they could make the best of it. Of course they did. Dumb optimism flourished when the sun was shining. People had been set to building temporary structures. And the act of moving their hands, doing any old thing, lulled them into thinking that things would all work out in the end. The young master called Rob had walked among them the day before and his men passed through constantly now, overseeing their progress. There was talk that soon they would be back in their homes and back to work again. Perhaps even before winter set in, they speculated, though the chill rattled their teeth, and hunger made their children whimper.

Treyna was figuring out where she wanted to set up her place of business under the new structures. She wanted a quiet corner where visitors could come to her without fear of being judged, though those now close enough to see comings and goings shoved their eyes away without commenting on her customers. Or on her either, she realized. She was doing a fair trade even without Jonas's oversight. Many people, men and women alike, sought the balm of her soothing hands and salves, even in this makeshift camp. Even stranger, her children found care and companionship among the other women and children in the tent city. They, too, were taken in without judgment. She made enough coin and traded food and goods to bring wealth to the people directly around her, so they never minded her as long as her visitors minded their manners, a preference she also shared.

Jonas had thrown himself wholeheartedly into the construction of the temporary shelter. She scarcely saw him, which suited her just fine. She didn't care much for him other than for his ability to keep away harm. He was never a physically abusive spouse—yes, he was her husband and not her father as he sometimes tried to pass for being. But she much preferred his neglect to his attention, whatever the type. Maybe her mother had recognized his non-violent tendencies before selling Treyna to him.

Jonas had had her working by age twelve, before she was even full grown. A few years after that, he had taken her as his wife. She was later than most girls in becoming fully a woman, thank the good gods, or else she would have had more children by now. She wondered, idly, where they were. They were innocent kids, but not hers. She bore them, true, but she was not their mother. Jonas named them, fed them, disciplined them, and otherwise owned them. And when it came time, she assumed he would do with them what he did with her. Make them profit him one way or another. Or maybe even outright sell them. She hoped they would not come to harm. They were sweet, though the middle one couldn't speak. Treyna had no memory of being a child herself. With remote curiosity, she sometimes watched them play or sleep together as they did, in a pile.

That, she didn't understand—how they could want to be near others while they slept, being touched while they were so vulnerable. She preferred not to be touched when she wasn't watching, alert, and eyes open. Oh, she didn't mind selling her services to the agamite miners. They were short, stocky people, silent by nature. Hard workers and deserving of her ministrations. They transacted their business and left her alone. They were tidy, too, though fingers were usually stained green from being with the agamite all day. It got up in the skin and didn't wash off after a time. If a miner held his or her fingers up to the light, sometimes there would be a slight sparkle of green, like they'd dipped their hands into a pond and couldn't dry them off. Ponds. Now that was something she hadn't seen in a while. Not since they'd come north above the snowline.

"Tell me about the good-looking one with the green eyes," Treyna had started out saying the other day, and the women in the camp had taken off with it and gossiped without any more prodding from her.

"You mean Ott. Half the girls here have batted eyes at him. He was never one to turn them away either." They smiled indulgently, and Treyna knew why. She'd felt his pull also, though his eyes were not as twinkly and his curving mouth not as flirtatious as they all described. He seemed downright wounded to her. Like an animal in a bad temper because of a wounded paw. She listened to their chuckling words about him and tried to decide whether she wanted to do anything about it. It was in her to try. She didn't have the natural instincts of a nursemaid, but she had learned over time how to tend to a body. And one as blessedly attractive as he was, broad shoulders atop a lean frame, had made her consider the effort worthwhile in his case. It wasn't just the body though. It was something else, like being god-kissed. A person just wanted to be around him. But still, tending to him would be something she'd be doing for him, not herself. Letting him heal himself with no benefit to her . . . because he'd heal up and then be gone. Though he was a soothing sight to see.

Treyna was drinking the weak but hot broth they served at the kitchen tent when two men from the big house walked by her tent. The master was not with them. She was now aware that the bigger of the men who had carried the kids from their broken-down carriage was the young master of the entire house. Not much to look at, she reckoned, though he carried some power in his step. Didn't like to throw it around. Hard to believe he was the owner of all this. The house, the land, and the mines themselves. They said his sick father still drew breath, but clearly this man was their master. She watched his men, not bothering to offer her services as they strode by.

They saw her, knew what she was about, and didn't bother themselves with it. Among them was a large one with a closely-trimmed beard. They averted their eyes when they passed her tent. She idly wished for more. She allowed herself a rare moment of fantasy, drawing her fingers over the fairly fine cloth on her table, taking out the thought once again—like a pretty stone from her pocket—that the young master's friend Ott would come by. He had such pretty green eyes and full mouth. The broadness to that one's shoulders said he was strong, but that strength was from use, not from breeding. Him, she wouldn't mind touching.

Footsteps halted outside her tent. She set her mug down with patience and acceptance, probably more than someone of her years ought to have, but for her, it was acquired. Low voices, not angry, but forceful, talked outside. The cloth sign she used to show that she was engaged with a customer wisped against the tent, and then the tent flap was pushed aside. A dark, bearded face appeared, his body filling the entryway; he was one of the men from the house who had just passed by.

Treyna always looked at their faces first because she knew what meanness looked like. She couldn't outright avoid it, but she could at the least prepare for it, and usually, could take herself out of her mind to be as far away from it as she could. It could be hate in the eyes, or just as often, a certain deadness, a lack of life in the gaze. Jonas could protect her when meanness tried to return, but the proof was in the violent first visit. And no one could protect her from that. Two times that she could remember, she'd had to turn away customers seeking her services for days while she recovered from bad sessions. Things like that, once lived through, were never far out of her mind, never forgotten. Especially when her will was weakened with hard spirits or ale. She found out the hard way that drink could bring the bad times back as though they were happening all over again here and now. She would never touch the stuff again. Cruelty had many faces, but only one personality. Everyone had a measure of it, true.

Except this one. This man showed none of that to her. She searched his brown eyes curiously until he dropped his gaze to his fingers, large hands with work-roughened knuckles. He picked at his fingernails restlessly until he realized what he was doing.

When he just stood there, she wondered if she would have to take the lead. She didn't take him for a man with shyness—sometimes they couldn't get the nerve to tell her what they wanted. But, suddenly, he put his coins on the table and came by her. He kicked off his boots, knelt in front of her on the blankets, putting his hands on her arms, and she felt her own face being studied as sure as she had studied his. Her heart pounded in her chest more than it usually did. Usually? Bah. Who was she fooling—just the good lady god Lutra knew—she never felt anything inside. This one. He was not ugly or rough, yet she shied away from his steady gaze and tried to set her eyes elsewhere.

His hand slid up her neck, thumb right in the tender part of her throat. He could see right through her and now feel her pounding pulse. Her breath increased, and she felt like a coward, a mountain ewe sheered clean of her coat, naked and left out in the open. She tried to shrug off the feeling, irritated with herself. But then she met his eyes. His thumb stroked her neck as he openly stared at her. His other hand smoothed her hair, gently as he might have been sitting in front of his fire at home petting a cat in his lap. She knew her eyes were moving back and forth in uncertainty. She must look like a child, she thought, eyes wide, trying to take in more things, just trying to figure things out. Like it was new to her.

He had a clean, outdoors smell. No fancy scent. No fine clothes. He was calm and steady, not bothered by her unease, yet not particularly aroused by it. He seemed to want to assure her of . . . she wasn't sure. Or maybe she just wanted him to seem that way. Suddenly, she *wanted*. And that in itself was new and disconcerting.

She wanted to please him—she wasn't sure why. When her hands parted his shirt cloth, she didn't immediately set to work manipulating his muscles, stroking the soreness from his flesh. Instead, she stood back and stretched her arms above her head, displaying herself, though he was already sold on her services. She wanted his eyes on her, running the length of her body. She wanted him to want her. She cursed inwardly, feeling a rush of . . . shame. She knew she was clean. But she wanted to be that kind of *clean* for him, to remind him of the new flush of the spring season, to soothe him, and to take whatever he could spare. She wanted to make the right sounds, to smell just right, to stay in his mind after he left as he would surely stay in hers. She didn't know why. Nothing made a grain of sense.

He lay down on his stomach on the blankets, his face turned toward her, meeting her eyes. She felt the world drop away and the breath catch in her throat as she began to stroke him, to ease the tightness from his shoulders and lower. She moved with him, uncontrollably, listening to his breathing and realizing that hers was the same. She shuddered.

When it was done, he lifted himself. She watched him fasten his lacings back up. She ran her eyes over him, willing him to stay. The boots went back on. He flicked his brown eyes back to her, where she lay on the blankets, breathing like she had run a race. His eyes only reached up her belly before he drew his eyes away.

Sometime after she heard the signal cloth being taken down outside the tent, she roused herself, cleaned off her hands, and drew her robe tighter against the chill. With a mostly steady hand, she took up her soup mug. It still had a bit of warmth to it.

CHAPTER 27

Rav was warm. She was dreaming, and in it, she was at home in the desert, the wide starry sky above her. She walked out of her tent where her younger sisters still slept. She took a deep breath, wrapped her arms around herself, flexing her bare feet in the sand warmed in the morning sun. Her bare legs stretched up to her hips, her smooth, flat stomach. Then, she knew it was a dream. And she woke.

She was very warm. The earth radiated heat down here, down where she never saw the sky. The light was from the stones—a constant light, not a flicker from a fire with life, but a steady, unchanging green glow. It was all from the stones. As was the warmth. She slept on her side on soft furs, the smell of which she could no longer distinguish in her nose. She remembered when she first got there, everything stank. Not a stink from a dead animal, but of smoke and chemicals that burned when she breathed and made water run from her eyes. She ran a hand over her swollen, aching belly. She had been very, very sick.

She sat up, meeting the large, glassy eyes of her keeper. He gestured for her to eat. Always demanding that she eat, that she drink. He was not cruel. He was, in fact, gentle in all interactions with her, as if he considered her fragile and . . . precious. And she, in turn, found that she was not repulsed by him. Not his brutish noises, not his odor. His skin was as rough as animal hide. Bluish, but still not as dark as hers.

She worried that breathing the air down here would eventually kill her. It had made her sick at first. Two months of living below ground had nearly killed Rav. Eating their food, drinking their water, all tainted with the green stone, had distended her belly. She was as swollen as a pregnant cow. She worried only that she would not see the open sky above her one last time before she was called home to the gods. *The Great Mother above*, she thought, again detached. She had been separated from her people, from humans, and from her gods. They said the Great Mother would call them to her in the end, and they would be cleansed. Purified. Rav no longer felt any connection with her former gods. There was only her keeper and the green glow of the rock. She wondered, when her life ended, if her old gods would be able to find her here under the ground. Or would she forever lie looking up at the earthen ceiling above her? Floating, floating, scraping her face against the craggy scruff.

He was watching her eat, satisfied with her appetite. She gestured at him again, with their hand signals that she learned. *Up? Can we go up?*

Later, he said. *You eat.* Always the same answer, yet she never stopped asking.

She watched him watching her, and when she was finished, he took her scraps and ate them. She drank the green water from the wooden cup, and he watched till it was gone. From his close attention while she drank, she knew that the water was the key to her existence underground. Drinking some of the rock, pulverized in the water, allowed her to breathe the stinging air. If it didn't kill her first.

She rubbed a hand down her arm wondering if her skin would eventually take on the same hue as her keeper's. So far, she had not changed. Her skin was still darker than his, the same color it had always been. She wondered briefly if there were others from the Keep underground with her. Sometimes she thought she heard voices carrying through the rock, but she had never seen others like herself. Humans. And her keeper did not allow others of his kind near her. She suspected they had no females of their kind, which was why he treated her with reverence. As if she were precious.

In all, Rav was not angry. All her life, she had expected to be traded to a warring neighbor in the south in exchange for a temporary, transitory peace in the desert. She might have been bartered to a former enemy at whose hand she could have experienced a much more violent arrangement than her current one. She did not curse her absent gods. She did not mourn the loss of her sisters or human companionship, though, strangely, she thought often of her beautiful, shifting friend Mel, the girl who looked different every time one looked at her. Sometimes brown haired, sometimes blonde. Sometimes plain like sand. Sometimes shimmering like the sun, like on the final night. Surely Mel was dead, too, like the girl called Liz. And like Rally, the young man that Rav had once allowed herself to think of as a future lover.

She knew that her keeper and his kind ate the dead. She swallowed, her stomach rebelling in queasiness. He, at least, had not consumed anything terrible in front of her. He joined the others of his kind in the great meeting hall somewhere far off in the maze of underground caves. She heard their gatherings through the rock. The guttural sounds of their communication traveled to her chamber though he desired to shield her from it. The idea of eating their enemies was not foreign to her. Some desert tribes held that custom, too. They believed they could absorb the strength of the warriors that they vanquished.

Rav missed the sky the most. Her people did not bury the dead. They burned the bodies so the ashes floated upward. Or they fed the bodies of their dead enemies to the animals. They did not dig holes in the sand to cover them up. Here, she was buried and alive, pining for air, for wind, for the embrace of the night sky and adornment of the stars. She locked her gaze on her keeper's face, unwilling to acknowledge the tear that escaped from the corner of her eye. A guttural cough came from his throat. Like the rest of his kind, he could not speak words, but *he saw her*. He understood her grief, though maybe not the cause, because he looked away, collecting her cup and leaving her alone again in their small shared chamber.

CHAPTER 28

Late in the day, as Ott climbed a ladder in the tent city, he felt Treyna's eyes burrowing holes into the back of his jacket. She stood in the doorway of her tent, unoccupied. Jonas, on the ladder next to him, was equally idle, unless you counted his mouth, which he exercised endlessly. Ott pulled another nail from his pocket with frozen fingers and pounded it into a wooden beam. He was avoiding Treyna, and she was stalking him. *Field mouse, meet mountain cat.* Below him in the muddy thoroughfare between the tents, another dark eyed girl threw him a glance as she passed by. As did the older woman with the girl. He frowned as he hammered, wondering when the attention had become a curse.

To distract himself, he turned his thoughts to earlier in the day when he had returned his nephews to the house. Rob was sitting at the kitchen table looking for all the world as if he belonged there. And Jenny, face flushed from the kitchen, seemed content. Baffled, Ott had said nothing, but suspected that they'd finally worked out their differences, whatever had kept them apart this long. Ott had never understood the reticence. As the old folks used to say, "If the girl's willing . . ." At least, that had been Ott's motto. Mostly. Until now.

Maybe Jenny was afraid for herself and her boys. Especially after her bastard of a husband. But Rob wouldn't hurt her, Ott knew. Rob would sooner hurt himself, and that was a lot easier to imagine, especially if either Rob or his sister persisted in tiptoeing around each other much longer. Rob had stayed for the late morning meal—Jenny's tasty, fluffy-white scratch bread—then suggested that Ott join the construction activity. Which was why he was here now.

Ott cursed himself now for not acknowledging them having overcome their obstacles and finally pairing up. He was just so frozen inside, his reactions as slow to build as a snowdrift without wind, in straight-down snow that fell like sugar. *Azerus*, that was called. Jenny and Rob. Together. Finally. Something they all could look on as a good thing. Ott should be happy. Happy for them. Lutra knew Jenny had suffered enough. Rob as well. Yet, Ott didn't have the good grace to push around his face so it looked like a smile. Somewhere inside of him, he supposed he *was* happy. But on the outside, on the surface, nothing. Belatedly, he realized he'd just smashed his thumb with the hammer. For one instant, he felt no pain. Then, it burned and throbbed. He cursed and sucked it into his mouth.

It was not entirely true that he felt nothing. There was a vast void in his soul, if he had a soul. The better part of it was nothing, true, but there was also . . . red. Pure, unadulterated fury lurking just below the coat of his numbness. In fact, he was fairly certain that it was the numbness alone that made him fit to be among other people right now. He had sometimes in his life cursed the goddess Lutra, their family diety, for his luck when, in fact, he'd had nothing but good luck for most of his life. He had never starved. His sister and her boys were healthy and among the living. He had had nothing with which to fault his deity in the past. Until now. And this was how the balance was restored—one swift tilt of scales and fortune was taken away.

Mel.

He could barely approach the edges of her name in his mind without feeling the lick of red fury spreading across his face, burning his nostrils, and blurring his vision. The anger was taking control of him more and more unless he gave up and let the numbness take him. If he forced all memories of her away, the blur of nothingness took over, buffering him from feeling anything at all.

Mel.

His mind touched the memory of her again, lingering over it just as his hands had slipped over the soft sheath of her dress that night at the Keep in the garden. Red fury rimmed his vision and blended with fiery images. His hands breaking bones, ripping tough hide from the face of a trog. His uncontrolled hands changed to mallets in his mind, smashing into the beasts. His feet on the chest of another as hands again gripped the head and twisted it from its neck. His hands, fueled by red fury.

Then, later, waking to Rob's uncertain gaze. Ott's hands, again, covered in dark, bluish blood. And the numb stupor that followed when the fury was gone. Even now, the flicker of memory sped Ott's pulse. He pushed it away. Ott, on the ladder on the lawn in front of Rob's house, hammer in hand, forced himself to keep moving. Numb. Numb was better. Around him, miners—builders, now—pounded nails into wood beams. What in Lutra's name did they think they were doing? Taking a walk in winter? The cold was going to come for them. And they were not in their homes. There was no doubt in Ott's mind that everyone outside would die. They would not be spared no matter how many of the poor souls prayed to Dovay, bear god of ruthless, unrelenting hope.

"Couple more of these. What do you think?" Jonas, the panderer, said at Ott's elbow. "As good as being under a roof." The older man's hand rubbed the beam. Ott grunted noncommittally, sensing the pretty-faced predator Treyna drawing closer to his ladder. He took a handful of iron nails from the stout miner on his right when the pail was held out to him. "Mark my words," Jonas continued. "The trogs have given up. They've retreated back into their tunnels now that the winter is setting in. What are they? Nothing but dumb, foul-smelling animals. How do we know this? Look at us. Then look at them. How do we look? That's right. We wear clothes. We have property. Currency. Wages."

Ott stoically considered how Jonas's wages were made by Treyna, by her toil.

But the man persisted, his bony features flushed with his vigor. "How many of them could there possibly be? Two times ten? A few dozen at most. If they are as big as they say, how can they possibly have homes underground? Where are their pups? Do they even have females? Perhaps they eat what they excrete. Who knows? They are beasts after all. And we—we are men! Far superior." He leaned toward Ott, tapping his own temple with a clean, uncalloused finger. "Superior intellect. Superior powers of reason. And . . . " He jabbed a finger at the sky. "Superior weapons. Superior gods."

Ott blinked, annoyed. He glanced at the man to his right, a stout miner who hammered on, oblivious.

"Will our gods desert us in this time of need? No. Absolutely not. Have we not tithed greatly enough with our efforts, with our sweat every day of our lives? Have we not lived cleanly, earning our just reward?"

Would the man not shut his mouth? Ott heard Treyna muttering to herself from the base of his ladder. He glanced at her, and found her looking up at him. She gestured at him with a mug of water, so he descended, realizing that hours of work had passed without him resting.

He drank, looking up at the very little progress his own efforts had made in that time.

Jonas, thankfully, had taken his drink inside the tents. Treyna handed a second cup to the man next to him. She had a beautiful face, Ott thought, in a detached way, the same way he had sometimes walked through a marketplace looking at goods he wasn't interested in buying, like girls at faraway inns who had sometimes blatantly offered themselves to him though he wasn't interested. He glanced at Treyna, but he felt not the smallest spark of interest. Though willing hands and body might get a rise out of his physical self, his mind was repulsed by the idea. Physical intimacy without emotional desire was no longer appealing to him. When had he become so fine, he wondered? But he knew since when.

Treyna, standing beside him with her shawl wrapped tightly around herself, muttered again. It sounded like she cursed. At Ott's look, she shrugged it off but stood her ground. The man next to him asked her for a refill, which she obliged him. Ott sipped his water slowly. She spoke suddenly, in a calm, clear voice, her pretty face smooth and serious. "It's not that I care much about them. I just want to do right by them. They're not really mine. By birth maybe, but not in any other way. But they're innocents."

He looked around, wondering if she was talking to him, if he hadn't stumbled suddenly into the middle of a conversation for which he'd not been present at the beginning. She had been looking off to the left of him over his shoulder, which further confused him, but then suddenly she looked directly at him.

"When we're dead and gone, I want those little ones looked after. The three of them, all. The middle one can't talk." She caught the surprise on his face. "Don't look at me like that. I know what we're facing. If the monsters don't get us, the winter will. And Lutra knows you're the man to survive it." She turned abruptly and left him frozen, staring at her retreating back.

CHAPTER 29

Mel wanted out of the cursed sled. Hour after hour passed. Then, finally, the first signs of life in this barren, icy wasteland arrived in the form of sound. Hammering. Hewing. Sounds of construction. Their horses were tired, but the sounds of activity lifted their hooves. Mel's head pounded; it had itched and swelled where the wound was drying. She could quell the pain, but she stubbornly did not. She was irritable, anxious, and raw. And she knew they all knew exactly what she felt. She could feel her mother's eyes on her even though her mother was wearing her Mask. And Mel was petulantly glad that she didn't have to meet anyone's eyes.

Because her father had commanded her not to wear her Mask, Mel shrank back from the sled windows as their sled carried them through the gates of the estate. Still, she saw the activity—people creating frames for shelter—and even through the thick, insulated sled windows, she could sense the bitter cold coming and knew that the shelters would not be enough to prevent deaths from exposure. Her body was being ridden hard by overwhelming emotion, cords of it whipping through her like flood waters. Without reining any of it in, she grew tired quickly and felt *used* by it, as unaccustomed as she was.

A fierce, bearded man on horseback escorted them through the gates. He had met their sled a couple miles out and rode alongside them all the way to the house. Though the man glowered, Mel took her cue from Guyse, who appeared at ease with the man, so she tried to calm nerves. The sled slowed to a stop in front of a massive stone mansion, even more imposing than the Keep at Cillary, with its dark balustrades and steeply sloped, brooding roof. Mel watched her parents, waiting for a cue, exposed and awkward without her Mask, uncertain of her role. She gingerly ran her fingertips across the dried bloody welt on her forehead as she considered the impression she would make, and again, questioned her father's intentions. It seemed uncharacteristically dramatic. Aggressive, even—an opening move in a game. What was the purpose? What did her father know that she did not? She touched her head again. At least she had managed to clean most of the dust off her face, though she could feel bits of rock still embedded in the wound. She would need a bowl of water and a cloth to wash it before she healed it.

By the front door was an entourage of maybe thirty men, women, and children who did not seem to be appropriately dressed for the harsh cold, but also didn't seem to be bothered much by it. Perhaps they were accustomed to it; not a single one of them shivered in the least. They stood, ready, in universal silence, equal parts reverence and fear on their faces, the unwavering faith that Mel and her parents would aid them.

The sled driver opened the door, and the first blast of dry icy air invaded the warm cabin, the cold devouring their sled's cocoon of heat in seconds with its vicious fingers. Guyse exited first, then turned to show deference to them. Her mother descended from the sled on a set of boxed steps. Mel crouched under the low ceiling, making her way to the door, but her father halted her with a gesture. She thought for a minute that he was going to save her, to allow her to cover her face. Instead, he paused only to fasten the Mask medallion around her neck to mark her as one of them. He left her cowl and veil discarded on the seat of the sled. Exposed, as much from emotion as from bitter cold, her face flushed as he exited the sled ahead of her.

"This is not a good idea," she said, trying to grasp the sleeve of his robe. She was too late and ended up catching nothing but air. She grabbed her coverings from the bench and followed him.

Blinking to clear her eyes from the sharp sting of cold air, she stepped down onto the wooden box. She thought she heard a gasp as someone saw the dried blood that ran down her face. A ripple of anxiety ran through the people. The sun was very bright, but she knew it wouldn't last. There was a scent in the wind that marked a storm, a great frozen beast looming that even she could feel. She cast her eyes down the snowy lawn at the people at work hammering, trying to stave off their panic with activity. Pointless effort. Except that perhaps it soothed them. The opposite of what Mel felt now. Her heart pounded, and she had trouble drawing a normal breath.

She stepped off the lowest step onto the cleared ground. A narrow path had been shoveled through the snow to the front door. The ground was frozen, but she sank into it—not with her feet, but her mind. She stood stock still. She was not prepared to feel this much. It was too much. She wasn't closed off and protected. She wasn't a person, but a mass of emotion and nerves, spilling over, like water seeking lower ground. She stood frozen in the path as she reached out to the people down the lawn. She could sink into the bare ground and follow along the bits of green current. She inhaled deeply, reaching, scenting, touching their sense of purpose, their anger, despair. Her mother gasped and was suddenly pulled along with Mel, as Mel punched into the earth with her mind. She raced from thread to thread of the green agamite stone. Jumping, twisting deeply, leaping blindly when there was no clear path to follow, and hitting the next tendril. She passed through the earth, deep underground, far down where it was not frozen.

She came up in the center of the activity, at the feet of a strong man wielding a hammer. He was a miner, his blood full of the stone, bits and tiny particles, motes in the streams of his veins. He stopped, frightened, although not sure why, seeing nothing to alarm him. Mel jumped from the ground into his green fingertips, into his arms, up through his neck, and into his eyes. She looked around, and then inhaled deeply, feeling the man's fingers curled around the handle of the hammer as he paused in his nailing, frozen, completely taken over by her. From inside, she moved his limbs. She turned him around slowly and stared. The familiar scent slammed into her lungs through his, his nostrils flaring as she looked directly into Ott's shocked eyes.

Could he see her? Did he know it was her?

Ott's green eyes locked on hers as though he saw her in the body of stocky miner next to him. His hammer fell from his fingers, and his face froze with shock, eyes open wide, unshaven chin going slack with confusion. With a sharp gasp, Mel withdrew and shrank back into herself. Back up the lawn by underground route, she slammed back into her own body.

Part 4

Reveal

CHAPTER 30

Standing at the foot of his ladder in the tent city, Ott struggled for air. "*Mel?*"

He whipped his head toward the house where he'd seen the sled go. They all had noticed its arrival as it passed through the gates, brought up by scowling Harro, Rob's man, on horseback. And then Ott was in motion, leaving his hammer forgotten where it lay half-covered in the icy mud. The miner by his side looked astonished as he recovered himself. Whatever it was that had been in the miner man's eyes, whatever he *hoped* it was, propelled Ott toward the big house.

Ott's body roared. His mind shut down, his legs powering him up the hill. He was afraid to hope, but more terrified of not knowing. He ran up the slope when the ruts in the snow would allow him, his feet sinking deeply where he stepped outside the track. His feet covered the distance, lungs straining to burst. After months, what felt like years, he couldn't get there fast enough. He knew she was up at the house, pulling him to her. It had to be her.

As he neared the sled, he found it empty. The massive front doors of the house were closed, so he ran around the side to the kitchen door. His footsteps pounded up the steps as he took them two at a time until he stood in the threshold on the worn stone floor that he'd known well since childhood.

"Nan? Where are they?" he asked the startled cook, her gray hair tucked under her cap. She looked up at him and started to smile, as she always did, but the look on his face stopped her cold. He probably looked like a lunatic. He had been working outside for hours and knew he was a mess. The full sprint through the snow had him sweating under his coat and breathing hard.

"Lutra take it. What's the matter, Matty?" she said, dropping her armful of bowls onto the immense wooden table, immediately coming around the counter at him in full protective hen mode though she came only up to his shoulder now.

"The sled that arrived . . . the Masks," he said. He could barely get the words out. He took a big breath. "Where are they?"

Nan answered right away, as always wanting to alleviate whatever discomfort he was in. He realized with some embarrassment that he was her favorite. He was even more of a favorite with her than Rob. More than any other child at the big house, even though he hadn't lived there. And he wondered how many times in the past he'd used this knowledge to his advantage. With Nan, with other people. Why hadn't he been more grateful? "In the hall with Rob and the master." She put a hand on his arm looking up into his face. "But you can't go in there."

"Why not?" He frowned, agitation bubbling up and making his skin itch. He had to know if *she* was in there with them. And why had she come with them? What was she doing here? He brushed Nan's hand off as gently as he could and paced for a second. She watched him, consternation wrinkling her sweet, old face.

"They've locked everyone out of the hall. From the inside. No one can go in."

CHAPTER 31

Mel was ready to jump out of her skin. She had seen him. She had smelled him. Ott. So close. In her nose and deep down into her chest. But she had to calm herself. She had to control herself even though he was so, so near. Her mind raced though she tried to make her face placid. She didn't care how it was possible—that she had had to come to the edge of the world to find him—*he was alive.*

She tried to stop her eyes from speeding from face to face in the room, as exposed as she was without a Mask. She, along with her parents and Guyse, had been led inside the gloomy manse to a large theater. Now they faced a crumpled, skeletal old man on a dais. Colubridan Robinet. She had studied and memorized his historically known facts. He perched in a fine-worked chair that was more a throne than anything Mel had ever seen in a book of tales. These were a people of a great and long tradition, as isolated as they were; they were fierce, proud, and stubborn. His ancient body was swaddled in furs and a rich, deep purple velvet. She expected him to wear a crown at his withered temples; this minor lord projected a formality and grandeur the likes of which she hadn't experienced since Lady Skance at the Keep, miles away and a lifetime ago.

Now everyone stared at her silently. No one said a word. They saw the blood on her head—the injury she had suffered at the hands of the locals at the port. Why would Ott be here of all places? She wanted to close her eyes, to pretend to be invisible, so she could think, maybe try to reach out to him again. Yet, she could not. The stone floor here was solid and non-porous; she sensed nothing, no veins of agamite, no green dust. She needed to put it out of her mind and focus on the old man in front of them. She had been struck—clearly, there was a threat to her kind here. They were not guaranteed the respect and treatment they'd been accustomed to in the past. So, she stood there, as still as she could, outwardly calm.

With a hand on her arm, her father displayed her to them, but she realized the people crowding the hall were not looking at the wound on her head but at her face. They had never seen a Mask, unmasked. No one had. Why should she be the first? Had her father seen something? She took a deep breath and began reigning herself in, battening down her mind against a wild storm of emotion. She could hear them then. They were talking; she simply hadn't been able to hear them over the cacophony of her own raging sensations. She tried to pick out voices, to distinguish words in the mishmash.

She is one of them? . . . She's so young, much too young. Is it a trick?

She gritted her teeth. Masks were not supposed to have motive. Yet her father clearly had one. She simply couldn't figure out what it was. She focused on each face that stared at her, and her Keep training returned to her at once. She would show them. She was not simply a Mask, but a Cillary Keep-trained one at that. They had their formalities and rituals here; she would prove that she could match them. She straightened her back, clarified the light that fell on her face from the dormer windows high above, so that her wound would be visible in detail to all those who looked at her. As she waited for the formal, traditional words of welcome, she sharpened her features, raised her height, and diverted attention to the wound, made it glisten slightly though it had been dry before. She thought she saw Guyse lift an eyebrow at her display.

The murmurs dwindled, and the old man on the dais cleared his throat to speak. The acoustics of the room carried his reedy, cracking voice to her. "I assume you have received a summons. I know that is the only condition of your attendance in a matter, that you Masks must first receive a call for assistance from someone." Without the formal greeting that was due to visitors or even the required blessing and call for respect to his household god, he began, his very first word even referring to himself. *I.* He dared speak of himself before all others.

There was no murmuring in the great hall, but Mel sensed shock at the man's lack of decorum, his lack of deference to them. His lack of humility. His pride. She searched his face for signs of senility but found none. With a shock, she realized that the younger man standing to the right of the dais was Ott's big friend.

Ott was truly here.

Seeing his friend was absolute confirmation. Ott's friend was related to this minor lord? Her heart pounded and soared. She tried to reign herself in and managed only to keep herself from running to him. Ott's friend was this old man's son, as his position at the man's right hand declared him. But what was that look on his face? The stoicism was hard to get past, but she saw frustration in the set of his jaw and schooled patience measured by the pulse at his neck.

The old man continued, "I am the head of this house still, as breath goes through my body. I have called for no one. Therefore your presence here is unwanted. That is all. You may go." The old man gestured to a nearby servant, who helped him descend the dais and make his way to a door off to the side of the great hall. As soon as the door closed behind them, the great hall erupted in chaos. Mel felt it swirl around her. A wave of uncertainty came from her mother, but from her father, there was nothing. Mel herself felt . . . she didn't know what. The people's outrage, fear, and nervousness licked her like flames. She was kindling, ready to combust.

She inhaled, ready to laugh, feeling the absurdity of the situation ready to consume her in a storm. She inhaled again, drawing the escalating emotion of the room into her. The great hall seemed to shrink suddenly. It wavered and contracted. Then, she did hear a sharp intake of breath from her father under his Mask. But she couldn't stop. She was eating it all, the chaos and discomfort, delicious to her, and as she did, calmness replaced chaos all around the room. She had never been this open before, this able to absorb people in such an enclosed space. She could feel, even, a draft of air sucking inward under the locked doors of the great hall, air coming from the hallway. It reached her nose, tendrils of it filling her lungs with that particular spicy aroma she'd missed all these months. It hit her chest, and she froze in her inhalation. She released the room, and a calm settled over it. Her mother, father, and Guyse stood frozen, turned toward her, staring.

At that moment, the young man to the side of the dais, Ott's friend, came toward them, quickly yet coolly, surprisingly without a trace of apprehension despite the tumult of the situation. Perhaps they bred them stronger up here in the frozen north. But his eyes gave him away. When he got closer, she saw they were lined with strain. His jaw was locked with tension.

He addressed all of them in a low voice that was cool and collected. "If you would, please retire to your chambers so that I might call upon you and discuss matters privately." His eyes passed over her open face without recognition. He didn't know her. But then, she wasn't surprised. She didn't look the same as she had at the Keep when she'd been costumed in her presentation finery and shining like a sun, and he had seen her only once.

Her father said with as great a show of deference as his cloaked body would allow, "As you wish." He pulled Mel's mask over her face, and they were escorted from the great hall.

CHAPTER 32

Ott paced the smooth dark stone floor of the hallway in his stocking feet trying not to slip. Twenty paces one way. Twenty paces back. He had gone back to the kitchen door and removed his coat and boots, momentarily chagrined when he realized he was tracking melted and dirty snow through the entire house. He vowed to never again be so self-obsessed as to not give a thought to the cares of others. At least when he could remember, he amended, realizing his flaw. He paused and turned around, wracked with a nervous fidget, then turned back the other way. He rubbed his cheek roughly, scratching his two-day beard. He took a sniff at his shirt and grimaced, wishing he'd taken time for a bath. Another waffling directional change, and then he resumed his footsteps. For pity's sake, when were they going to come out?

A little housemaid shot him a surprised smile. She stopped in confusion when he stared at her, frozen mid-step. Her brown curls were tucked under a knit white cap that identified her station. Then she turned and continued down to the east wing, casting him a narrow-eyed look over her shoulder. Ott froze, and then jogged after her, kicking himself. Marget was her name. He'd once given her a flower. A peck on the cheek in the east wing where she worked. That was where high-ranking guests usually were housed. He followed her retreating figure, her thin shoulders in her house uniform. He searched his memory, fairly certain a kiss was all he'd done with her, cursing himself for being such an idiot. Now every past flirtation tormented him. He caught up to her and laid a hand on her narrow shoulder. Even that felt awkward. What was wrong with him? Had he lost all feeling of being at ease in his own skin?

In answer to his query, she said, peering up at him, "The Masks? There are three of them. I've never seen a Mask up close before. Kind of scary creatures, aren't they? Little bit ghostlike. Gives me the willies and makes me wonder what's under there. Not human, that's for certain. They don't talk very much. They say they can sense what you're thinking and get inside of your very thoughts to see if you're telling the truth or not." She gave a little shiver that would have made any other man want to put his arm around her. "They also have a man servant. Tall as you've never seen, broad as you through the shoulders, and what a scowl on him. Looks like Dovay himself. Great bear of a fellow. There's two with the Masks covering their faces. Don't know if they were men or women, can't see their faces you know, and they're all the same height. And a tall young lady whose face wasn't even covered up."

Marget was alive with the gossip. He was having trouble following her account, whether there were two or three Masks. Her pretty eyes were wide and bright, but he wanted to know about only one thing. One person. He asked, "There was a younger woman with them?"

"I saw her myself. Quite pretty, actually. You know, if she had her hair done up and the right clothes, she might have been quite beautiful. Looked a bit done in though. She had a lump the size of a melon above her eye." Marget gestured a lump approximately as big as a summer melon.

"A lump?" Ott repeated, blankly.

She tapped a small finger to her brow, and amended her description "Big as an egg. Like my little brother got from a flatball. You could see where the dried blood had gushed right out of it right down the side of her face. Don't know what happened. I imagine they're talking about it right now in the great hall."

He thanked her and ran back like a headless loonybird just in time to see the doors of the great hall open and people start to stream out. Where was she? He combed through them, swimming his way into the room but found no one, not even Rob. Ott spun in circles, looking from face to face. Nothing, just a blank calmness that confused him. What was the outcome of the meeting with the Masks, he wondered. He swore in frustration. Several stragglers looked at him with curiosity, but he brushed past them. He rubbed a hand through his hair. Then, he turned back to the east wing, jogging on the hard stone floor and slipping on a spot where someone had tracked in snow. He could feel Mel here somewhere, but damned if he knew where to find her in this maze.

So close. So intensely frustrating.

He cursed and nearly growled. The edges of his vision became tinted with red, though he didn't know why the battle lust was coming now. He didn't care—he just wanted to find her.

He reached the east wing guest quarters and slammed open the heavy wooden door without so much as a warning knock or shout. He skidded to a halt, a trickle of sweat dripping down his face in front of his ear. He froze, realizing belatedly that the door had been locked. Solidly barred. And he had broken through it without a second thought. Staring back at the door, he saw the solid iron latch destroyed in its setting, wrenched apart by one push of his hand. Five faces stared at him. Scratch that. Make it three Masks, another man, and Rob, looking grim and tight-jawed. Three heads swathed in smooth black cloth. Blank like a godless death. All turned toward him.

Blood drained from his head, and the red abruptly receded from his vision. Masks here in this room standing not more than a few steps away. They were the stuff of spooky tales that made children quake in their beds at night. Except Masks walked about during the day, looking surreal, casually standing about on the muted, tasteful colors of the woven rug in the otherwise cozy sitting room. *Three wraiths come for tea . . .* It was the beginning of a joke that fell short of funny. They were soulless judges, drifting, floating almost above ground in their ghostly cloaks, coming when called. Summoned like evil spirits on a curse. Inhuman. Faceless. His mouth dried up.

Rob cursed finally, invoking the conniving snake god of his father and breaking the silence, "Colubrid swallow it. What are you doing here, Ott?"

Ott knuckled back a rivulet of sweat from his jaw, floundered, and said, "H . . . hello."

Three hoods empty of all but darkness met his gaze. Dizziness swept over him as his red sight receded further, leaving black spots in his vision, threatening to take his consciousness. He hadn't eaten or slept well in days, maybe weeks. What a kick in the pride it would be to faint in front of them. To leave himself vulnerable in the face of . . . he faltered. Why had it been so important to find them? His mind drained to an utter blank.

Rob cursed again and rounded on him. He grabbed him by his arm and yanked him out of the room. "Whatever it is, man, we'll deal with it. *But later,*" the big man said. He guided Ott back out to the hallway, a big hand clamped under Ott's elbow, and then suddenly spun him around and hooked an arm around Ott's neck and pulled him close and leaned into Ott so they were forehead to forehead. Like when they were kids. "Please," Rob said. "Let me do this. I need to do this. For all our sakes."

Ott frowned, confused. Whatever business Rob had with the Masks, Ott wasn't aware of it. But he'd never sensed a greater need than now in his friend. The big man's face was suffused with color as he ground his teeth together. Lutra knew Rob had stood by patiently enough all those days after they left the Keep, on the road when Ott was barely able to step one foot in front of the other.

Pull it together, you hopeless imbecile.

Inconstant, yet always buffered by the sweet shelter of seemingly endless good luck—that was Ott. When had he ever let fate roll toward his friend Rob? Rob, who had more than his share of downright bad luck and dealing with the fallout from Ott's thoughtless behavior their entire lives. Well, his friend needed him now. Uncertain and still unsteady, Ott nodded once, then twice.

Rob let out a breath. "Wait in my room. Have a soak. Get some food. You need to eat. Drink. Whatever you need, as always. Just wait. It might be a while." With a final squeeze of his large hand on the back of Ott's neck, not unlike an embrace, Rob abruptly turned and re-entered the room with the awaiting, awful visitors. In the chamber, they loomed, cloaked and silent, judging.

CHAPTER 33

Mel froze.

Behind her Mask, she was hidden, but the sight of Ott, the much-longed-for, spiced aroma of him staggered her. The heavy draping clung to her nose as she inhaled sharply. Confronted with the sight of Ott after so long, this close, and as exposed to emotion as she was, she was struck still like stone. She was immobile and mute, unable to do anything but breathe as she stood there.

When she finally reconnected her mind with her legs, she stepped forward. Only to find a strong hand on her arm. She tried to shake it off, instantly angry with her father. But when she looked up, it was Guyse. And he was frowning, his dark, angry eyebrows pulled down with a startling comprehension. He knew what she was feeling? It shouldn't have been that much of a shock—she was broadcasting her emotions broadly enough for all of them to know. But it was a surprise, an invasive and humiliating experience that they all knew her inner turmoil was overcoming her; it made her weak in their eyes.

"Not now," Guyse said tersely, his deep voice a rough growl. He stared at her, assessing and cold, his menace barely in check. Mel knew suddenly, he was there not to protect them all, not to guard them, but to watch her. To keep eyes specifically on her. They didn't trust her. It was enough to make her stomach drop. How did they know? She was briefly cowed by the thought. She wasn't halted by his arm for long, but long enough for Rob to take Ott out of the room and disappear. But he was here. Ott was here.

She took another step forward, ready to throw off Guyse's grip. His large fingers dug into her arm, and she turned toward him, ready to . . . what? Yell. Attack. Howl?

"Stop," Guyse hissed into her ear. "Not for yourself. But for the lives of others."

Her head snapped up as she took him in with wide, shocked eyes behind her Mask.

"If you cannot think of the consequences of your actions for yourself, think at least of the people outside these walls. They will die if we do not help them reach some sort of agreement." His large fingers on her arm loosened, and his voice softened, at odds with his rough appearance. "Please, Ley'Amelan," he said using her proper name, formally, softly and yet with a strange familiarity that brought a crease to her brow. "See this through," he murmured.

Under her Mask, she flushed up through her neck to her ears in further humiliation. She stilled herself only with the promise that she would find Ott as soon as she was done here. She calmed herself. She set her shoulders. "Of course," she said stiffly to Guyse, willing control to color her voice. Determination to follow through with the commitment. Yes, she would serve these people. Just as her parents were. Just as generations of Masks had done before her. Overall, she was insignificant in herself, but whole and infinite in her service. Individually, she was a failure as a Mask. She fought tears and allowed Guyse to lead her after the others to the seclusion of the adjoining room.

CHAPTER 34

In Rob's quarters, Ott tried to eat but settled for drinking half a mug of dark ale off the tray that had been brought to him. It calmed him enough to turn the crank above the stone bath that would signal a fire downstairs and eventually allow hot water to flow through the pipe and fill it. He sat in an oversized chair by the fire, elbows on his knees, head in his hands while he tried to think. Three Masks, a guard, and Rob. But where was Mel? He rubbed his temple and followed the line of scruff down the side of his face to his chin. He was insane. She wasn't here. What had he been thinking? Just him and his crazed, hopeful mind standing out in the cold sunshine hammering away, wishing she were here. His chest contracted. He didn't know which thoughts to try to banish. Either she was here, but he wasn't able to find her. Or he was hallucinating. In the bathing room, the water had started to flow into the basin.

He downed the rest of his tankard and wiped his mouth with the back of his grime-covered hand. Sweat, snow muck, and sawdust mixed together. His fingers smelled like metal from the construction nails, his fingernails cracked and uneven, but he ran them through his hair anyway and rubbed his gritty scalp. He cursed in disgust at himself and caught his reflection in a mirror across the room. He was thin. Gaunt. Hollow in the face with deep shadows under the slashes of his cheekbones. His shirt was hanging off him in a strange way like he wasn't so much a living, breathing person as an excuse to hang some dirty clothes out to air. He stood and stripped them off, discarding them in a pile on the floor, watching his wretched reflection in the glass in a detached manner. Shadowed collar bones. Jutting elbows. Pronounced ribs. Hip bones that he'd never seen before. Lutra take a walk in winter. When had he last eaten? He remembered the smell of fresh bread at his sister's house. But had he eaten any of it? Who had been guiding him, moving his body around, while he had been away inside of himself? No one, apparently.

He poured himself another pint from the pitcher, already feeling the effects of the first on his empty stomach. He took the dark ale with him, walking barefoot. He stepped over the tub's smooth edge and lowered himself into the steaming bath, cringing and slowing as the water reached his thighs until he became accustomed enough sink all the way in. The last water dripped in from the pipe, the exact right amount to pour for a bath having been measured out decades ago. Somewhere in the house, he knew servants observed the water temperature and pressure, making sure that everything flowed smoothly. He had traversed the bowels of the house with Rob when they were children, when Rob particularly wanted not to be found. With Ott his constant companion. The brother that he'd never had. More than a brother. A friend. Always.

He pictured Rob in that room alone facing off with the three Masks and their guard. As if they needed a guard. The thought of the Masks made his stomach lurch a little. Inhuman. Gods among men, some thought, yet cruelly detached. He'd heard stories of them heartlessly judging others, making decisions that gave lands from one family and destroyed another. If there were any *true* justice or law in the land, his sister wouldn't be living in near poverty. His family would be thriving and not at the end of its course. He would have a place in the world instead of drifting away. He could feel himself even now slipping away a little and struggled to raise himself before the ale stupor took him completely out of his body. He grabbed the coarse brown soap and scrubbed himself all over including his scalp. Then he slid under the steaming water and rinsed off, almost losing the air in his lungs as the hot water hit his face and went over his head. He stayed under a little too long and rose up like a *whaleri* out of the ocean, gasping for breath. Then he leaned back propped against the sloping stone, eyelids slumping down, and thought fleetingly about scraping a razor over his face before he gave up and went limp, his body sagging and his mind floating.

Sometime later Ott heard Rob come into the room. The water in the bath was still warm. He wasn't sure how long he'd been asleep, but he was deadly thirsty.

Funny how you could die of thirst in a hot bath.

The outer door closed, and Ott heard footsteps trail across the room and stop at the entrance to the bathing room behind him. "I'm awake," he said without bothering to turn, and sounding gruffer than he intended, words a little more slurred than he thought they might be. His throat had dried up and it took two tries to get a sound out. "Haven't drowned yet." Though he was parched from the heat and the alcohol.

Footsteps came into the room and approached the side of the tub into Ott's line of sight, but they sounded wrong. They were too light, too hesitant. Ott opened his eyes, suddenly on alert, red flaring up on the edges of his vision. He saw the robes first. Long black cloth draping to the floor. The dark cloth swept against the stone, muffling the steps. Disbelief reigned as he tracked upward. He uttered a curse and cowered against the side of the tub, scrambling without success for something to use as a weapon. The water sloshed over the edge of the tub as he raised his eyes thinking he would again meet that faceless hood.

And he blinked, stunned again.

Instead of the ghastly veil, he saw Mel's face. Or what looked like Mel. Because it couldn't be her. Could it? Whatever hovered above that ghastly black apparition was a damned nightmare, a disembodied head adhered to a Mask. Dried blood led down the left side of her face in ribbons from a knot of swollen flesh on her forehead. Her hair was dark brown, darker than he remembered. She was pale, very pale. Her mouth was drawn in a straight, tense slash. And her dark eyes held . . . fear.

"What have you done to her?" he demanded, gravelly throat disguising the quake of fear in his voice, alcohol and exhaustion confusing his thoughts.

Had they killed her? They've killed her! And now one of them wore her head as its face.

He grabbed a towel and wrapped it around his waist as he propelled himself out of the tub, unable to bear crouching below the thing any longer as it levitated above him. Confusion crossed its face. The face looked down at the cloaked body, and then her eyebrows shot up.

"Wait," it said. Then, "Please. Wait," again, more frantically.

Even his alcohol-addled brain recognized that it *was* Mel's voice, though more ragged than he'd thought possible. Thin, pale fingers swam out from the cloak's arms and clawed at the throat of the cloak. They wrenched at the Mask's medallion and undid the clasp till it dropped on the floor with a thunk. Pale fingers connected to arms that undid the ties of the cloak and ripped at it frantically. When the ties were undone, the hands pulled the sides of the cloth, parted it until it too went to the floor. Slim neck. Deep crevice the size of his thumbprint at the base of her throat. Smooth skin to a slender torso under a sleeveless tunic. Long pants that hung low on hips and flowed downward over the curves of long legs. It was a woman under the Mask. It was a body that he'd once held in his arms.

Mel.

He stood shocked and dripping water on the floor as seconds ticked by. His mind churned as he struggled to connect the facts and failing. She'd used a Mask as a disguise to come to him? She was their prisoner and had escaped? No, that didn't make sense. She had been taken by the trogs during the attack on the Keep? That didn't work either. She was here. Real and standing in front of him now. Alive. And real.

He didn't intend to lunge at her; he was soaking wet. At first, he simply snaked the fingers of his free hand toward her. He spidered them toward her shoulder and then grasped her, her slender bones and smooth skin. Where they touched, his skin tingled, flooding prickles up his arm and into his chest. Finding her as real and solid as he hoped but still couldn't quite believe, he swore again, half curse, half prayer. His vision blurred for a second and he had to close his eyes. Then he swooped, wrapped both arms tightly around her and tucked her close into his hollow chest against his dripping wet skin.

CHAPTER 35

Mel had stared at Ott's face hungrily while he lay covered by murky bath water. She had been longing to see his face for so many months, and now here he was. He was thin and wretched-looking; his eyes were closed as he dozed in the bath, the blue stone of the bath turning the water blue, making his skin look more bloodless and corpselike. He looked half-dead, his scruff-covered face gaunt and lined with exhaustion.

That in itself was alarming, but more than that, she was afraid that he would resent her for not finding him during all the time they'd been separated, for not telling him she was alive—though she hadn't known where to find him. And she was afraid he would hate her for not telling him the truth about herself, that she was a Mask. But then he shot straight up, covered himself with a towel and after a minute, had pulled her into his arms. Her hands wrapped around his back, feeling bones and sinew.

"I'm sorry. So sorry," was all she could say against the bare skin of his chest. She inhaled his aroma, trying to drink it in as they held each other, but her arms were not tight enough to dispel the disbelief of being with him again. Her mouth opened against his skin as she apologized again, thinking he hadn't heard her. Bath water soaked the fabric of her shirt. He rested his chin on the top of her head and made soft shushing noises as he stroked her hair with his damp palm.

"It's you," he kept repeating, his hand lightly touching her hair, the back of her neck, her shoulder. When he pulled back to look at her face with a puzzled expression, the towel between them started to slip. He realized it, made a grab for it, and flushed profusely up through his neck and grizzled face as he caught it with one hand. His other hand locked with hers, fingers twined together, and he refused to let go, letting one hand do the task of covering himself with the towel instead. She felt a half smile lift her cheek. When had she last smiled? The muscles of her face found the gesture foreign, forgotten. She leaned into him, pressed her lips gently into the deep seam that ran down the length of him from sternum to navel and watched the shiver pass through him. She felt herself flush with heat all the way up to the throbbing wound on her forehead.

His fingers on her cheek lifted her gaze to him. He said, "What did they do to you?" His eyes were on her forehead, focused on the bloody wound that her father had refused to let her heal. She was embarrassed by it and wished she had remembered to fix it before she stumbled into the room.

She shook her head. "It's nothing."

His eyebrows came down. "It's not nothing."

She was frowning more about him than herself. He was so thin, just the bones of the person he'd been a few months ago. She ducked her head, tentatively reaching her free hand toward the sore spot on her head where the stone had hit her. She risked a glance upward at him. She had seen his reaction to her Mask. He could still hate her when he realized what she was. She faltered, wondering if there were a way to avoid telling him. But his scent in her nostrils, that savory scent, the touch of his fingers in hers, and the steady, green, agamite-colored eyes so focused on her demanded that she tell him the truth.

His fingers twisted a strand of her hair around his finger. He was staring at it with a puzzled expression, as if not trusting his own memory. She knew what he was thinking. It was not the color hair that he remembered. She owed it to him. The truth. *This is going to upset you . . . The thing is . . . I'm a Mask . . .* She attempted, then rejected several beginnings silently.

She bit the inside of her lip and cleared her throat. "About that . . . "

"Wait," he said. He took her hand and led her back to the dressing room where he hurriedly dried off and pulled on a pair of pants while she turned her back to afford him a little privacy. When he came back to her, she found it hard to meet his gaze. She focused on the scar on the underside of his chin. His nearness made her eyelids half close and her breath come fast. Heat, again, washed over her, up her cheeks into her hair, into the tips of her ears. When he stroked his hand along her jaw, against the soft skin behind her ear, and cradled her face in his hand, she lost all semblance of control and wrapped her arms around him, pulling his face to hers. She would never let him go.

Uncontrollably, she started to contract. Everything about her, mind and body. The muscles throughout her entire body seemed to convulse, to spasm. Inward further and further she clenched, drawing on the scent, on the tidal waves of emotion. She gathered it in until she was nothing but a speck within herself.

Then, she exploded. Out, farther and farther, feeling a wash of raw and powerful love, terror, pain, and joy whip out of herself.

Her back arched, and she shouted soundlessly as ripples of energy exploded. Every particle of herself vibrated and hummed. The wound from the agamite-encrusted stone on her forehead healed in the wave. Skin reconnected and absorbed the flecks of green stone left there. She took the stone into herself. And burst, from the inside out. And she knew without having to open her eyes that she was golden.

CHAPTER 36

Later, much later, Ott was dying in his dreams. Nothing could save him. He was alone and adrift. He thought he had found Mel and had taken her into his arms only to find her dripping away like ice melting into water, the smooth deathlike veil of a Mask in her place. His luck had run out; it was over. He woke with a gasp in a sweat-drenched tangle of blankets and looked over at the sleeping woman next to him.

Mel.

Smooth, smooth golden skin. Sun-drenched hair. He'd gone to sleep with a wounded, broken Mel and had woken up with a goddess, Lutra forgive him again for his blasphemy. Mel stirred and turned over to face him, blankets draped low across her. She was stunning. He drew a sharp intake of air. Her forehead injury was gone, as were all traces of blood. Her sleepy eyes fluttered, and then flared wide open at his unblinking stare. He wanted her. He hadn't forced himself on her, but he wanted her.

"I could use a skin to prevent pregnancy," he offered. He was fighting the urge to touch her, to get under her skin. And he cursed himself when a frown crossed her smooth face. Lovely dark eyes blinked once. *Of all the dumb, clod-kicking things he could have said* . . . She pulled up the blankets to cover herself though she was still clothed, but stopped, looking embarrassed, a flush seeping up her neck.

"I can't become . . . I can't have a child unless I, um . . . " She avoided meeting his eyes while speaking of her Mask capabilities. "To conceive, I have to meditate. I have to go within myself to open certain . . . passages that have been closed off. Blocked. If I wanted to have a . . . " She trailed off nervously, watching him closely for his response. He could feel his eyebrows shooting upward. He hadn't known that Masks had that much control over themselves . . . to be able to manipulate their bodies in such a way. As if they were gods. A shiver ran through him, which she saw. That frightening red tinge from strong emotion—any strong emotion, he was realizing—was back around his vision. But he held himself still in the bed next to her waiting, hoping that he was indeed still lucky and Lutra blessed, that the whole nightmare about the Masks was his drunken, fearful imagination.

"Ott," she then said in a low, quiet voice. *No such luck.*

He sighed and rolled onto his back, lifting an arm to cover his face. At least the red tint went away when his eyes were shut. "You're a Mask," he said flatly. He wished there were some way to stall her answer, to freeze them in this one moment in time. To stop everything. To halt the relentless flow of time and capture it in eternal ice. Now, before she said the inevitable and changed everything between them.

"Yes . . . I mean, *no*," she said. What was that in her voice? Denial? Confusion? Either way, she had said yes. And he had seen her in the Mask with his own eyes, whether or not he wanted to believe what his eyes had been telling him.

"Either you are or you aren't, *my lovely*. Which is it?" he said, still unable to bring himself to look at her. That falsely flirtatious tone had escaped him without him intending it. My lovely. He'd spoken to her as if she were a barmaid. Not his Mel, the one he'd been dreaming about, fantasizing about for months. Head pressed into the pillow, he was sinking into a dark abyss. He could feel his bones caving in on themselves. He felt the blankets across his belly move and thought she might be leaving the bed. Getting her shoes back on. Putting that damned creepy cloak over her skin like a shroud locking her away from him forever. All for the best, probably, he tried to tell himself. It was better that she leave now that she could see what an uncouth, cowardly bastard he truly could be. Except the minor detail of his heart being ripped directly out of his chest.

Instead, he next heard her soft voice nearby his ear, and felt her breath on the arm that was covering his face.

"It's not fair, is it," she said.

He frowned, momentarily flummoxed. "To which of the many candidate parts of this . . . situation are you referring?" He lifted his arm, finally, to look at her, but was still startled by her proximity. She was kneeling on the bed next to him, her knees at the corner of his pillow, but looming above him so that as he looked up, he saw her face beyond the lovely, distracting swells of her breasts underneath her shirt. A red halo flared to life around her. His mouth went dry. Unconsciously, he found himself slipping a hand over her thigh to draw her closer. She leaned over to him so they were nearly nose to nose. And he choked when she suddenly threw her leg over his hips, straddled him, and brought herself down firmly on the blanket that covered him. His hands were on her thighs again, but she interlocked her fingers in his and pressed both of his hands up by his head. Hinging her hips on his.

"OK. I can die now," he said, as her golden-tipped hair hung around their faces in a curtain. But she studied him with a seriousness that robbed him of his thoughts and words altogether.

"I think I can help you," she said finally.

He was distracted by her closeness. All that golden skin. Turning orange in his red-tinted vision, he noticed with some anxiety. The tint was flooding his eyes due to his lust. Desire. Whatever he wanted to call it. It was starting to surge. Uncontrollably. The thing that happened when he started ripping heads off other things. With a tinge of panic, he lurched, trying to roll away. But she clamped down on him with her legs. *My, she was strong for such a soft, skinny little thing.*

"Wait," she said, then kissed him until he was docile. Pliant. Limp. For the most part.

"Kissing is good for the panic," he said. "More of that." He groaned when she finally broke away and sat back. But she was serious again.

"Ott, I'm a Mask," she said.

"More panic," he said. "Lots of panic coming now. Heaps of it. Blizzards of it." But he remained as still as he could under her.

She waved her hand between them as if to clear away what she'd just said. "I mean, I'm Mask-trained. But I'm not a Mask. How could I be when I love . . . when, I'm too emotional. Too sensitive of others. I'm not a Mask." She said the last part with certainty. He waited.

She went on, "Yes, I'm here as part of the delegation. I'm here on a task. But it's my first task. Kind of a trial one. But I don't know what I'm doing. I don't belong here. Well, I know I belong here. " she said, laying a hand on the concave muscles and skin above his navel. "But I don't know what I'm doing here." She waved a hand somewhere over her shoulder. The gesture made the lovely parts of her body move in such a way that nearly prevented him from hearing what she was saying. But dumb as he was, he had heard enough and was stunned.

She'd just as well said she loved him. Well, just as good as said it although she'd stuttered and interrupted herself. He could say it back to her, take the upper hand, and be the one to say it first. Except everything was red again. Red like battle fury, apparently also brought on by lust. He couldn't win. It was either all red or else it was black death and despair when the red was gone.

So instead, he said, "What's not fair?"

She locked eyes with him, suddenly all seriousness again. "It's not fair that I was able to heal myself. And you are still wounded."

He lay back, letting her meaning sink in. She was whole. Perfect. Straddling him, a veritable goddess hovering above him, he silently apologized to Lutra *again* for his blasphemy in comparing the two. It was just that one was so unapologetically immediate. Nearby. In hand, so to speak, he thought as his hand involuntarily wandered over her hip. But no matter how she made him feel, she hadn't been able to make him whole just by letting him be with her. No one could do that. Except maybe the goddess Lutra herself, but her domain was his good luck. Charisma. Lutra gave him sociability and ease. Family and community. She didn't repair souls when they had holes in them like his, though he could pray and wish and hope all he wanted. Lutra might repair the pots in his sister's kitchen for all that he prayed. But no, that was blasphemy, and he wouldn't risk that again.

And Mel, though she was here now, Mel knew he was broken inside, in his mind. She would probably leave him because of it. He would never be good enough for her.

He closed his eyes and let himself sink back into the abyss. "OK, I can die now," he said again, though this time without any will to continue. He let himself wallow in it, feel the dark fingers of the depressive sickness trickle into his mind and down into his belly. Losing her the first time had nearly killed his will to live, while exposure to the trogs had brought the battle fury out of him. He was someone else now, not the same lucky bastard as he'd been before this whole mess had started. He was adrift and alone, out of his body, no longer able to feel his own skin, never mind the weight of Mel's body on his hips, wherever their bodies were. Somewhere in a bed together. In Rob's quarters. In a big house in a frozen land.

He floated away.

CHAPTER 37

Staring down at the unconscious Ott, Mel took advantage of the situation; she should have warned him first, but he might not have agreed to it or even understood it, had she been able to put it into words. She wasn't going to heal him—not in the conventional sense with poultices and herbs and prayer. He didn't have a broken body, so much as an agamite infection that poisoned his spirit and his mind. She was going to *take his pain*, just as she had done for Liz, her dead friend from the Keep, in those precious final moments. At least, that was Mel's intent, though she wasn't sure if she could do it again, now that it was even more important to her. Everything rested on this one task.

It had been easy to get him to slip away. He was half-starved and exhausted. All he had needed was suggestion. No *pushing* involved. She had seen it in his face at first glance. His face. She leaned forward over him and watched him drift behind closed eyelids, his mouth slightly slack. Without the tension that had been webbing across his face, he looked like a boy. His whole countenance pleased her. He had a nice mouth. And she liked the shadow on his jawline, liked how it felt against her neck. Her skin had been rubbed raw again and again by his kisses before healing each time. He had fed her needs. Now, she would give some of that nourishment back to him.

She took his hands in hers and thought for a minute. He was out there by himself, floating like a toy boat in a river tied to the bank by only a precariously thin string. She closed her eyes and reached out to him with her mind. She felt the river of his despair coursing around them. She pondered for a minute. With Liz, the connection had been fast and easy, without thought, without any imagery, maybe because poor feisty Liz had been at the end of her life, weak and dying, no barriers or resistance left to surpass. Maybe because death had no imagery. Or maybe because death was imagery in itself. And though he might feel like it, Ott was not close to death. Not by a long shot.

More physical contact.

Mel lifted herself up on her haunches and pulled the blankets away from them. Then she laid herself on Ott, from toes to forehead: her toes on his shins, her forehead buried in his neck. Who knew if it was the right thing to do, but it felt nice. She fought nervousness that bubbled up with the urge to giggle. Calm yourself, stupid.

He breathed evenly, drifting somewhere far away. She threaded her fingers through his rumpled hair and clamped her elbows close to the sides of his face, scratching the sensitive insides of her arms with his beard stubble. And shut her eyes. And dove into him.

The current threatened to drag her away. The force of it surprised her. Seen from afar, it had looked like an ordinary river, almost smooth on the surface. But now that she was in it, she could feel its strength. She treaded in place, thrashing her legs to keep her head above the surface. When she pushed her hands through it, the water was black and thin. She pulsed her legs with an extra stroke and attempted to breach.

Where was he? There. She saw him, floating on his back. Placid. Adrift.

She stroked her arms and legs cross-current and tried to get nearer to him. But she realized before long that it was futile. Her limbs grew heavy, exhausted.

But what if she simply stopped trying to resist it?

To answer her own question, she paused for courage, then ducked her head underwater and . . . took a breath. Water flowed into her like air. Because it was not water. It was pain. Pure, black pain. She opened her eyes under the surface, but saw nothing in the inky depths. She fought panic as she sank deeper and deeper.

I can breathe. I can breathe. No panic. I am smooth, calm. Breathe in, breathe out.

Her feet touched the bottom. She could still see nothing. She tried closing her eyes, but the weight of the water on her shut eyelids was worse than blinking repeatedly and seeing nothing.

Wait, not nothing. She saw . . . something. With each breath out, she saw a little something. A light that came with each breath out of her mouth. She observed it. Thought about it. Then tested it. Breathe in blackness. Breathe out clean and bright light. She measured the vastness of the river around her. Then set her shoulders, dug her heels into the riverbed, and inhaled for all she was worth.

And inhaled. And inhaled.

The first exhale created a clear protective bubble around Mel. She saw the clean, dun-colored sand of the riverbed under her feet. She inhaled again, closing her eyes, and pushing beyond capacity. She ignored her physical limitations and pulled the black liquid into her emotional self, into her inside space, which, she found, didn't have the same constraints. She burst through the hull of the inner seed of herself and found . . . more space. Green fields that went on and on, crossing each other lengthwise and across and through and other ways she had no words for.

And exhaled. For minutes. Hours? Days?

She heard a rumble of male laughter. Ott's laughter swirled around her, just as the inky black fluid swirled around them as if someone had let the stopper out of the tub, and it was all swirling down the drain pipe. He floated by her, catching her arm. She locked her grasp onto him, hand on forearm, hers to his, and his to hers.

CHAPTER 38

When Ott opened his eyes, he felt as if he'd been away for a very long time. Yet, Mel still lay on top of him. And to his embarrassment, he found that he was holding her tightly, rocking his hips against hers while they slept. But were they asleep? He didn't know. He started to draw away from her, but she looked at him with what seemed to be a self-satisfied grin on her lovely, golden face. Gods above, it was like she carried the sunshine with her. She laughed. Her whole body spasmed with her mirth, sending him into an uncontrollable frenzy of lust and . . . joy. She shook her head and it looked like a sheen of glittery agamite-green dust left her hair and floated away in the morning sunlight.

He lost himself in laughter. And took her with him.

A little while later, still drowsy, he watched her leave the bed in perfect complacency. He knew she would be right back, and she was, bearing the tray of food that he had not been able to eat earlier. She sat on the edge of the bed, balancing the tray next to her.

"I'm going to feed you now," she said.

He watched her through heavy-lidded eyes as she broke off a piece of bread and placed it in his mouth. He had a sense of something momentous occurring, some ritual of which he could barely grasp the gravity. No ritual that he had ever heard of among his own people. Maybe it was from hers. Maybe it was their own. The bread was heavy with grains and fresh baked that morning, he guessed. Flavor flooded his mouth. He found that he was hungry for the first time since . . . since when? Before the Keep. She waited until he swallowed the first bite. Then, bite by bite, fed him cheese, fruit, meat, more bread, and ale from the tray.

"What are you doing to me?" he groaned, lying back, finally full.

She paused, feeding herself then. "Was that a complaint?"

"No, my love," he said softly, this time meaning it with every ounce of himself. *My love*. His Mel. He liked to watch her eat. He folded his arms behind his head, eyes firmly on her until he suddenly noticed that his arms felt different. Fuller, heavier, no longer wasted. He brought one up and examined it. Thick ropes of muscles wove around his arm, and no bones protruded from his elbow and wrist joints anymore. Then, the other. Yes, definitely, his arms were thicker. He pushed the blankets back from his belly earning a squeak from Mel as she caught the teetering tray of food that he'd knocked off balance. He smoothed a hand down his abdomen. No longer caved in. Smooth and thickly muscled. Healthy. No. *More* than healthy. Then, he noticed his feet pressing the foot board of the bed. Rob's extra-long, specially built, big bed. He whipped the blankets off and leaped to the floor. Mel pushed the tray aside and watched him with an amused quirk to her eyebrow. Ott wobbled, his sense of balance thrown off by his altered perspective. He was taller by a good three inches.

"What did you do to me?" he wondered out loud. "I'm taller."

"I don't know," Mel said shrugging, biting into a chunk of bread. "Maybe you're just standing up straighter. You were kind of slouching when I got here. You know, hunched over." She demonstrated. Very distracting.

He held up his dirty old shirt from where he'd discarded it in a pile on the floor. "Look, the sleeves are too short."

"Maybe they shrank. From the grime. Sweat. You know, man detritus."

"And the pants, too?" he said, holding them against his body. The bottom of the legs were above his ankles.

She said through a mouthful, "They're not exactly lying smoothly."

He looked down again and saw the pants were tenting outrageously at his groin. "Definitely your fault," he said, tossing them aside, reaching for her, no longer caring about his altered appearance.

She said with a drowsy smile, "We're never leaving this room, are we?"

He looked around and noticed it was nighttime. He wondered where Rob had gone. And wondered how to broach the subject of the Mask delegation with Mel. He still got a shiver up his spine thinking about them, never mind her with them. He didn't want them anywhere near here. He turned on his side and found she was eying him, as if reading his mind and deciding which parts of his insanity to address first.

Could she do that—read his mind?

"What it comes down to, basically," she said, apropos of nothing other than his thoughts, "is that your friend Rob wants to continue with the plans for sending a delegation of negotiators to the creatures despite what his father wants."

Ott sat up quickly. "You can do that? You can read my mind?!"

She patted his leg soothingly. "Heal myself, yes. Change my hair color, yes. Make you . . . taller, yes, apparently that, too. Read your mind, probably not for another fifteen years. It's not your mind, Ott. It's your face." She gave him a sly smile, and he thought, feeling some silliness, *she loves me.* Then she continued, somberly, "I think that you and I both need to go with them. With the delegation to the mine."

At that, his mind clamped down. The thought of her near the trogs nearly made him lose all the food in his stomach, though oddly, his vision remained red-free. His skin still crawled. Thoughts of the pickled head they'd brought back with them to Rob's father crossed his mind. He knew what it took to destroy just one of the beasts. They were savages. Monsters. If they got her . . .

"My mother is a healer," Mel said, once again throwing him off his train of thought. She seemed to have a knack for doing that. Or maybe his thoughts weren't as single-tracked and steadfast as he liked to believe. Then, a quake went through his mind.

"Your mother is . . . a Mask?" Somehow, he couldn't imagine it. A faceless, cloaked thing feeding a baby. Bathing it. Clothing it. Rocking it to sleep at night. Lutra on a spit. Did they even do those things?

Then, another kick in the gut. "My mother and father are here with me."

Suddenly it struck him who the three cloaked figures had been—Mel *and her parents.* Ott swallowed this new piece of information about as easily as gulping down his own tongue. Same effect, apparently. He sat, while his mind flipped over one hundred and one useless thoughts, unable to speak. Was he going to have to approach them with an offer of marriage for their daughter? It was the traditional thing to do among his people. Good gods, maybe they didn't even have marriage among Masks. The thought of not being with Mel, and her alone, made the red tint flood back into his vision. His heart pounded. He ran a hand across his forehead and discovered that a sweat had broken out. His breathing ramped up and his chest squeezed enough that he feared apoplexy.

She knocked on his forehead not too gently with her knuckles. "Hello in there?" And when he met her eyes, she said, "Yes. That's right. It's me. The girl in your lap. Yes? Hi? You remember me?"

"Damn," he said, trying to breathe slower and rein in the panic. "I'm going to have to meet your parents, aren't I?" He wasn't sure which was more anxiety-causing, the fact that they were Masks or that they were the parents of a woman he'd just been with. For hours. Of all the girls he'd romanced, he'd never had a situation like this: one in which he needed to charm the mother and father. A wooing situation in which he actually cared about the outcome. He didn't think he had enough charm or luck to win over a thousand faceless Masks, never mind her parents.

"Breathe, Ott," she said stroking his face with her fingertips. She gently pressed her fingertips into the spaces under his cheekbones, and suddenly the panic seeped out of him. His breathing slowed down, and the red receded again from his vision.

He sighed, contentment flooding into the space left by what she had taken away. "I think you may be good for me."

"You think so?" Her words were serious, but her smile was sweet. "And anyway," she went on as if his attack had never happened, "You need to meet my mother and father if you'll be going with us. My parents already know what is transpiring between you and me. They know I'm here with you now."

He sat up again, this time taking her with him. "How do they know? They're not . . . witnessing any of this . . . in any way, are they?" He waved his fingers vaguely at his temple, miming some kind of mental ability that he didn't know what to name.

She shook her head. "No. I told them I was coming to you."

"They didn't mind?" He looked at her closely. Something crossed her face. Regret? Sadness? Then she gave him a smile that knocked him flat.

"It wasn't their choice to make," she said simply. And as she leaned in to kiss him, she added, "And for me, there was no choice at all."

CHAPTER 39

Across the fields, Rob woke up before the dawn wondering what his choices were. He fought the urge to pace, certain the floors of the battered old house would squeak, and he didn't want to wake Jenny. She lay curled on her side next to him in the blankets while he sat next to her propped against the headboard. In the dark, he listened to the soft sounds of her breathing and wondered at the abrupt change of fortune that had brought him here. He resisted also the urge to stroke the dark curls of her hair, touch her skin, and wake her. Just to make sure this was real and not another one of his thousands of dreams.

Colubrid, snake god of his father, though never merciful, be merciful now. Make this be not a dream.

Though, he had never seen the inside of Jenny's bedroom before, so surely it was not a dream. She seemed to like purple, he noted, almost excessively. His Jenny. The rush of sensation those two simple words together brought him was almost overwhelming, so intense that he had to push the thought away and approach it slowly, taking it out little by little. It took his breath away every time. He didn't trust it to be real. Yet, here he was with her now.

Her hand shot out and stroked his side. "Hold me, you lout. Before we both wake up," her voice, luxurious with sleep and desire, commanded. A hoarse chuckle escaped him as he moved toward her and took her in his arms.

The night before, he'd hardly finished meeting with the Masks at the house before he had thrown on his coat and boots, climbed the snow-covered hill, and gone across the field toward her house. The sun had been up and her boys still awake when he'd arrived. Whatever they thought of his presence still in their sitting room when they'd finally settled down and gone to sleep, they didn't say anything about it. Maybe they figured that because Ott wasn't there, he was looking after them. Whatever the case, he would never forget the feeling of banking the fire in the sitting room and then being led by Jenny in the darkness to sleep beside her in her room. Her room. How many times had he wondered what it would be like?

She kissed him with a soft gasp.

What seemed like a few minutes later, though he must have fallen back asleep, Rob heard heavy footsteps pound up the front steps. The front door was thrown open, and the footsteps came into the sitting room. He jumped out of bed with a curse and punched his legs into his outer, long pants, not bothering to tie them up tightly at the waist before he threw open the door to Jenny's bedroom and flew into the sitting room. He heard Jenny stir, get out of bed. He wanted to keep her behind him, keep her safe, but the door had swung wide open behind him, so he did the best he could by blocking her with his body.

The sun was up now, and whoever it was now standing just inside the house had left the door open behind him. All Rob could see was the outline of a huge male with the light behind him. The man wore boots just like Rob owned. A blast of chilly air followed him in from outside, and then another person came in—a smaller figure, a female who was more tentative.

Rob tensed and crouched low, ready to defend. He scanned the room for a weapon but found only the metal poker by the fireplace. It would have to do. He could reach it in a couple quick steps. Jenny stepped out of the bedroom around him, and he moved to block her, but she was faster. And she was armed with a homemade pipe gun. Squinting into the sunlight at the intruder, she planted herself next to him on the side that was closer to the boys' room, just as their door open to reveal a sleepy-eyed Jamie. Her youngest boy took one look at Rob, then the intruders, and squealed with delight, pitching himself at the huge figure . . . who caught the boy up and swung him around.

CHAPTER 40

Rob froze in confusion, but Jenny lowered her gun and shouted, "You stupid mutt, I could have killed you!" She tucked the gun back inside her room by the door, and then tightened the belt of the robe around her. Rob frowned. The female behind Ott came in, closing the door behind her. Sudden relief from the angled sunlight brought them into focus. Ott. And, gods, his girl from the Keep. Not dead after all, apparently, Rob thought with some surprise. And where the hell had she come from in this weather? Surely not the mines. Then, staring at her, he realized she was the Mask girl, the one with the uncovered head. Ott locked fingers with the girl and brought her next to him, balancing his little nephew in the crook of his other arm. He didn't seem likely to let the girl's hand go any time soon, especially the way he kept throwing his gaze toward her. Rob knew the feeling.

"Great goddess apart," Jenny said on an exhalation. "You're lovely." She was staring at her brother's girl, mouth slightly agape. Ott did the introductions, dusting off manners they hadn't seen in a while.

"Glad to see you're alive and well," Rob told Mel with a little bite to his voice. The girl blanched and gave what seemed to be an apologetic shrug. Rob should have brushed it off, but he knew how much his friend had suffered and, in fact, how much he had suffered along with Ott. It was hard to let go of the bitterness so suddenly, despite how well Ott was looking. Apparently, the two of them must have done a little healing together, he thought with an inward snort.

But Jenny took Mel aside to the kitchen, where she was starting breakfast for her clamoring boys, the two older of whom had by now tumbled out of their beds and joined their little brother. The two women's heads were together in a way that made Rob a little nervous. Ridiculous, he thought, still feeling hesitant about his new . . . understanding with Jenny. Gods, he hoped it was more than temporary for her. It would kill him if she grew tired of him. He couldn't bear to think about it, and pushed it out of his mind, as he was so good at doing when things made him uncomfortable. But he was glad Jenny didn't seem to feel any jealousy, and in fact, seemed to welcome her brother's chosen . . . *Chosen?* Rob suddenly wondered why that word had popped into his head. It was an old fashioned term. No longer used since official marriages—and more common divorces—had come into fashion. But, whatever the case, dealing with trivialities was a comfort, but it meant he was skirting the issues at hand.

Ott took him aside, but Rob spoke first. "You have some explaining to do?" Rob asked him, gesturing at the clothes Ott had commandeered from his closet. He didn't remember his clothes ever fitting Ott in the past, but they seemed to fit him fine now that Ott was finally standing up straight, finally eye-to-eye with Rob as he should have been their whole lives. His friend looked . . . whole.

Ott shrugged. "Yesterday, you told me to bathe. My clothes were pretty much done for." But he gestured at Jenny's bedroom door. "What about yourself? Got some explaining to do of your own? She's my sister, Rob."

Rob shrugged uncomfortably for a minute, looking at his own bare feet. But when he looked up, he saw Ott was wearing a big dirt-eating grin.

"About time," Ott said, adding in a curse for flavor. A silence passed between them for a minute while they digested their new, expanded connection with each other, throat clearing and toe scuffling. It was good to have the old Ott back again. When they were both more comfortable, Ott changed tactics. "How are we going to do this thing with the trogs? What do you know? What have you heard?"

Rob knew he was talking about the delegation. He pulled out the thoughts he'd been mulling over when he'd first woken up that morning. "First, we need to move Jenny and the boys to the house. We need to get them in closer. It's not safe out here."

Ott nodded, and then cast a furtive glance at his sister. He told Rob, "She's been holding this house together by willpower alone. You're the one who gets to tell her."

Now it was Rob who cursed, though without any real venom. Then he smiled, thinking how he'd like to have her in his bed at the house. And how he would convince her that she would like it, too.

"I don't want to know what that expression on your face means," Ott said with a shudder. "But if you're thinking what I think you're thinking, please stop right now."

"Your mouth. Shut it," Rob muttered, but knew he was unable to hide his smile and wouldn't have been able to under any circumstance. Then he grew serious again. "I need to stay back on this one. I can't go with you to the mine," he said returning to the trogs. "The old man is against any kind of communication with them, but we have to get the Masks out there to the mine entrance and see if . . . gods, I don't know."

Rob ran a hand across his face and went on, "If we can work out some kind of agreement. I don't know what we have to barter with if they're already controlling the mine, but I don't know what they want either." He looked at Ott, then abruptly took his shoulder and turned him away from the kitchen. He lowered his voice. "I need you to go with them. I've seen what you can do. You and their man Guyse can escort them. The Masks trust him. I trust you. But I can't be there. I need to stay here if something happens. The people need to be protected." Their faces close together, Ott met his eyes and nodded.

"As for your girl," Rob continued. "I know you're not going to want her near them . . . but I think you're going to need her." Ott started to protest, but Rob cut him off. "She's one of them. She's a Mask."

"No, she's not—" Ott's first instinct was to deny it. Like it was a childhood insult flung during a fight.

Rob shot him a look. "Are you sure you're thinking with your actual head? You saw the cloak. And if she's one of them, you know she's not fragile. She's got their abilities. Whatever they are, they're built for jobs like this."

Ott kept silent, scowling. Rob knew his friend had to be feeling a natural aversion to the Masks. He knew because he felt it himself. They'd been raised with it: suspicion and fear of all outsiders, never mind the black, cloaked, soulless ones. It was hard to be in the same room as the damned things. Silent and cold. Still as death. Rob cast a look over to Mel and Jenny, heads still together in the kitchen.

It was difficult to reconcile this pretty yellow-haired girl with being a Mask, yet she was one of them. Even Ott had to admit it to himself, no matter what his body was telling him. Rob wondered whether the shine of

Ott's infatuation would fade over time as it had with all the other girls, no matter that he had suffered over this one. Rob had seen the bloom fade on Ott's romances, time and time again. He just hoped it would fade before she was killed or left him. That, Rob couldn't take. To see Ott suffer as he had . . . it had nearly killed them both.

His eyes rested on Jenny again, just as she lifted her face and beckoned them both to the kitchen table. He would see her and her boys safely packed away at his house. He pulled on a shirt as he approached her, his barefooted steps muffled and swallowed by the sound of three young boys eating. He cleared his throat with the intent to be heard clearly, wanting to order her to follow his will, to demand and boss and hear no words of opposition. He was utterly, absolutely in charge. He would be the man here, as damned well as he knew how. He would tell her what needed to be done in the din of the breakfast sounds, so that none of the others would overhear the authority that he had over her now. She had always been a strong-minded girl and was the same even now, as a grown woman. She would resent his superiority at first, but she would get over it faster if no others witnessed it. As his chosen mate, as his woman, she would have to submit to his higher authority.

But as Rob's rotten luck would have it, at that moment, all eyes turned to him and their voices dimmed. Jenny's eyes met his, and all else dropped away. He stammered, his first words coming out in a manner that would have earned him a certain beating had he still been a boy before his father. "Uh . . . would . . . " He tried again, while she waited patiently. "Do you think you might like to come with the boys to . . . " He scratched his head, casting about for some thread of thought to follow. "There's plenty of room, of course, you know. What with the . . . extra rooms."

"Nicely done," Ott muttered, eyes bulging with disbelief at Rob's utter fumbling of the job.

"Sorry?" Jenny said, spoon in mid-air.

Rob, to his abject humiliation, felt himself reddening all the way up to his forehead. "What I mean to say is, would you and the boys . . . and you, too, as well. Of course you. All of you, actually. Together, although there's room for you to be apart. You wouldn't actually have to, you know, stay together as a group. Though you might, if you like. Though, I would hope that you and I . . . uh . . . Would you like to live at the house? My house? Well, the big house."

Jenny froze, a frown of concentration creasing her forehead. She was leaning forward as if straining to hear a faraway sound. He wondered if he had actually completed his question. Out loud. Had he managed to include all the relevant details and pertinent information in his offer? He wanted to bang something in frustration. And he would have, if he hadn't lost all feeling in his hands and feet. *Damnit. Grab your balls in one hand, man*, he told himself. And tried again.

"I'd like it if you and the boys would come live in my house," Rob said. "And you two, as well." He nodded at Ott and his girl. "Though I want my room back, if it's all the same to you."

He was met with silence. Absolute, straight snow-falling silence. The boys eyed each other in apprehension. Ott and his girl were watching Jenny, but Rob couldn't bring himself to look at her face. If he were met with with stubborn, frozen anger, he wasn't sure what he was going to do. All signs pointed to him gathering up the rest of his clothes and leaving her house silently and never looking back.

Her spoon clattered violently into her bowl. She was the most astounding female he'd ever known and he cringed and waited for her final words on the matter, however harsh they might be.

"Boys, finish your breakfast," she said. "and pack up your things. We're leaving this wretched shack."

CHAPTER 41

Colubridan Robinet, the lord and master of the northernmost manor of the realm—once familiarly called Col Rob by those who knew him, raised him, and watched him turn from youth into man—was finishing his breakfast in his room. He took it sitting up at his chair near the fireplace lately, his heavy mantle wrapped around his legs. *Ahh, but the fire was warm.* His breakfast was quite good, better than he remembered it ever having been earlier in life. His cook staff worked nothing short of miracles using the dregs which remained . But perhaps everything seemed sweeter on his tongue at this late stage in his life. Much more so than he'd ever experienced as a youth.

Lately, his thoughts had been turning more and more to his childhood, his three older brothers and two sisters, his father and his mother. They had once lived the privileged life of a wealthy family in Port Navio. No, not a soul here in the snowlands knew that he was originally from the port city; no one alive was left to remember it. His brothers and sisters were all dead, as were his mother and father. Servants from his youth were all dead, too. But they were all so replaceable. Sometimes it slipped his mind which ones he had now. He'd collected them over the years. He had adored them like pets while they lasted, but they all died so damnably fast. The expanse of servant gravestones in the burial place behind the house grew as decades rolled by, while his lord Colubrid, the snake god, allowed him to molt yet another metaphorical skin and live on. His life had stretched ahead, longer and leaner than ever.

He coughed hoarsely and was grateful when Charl, his young manservant, brought a cloth to wipe his mouth. Col Rob waved him off when the servant sought to raise him up and restack his bones in better order in his chair. He nodded, however, when the boy removed his breakfast tray. Good lives he gave them, just as he did his agamite miners. Nice, strong, stone and wood houses. Shelter from the godforsaken endless winter. A good living. And a means to provide for themselves. The ability to flourish, if they put themselves forth, to make men of themselves as much as they could, to draw themselves wives and create offspring. Was he not a good lord? A just and constant lord?

He thought with a certain flicker of anticipation about the coming days. He gestured for Charl to bring his game table. There was nothing in the world he enjoyed more than a good game of strategy. Dodge, feint, thrust. A distraction to the edge of the board. A subterfuge. It brought him alive. Col Rob felt blessed he'd had the patience and foresight to train Charl to play the game when the boy was just a freckled, blond hatchling at Col Rob's knee. The servant had good concentration and showed a keen and facile intellect. Col Rob was proud the first time the boy had beaten him at the game. And, in fact, he had presented the boy with a banner bearing Col Rob's family colors that very afternoon. What an accomplishment that had been. To have cultivated such ability in the boy. Even now, Col Rob felt the tingle of pride as he looked across the table at his manservant.

Charl opened with a quiet, standard move. A *chan* slightly to the right of center, two paces ahead. Could mean anything. Very generic. Very deceptive in its banality. Col Rob decided to let the servant take the lead, and mirrored him.

Charl said, "I have the cadre in position, as you directed." He moved his *boneye* diagonally out to the left. *Ah, now there was an aggressive move.*

"Very good," Col Rob said. "Move ahead tomorrow afternoon in the noonday sun. Might as well not freeze off their toes. The trogs know not whether the sun shines while they burrow around under the dirt." He positioned his *chool*, fashioned in the likeness of the snake god, to the side of Charl's *baneye*. In two moves, he would have the boy cornered.

"My father leads them," Charl said with a note of pride. He took a moment before he made his next move. Lunet, the lady piece, fleeing to the side. He was on the defensive already.

"Of course. He will do well," Col Rob said. "An adept and truly well-placed man."

"What would you like me to do with the others?" The servant didn't meet his eye, but Col Rob knew he was referring to the soulless ones, the Masks. He scoffed inwardly at their tactics. Amateurs. Displaying the bloodied face of that young girl. He didn't believe their ploy for a minute. Whether she was a hired pawn or one of them was irrelevant. He knew they could alter their appearances. It was a clumsy trick that used light and shadow to create illusion. There was nothing mystical or magical about it. Instead, he'd pretended that he hadn't been the one to summon them. That he was senile and incompetent. Let them think that his adulterous wife's son was at the reins. Lovely insect that she'd been, her family one of the strongest pillars of the house of Insectoj. True to their nature, she had never been completely his. And true to his nature, he had not expected it to be so. And yes, his so-called son Rob was just as much a pawn as the rest of them.

He had Charl cornered now. In three more turns, the game was over. He moved his guard, the *rib*, to the left and gave the boy an opening and a chance to redeem himself.

"Do nothing," he said. "Let them stay penned here for a while and stew. The storms are not expected to move in for another week. The people will be fine outside while the Masks determine their next approach." He hoped to his god that the Masks' next move would be more entertaining than the first feeble show. He'd expected them to be better adversaries. Instead, he had bested them in his first turn. Luckily, he had not pulled out the stops at first. Though he had given them more than they were prepared for.

Charl accepted his statement and took the opening that Col Rob had left him. *Good boy*. Charl knocked Col Rob's game piece to the side and smiled boldly with the final stroke.

"Well done, lad," Col Rob said.

"Shall we play again, sir?"

"No, not for now. I think I might rest," he said contentedly. The boy nodded. Col Rob watched his servant clean up the pieces and move the game table aside, and took pride in the boy's victory.

CHAPTER 42

"I'm nervous as a cat," Ott said, looking the part.

Mel watched him run a finger around the inside of his collar. She matched him stride for stride down the hallway to her parents' quarters in Rob's house. Not an easy feat. The man was walking fast and his legs were longer now. He had adjusted well to his new stride, although did not seem entirely accustomed to the feel of the fine clothes that he'd borrowed from Rob. Ott yanked smooth the front of the light green tailored shirt and tucked it into his heavy, corded brown pants.

Mel still wasn't sure how she had made his change in stature come about. It had been a side effect of the cleansing. A nice surprise, she thought, eying his larger frame with admiration, though she had liked him plenty enough before. Nothing she'd ever read in her mother's library had pointed toward changing the appearance of others. She thought about the agamite granules that had been absorbed into the now-healed wound on her forehead, about the ribbons of the stuff that ran through the ground here, and the color of Ott's eyes.

She'd have to ask one of her parents, if she got the chance. If she could bring it up between, *It seems I don't want to be a Mask after all.* And, *This is the man I love.* And also, *I can't seem to bring myself to be more than two feet away from him at any time.* It certainly felt that way. She'd been across the room from him at his sister's house, although he'd had his eyes on her nearly the entire time.

"I wouldn't call you a cat. More like a hound," she said giving him a look from under her lashes. As a reward, she found herself pushed into an alcove in the hallway and pressed into a hanging tapestry. Ott's arms braced against the wall, caging her in. She was trapped in a good way, a very good way. His mouth found hers roughly, and she closed her eyes, matching his ardor. Funny how something could feel both familiar and new at the same time.

When they broke apart, he said, "I wish you would think about not coming to the mines."

She felt her temper immediately flare up, and enjoyed the accompanying lick of heat. If she had been a lesser woman, she would have accused him of kissing her on purpose to distract her into doing what he wanted—not going with the delegation. But honestly, the two events were separate. She could see it in his face. Lust and attraction. Concern for her. Two separate, yet ever-present layers. But she was still angry. And though anger was something foreign and new to her, she loved it. Every outrageous emotion. There would be no more banking the embers of her feelings behind a Mask. She let the anger ride over her and appear on her face.

He stroked her cheek with one large knuckle. "By your deafening silence, I see you have no more to say on the subject," he said. "And neither do I."

She smiled, anger and wily manipulation sharing time with what she knew she could never fail to feel for him . . . tenderness and, well, love. All those things she would have been forced to deny feeling before. He gave a groan as she snaked a hand up the back of his neck over the collar that had been bothering him so much, and drew his mouth back to hers.

"Are you ready to do this?" she asked him, her voice low as she tried to stay on task. When his arousal-hazy eyes met hers with an entirely different *this* in mind, she clarified, "Meet my parents." And she was met with another groan. This one, in which the lust wilted, and his eyes cleared as he blinked and immediately tensed up again. He rolled his shoulders, partly untucking Rob's shirt again. She helped him smooth it, and he took her hand.

"Ready enough," he said.

There was a sense that they had to do this. They had to do this strange, formal presentation of him to her parents because of the uncertainty of the outcome from their meeting with the trogs. Mel wasn't naive enough to try to fool herself into thinking that it would all work out for the best, that they would come away from the mine entrance and the trogs unscathed and with satisfaction on the parts of all sides involved. The violence and death at the Keep was too fresh in her mind for that. If something were to happen to herself or Ott . . .

She drew a deep, shuddering breath that caused him to tighten his grip on her hand. She looked at their hands—his large, weather-roughened hand that engulfed hers. The skin of their palms was pressed together, but still didn't feel close enough to her. She came to a halt outside the chambers where her parents were sequestered and lifted Ott's hand to her face. She met his green eyes as she pressed her mouth against his knuckles, breathing the scent of him in. She knew now that his scent wasn't something that he wore. It was just him. It was the way he was, and she hoped that she wore some of it on her skin.

CHAPTER 43

Her mother and father were seated, and attired in their cloaks, but their cowls were not raised and veils not in place. She had sent word to them the night before that she would be bringing Ott, her *chosen*, to meet them at dawn before they all embarked on the task. Though she hadn't asked them to, her parents were obviously seeking to ease Ott's discomfort by showing their faces. They were aware of how Masks were viewed in this part of the world. There was, however, no mistaking the sense of urgency in the room. After this little bit of greeting was taken care of, they would be leaving together for the mine entrance, a good distance away. The time it took for the journey by sled was reserved for planning, for strategizing, for information exchange about the trogs, not for dealing with their daughter's chosen mate.

"Please enter," her mother said, rising and embracing Mel. Her father kept his distance but inclined his head in their direction, and his face was arranged with a . . . pleasant expression, which shocked Mel in itself. Their guard Guyse lingered at the window, his dark and massive height disappearing into the rich darkness of the heavy curtains around the window glass. But Mel felt his eyes on her, and then on Ott, assessing them together.

Mel made the introductions, and her mother was generous enough to take Ott's hand. She knew it was not something to be taken lightly, to be touched by a Mask, by the mother of his . . . Mel wasn't entirely sure in what terms Ott thought of her. He cleared his throat. He looked intensely nervous for a minute, looming at the edge of the carpet in the sitting room. Then she felt something change in the room, almost as if there were a physical lever or handle pushed.

Ott surprised her by suddenly dipping a stiff bow and by saying formally, "Ley'Ana. Ley'Albaer," he said facing them, without the slightest hesitation over what had to be strange-sounding names for him. "I thank you for the honor of your audience this morning. I have been blessed by the acquaintance and affection of your daughter. Please accept my application for her hand, so that we may be joined in holy union and in the eyes of our society." He added, "Or however is deemed fit by your rules and customs."

Mel gaped at him. Whatever she had been expecting, that wasn't it. And the silence that met Ott's words was telling of the surprise her parents felt as well. A glance passed between them, but Mel didn't know what it meant. She was too stunned to think much of anything. He wanted to marry her? And why was he asking them instead of her? She had the overwhelming urge to punch him in the arm. Or wrap her arms around him. Either one. Maybe both.

Her father spoke first, starting with an uncharacteristic throat clear. "Well, this is certainly a morning for new undertakings. We appreciate your candor, Mattieus Ottick. And we will consider your well-tendered request."

Mel felt her eyebrows shoot up on hearing Ott's full name for the first time. Someone had been doing his research, and it was obviously not her. She wondered what else she didn't know about him. And she realized with embarrassment that what she didn't know about him was certainly more than she could claim to know about him. Ott bowed again, and she stared at him like he was a stranger.

Her father continued, "We have some preparations to complete before our departure. If you will excuse us." Mel felt her mother's considering eyes on her, assessing her sudden alliance with this stranger. Undoubtedly, they had to settle themselves, which included donning their masks, something they'd prefer to do without an audience. Mel felt restless, not joining them. She still had one foot in their world, but she preferred to remain half-apart from them. Or so she thought. When the door closed behind them after they filed out followed by Guyse, Mel turned to Ott, narrowing her eyes. To his credit, he looked sheepish, shrugging his big shoulders, running a hand across his freshly shaven jaw.

"Did you just ask me to marry you?" she said.

He swallowed. "In a way."

"Yes," she said with narrowed eyes. "In a way." He sat in the chair her mother had occupied, took her hand, and pulled her between his knees.

"You're angry," he said. It was more of a question, hesitation and uncertainty in the rise of his voice. Unknowingly, his fingers tightened their hold on hers. She felt his fear and a kind of power over him, which she didn't necessarily want. It discomfited her that his entire future happiness rested on simple words that needed to come from her throat, from her tongue, from her lips.

She shook her head. "No."

He swallowed and looked a little sick. "No, you won't marry me?"

"No. I mean, no, I'm not mad," she clarified. He exhaled.

"So, you would marry me?" While she thought about it, wrestling with her uncertainty, he said, "Do Masks marry?"

"I'm not a Mask anymore," she said immediately, though more to convince herself of it than anyone else. Then she shrugged, realizing it wasn't a question of what she was, but rather what convention she'd been raised with. "Yes, some marry."

"Like your parents," he said. And then looked astounded when she told him they weren't married. "Not married?" He looked baffled, and she felt a divide widen between them. She realized that she knew nothing about him or his own parents. The fact was, she would marry him, in whatever belief system he chose. The fact was, she felt married to him already, in a way. She wasn't certain if she was ready to say the words aloud in front of witnesses. Words felt empty to her. She wanted to show him by her commitment, by her unfailing, steady presence by his side as years rolled by. But, looking down as his face, already etched in her mind, imprinted on her, she knew he needed the words. It was this task that they were doing this morning that heightened his sense of purpose and desire for her commitment. It was this godforsaken task of meeting with the trogs and seeing what their demands were. The word *suicide* floated into her mind. They might fail. He needed to hear the words from her, as uncomfortable as they made her feel. As forced as they felt.

"Yes, I would marry you," she said. Another big gush of air escaped from his lungs, a breath of relief released. Then she gave what she knew had to be a wicked grin, "If you ever asked me."

Before he could respond, the door swung open and her father said, "Ley'Amelan, we would have you join us now." It was not a question. And Mel's heart sank. If her parents insisted that she take up her Mask again, she would not deny them, at least for this task. She had committed to it from the start. She had taken the oath, and if she were held to it by others, by her parents, she would cave to the tradition ingrained in her. But, she would find a way to make it all work. To be a Mask and to stay with Ott. She looked down at Ott's face again, who was still stunned by her last words, his green eyes curtained by thick lashes, the scruff on his sun-darkened chin, the scar under it that she had attended with her lips earlier that morning. Her chosen.

She dropped his hand and moved back one step. "I'll return in a moment," she told him. Her promise to him, whether he knew it or not. Then she followed her father into the other chamber.

Her mother, father, and Guyse faced her as she stood in the doorway. She closed it gently behind her, feeling the wood that had worn to smoothness over time. In a burst of nervousness, she suddenly sensed the moisture still trapped in the grain of the wood, the minute particles of agamite, still in those veins. It connected her to the entire house, its life, the people in it, and the land beneath it. The rush of sensation flooded through her, yet she withstood it calmly this time, as if the previous deluge of it had already carved its course through her and now she was a ready conduit. In the room outside, she felt Ott receive the rush of energy as well. He sat up straighter in his chair, tightened his fingers on the chair's arms, and inhaled deeply in surprise.

Then it receded, and she turned to face her parents.

"I expect you think this is rather sudden," she said. A bit of a weak opening, she admitted even to herself. Her parents remained emotionless outwardly, but to her surprise, the corners of Guyse's mouth quirked up in a smile. She glanced at him, took him in peripherally, his heavy brow, dark skin, and glittering black eyes that . . . flashed abruptly to blue, then black again. She blinked, and fought the urge to let her jaw drop open. It was not Guyse. It was Jenks. Or rather, Guyse was Jenks?

She struggled to reconcile the shape-shifter and loner Jenks with the dark, scowling Guyse. Jenks had shifted into an old man for her while standing in the sitting room of his herb-filled cabin outside of the settlement. Jenks was Guyse, her parents' escort and guard? She wondered, now, how often he had loomed in the corners of her life, taking on the shape of one or another of the fixed people in her life. It would explain a great many unanswered questions in her mind.

"Hmm, yes. Jenks," her father said. A strange quality that Mel did not understand entered his voice. She saw a twitch of her father's eye that none but those who were Mask-trained would have detected. Irritation? Jealousy? But whatever the case, it was absolute acknowledgment to her that Guyse was, in fact, Jenks.

Guyse and Jenks were the same person.

Mel's mother spoke suddenly, "Mel, there's a specific reason why your father would not give your . . . Ott an answer to his question. His request. It's not that we disapprove of the young man, nor is it any reflection or judgment on your behavior since you've returned from your time away from us." Mel frowned, struggling to comprehend. This was not the conversation she imagined having with them before she'd entered the room. She held her hands calmly in front of her body though doing so was a challenge. She had always been a fidgeter, which they knew. Guyse—no, Jenks—smiled again. Now that she had seen the blue eyes twinkling behind the black ones, she could imagine his face behind the scowling, rough façade.

"You know this young man from your experiences at the Keep, I assume," her mother continued, cautiously. "Judging by your emotional response and the color of your skin." Mel nodded, curiously devoid of embarrassment for once. She couldn't have hid what she felt even if she'd tried. And she wasn't ashamed of it.

"In fact," her father interjected, "We think your young man is a perfectly . . . suitable . . . partner for you, if you so desire each other."

Why did her father chose his words so carefully. Suitable? Mel still wasn't sure what she was suited for. Maybe now she would find her role. Perhaps it would have something to do with how she had cleansed Ott, how she had taken his pain. It was a healing of sorts. But now she had been relegated to the ranks of the healers that her father looked down on. She remembered that conversation she'd overheard between her mother and him at the settlement when they discussed what they thought her future might hold. Whether she might be like Jenks, who was a blood relation to her. Whether she might be just a healer out among common people outside of the settlement instead of full Masks like they were. And then she realized that she didn't care. Her whole world had been tipped on its ear. Dunked upside down into its baptismal stream, so to speak. And that black inky stream had been made of pain, Ott's pain. Suddenly, she could think of *no better purpose* for her life.

She straightened her shoulders and faced her parents.

"In fact," her father was saying. "I cannot give my approval of your union with Mattieus Ottick . . . with Ott," he amended more gently and with more care than she remembered him ever applying to any words, "because, as it is, while it is true that I'm your known father, I am not your blood father. Jenks is."

Part 5

Oppose

CHAPTER 44

Harro found himself in the tent city with the woman again. She wasn't like any of his past females. For one thing, she was much younger than the others, much younger than he was. Her skin was firm, soft, and unmarked other than the faint webbed marks from bearing children. She was different. This was the third time he'd come to her in as many days. He realized she could easily become a regular woman for him. If he were honest with himself, he might as well admit she already was.

He liked the feel of her small body under his fingers, on her hips where she liked him to rest his hands. And he knew he satisfied her in a way that was wholly new to her. He could see it in her face. There was surprise, astonishment, and trust, like he saw in the body language of horses that he'd tamed. People weren't that much different from animals, himself included. He had already grown accustomed to the way her skin and hair smelled, her own unique scent—apart from the smells from her balms, her salves, and what she did to earn a wage. Her scent was all over the tent and on his skin after he left her; it had become something that he craved, something that he could think about when he was other places, something that was fixed in his mind.

In her tent, he ran a hand over her arm, pushing her sorrel-colored hair forward over her shoulder. The back of her neck was pale and smooth like the rest of her. He ran his fingers over it, and she let her head fall forward. She let him touch the vulnerable and delicate bones of her spine. He explored gently, still caught up by the newness of her. She was letting him stay longer, too. He could only think it was bad for her trade, letting him take up time when she could be seeing others to earn her coins. He thought about it without jealousy. He made no claims of ownership and knew only that when they were in her tent with the flap down, they belonged to each other. Apart, she was herself, and he was himself.

He still paid her; his money still defined their relationship. They didn't speak much—just brief words of greeting when he arrived, though he saw something in her eyes light up when she saw him. The light might not have showed in his own eyes—his was a darker, grimmer nature, more hidden from the eyes of others—but he knew his actions spoke for him. He couldn't help that. He thought she was beautiful. He thought a lot of things were beautiful—the open sky, clouds around the moon, and most animals. She had a quality about her that was just like one of the animals which he used to tend. Not like the people he dealt with in the big house. Not like people in the marketplace. Not like the other people in the tent city. He didn't know how she could have lived the life she had and still have that innocent, open quality about her. It was a quality she could take with her into a long future and die a smooth-faced old woman. She was special.

He put a hand on her shoulder, dwarfing it with his large palm as he gently pushed her onto her back. She met his gaze with her sharp gray eyes, big cat-like eyes heavy with color like a snow storm that hadn't arrived yet. He could almost smell the crispness in the air, feel it sting the inside of his nostrils. Her eyes moved constantly, over his face, his beard, to his mouth. He stroked her hair with his hand, watching her eyelids relax, her blinks become longer and slower. He stopped stroking her hair and instead, smoothed his hand over her face, encouraging her to close her eyes completely. She complied and kept her eyes shut, but her arms reached up and her hands clasped around his neck drawing him closer.

Their mouths touched for the first time. Very softly, very gently. When he drew back, her eyes flashed open. That same intensely astonished expression flashed across her face. If he had a heart for humans buried somewhere in his thick chest, she might have broken it with that look.

"Have you never been kissed?" he asked gruffly.

A flicker of confusion and wonder crossed her face then. He guessed the answer was no when she said nothing. She was breathing hard, like she might break. Or panic and flee. He backed off her mouth then, and stroked her red-brown hair until she was easy and calm again. He made no other move. He figured she had as many thoughts in her head as he did. Although the gray was starting to weave on his chin where he often touched his beard when he was trying to think, she'd seen her fair share of things to age her mind well beyond her numbered years. Of that, he was sure.

His mind took him to his last conversation with Rob, who had asked him to stay at the house instead of going with the delegation to the mine. Harro wanted to be part of the escort as was his duty, but it would be best if their own bit of underhandedness, of sending the Masks to meet the trogs, went undiscovered as long as possible. If Rob were a usurper or a patricide, Harro would be proud to wear his colors. In all honesty, Harro couldn't be more proud of Rob if the man were his own son or if Rob were king-in-waiting. But Col Rob wasn't a king, and there would be no upstart to his throne. Just death waiting at the door to do his job and move on to battle the next old man . . .

But it was giving too much of an upper hand to Rob's father if Harro left on horseback with the Masks. Col Rob might be withering in his nightgown, but he was no fool and was not to be treated with anything but wariness. He was like a snake, lying coiled, ready to spring. Just as venomous, too. Harro knew how to wait patiently, as was the way of all people in this eternal winter climate, and the best way of doing so was to keep busy. So instead, Harro had taken his idle hands elsewhere, to be employed otherwise, running over the skin of this small woman in her tent.

With a grunt, Harro sat up. When he reached for his shirt, he was stayed by her hand on his arm.

"Once more?" she said sitting up behind him.

When he turned to her, she cautiously offered her face up to him. He leaned and gently pressed his mouth on hers. Soft lips, lax and pliant, not firm, not demanding, not at all skilled on her part. Just a gentle press of flesh against flesh. She tasted like fresh bread and warm soup. Herbs and young skin. Then he pulled away and tugged his shirt fully over his head till it dropped across him. He reached for his boots, dragging them across the tent floor, his legs splayed out across the blankets on the floor where he and she had lain side by side. He could feel her eyes on him, drifting across his shoulders. His money lay in a scattered pile on her table.

As he stood to heave his thick coat across his shoulders, she dropped her eyes finally and gathered her cloak around herself to brace for the cold that would come when he opened the tent flap. He patted his pockets. Clasped his buckles. Pulled his hood over his head. Fastened his gloves. Patted his coat pockets again. He wanted to leave her with something other than his coins. Finding nothing in his pockets the third time searching, he put his hand on the tent flap to draw it back. Then paused.

"What do they call you?" he asked.

Her head came up sharply, and her gray eyes met his. "Treyna."

He nodded, watching her. Then he pushed back the tent flap and left, exposing her to the resulting blast of chilly air.

CHAPTER 45

Jenny was trying to be irritated at once again being left behind by her brother; she should have felt more upset, but honestly she was too busy. Somehow, she had collected three more children in addition to her own three. Plus it was impossible to be irritated when she was so blessedly happy. Waking up next to a lovely, warm body could do that to a person.

Actually, it was her warm body in Rob's bed, but that was splitting hairs. Her clothes were in his dressing room. Her brush was on the table by his mirror. She'd shared a bed before with that other man who had called himself her husband, but their bed was never a source of the infinite peace that Jenny had felt on waking this morning. Stretching her arms out, unfurling her spine, and arching down to the souls of her feet, feeling the indescribable rush of emotion on seeing Rob's face, and watching him watch her while she woke was an entirely new experience for her. She had pushed back her mass of matted morning hair, unembarrassed, and had laid her head back on her pillow, for once not worrying about her boys. Her children were in the room across the hall with the others being attended to by Mallie, a trusted young housemaid.

"Do you mind that we can't have children?" Jenny had finally asked Rob that morning. He knew how the birth of her youngest boy had damaged her so that she couldn't bear any more. She would never carry his child—she would have wanted to if he wanted it. She cringed, realizing belatedly that there was no good answer to the question she'd asked.

But he had given her a soft smile and said, "What's wrong with the ones we have now?"

Now she knew why her brother looked completely healed, like he was a new man since he'd found Mel. This was how Rob made her feel. That was how Mel made her brother feel. And for that alone, for loving her brother so well, Jenny rejoiced in the fact that her brother had found Mel. It was hard not to smile just thinking about her. There was something about her . . . Jenny had felt a lightening of the tension that normally bound her when Mel had come into her kitchen and touched her hand.

Nearly a head taller than Jenny and blond where Jenny was dark, yet soothing like a sister. The girl was a walking, talking dose of *carrow*, that root, when boiled, that eased the frantic workings of the mind. Jenny had tried tea made of it once or twice with some success but had realized soon after that she would have to administer it daily for the rest of her life in order to feel any lasting comfort. So, she had given it up. But this girl, Mel, had drained the anxiety right out of her. And it was still gone. Or maybe it was the effect of waking up in Rob's bed. Jenny would have to see how long the sense of ease lasted, she thought with a sly smile to herself.

Now it was mid-morning, and Jenny was up to her elbows in soapy water.

"Now, my sweet, tip your head back so you don't get the soap in your eyes. This soap can sting you if you're not careful," Jenny said to the littlest one brought in from the tent city, a boy who obeyed docilely yet had wide, inquisitive eyes. She and Mallie were taking turns at the wash tub trying to delouse the children who'd recently joined her boys. They'd had to shave the children's heads clean, even the middle one who was a girl, so all of the children looked like Jenny's boys now, not an errant lock or curl among them. Rob had brought the new additions up to the house from the tent city. She wondered who the families were who had given them up, but Rob didn't elaborate. The three children were decently fed, although timid from exhaustion, and perhaps from untold horrors they'd seen or, Lutra protect them, experienced in their short lives.

"She doesn't talk," the little boy in the tub said, pointing to his sister, who was clinging to the side of the tub watching both Jenny and her soaking brother intently.

"Not a word?" Jenny said, with furrowed brow at him, which she carefully hid from the little girl.

"Not a word," the little boy confirmed with a solemnity beyond his years. "She's my sister," he added.

"Is she now?" Jenny said, turning to give the little girl a quick wink.

"Yes, and he's my brother," the boy said pointing to the other one who had been brought in with them. She wasn't sure how they could be from the same family. They were clearly all very close in age, around five to six years old maybe, yet their coloring differed greatly.

"Very good," Jenny pronounced, not knowing exactly what else to say. Yet, what she said seemed enough for the boy. Perhaps the children had been collected together, just as they were now thrown together and given into her and Mallie's care. They were clearly used to being with each other. She'd seen them sleep in a single bed, cuddled together like triplets. That was fine for now, especially with the turmoil of the camp, but as the little girl grew older, she'd certainly want—need—her privacy. One day, she'd wake up a young woman, and young women needed their privacy and the space to keep their thoughts to themselves. Jenny would make sure—.

Jenny sat back on her heels suddenly, startled that she'd sent her thoughts so far ahead. She didn't know what the future held for these children. Yet, she was already envisioning a future in which they were hers. A bit foolish to bond with fosters so quickly. For all Jenny knew, their mothers could want them back when the weather turned warmer. When they had their homes back over there across Gasgun Lake. When the mines were being worked again. She didn't relish the thought of that heartache, but she couldn't force herself to deny them any affection, as temporary as it might be, as great as the cost might be to her in the long run. The mines would get up and running one day.

At that thought, her heart quaked again, chest tightening. She thought of her brother and his new beloved crossing the snow with the Masks to try to meet with the trogs. She wasn't sure which was the hardest pill to swallow, that her brother was with the Masks, or that he would be facing the trogs, those beasts straight out of bad dreams. She hoped beyond hope that they would arrive at the mine entrance only to find it deserted, the trogs gone. Evaporated like ice turning to water vapor in spring. Like the memory of bitter cold, impossible to conjure in the middle of a warm summer day. Like . . . *pah*. She knew it wasn't going to be that easy. She, Jenny, had found a pocket of ease in her life, and she wished to stay in it as long as possible. And she wanted everyone she loved in it with her.

She sent a silent prayer to Lutra to protect her brother and Mel, in the name of hearth and home. She prayed for Ott's unfailing luck to stay with him and to protect him. Then she sent a tentative prayer to Dovay, the bear god, to aid them. Although she wasn't certain the bear was to whom Rob sent his words of need, she suspected that it would do well enough. Certainly, the man was like a bear. He had waited patiently enough for her to come to him. More patiently than she.

"All right. Out you go," Jenny said, lifting the boy out of the tub and swaddling him in a thick cloth. He giggled when she swooped him up in her arms and rocked him. She bellowed a lullaby in a voice fit for outdoors, pretending he was a newborn and a deaf one at that. His giggles turned into full-blown shrieks of laughter, and when she plunked him down on the soft rug, she spied a smile lifting the corners of his sister's pale mouth.

CHAPTER 46

Guyse, in the shape-shifter skin he now wore instead of Jenks, scanned the crystalline, snow-covered terrain. They were in sight of the mine. Its adit, or entrance, was marked by enormous wooden side beams and an equally massive lintel bracing the top. Crouched on the crest above the valley that led up to the mine, Guyse observed the cleanliness of the snow around the entrance; there'd been no creatures in or out of the shaft since the last snowfall four days earlier. In fact, the snow all around looked pristine except for their own prints. Not a big surprise—the trogs were subterranean dwellers. They probably traveled underground as well.

He broadcast a short series of hand gestures to convey to Ott that his cursory search had yielded no others in the immediate vicinity. Finding the trogs would not be a difficulty. Ley'Albaer, the *so-called* seer, had outlined a plan for contacting the trogs which was simple enough. They would approach the mine shaft and enter it. All of them. Together. Ley'Albaer, his brother and his lifelong rival for Ana's affections, and Ana. Mel and her Mel's newly-chosen mate Ott. Guyse gritted his teeth and tried to assume the devil-may-care attitude that was coupled with and embedded in Jenks's skin. It didn't work. Guyse's jaw popped, and he worked it from side to side to loosen it. So many things could go wrong with this *simple* plan.

Inhabiting Guyse's skin made him crack his knuckles and roll his neck. Being in this man's skin amplified his sense of ownership over the two women and his need to protect them. Shifting had always worked that way as long as he could remember. Personality changes occurred along with the physical changes in his appearance. Inhabiting the kindly, but detached, form of Jenks was the only way he could bear living so close to Ana when he could not be with her, have her, touch her, possess her. And with Mel, he had been able to be objectively removed, a distant, all-seeing benevolent presence. A hermit grandfather, mildly curious about his own daughter. Otherwise, the pain was too great.

Neither the skin of Guyse nor of Jenks was his true form. In actuality, and ironically, he looked much like his older blooded brother Ley'Albaer, though he would never—not on his life—curse the family resemblance that had made him acceptable to Ana. She had willingly conceived Mel with him when Ley'Albaer had refused. His older brother eschewed sexual acts saying they clouded his thoughts. He preferred to exist without physical intimacy and to remain entirely celibate. Later, however, Ley'Albaer had willingly assumed the role of Mel's father. Ana had received the child that she wanted, a daughter who looked like Ley'Albaer. And Guyse had done it willingly, just for the chance to be with the woman he loved—if only for the few times until the baby took hold in Ana's womb. He held the memories in the deepest, most sacred part of his soul, and took them out only when he felt the need to reward or punish himself.

He stood up cautiously on the icy crest—he was dressed in dark clothing for their underground mission—and did a quick scan, circling once to look in every direction. No dark figures. No shadow. No movement. Nothing but reflective whiteness in all directions. He set his narrow board on the edge of the crest, anchored a foot on it, and shoved off, surfing down the snow toward the others. He swayed in a gentle ribbon pattern down the crest, then turned to skid to a stop, lithely jumping off his board and stowing in the back of the sled.

"Our path is clear," he told them.

They gathered in a loose half-circle around his brother Ley'Albaer, who met each of their eyes. Guyse watched his brother, who said, "Each of you has a role. Do not hesitate to do what is necessary. We must obtain these people's requirements for a peaceful resolution. Without conflict. I have seen what lies ahead. And there will be a negotiation that leads to a situation that is beneficial to both parties. How we convey this message now determines the future. Be strong." Ley'Albaer looked at Mel. Then, he looked solely at Ana and reminded her of their oath as Masks, "Impartiality. Diligence. Fair-mindedness."

Ana inclined her masked face, nodding once. Guyse wished he could see her expression just then. He wished she would look right at him and not at his brother. He wished she would look at him as a woman looked at her mate. Just then, he was glad he couldn't see her face. She probably had exactly that expression on her sweet face now as she looked at his brother.

They silently gathered behind Guyse and headed toward the entrance.

He would be leading them, weapon drawn, into the mine. After him came the three other Masks. Ott, whose vision was not as strong as that of the others, would take the rear. Mel had opted not to cloak herself, he realized with a mixture of pride and sadness. She was more like him than he'd realized before their talk at the house in the woods. For safety, he wished that she had covered herself. He didn't want them to recognize her from the attack on the Keep or even to see that she was young and female. But she was like him, his inner self insisted. Once deciding that she could not fulfill the obligations that the Mask demanded, she would not submit to it. Or, perhaps, she could not tolerate the lie of wearing it when she had to know in her heart of hearts that she could never fully be a Mask.

He saw how she was with Ott. And he admired her for it. He warmed to her humanity and her emotion, the craziness that neither of them could deny. He pitied her that the truth separated her from all she'd ever known and from what she had been raised to be. But the truth also opened up the world to her in a way that he himself held close. And that world was one of sensation and feeling, of loss and suffering. And love.

"Hold here," he said immediately inside the mine. He allowed them time to adjust their eyes, and for Ott to remove some of his bulkier outer garments. The Masks adjusted their body temperatures accordingly. It was much warmer inside than out, due in part to underground heat and in part to the green stone itself. There was a strong stench of chemicals and burning that he wasn't sure had to do with the stone. The harsh odor made the eyes water. Maybe it was the trogs themselves that emitted it. Mel tossed her head as if to shake it off. Then he saw her set her shoulders with a stubbornness that sent another tingle of pride up his spine. *She is so like her mother*, he thought.

Though it was hardly the time for reminiscing, he caught himself thinking about Mel as a child. She had been frenetic compared to the sedate children in the settlement, not that there were many others. She had always been different. Running, jumping, saying things aloud that would have remained unspoken by the others. She was both an irritant and a salve at the same time. Ana and Ley'Albaer had tried to deny it, tried to raise her as if she were just one of them, but she was *his* legacy. No matter what Ley'Albaer claimed to see in the future that lay ahead, he had not accounted for Mel's nature taking after his, her blooded father's.

He had eavesdropped on some of Ana and Ley'Albaer's conversations about Mel. He had stood quietly outside Ana's house listening at the window as he dropped some necessity at her doorstep: fresh milk, vegetable trade, or some other sought-after commodity from Port Navio. They thought she could be trained to be a common healer, at the most. He had listened to their hopes and fears for Mel, and, as his lack of role in her life dictated, had walked away from them. He was the surrogate father, nothing more.

His eyes drifted to the ramrod-straight set of shoulders on his daughter as she came to stand beside him in the darkness of the mine. Her eyes glittered in the ambient light from the stone. Her preternaturally gold-tipped hair gleamed. And he felt with every last fiber of his being—no matter what skin he wore, with all that was purely and essentially him—if anyone harmed even a hair on her head, he would shred every last one of them to blood and bone, trog or human.

CHAPTER 47

Ott stood at the back of the group, his hackles up. He didn't like the harsh chemical smell of the dank air inside the mine. He didn't like stumbling around in the dark; the dirt and their slow descent made him feel that he was being buried alive, slipping down into the earth, scrabbling on the loose rocks on the floor. He didn't like the two Masked figures in front of him—not that he minded the people inside much anymore, just the unsettling effect on him of the fabric itself, the swirling sound of it and the lack of sound from their footfalls. And most of all, he didn't like Mel walking up ahead so far away from him.

He could see her only if the two Masks between them swayed in the same direction as they stepped. Then he caught a glimpse of Mel's hair or sometimes her slim shoulder. He strained to see more, to reassure himself that she was still with them. She followed behind Guyse, that hulking mountain of a man, who was leading them on this fool's errand. As it turned out, Guyse was her father. However that worked. He still had trouble grasping how it was possible. For now, he bit his lip and kept his mouth shut, and dealt with the distance between Mel and him. He didn't want to demand that she come back near him—and insult her abilities—though he was crawling out of his skin with want.

He'd already unsettled them all with his early morning marriage proposal, or whatever it was. Mel didn't seem overly pleased with him. *And she'd never actually said yes either.* He'd woken up that morning with the crazy idea in his head. He'd felt the necessity driving him to say it, to commit to the formal words, to lay out his emotion in front of her parents. Lutra's luck had it, "her parents" had all been in the room at the time—all three of them, including Guyse. Mel seemed bowled over by the revelation, and he hadn't had a chance to take her in his arms and ask how she was taking it.

He tilted his head trying to see more of her. It had to be rough, thinking one man was your father your whole life, then learning it wasn't true. And Ott didn't exactly get it. Mel didn't look like Guyse. The guy was actually kind of an ugly brute, although Ott wouldn't for his life want to insult the man. Big and hairy though Guyse was, he seemed to know how to handle himself in a situation like this, and that was all that mattered to Ott. Although he still didn't *like* any of it. The whole situation. It stank down here, kind of like the back end of a goat . . . dipped in pitch . . . and lit on fire.

Ott gripped the handle of his axe, which felt neither comfortable nor right in his hands. Rob had brought the tool out of the wood shed behind the big house, insisting that Ott carry it. Something in his friend's face, the weary set of his expression—grim determination? helpless fear?—nagged at Ott until he'd taken the heavy tool. No, *weapon*. Now it was a weapon. He fingered the heavily grained haft and then tightened his grip.

He paused a minute to scrutinize the mine entrance over his shoulder as it disappeared behind them, taking with it the last rays of natural light. *Curse it*, he thought. If he had thought he'd been on edge this morning before his ridiculous proposal of marriage, then he was ten times that edgy now. And he couldn't see a blasted thing in this brown-tinted light of the mine. The air was stifling with a smell that reminded him of the awful night at the Keep. He didn't entirely remember the details, just bits and pieces and bad smells and sounds. *And Lutra on a spit, why hadn't she said yes?* That way, if something bad happened . . . at least he'd know for sure that they were together, that somehow they'd made it official in the eyes of . . . well, he didn't know. He caught a glimpse of her wiry shoulders and marveled again at how she didn't feel the chill in the air. It made him shiver and want to pull her close, but she didn't need him. He still wished he could pull her close and put his mouth on her skin, just breathe into the hollow at the base of her throat to get some reassurance that she was all right. She was little more than ten feet away, but it might as well have been a mile.

While Ott was gnashing his teeth, they reached a branch in the mine shaft where it branched left and right. Guyse told them to wait while he scouted ahead. Ott had visited this very mine several times as a child, having been taken on tours with Rob and his father. Back then it had been full of activity, teeming with workers and bustling with life, even as dank and cold as it was. On their visit, the mine had been well-lit, and the noise of wheeled carts had rumbled up and down along the shaft. He knew the workers were normally fastidious for the sake of safety. The dust-covered, hastily discarded pickaxes and shovels on the mine floor were a stark reminder of the events that led them to abandon it. Now it was a graveyard. A tomb.

Ott wrinkled his nose, sniffing the caustic air. He'd more than bet they'd find the filthy trogs if they headed right and took the smaller of the two branches. To the left, the mine floor seemed fairly level, like it led straight through the mountain, but the branch to the right sloped down, the rocky floor descending into the dark, dimly lit by the softly glowing bits of stone. Ott swore under his breath, but loud enough that they all heard him. They paused, looking at him in question, and he was forced to shake his head that it was nothing.

He had cursed because he had realized that he saw the dim light as brown. He shook his head again. *What an idiot.* Agamite was green. Therefore, the light would have to be green, too. It was his red-tinted vision returning, his red battle haze bleeding into his eyes because he was on edge. Red mixed with the natural green light of the agamite to cause the sick brown tainting his vision now. He gritted his teeth. Nothing he could do about it. No time to stop for calming breaths or healing time with Mel. The thought forced a stupid grin to his face, the red receded from his vision accordingly, and the unseemliness of the thought made him quickly wipe the telling smile off his face as the big body of Mel's blooded father loomed toward them in the dark channel.

Guyse drew near and pointed toward the right-hand branch of the mine. He held his hand up straight, fingers toward the ceiling, wide palm a warning to them all. *Take it slow. Use caution.* And Ott found out why as they made their way forward. The ceiling dropped low and the shaft narrowed. Both he and Guyse had to duck their heads and walk crouched. The Masks between them were all much shorter. Ott could feel either side of the corridor when he put his arms out; it was wide enough for two smaller men to pass shoulder to shoulder. This part of the mine must have been carved out very slowly. Probably it was not as old as the other, wider branch, but a newly explored vein of agamite scattered throughout the walls and ceiling around them, providing a dim glow.

The smell grew stronger. Ott heard Mel cough once, the breathy, non-vocal sound of her voice ringing like a tuning fork through him, speeding up his heart. The urge to touch her, to reach out and make skin-to-skin contact raced through him, barely held in check. If she coughed, it meant she wasn't controlling her breathing the way her parents were, filtering out the dust and chemical stench. They'd warned him that it would get bad and that he might have to turn back if it got toxic. He wanted to stop them to check on her, but Guyse kept moving forward.

The glow of the rock—whatever color it was supposed to be—cast the rest of the group in silhouettes ahead of him. He thought the person directly in front of him was Mel's mother, though he wasn't absolutely sure. Along with the stench, a nervous jangle in his bones was making him twitchy and it was getting worse. But they weren't here to fight. They were here to try to talk. It was absolutely, positively, a non-violent, peace-keeping mission.

They were supposed to make contact and to demonstrate immediately, by their lack of serious weaponry, that they meant no harm. It was imperative to communicate that they wanted peace, and they needed to know the creatures' demands. He could kick himself. Why hadn't he insisted that Mel stay back at the sled in relative safety? The thought of something happening to her caused fear to ripple through him. Now that he knew with certainty that she returned his feelings, at least enough to lie with him, to let him touch her, embrace her, kiss her . . .

He gulped air and tried to steady himself. And whatever had been wrong with him, whatever had been eating him up inside and turning him black as winter, she'd cured it. Losing her after that was an impossibility. Thinking about it threatened to tear him apart where he stood. He shook his head to get himself back into the present. He needed to focus on what lay ahead.

The tunnel opened up without much warning, and they spilled into a natural cavern.

CHAPTER 48

In the gaping underground chamber, more than 100 feet wide, Ott's eyes followed the crusty white ceiling across to the other side of the room where a group of a dozen chuffing trogs stood in loose formation. He swallowed. He'd known there were a lot of them, but he thought just a few trogs would meet them. A handful. Maybe, a couple. Not this many. Their small delegation was outnumbered and could be easily overpowered by a dozen of these brutes. Overpowered? Slaughtered, more likely.

Guyse moved them farther into the room in single file at a slow and non-threatening pace. Ott kept his eyes narrowed on the trogs, watching them for the slightest hint of threat. The beasts were motionless, other than their raspy breathing, watching Ott and the others just as warily as they were being watched.

Gods above, Ott thought, *they are huge.*

His memory of them was vague and clouded by battle haze. But now, here, standing within hurling distance, they were animalistic menace personified. Gnarled, gray-skinned hands clutched heavy axe hafts and spears. Their bodies barely clad in furs and leather, feet bare, not hoofed, but gods above, they might as well have been. Their skin was more hide than human. They shifted their weight, one or two of them at a time, so that they seemed to undulate, ready to lunge across the rapidly shrinking space between the two delegations. And the smell. Unholy rot. Lutra on a spit, Ott didn't want to feel the nervous buzzing throughout his legs, but it was there. His fingers itched to grasp Mel's shoulder and pull her behind him.

The delegation advanced slowly. At about 20 paces into the cavern, Ott had a sickening sensation. He heard a sound behind him and saw the trogs leap into motion at the same time. "Wait. Stop. This is wrong," Ott started to say at the same time an arrow took one of the trogs in the throat and dropped it.

An arrow? And one that had come from *behind* Ott?

A whistle cut through the air, interrupting him before he could form any words. Had he imagined that? Then he heard the clatter of wood against the rock floor just a few steps ahead of himself. It sounded like the handle of a shovel hitting the rocky cavern wall. He hadn't seen any tools in the cavern. He felt as if he were seeing only half of what was unfolding before him. Then Guyse uttered a guttural shout. Ott couldn't make out what he said. Mel's mother and father suddenly pushed Ott back, knocking him back a few steps. They shoved him solidly, using their preternatural strength, retreating back into the tunnel from which they had come.

The trogs crossed the cavern toward them now, leaping on all fours like great cats, bracing their hands to spring off the rocky cavern floor. Ott scrambled to get his feet under him. When his legs cooperated, he ran with the others back toward the tunnel. He had the fleeting impression of other people ahead of them in the tunnel, but that couldn't possibly be right. Trapped from behind and more ahead? They scrambled and clawed, but they made it back to the tunnel, plunging into it without encountering anyone. He must have been mistaken. He turned his head, trying to see how closely they were being pursued.

"Get them between us!" Guyse bellowed at him, pointing at Mel and her parents. Between the dimness and the confusion of cloaked bodies coming back up the tunnel toward him, Ott couldn't see a damned thing. He heard and felt the swirling cloth of their cloaks and had the heavy smell of dust and sweat in his nose. Shuffling footsteps told him there were more bodies crowding the mine shaft than just their own. The stench turned gamey and sweaty; it mixed with dust that clouded his eyes and coated his throat. The narrow tunnel filled with guttural grunts and hoarse breathing—the trogs were inside it with them. Red vision flaring, Ott put out an arm and shoved one of the Masks back behind him. The handle of a shovel hit him in the jaw as he reached for the other Mask. He grunted from the impact, and then pulled the second Mask behind him as well, batting the wooden handle away as it almost hit him again. The Mask, Mel's father, was gripping the shovel tightly.

"Keep your bloody shovel. Just get behind me," Ott grunted and turned, coughing and squinting in the faint light for Mel and Guyse. He held up his ridiculous wood axe, balanced in two hands and ready. The tunnel was obscured by the dust of their hasty, shuffling footprints.

Oh, no. Ott's mind caught up to his eyes. That was no shovel that had been in Mel's father's hands. On the fabric of the man's cloak, a dark shadow soaked his midsection where his hands grasped the protruding wood. What Ott had thought was a shovel was the haft of a spear. The whistling noise he had heard earlier suddenly made terrible sense. Mel's father had caught a spear that had narrowly missed Guyse and Mel.

Guyse cursed loudly and then shouted again, "Get back! Go back." His looming form suddenly emerged from the dust cloud, running at full speed. He waved his arms at them, striating the smoky dust with his choppy arm slashes. "The trogs are collapsing the tunnel. They ripped out the supports. It's going to—" His words were cut off by the deep rumble of the tunnel behind him. A thicker cloud chased him, threatening to swallow him up. There was no way he and Ott could both fit through the tunnel. They were both big men, too big to pass each other in the narrow tunnel.

"Where's Mel?" Ott screamed at him over the sound of the cave collapsing. Guyse's rough hands shoved him off balance, pivoted him, and propelled him back toward the branch. Ott tried to dig his heels in, struggling to stop. "Stop! Where's Mel?" he bellowed again.

"Move. Or we're going to die," Guyse barked.

Ott didn't care. He struggled to turn back, trogs be damned, but Guyse lowered his body, shoved his shoulder into Ott's ribs, and drove him across the mine floor back to the branch. Ott's widened eyes saw the two Masks in front of him reach the greater mine shaft just before he was pushed through by Guyse. He turned to attack Guyse, to demand that they go back, when a huge plume of dust exploded from the tunnel they'd just left.

Ott heard a hoarse scream piercing two octaves and then realized one was his own while the other came from Mel's mother. He wrenched his face around just in time to see her take an arrow through the chest. He threw an arm out as if to stop it from happening though he was half the distance of the tunnel away. The arrow pierced the fabric of her cloak below her left shoulder. She fell back, arms out straight, and hit the mine floor from the force of the arrow. She bounced once and scattered the loose rock. Then, she lay still.

Ott swiveled toward the tunnel they had not taken. He saw a human archer nock another arrow and take aim at him, Ott clearly in his sights.

Ott raged, anger and frustration overwhelming him in a bloody, crimson wave. He charged, wielding the axe with both hands in an arc over his shoulder. Then he sprang, hips connecting to taut thigh muscles, corded to knees and shins. His calves pistoned down to ankles and feet pounding the dirt, releasing the coiled spring of his body and he flew fully splayed and horizontal through the air to take down the archer. The terror on the man's face was bathed in red, the last sight Ott remembered.

CHAPTER 49

Guyse saw nothing but Ana. He held her in his arms after gently removing her veil and pushing back the cowl from her soft hair. Had his dreams ever come true, it would have been her veil on their wedding day that he pushed back.

She was dying, and Guyse had no words for her. Nothing would come out of him; it was all trapped where he'd hidden it for so long. Volumes and volumes of words in the endless library of his soul. For her alone. He stroked her cheek with shaky fingertips and held her hand as she struggled to breathe. He murmured wordlessly as her eyes sought his face. No, not *his* face. He took a gasping breath himself, stilled himself, and gave her the only thing he had left to give her. He shifted, pushing outward with his energy, forcing it to mold the surface of his skin, and assumed the face of his blooded brother Ley'Albaer who lay leaking his own life's blood onto the cavern floor.

Guyse leaned down so that Ana could see him and could focus her dimming eyes on the face of her beloved. With the voice of Ley'Albaer, he spoke soft words to her, words of love and everlasting devotion. The voice was his brother's, but the words were his own. She relaxed and a small sigh escaped her mouth. Her heart slowed, and he listened to it closely, with head bent low, memorizing each last beat. He regretted that she was the healer among them. He could do nothing for her except to hold her and pretend to be the man she loved. He pressed his lips against her cheek, her forehead, and, after her eyes slowly closed, her lips.

He embraced her after she was gone.

He sat for hours, surrounded by the bodies of his brother, Ana, and the unconscious, but still-living body of his daughter's chosen mate. Mel, his blooded daughter, was also gone, swallowed by the mine. Remains of the archers, their human attackers, lay in tatters around his daughter's mate; it had been a gruesome slaughter. Looking upon the bodies now, there was no telling how many of them there had been. Ott sprawled among them, unconscious but breathing and drenched in the fluids of those who had died at his hand. Guyse could hear Ott's breathing and feel the beat of the sleeping warrior's heart from across the cavern.

What kind of beast was this boy who wore the skin of a man, yet attacked with the ferocity of a mindless devil? Who was the man his daughter had brought to them? A savior, but too late for his Ana. Most likely too late for his daughter. Guyse had promised Ana with everything in him that he would protect Mel. He would avenge them. But now, he did not want to go on. Not without Ana. Without her he was nothing. By the grace of God, he hoped that Mel was dead already and not suffering in the hands of the trogs.

But it was too late for Ana.

I'm not Guyse, he thought, as he realized in his grief that he had reverted back to his natural shape, his skin that was not a skin. It was not a façade, but himself. His true self. He had not been without a disguise for decades. And now, revealed and raw, bared in the darkness of the cavern and utterly alone, without family and without love, he wept.

CHAPTER 50

"Wake up," Ott said as he roughly slapped the man's cheek with a filthy hand. Ott watched his hand capture the man's chin and yank it upward. Dried blood, caked solid with dirt, cracked across the knuckles wherever the skin bent or creased. Ott had awoken weak and exhausted in a pool of darkly thickening blood that wasn't his own, but was of his own making. He'd killed many.

This morning, he had thought their enemies were trogs. After he got a long, hard look at the damage he'd caused, he wasn't sure who they were fighting. These bodies were humans. One of them was Haught the houseman, brother of Harro, Rob's trusted man. Haught was also tall and dark though clean-shaven while Harro was always grizzled and bearded. But it was sorry shape Ott had left him in, with limbs broken off, neck at a bad angle. Not that he remembered doing it. But who else was here to blame? Who else here looked like a bloodied sea creature in an ocean of gore?

Ott shook his head to try to clear his thoughts. Haught had been close to Rob's father, Col Rob. The old man was always a schemer, always a vicious tyrant and ready with the switch where Rob was concerned. Was the old man still manipulating and trying to control things from his deathbed?

"Wake up," Ott said again, jerking the man's chin. When the wiry man on the floor started to stir, Ott said, "Who are you?"

The man blinked coal-black, weary eyes. He looked like Mel, slight of build and wiry, except male and a thousand times more worn out, a thousand steps older. "I'm Guyse," he said.

"No, you're not," Ott told him, cracking the dried blood on his knuckles as he made a fist and narrowed his eyes. "I ask you again. Who are you?"

The man sat up gingerly, propping a hand behind his slender body. "You know me as Guyse."

Ott stared at him. And whether it was exhaustion in the wake of his departed battle haze or whether it was his remaining two bits of brain, Ott let himself believe the man. For one thing, the man was lying curled protectively around the body of Mel's mother. Their two faces, when combined together, even in repose or death, unmistakably resembled Mel. For another thing, Ott had no idea what Masks could do. He'd seen his intended—yes, he thought of her that way—taken away from him by beasts. Yet again. He'd experienced his own transformation into a berserker twice now. He could believe a Mask was able to change his physical appearance.

"I need you to be Guyse," Ott said, determination sounding in his voice.

"I'm not Guyse," the man said tiredly.

Ott waved his hand derisively and began pacing. "I don't care who you are. I *need* you to be Guyse. Change back. Or whatever you do."

"I can't," the man said. His eyes looked like Mel's.

Ott bent over him suddenly, grasped him by the front of his shirt, and hauled him to his feet. "You can. *And you will.* You've lost your . . . you've lost Mel's mother. I realize that. And I can't imagine—" He steeled himself, staring directly into the man's eyes, almost nose to nose. He ground out the words, "I *will not lose Mel.* So, I need you to be Guyse. I need you to take the sled and go back to the big house and tell Rob what's happened. I need supplies. I'll take what we have now out of the sled. But I need more food. Water. People to help me dig out the tunnel." He left the fear unspoken that those at the big house had schemed to kill them, the delegation. Perhaps they would not be inclined to aid him now. He forged ahead, tamping down the anxiety, and willing Guyse to do as he commanded.

The man's eyes widened. "You can't dig it out. You won't be able to. It's half a mountain in there."

"I'll need at least ten people in rotating shifts. I can have some of them carrying out debris in wagons. We'll need shovels and pickaxes. More beams to shore up the roof, if possible. And I need some miners who can tell me how to do it. Get me miners."

"We can't get her through there," the man insisted. "It's blocked. It's impossible."

Ott glared, gripping the man's shirtfront tighter, pulling him closer. "*I will not leave here without her.*" He dropped the smaller man on his feet and resumed pacing, thinking about the supplies and how much time it might take to re-tunnel through the ground till they found clear passage. They needed to haul these bodies out, which meant getting some hand carts. When he turned back around, he met Guyse face-to-face. The old Guyse. The big and gnarled one with the heavy brow, though he looked as if he'd aged thirty years in the last day.

"I'll go," Guyse said brokenly, gently lifting Ana's body to take with him. "I'll clear out the sled for you."

Ott watched him cradle the body of the woman he loved. Ott's mouth dried up. Then, he nodded curtly. "I'll start digging."

CHAPTER 51

Pain streaked across Rav's belly, lancing into her lower back, fiery fingers gripping her. She grunted wordlessly, pushing a thin tape of air out her mouth through her gritted teeth. A sheen of sweat covered her, and she alternated between flashes of heat and chills. Her belly, swollen with agamite poisoning, threatened to burst and rip her apart from the inside out. But it was too soon, she thought, feverish and hallucinating. Was she with child or not? *No, she was not.* Her keeper had not touched her, though she had expected it, braced herself for it. But then, he had not. She kicked off her fur coverings and curled tighter on her side. The pain slackened for a bit, leaving a sick feeling in its place. But she was helpless and getting weaker.

Her keeper paced restlessly at the foot of the bed. *What do you need?* He asked her with his crude hand signs.

She waved him off, gestured for him to go away, but he shook his great, coarse head and stared at her with eyes she'd grown to learn held some intelligence.

I won't leave, he said. *I'm not leaving you.*

She groaned and shut her eyes. If she had known any curse words, she would have used them now. But her people didn't curse. Whatever happened, it was as the Great Mother intended. There was no denying the fate of an individual person. It had all been told ahead what would happen. Her role was to accept her fate and move with the flow of time.

Another spike of pain shot across her midsection, and she cursed loudly with the profane words she had heard spoken at the Keep.

The big idiot of a male at her feet froze. He gripped one of his large hands in the other. She would gladly have given him even a fraction of the pain to hold for her. *How can I help you? What can I do for you?*

Nothing. Go away, she replied glaring.

The pain and fever took her again, and she imagined the horrible swelling in her belly to be a child. Surely, it was a child and she had merely blocked out the horror of its conception? He looked pained and confused, whether for the loss of her or for the loss of his offspring, she didn't know. But she was dying, she was ready to admit. And she was absurdly glad for his suffering, ready to laugh for the first time since she had come below ground. At last he understood things on her terms. *Do you have a midwife?* she tried to ask, but he only looked confused at the signs. She had to make it up because she didn't know how to sign it in his words. *Do your people have a female who helps bring children into the world?* She tried again as pain sliced through her.

He still looked at a loss, his intelligent face contorted as he observed her pain. But he shook his head. She was about to try again when he abruptly signed, We don't have females of our kind.

She was stunned into silence, into stillness, as his meaning took hold in her mind. He sank to his knees beside the bed, still looming, but more at the level of her gaze. He started signing rapidly then, so fast that she had to shake her head and tell him to slow down.

It's our curse, he said, signing too rapidly for her to catch every word. *It has to do with the beginning of my kind. We worked in the mines for generations. Forever. We were enslaved in the mines. Our suffering forced us to come below ground, to retreat where we could live freely. But our curse is that we produce males only. We take females from above ground to mate. That is how we continue. We steal ones like you.* He looked away from her and then apologized with a hopeless shrug of his heavy shoulders, skin like the gray hide of a desert plains animal.

Rav closed her eyes. It was absurd that she should understand and commiserate with him. She was the victim. The hostage. The stolen good. The person who had been denied a choice. She was the one who was being physically torn apart from her womb outward. And with that, she buckled in the grip of a pain more intense than the others. Her vision went white with agony, and she felt the wetness leak from between her legs. She must have cried out, but all she heard was the frantic noise from her keeper as he rushed from their small chamber.

Time passed. Hazy, sick time, laced with pain.

She thought she had died and been called up to the Great Mother because there was a woman sitting next to her, comforting her, holding her sweat-drenched hand. The ache across her belly was terrible, the skin stretched tighter than the skin of a drum head. The imagined child inside her twisted and turned and writhed in discomfort, mirroring her own outward tortured display. The Great Mother's face was lovely. Sun-kissed. A halo of light-drenched hair around her face. Like her friend Mel. Rav gave in to the relief that washed over her and let go. She slept.

Later, when she woke, she was astounded to find she was still underground, still captive in the dirt chamber of her beast-like keeper. He was no longer here. She looked around and discovered Mel sitting next to her, their hands wrapped tightly together, golden fingers meshed with Rav's dark ones.

"I'm alive?" Rav asked.

"Imagine *my* surprise," Mel said. She smiled wanly, strained and pale with anxiety. Then they embraced like long-lost sisters.

"But how did you come to be here?"

Mel shrugged, looking unhappy. She was covered with dust and not outwardly injured, but she held her head as if she were in a great deal of pain. Rav knew that feeling, when her head was full of thunder. "Like you, I think. I was caught. Captured and brought here."

Rav sat up suddenly, running a hand over her relatively smooth belly. "Did I have the child? Did I lose it?" She was surprised to be anxious at the thought.

"There's no child," Mel said and, with the tensing of her neck, pushed aside her own discomfort. She seemed to hesitate, as if she were going to say more. But Rav couldn't wait and interrupted her.

"But my womb grew and grew though I had not been violated. It grew from magic and from the stone's poisoning. I thought there was a child. Why is my belly small?"

Mel looked uneasy, but then said, "I'm sure it seemed so, with the size of your belly, but there's no baby. There's no child now. But there may be one day. I . . . I took your pain, Rav." Rav sucked in a breath and stared at her friend in astonishment and, at first, disbelief. But then she examined herself. No knives of pain, no all-consuming terror, no being ripped apart from the inside out. *Consumed her pain?*

"You are a paineater. Why did you not tell me?" Visions from the stories her people told flooded her mind. Great healers who could eat the pain and suffering right out of a person's body. With a paineater, anything could be endured, all suffering could be alleviated. A tribe could survive and flourish in the worst of conditions. And a paineater as powerful as the Great Mother could cleanse all evils. Mel creased her forehead at the term, which told Rav her friend had never heard the word before.

"I don't know what that is." Mel shook her head, light colored hair falling on her shoulders. "I didn't know I could do this. Until recently."

"Paineaters are great healers," Rav said cautiously. "But I've never met one." *Until you*, she thought. Beyond the strain in Mel's face, there was a look of something that had not been there at the Keep. A lot of sand had shifted between then and now. Things had changed. For both of them. Rav's hand went to her belly, smooth now, and not uncomfortable.

Mel said she might still have a child one day, and Rav believed her. She was glad for the well-being of her future child, whenever it came, no matter who had fathered it. *She was the mother.* When Rav looked up, her friend was staring at her intently, dark brown eyes unwavering, unspoken words clearly fighting to come out.

Mel hesitated one more time, looking at Rav and then at her keeper, but then said, "When I . . . took your pain, I met your child that will be. She's not here now, but she will be one day. I saw the face, the eyes, the shape of the head, and the mouth. I took pain from you, and I took the pain from your child. I freed you of the poison. That's why your belly shrank and why it doesn't hurt anymore. I took what was writhing and festering and killing you. What's left is just the impression of your future child. And Rav . . . " Her voice faded and she looked away rubbing a hand to her neck.

"Tell me it all. I want to hear it. What did you see? What do you know?" Rav demanded, tightening her grip on Mel's smooth, cool fingers.

Mel took a deep breath, clearly telling only a half-truth. "Your daughter will be lovely, Rav. She will be perfect. Absolutely, completely well. And healthy. And utterly human."

CHAPTER 52

Rob was ten paces from entering the back of the house through the kitchens when he heard the first screams. The terror-filled shrieks carried up the snowy lawn from the tent city. The daylight was fading though it was still early. He had heard nothing from Ott or the delegation of Masks since dawn that morning. He had walked through the tent city restlessly, checking on the construction of the temporary shelters, and then finally had turned back to the house. The first screams turned him in his tracks and sent him scrambling back down the lawn.

Harro advanced on him from out of the shadows, caught him by the arm, and pivoted him back toward the house. "Trogs," the stableman panted hoarsely. "They're attacking the tents. We need weapons. Go back to the house and secure it. Arm yourself."

Rob let himself be led for a good ten more steps before he put his legs into it and powered back up to the house. He went to the wood shed, which had been converted into a temporary armory—as much as it could be with their lack of weaponry. He grabbed a roughly-fashioned metal blade, wondering if he could pretend to have any skill with it. He turned to follow Harro back toward the tent city, but the stableman grabbed his arm again in a tight grip.

"You must protect the house. Secure it," the big man growled at him, his beard darkening his face like a mask. "You are the master now." Then he turned, stepping quickly into the dusk, leaving Rob, who hesitated another minute before running to the house.

Rob's explosive entrance froze all activity in the bustling kitchen. His shouted orders caused hands to grab whatever weapons could be found—carving knives, fireplace irons, and heavy pans. The kitchen maids slammed shut and shuttered the windows. Feet pounded down hallways and up staircases to spread the urgency, to allow noses to be pressed against the glass looking for inhumanly large shadows on the blue-white snow of the lawn under black trees.

A scream erupted from inside the house, which nearly stopped Rob's heart, but then a pointed finger turned all eyes toward the tent city where flames now shot upward in the darkening sky. Rob halted and rubbed a hand across his face, feeling the anguish of the people in the tents as if it were his own. There was no time to douse the flames with snow while the trogs butchered the people in them. Rob needed to get them out of there immediately.

Then, as luck would have it, the perfect envoy crossed his path; the houseboy Charl stood at the windows with the others, gripping the high sill with white knuckled hands. The young man was quick and smart. He would need to be. Rob laid a hand on his shoulder and drew him away from the others.

"Charl, are you up for a task?"

Fear, glinting in the young man's blue eyes quickly galvanized to anger, then to action. "Whatever you need, sir."

"I need you to locate your Uncle Harro." The young man's brow furrowed. "He's down among the tents." His eyes widened. "I need to you find him. Carefully. And tell him to get the people up here into the house. Evacuate the tent city. Those people need to be up here. We'll house them in the great hall." *Whoever is left*, he almost added, but bit that thought back along with a curse that he had not done this sooner. "Can you do this?" he asked Charl.

Thoughts seemed to flash across the young man's face as he considered the danger, the excitement, and the honor. And the danger again. "Can I have a weapon?" he asked.

Rob immediately unbuckled his belt with its sheathed dagger attached. It was just a hunting knife, one that he always carried, but he had his rough hewn metal sword now. Charl could make better use of the knife, so Rob strapped it around the young man's narrow waist, notching it tighter. It still hung low, but it wouldn't impede his speed or stealth.

"You understand what you must do?" Rob asked, suddenly more concerned for Charl's safety than finding Harro. At least, at this moment, the young man in front of him was the life he most wanted to protect—the young life that was currently not in danger until Rob decided to send him into it.

Charl nodded resolutely, firm and steadfast. "I'll do it."

Rob gripped the nape of the young man's neck, just as he had done to Ott earlier. He nearly changed his mind. Then he nodded. "Good man," he told Charl, who straightened his shoulders more—shoulders that might not be done filling out. Rob spared a heartbeat for a prayer that they would both live to see him full-grown. "Go out the back. Keep to the trees. Do not attack a trog unless to defend yourself. I repeat, do not approach them unnecessarily. Do your task. Find your uncle. Save the people down there in those tents." Charl nodded again, and then ran down the hall toward the kitchen and the back door.

Rob watched him go. More than likely, the young man's father, that refined houseman Haught, was already down there. Most of the strong-backed men and women from the house had been at the camp constructing the now-useless wood-framed shelters alongside the miners—most of them were down there still, facing the trogs now. Then Rob gritted his teeth and headed toward the side staircase, pounding down the stone steps in a heavy torrent of footfalls.

He needed to make sure the cellar and lowest floor were secured. An image of the gaping black pit in the ruins of Cillary Keep flooded his mind. The trogs had broken into the Keep by coming up through the ground, by tunneling somehow up through the foundation itself. The floor of the cellar here was hard, tamped dirt covered by slabs of stone that had been cut from a mountain. Impenetrable by most standards, but Rob didn't know for certain if the trogs could be kept out. He couldn't live with the thought of the trogs pushing up through the earth directly into the house, *his house*.

He passed an older serving man in the stairwell. The man was moving with purpose, clearly aware of the situation outside. "Have you checked on your lady friend and her children?" the man called to him. Rob halted in his tracks, already a flight of steps above the man. Jenny?

"Why? I saw them upstairs," he shouted downward, thinking back to earlier in the day. Gods. It was night now, and he hadn't seen Jenny since morning when they'd left their room.

"Good. I hadn't seen her return to the house." The man was tilting his neck to send his voice upward to Rob. The man started back down the steps, but stopped at Rob's frantic shout.

"What do you mean *'return to the house'*?"

"She went down to the tents this afternoon because one of the younger children left something there—a poppet or a dolly or some such thing. He said he wouldn't be able to sleep without it. So she took him and—"

Rob cursed, shouting at the man to check the cellar for him, and pushed himself the rest of the way up the stairs, gripping the handrail and yanking upward when his own feet were too slow. He raced to the room where Jenny had planned to keep the children during the day, running down the hall and startling several people who were already frightened. They clung to the walls out of his way. His footsteps took him to the playroom where he flung open the door. He counted Jenny's three sons, plus two more children they'd brought up the lawn. His eyes sought Jenny, the shape of her back, her dark hair pulled back in a tie. He found a woman's back as she knelt over the children. But the woman wasn't Jenny.

"She's not back yet," the nursemaid said with a quaver of uncertainty. "When I heard the door just now, I thought you would be her." The children's eyes were all wide with fear, but he couldn't offer them a calming word. Not when he couldn't soothe himself—not when his chest threatened to cave in on itself and the blood rushed away from his head.

In his moment of abject terror, Rob covered his face and prayed. Not to Lutra, the otter goddess, for luck. Not to Dovay, the bear god, for patience. Not to the one god of the frighteningly powerful Masks. But to his own long-dead and departed mother. He prayed for Jenny's safety, and selfishly, he prayed for comfort for himself, for something in the great, vast world beyond his experience to help him find the strength to stand and to alleviate the crippling fear in his chest.

If the threads of the world were somehow held together so that the woman he loved were protected and returned safely into his care, he'd find it in himself to believe once more, to have faith, to . . . cherish the good things that he'd been given the chance to receive, the good things that far outweighed all the evil that had been done to him as a child. And so, he sent fervent pleas to the memory of his mother, the last-known benevolent presence in his life.

CHAPTER 53

Ott's hands were bleeding.

In the collapsed mineshaft, he had grabbed a shovel at first, but the metal blade scrabbled uselessly across the larger rock fragments. Then, he'd tried a pickaxe, but had thrown that aside as well because the stones were too loose. Nothing worked as well or as fast as his hands, though misery heaped on misery as he smashed his fingers between stones trying to pry them out. And he needed his hands to last.

His shirt had already been half ripped to shreds, so he stripped the rest of it off, tearing it to bind his hands. He tried not to think of the bodies in the chamber behind him where their blood seeped into the dirt floor, but it was either that or think about Mel. He caught a sob in his throat, refusing to let it out. He couldn't remember how long ago he had last eaten or had drunk. Right—it had been back at the big house, sitting across a small table in the room he had shared *with Mel*. A bowl of hot cooked oats. Strong tea. A hunk of cold, smoked meat. He would have to stop soon and eat from the supplies Guyse had left inside the entrance. He would have to start a fire and melt some snow to drink. *What was Mel doing?* Was she somewhere where there was food or drink? What were they doing to her? He could barely think of feeding himself.

He shuddered. His legs suddenly collapsed and caused him to sprawl on hands and knees, prostrate in front of the pile of rocks that barred him from her. He looked up at the wall of boulders and stones and failed to see any progress despite the pile forming from rocks he'd removed and the blood welling on his dusty knuckles. He hung his head and wondered where his battle fury was now. Could it propel him through a wall of rock? How far could fury carry him against a mountain? Where was it when he needed it? But no, his vision was normal, no red, just the pale green glow of the stones. Even numbness would have helped at this point, but no, again; he was so wretchedly sensitive he felt every granule of the green-crusted rock around him. He almost wished it would all cave in and crush him. But then, what would happen to Mel if no one were coming for her?

So, he pushed himself to his feet and traced the edge of the next stone with his raw, swollen fingertips.

CHAPTER 54

The tent city churned with sounds of struggle. The clang of metal on metal combined with the hoarse cries of human combatants and their trog counterparts. And alongside that were the moans of the wounded and dying.

The stableman Harro grunted from a blow to his chest. He had blocked the better part of it, but it was a sizeable strike that smashed his arm back into his sternum. He shoved his attacker back and kept an eye on the man behind him who wasn't doing badly considering he was a miner, not a fighter. The shorter man was steady in his bearing and stocky with his weight centered lower in the legs than Harro; and he kept his back to Harro's back as they blocked blows from the trogs' heavy axes.

For a minute, Harro could almost imagine his older brother Haught behind him, the way they had played as boys then played harder as young men. Haught was taller than the miner and more skilled, and he preferred a bow and some distance from his assailants. Well, he was here somewhere in this tent city, and Harro would find him. For now the miner would do.

The trogs came at them one after another in a steady stream of animal hide and blood, their harsh breath sounding like that of bulls charging, their thick-skinned faces shadowed in gray skin and grimaces. Residents of the tent city fled screaming. Others cowered in terror, unable to move. Those were the ones that the trogs hauled off, lifting them over their shoulders, jogging easily back to the gaping hole in the center of the tents, and plunging downward into the foul blackness. Then another trog would take the place of the previous. They were in seemingly endless supply, inexhaustible in their strength and thorough in their taking of the tent city. A smell like acid burned the inside of Harro's nose, but he didn't pause to wipe either that or his sweat-drenched hair from his face and beard.

Off to Harro's left, fire erupted near the cooking tents. Flames licked upward, feeding greedily on the flammable cloth and furs inside them. The stench of burning hair and smoke mingled with the sharp, sulfurous fumes rising from underground. A trog with a leather harness strapped over his massive gray chest accelerated toward Harro with a great, wheezing roar, nostrils flared, eye whites bright in the darkness. Bare, rough-skinned feet pounded through the mud taking steps as long as a man was tall. Sinewed arms hefted a great axe toward Harro's head, aiming to cleave it from his shoulders.

"Feint to the right!" Harro shouted to the miner at his back. He hoped the man would realize that he meant the man's right, Harro's left. But they separated, parting in opposite directions. The trog's axe blade sank into the miner's shoulder, hacking downward and out to the side of his chest, nearly severing the entire arm from the body before the axe went to the ground. Harro cursed, then tamped down his chagrin at the loss of the man and used the trog's momentum to spin the beast and plant his own weapon into the back of its neck. He didn't pause to wrench the weapon out, but left it. It wasn't a very good weapon, and he re-armed himself with a sword from another fallen miner who wouldn't have use for it any longer.

Now mobile, not tied down to a partner or single combatant, Harro moved quickly through the camp assessing damage, urging the fallen to stand if they could, and putting his foot into the seat of the pants of those who were too scared to move. He unwittingly spurred others, who like him were moved to act and who were unencumbered by doubt or terror. They picked up what weapons they could find and gathered others to them, collecting those who were able to walk or run. They banded together and, it seemed to Harro, gained some momentum against the trogs, whom they now fought in small groups, which balanced the odds a little better against the massive creatures. Three men could successfully hold off a trog.

He thought if they put their backs to the fire and pushed outward, they had a chance at creating a solid front. Now they had some fifty men and women in their effort. With some luck, they might be able to sweep the snarling, grunting trogs back to their hole as long as they moved slowly and stayed together. They had to pay attention to the fire, but they could use it to their advantage. It was the only thing more powerful than the trogs at the moment. And together, they had less to fear. The beasts were still terrible to behold, but when there was a man to either side of him, Harro felt bolstered and forged ahead.

And then at last it seemed that fewer trogs were climbing out of their hellish hole. The beasts pitched themselves back into it—not hesitating at the edge, just jumping down into the blackness. Harro couldn't tell how they were talking to each other, but they seemed as a whole to be retreating suddenly. They turned their thick-skinned gray backs, slick with sweat, toward him before they disappeared down the gaping hole that was a good three men across and just as wide. How in damnation had they dug a cavity that large and that quickly? Some kind of explosive? But no, Harro hadn't heard anything, hadn't felt the ground tremble in the minutes leading up to the attack.

Harro wondered if the tide had turned in the favor of the humans. His fellow men were throwing snow on the embers of the burning tents. The hissing of fast melting ice into water vapor rose up as the grunts of beasts and dying people faded. Harro paused to look around him, still too tight with fighting ardor to lower his weapon. His eyes skimmed the tents in the darkness, picking out the dark shadows that leapt between the fabric to see which were caused by the dying fire and which could be an intruder.

If the trogs were retreating, the people would need every last human to tend to the wounded and to retrieve the bodies. Corpses, blackish-brown, both human and trog, lay covered in mud. Harro wondered with a sudden, heaving shudder how many he had stepped upon unaware. He had heard that the trogs took the dead as well as the living. And as long as he was here to prevent it, they would get none of these people for their supper.

Then the pit opened up like the lancing of a diseased boil as trogs surged over them all in a tide of gray skin and snarling mouths.

CHAPTER 55

With the reins of the sled in his hands, Guyse drove the sled through the gates as he reached the big house. He was as grim and silent as the remains of the two Masks he chauffeured. A houseman ran out to him before he came to a full stop. Guyse, in a fugue state of misery, was interrogated thoroughly, menaced with a spear that looked more like a cooking spit, and then let go with an abrupt and sharp intake of breath as the man caught sight of the sled's silent passengers. Two dead Masks, still impaled by arrow and trog-made spear, slumped across the bench inside the glass-enclosed sled. As the houseman stepped back, more aghast that the inhuman Masks were mortal—had been mortal—as any man, Guyse urged the sled forward, and drove the horses around to the back of the big house.

Mel was buried in the mine and certainly dead; Ott was on a hopeless mission. All Guyse had now were the bodies of his brother. And Ana.

Frozen as it was, the ground was too hard to inter the bodies, but it was not too cold to light a pyre. Guyse wanted the primordial comfort of standing in front of a fire. He wanted to see the ashes rise up toward the heavens. He wanted to burn the wooden weapons that had killed them along with their bodies. So, he found a place away from the house and away from the trees that wouldn't disturb the other burial sites. In the frigid night, air puffing from his mouth in clouds of white vapor, he transferred wood from the wood shed and constructed a makeshift platform, then padded it with kindling and some pitch he found in a holding tank on the far side of the house. In the darkness, with the moon shining on the snow, he lifted the two bodies of his beloved and his brother and laid them next to each other. Then he struck tinder and stepped backward, stumbling over snow. The flames licked up the dry wood, and he felt the heat on his face. The fire quickly became bright, and he closed his eyes.

His only consolation was that nothing had been left unsaid between Ana and him. He remembered the way she looked. The well-guarded expression of her eyes. The silken texture of her hair. The way her smooth face covered a multitude of emotions, a tidal wave arriving under the surface of placid waters. She'd known from the very beginning how he felt about her. And he had known how she'd felt about him. Though she hadn't loved him, she had let him love her. Yet, here he was, with so much more life left than she had had. He felt cheated. He would wrap up his images of her to keep them safely preserved in his mind till his days ran out.

Then he closed the part of his mind that contained Ana, and conjured thoughts of his older brother. An older brother who would now never stay older than him, yet remain frozen at his prime intellect, the pinnacle of his usefulness, the height of Ana's love for him. It had been nearly impossible to exist as Ley'Albaer's younger brother, to have come out of the same womb as him, and to have been so entirely a failure in comparison. Their parents had lauded Ley'Albaer's every accomplishment and indulged his insensitive, bookish nature—and had feared Guyse since the moment he'd performed his first shift in the cradle and changed himself into a boy-cat.

Yet, Guyse still loved them all. It was his nature to love and to forgive, as much as he craved both love and forgiveness from others. He imagined that he had it now, though all of them were now dead and departed from this world. Guyse had been raised to believe in a single, omniscient god, but he often invoked the gods of the people around him, depending on the skin he wore. Now, he prayed to all of them, and hoped with his entire being that he might see his Ana again someday.

But if not, he understood the reason. And he accepted it.

Then, he opened his eyes to watch as they left him forever, as ash rose into the night sky.

CHAPTER 56

A trog came for Mel not long after she took Rav's pain. She hadn't told Rav that the father of her future *human* child would be her keeper, the beast; Mel didn't understand it. Rav had slipped into a deep sleep, lulled by Mel's presence and respite from pain, and when the trog came for Mel, she refused to scream and wake her. She had known that eventually one of them would come for her. Heavy footsteps sounded on the tamped earth in the tunnel outside Rav's room.

Now? Is it happening now? Is this it?

She lurched to her feet. There was only one way out of the room. The trog lunged, grabbed her arm in its thick-hided hand, and dragged her down the tunnel. She dug her heels into the floor and flailed, hitting and kicking to no avail. She was pulled, feet scuffling, through more dank underground twists to a chamber that had a pile of rugs and furs like the ones that Rav had been lying on. A bed.

Mel looked around with wild-eyed dread. Just a pile of rugs illuminated by the green glowing walls. She knew exactly what was expected of her and knowing what was about to happen only amplified her panic. Rav had said they had no females of their own. They wanted human females to bear their young. Willingly or not. *Definitely not willing.* She redoubled her efforts in struggling but hardly seemed to budge the trog. His grip on her remained the same. She was succeeding only in injuring her own arm where she fought the huge manacle of his hand.

She screamed incoherent words; none made sense, but all of them meant the same thing. Her fingernails didn't make a scratch in his thick hide. Her forehead didn't even cause him to flinch when she butted his chest. He was a filthy stone wall. She didn't care what he smelled like or what he was made of, if he was dirt-encrusted or clean, or whether he was just following a biological urge to procreate or to dominate. She just wanted to get free. Truly, she was damned, whether she lived through this or not.

Why was she being punished? Was it because she'd gone away from her training and denied her role as a Mask? Guilty, she thought. The guilt was crushing, but it in no way justified being raped. She could find better ways of punishing herself. And why, if she were meant to be a Mask, had she been rewarded in finding Ott just when she had given it up? Because finding love was the biggest reward, the most positive, fulfilling point of her life. Maybe it was *the very meaning of life*. To be fulfilled by emotion and justified by being the recipient of that emotion equally returned. Freely exchanged. In all of her jumbled, frantic thoughts, the one that most often came to the surface was to wonder whether it made things better or worse that she had been with Ott, experienced his caresses, and still could feel the lingering sensation of his mouth on her skin. It was worse, much worse. And she couldn't even shut down her mind and escape into numbness. She was escalating into panic, climbing its steep cliffs, heartbeat erratic, her breaths gulps between screams.

Since entering the mines, the familiar dizziness had assaulted her. She experienced that same loss of control over her emotions and ability to divert her strength and energy. Her loss of self-control had begun in the forest outside Cillary Keep. Meeting Ott had compounded it. The effort of taking Rav's pain furthered the loss of control more. But now, terror was finishing the job. It was the same wretchedness that she had felt earlier in the summer when the trog had grabbed her out of the carriage outside of the Keep. The stench in her nose and muddling confusion in her mind made strengthening her limbs impossible, but she still intended to fight. Whatever she had left in her, she would use it against the trog.

But God, she was terrified.

He loomed over her, overwhelming her nose with his odor. The sound of his rasping breath through thick nostrils. The strange bluish skin that reminded her of the blue-leaved trees at the Keep. It's happening all over again, she thought. Her abduction. The harsh reality that the end of her life was near. Although this time, there was no Ott to help her get free. No one to drop a boulder on its misshapen, enlarged head.

She fought back as the trog ripped open first her shirt, then her loose-legged pants.

NO. NO. NO.

She said it a thousand times aloud and in her head, imprinting the word over and over, the next one arriving before the previous one faded. It was all she could think. She screamed with anger as he shoved her onto the rugs and trapped her there with one arm while he shoved his leather pants open. She raged as he lowered his body onto hers. She panted and bucked against him, thrashing her legs. She tried diverting her strength to her limbs to push him off, but moved him only a fraction of an inch, even powered by fear and adrenaline.

She *pushed* at him, trying to contain her terror, trying to shut out his hoarse breathing on her neck. He was so huge that her feet kicked at his gnarled kneecaps. He pressed weight on the tops of her feet, kneeling on them to keep her in place. Their skin met, knees to feet, his chest against her face, his chin on the top of her head, and suddenly, at all the places where they touched, Mel felt the agamite in his blood. He was saturated with it, through and through; not a single particle of the trog was free of it.

Agamite. Like threads of it in the ground outside the big house. Like particles of it in the wood in the sled. Like Ott's green eyes. She reached with her mind, and punched through the agamite, using the chips of it that had gone into her forehead and been absorbed into her blood as a conduit through the trog's bluish gray skin and into his blood.

It's the agamite, she realized, slowing down thought, time, and motion. It was the same as the blue of the tree leaves at the Keep, like Jenks's experiments with the colored water drawn up through the flower stems. Agamite was what determined the color of the trog's thick skin. There was agamite running through his veins just as sure as there was running up into the trees around Cillary Keep. How did it get into them? Was it eaten? Inhaled? And why? Maybe to enhance their strength, their terrible size and power. Maybe to survive underground.

"Whatever your reason, you're my puppet now," she said through gritted teeth.

Time regained its true tempo. She had been inside Ott's private hell, the dark inky river in which he'd nearly drowned. Because of him, she knew pain and she knew rage. She recognized it in the trog and she looked forward to embracing it closely within her. And now, she punched through the trog's blood, coalescing the agamite into a tight, mental fist. She gathered it in a huge inhalation and she shook him, racking his body and brain as she controlled the agamite and drew it through his body toward her. Above her, stunned and scrambled inside, he seized up and fell off her. He lay on his back, eyes rolling in shock. He struggled to get off the bed, but his limbs betrayed him, stiff at his sides. She wasn't finished with him. *No, not by a long shot.*

Rage still gripped her. Whatever his race needed to survive, whatever this one thought he was going to take, it was not her. Never. And, so help her, if she had to she would make every last one of them know it before she was finished.

She needed the skin-to-skin contact. More skin. More points where she could call the agamite out of him. She climbed up so she knelt on his chest, hands to either side of his face, her clothes hanging in tatters off her shoulders and back. With her head bent down she closed her eyes and tore into him viciously, calling every particle of agamite to her, charging each to vibrate and whip into a million tempests. Between her hands, his head shook. Under her knees, his ribs rattled and creaked. She clamped her teeth together in fury and concentration, gathering everything in him to her. Further. Then, even further, and she heard his bones begin to shatter, one by one. She twirled and twisted the mineral in her mental grip, like the clenching of her jaw. Tighter and tighter, faster and faster.

And then abruptly, like the dispersing of a tornado's fury, she let it all go.

The shockwave rolled outward from her leaving a mind-obliterating vacuum in its wake. She felt it spread into the earthen walls of the ground around her, traveling farther and farther away. Mel's spine arched. Her head and arms were flung backwards. Her knees sank through the liquefying remains of her attacker to meet the drenched furs underneath.

Part 6

Ascend

CHAPTER 57

Harro was certain this was his last hour, here and now in the tent city which they were losing to the trogs.

My life is done. And it was all for shit.

The trogs swarmed over the edge of the pit and flowed toward him in a vast, dark, snarling tide. The mass of bodies was taller than him by a head and as broad across as the pit itself. It was a solid wave of trogs coming to sweep him away, take his life, and trample his flesh into the filthy mud. He had always hoped that when his time was up he'd face it stoically and with acceptance. Instead, to his dismay, he felt self-pity. Though he stood with a small band of men, he felt absolutely, utterly alone. Humans now numbered about forty. Many of them had fallen when three trogs pushed through their weakening line and dragged some into the dying tent fire's flames. The fire was not burning as hotly as before, but a fire was still a fire when it came to flesh. It still boiled and melted. *It still made you scream.*

Where was his brother Haught? Perhaps his cold, better-looking brother had taken his wife and his son away from this mess. He and his brother were the last of their family. Stablemen, servants, men-at-arms, but always favored at the big house: they had always been more than simply servants. Harro's brother Haught was an arrogant man though, arguably, he had much cause for pride. Perhaps Col Rob had kept the boy Charl close to him because the boy was a favorite up at the big house. Harro wished his brother had kept his progeny far away from the old man. But staying in the old man's good graces had let them have a lives far better than those of stablemen. Better even than Harro's life, though he had eventually gotten inside the house as well. Harro wished his brother well and preferred not to think of him as one of the muddy corpses at his feet.

And what about Treyna? . . . But he had no time for more thought in that direction. The trogs surged forward, and all thoughts of life and brotherhood and women fled in the face of self-preservation and self-pity. Harro was brought to his knees by blows from the taller beasts. With his last efforts, he blocked inhumanly powerful blow after blow. He kept nothing in reserve. There was no point in saving anything for later. There would be no later. The mud splashed up into his eyes, across his beard and into his mouth. Tears ran into sweat.

He waited for the finishing blow, but somehow, it never came.

Instead, he heard cheers. Shouts of astonishment, disbelief, and pure relief. Bellows erupted from the trogs as they clutched their heads and stumbled. Yet they weren't the only ones suffering from an invisible onslaught. The miners were also temporarily felled, hands to their heads, ears, chests, dropping to the ground and writhing in pain. The trogs turned on their heels and fled back to the pit, some dropping their spears and axes where they stood, simply abandoning the fight. Harro didn't feel a thing. He was numb.

But I was dead, wasn't I?

Harro felt oddly cheated, kneeling in the muck, looking around in bewilderment at his strange and sudden reversal of a loss that had seemed inevitable. Slowly, the miners regained their senses. They stood haltingly, slick and covered in mud, turning to help each other up. Self, then brother next. The blood thumped in Harro's temples. He thought he might pass out. Then, a hand was extended to him. He looked at it uncomprehendingly, then took it and stood up.

"We won!" a hoarse voice shouted. More cries went up, and Harro struggled to comprehend the exhilaration in them. He felt no joy or elation. Only weariness. He staggered to his feet and looked around at the mud-covered faces, some mirroring his own confusion. They stood alone, no trogs among them.

"Harro? Where is Harro?" someone called. It was a man's voice, young and full of fear blended with anger. Through the tangle of survivors, Harro could see his nephew Charl with a dagger strapped to his side. It looked like Rob's dagger and it was unsheathed and clean-looking, Harro noted. That was good.

"I'm here," he tried to say. He had to clear his throat more than once before any sound came out. When it did, it was still only a croak, but his words were taken up by others. "He's here. This way. Come this way." The shouts went up and carried Charl back to him.

The boy—no, the young man—came to him. Charl was nearly Harro's height, though his eyes were wide and panicky as a child's would be on a night such as this. "To the house," his nephew said. "We have to get the people to the house, uncle. The master says . . . Rob says to bring all the people to the great hall. We have to get them to the house." He was repeating himself, caught out loud in a mantra he had probably been saying to himself over and over.

"All right," Harro said nodding, trying to soothe the boy into silence. He wouldn't touch him and humiliate him. He wouldn't put a hand on his shoulder and splash mud and the blood of beasts on Charl's clean clothes. Charl looked somewhat appeased then, his message delivered and his burden lifted.

And where was his brother Haught? Harro wondered, again, but couldn't ask. Instead, he heaped more responsibility on the boy and commanded him to guide the first group of survivors they found toward the house. The boy always did well when given a task. And they needed help. Otherwise, they would stumble around the lawn all night.

Harro set them off in the first group, his nephew leading the way. The miners— fighters, now—sank into shocked silence and for the most part, let themselves be led away like children. Like tired horses. The few clear-headed ones started going through the remaining tents in the shantytown with Harro. The punch of fists into fabric sounded around him as they made their way through, checking each tent.

Harro himself checked Treyna's, but it was empty. Her panderer Jonas lay dead in the mud outside her tent, but the woman herself was gone. His woman, if he had any right to claim her. Harro clenched his jaw and continued onward, not allowing himself any time to speculate. But two tents later, he abruptly went back. He brushed back the flap and stood just inside her tent staring at the dishevelment. Her table was knocked over. He did the best he could to clean his hands. He gathered up the fancy cloth she used as a tablecloth and fashioned it into a sack. A few trinkets were all he found, so he put those, her scarves, and her soup bowl into the sack telling himself that she would probably want them back.

The shouts went up while he was making his way out of the tent. He tensed, waiting to hear if the bastard trogs had returned, but the shouting rang out again, this time more clearly. "We got one!"

Clutching the tablecloth tightly, trying to hold it away from his grimy self, Harro barged down the muddy thoroughfare toward the voices. He pushed his way through the people gathered to gawk. They had a trog, bound by leathers around his hands, feet, and knees. It was on its back in the mud, and they were dragging it, stopping only to shove back another person who ventured close enough to kick it in the ribs, its big knobby head, or whatever part of it they could.

"Where are you taking it?" he demanded. They stopped, eying him with a mixture of fear and respect. Probably had something to do with the blood running down into his boots.

"To the house," one said. "We're taking it up there."

"No," Harro immediately said. It was a bad idea, a very bad idea. All those children and people at the house. Or even Nan the old cook, whose kitchen was near-sacred grounds. A trog within the same walls? He couldn't even think of it. He would not allow it. He said, "Take it to the old root cellar. The one out back."

There was an old cellar back from the house toward the burial grounds. It had been primarily storage until someone realized how idiotic it was to have food storage so far away from the house. It had taken only one winter to realize that error. They could convert the cellar into a makeshift jail. They could throw the trog in there as long as he was still trussed up. Though someone would have to watch the bastard at all times. The trog would be in his element underground. The old root cellar had a dirt floor.

Harro sighed. Opening up the old root cellar would not be a good thing. Someone had to find Rob and tell him. Finding no better option, Harro decided he would do it.

CHAPTER 58

Rob nearly lost the contents of his stomach. As much as he itched to storm down to the tent village shouting for Jenny and the boy, he couldn't go. *Someone* had to stay at the house. Someone had to make sure everyone kept inside and stayed sane. Though he wasn't sure how well he was doing at that job. He had his whole useless body pressed against the window, trying to see anything outside, and he was ready to flay the skin off the next person who spoke to him. All he could see were flames in the distance. Harro was down there. Other members of the household staff were supervising the security of the basement on his command. It was up to Rob to hold it together. It was his eternal bad luck, his duty. Then more screams went up, and his heart jumped up into his throat as he sprinted downstairs to find out the cause.

Damn it all to hell.

Screams could mean the kitchen staff had learned something bad had happened to Ott. There was still no word from the mine entrance, and Rob felt sick about it.

But, no. The panic was just a fire that had broken out behind the house out in the graveyard. Some fool had set a fire out by the burial grounds, alarming everyone. Rob would see to that later, whoever had started it. With Rob hovering just inside the kitchen door, a terrified houseman had gone out to check and reported that it was just a pile of brush and twigs. A bonfire. Someone setting a beacon. And someone would receive his harshest words for frightening the house people unnecessarily. But later. All that mattered now was that it was not a threat. As long as these flames were human-caused and no one had been harmed, it didn't matter. He had more pressing matters to deal with—for one, an army of trogs killing his people on his lawn. And for another matter, Jenny missing.

Rob thought about all the times with her yet to come that might now be stolen from him. All the times he wanted to wake up next to her that might have been taken away. They'd had two mornings together in two days, one at her house and the other in his room earlier that morning. What an idiot. He sank down on a wooden bench in the hallway outside their room.

"Sir?"

He looked up without recognition at the man in front of him. Then his eyes cleared. One of Col Rob's young assistants was standing in front of Rob looking like he'd rather be someplace else. Probably because of the expression on Rob's face, which he tried to smooth away. "What is it?"

"Your father wants to see you." It came out in a cringing rush. The strained relationship between Rob and his father was public knowledge within the house.

Let him wait. He was damned if anyone thought he was going to see the old man right now. Rob clenched his jaw. His teeth made an uncomfortable grinding noise. "Thank you." But the young man just stood there as if waiting for Rob to accompany him. Rob shot him another look, pure murder this time, and the young man twitched and scrambled away at almost a full trot.

Rob concentrated on breathing and trying to stop his head from exploding, but just a few minutes later he was interrupted again by heavy footsteps coming down the hall, a lot of people, and urgent voices. *What fresh panic now?* He briefly gripped a handful of his own hair to steady himself, then let go and stood up to meet whatever it was coming for him.

The outlines of bodies became clearer. Mostly housemen, some of whom Rob didn't recognize, moving toward him quickly in a tight phalanx. He frowned as they drew nearer, not sensing their intent and feeling vaguely threatened. Through his suspicious squint, he saw a short, dark-haired head in their midst, and his chest lurched with hope. The men abruptly parted, pushed from within, and Jenny shot out, her face tense with fear, propelling herself toward Rob and wrapping her arms around his chest.

"Thank you. Thank you," Rob murmured hoarsely to no one in particular, burying his face in the top of Jenny's hair. *She's not gone. I didn't lose her*, was all he could think over and over.

"I'm sorry. I'm so sorry," she said, her voice muffled by his shirt. "We went to get Jack's doll. He said he couldn't sleep without it. It's his bear doll. I didn't know there was going to be a surprise attack."

"Of course you didn't know there was going to be a surprise attack," he murmured, stroking her hair, not knowing who Jack was and not really caring. "Nobody knew."

"I've never been so scared in my whole life," she said looking up at him, her dark eyes shiny. "And it wasn't about dying. It was that I couldn't get back to you." Her chin quivered, and it looked like she clamped her teeth together to keep from crying.

He knew the feeling. However, his particular brand of stupidity kept him mute, unable to put words together to tell her that he felt the same way, that he felt like he'd lost years off his life wondering if she were all right. And that life, even a shortened one, would not have been worth much of anything without her. Instead, he nodded and held her closer, tucking her head under his chin.

One of the housemen brought up a small boy behind her, and Rob recognized him as one of the children they'd brought in from the tent city earlier, except now his head was shaven clean just like Jenny's boys. His eyes were wide and deep set in a small, pale face. Jenny disengaged herself from Rob, causing him a small spike of anxiety. He watched her take the boy, who clung to her, and thank the men who escorted her. Rob nodded at them, finding himself unable to produce words. In turn, they seemed reluctant to leave and milled around with incongruously gentle expressions on their rough faces as they watched the reunion. Jenny went to the nursemaid and the other children. Rob followed, less than a step behind.

The maid was relieved to the point of tears, but she quickly dried them, holding them back in true northerner fashion. The other children surrounded Jenny as she got down on her knees, so they could throw their arms around her neck. Five pairs of arms. The maid had the little boy called Jack, alternately hugging him and checking him over for injury.

"Go rest," Rob told the nursemaid firmly, the roughness in his voice caused by tightness in his chest. "We'll have some other people up here with the children as quick as we can." She shook her head, but he insisted. "You can come back whenever you want, but you need to go rest. Eat. Take care of yourself. We'll get Marget to help," So she nodded slowly, giving in, exhaustion lining her face. Rob knew the feeling. But he wasn't ready to rest yet either.

He stood for a minute watching Jenny calm the children. He felt inept and as out of place as the housemen loitering around, though it was his own house and they were his men. He needed to get back to checking the house, to waiting for word on survivors.

He moved to the side of the room, his hands behind his back, looking at her, at the sweet slope of her neck and her gentle hands on their faces. She was small and soft and unharmed. *He needed to get her alone.* It was an inappropriate urge, but he couldn't deny the overwhelming thought that neither of them would feel whole again until he could be with her. But she was undeniably exhausted and hungry and traumatized. And there was no time for his weakness, his desperation for reassurance.

He fidgeted in the corner until Marget, the young housemaid with the quick smile, arrived with three others to help with the children. Then Jenny stood up looking truly done in with her shoulders slumping. Rob sent the idle housemen to the great hall, hoping the preparations for the evacuees were well underway. He'd have to go check in a minute. But for now he was finally alone with Jenny. He put his arm lightly around her shoulders and guided her across the hall to their room.

She stopped inside the room and just stood there looking blank and forlorn when he turned to shut the door behind them. With her back turned toward him, she started to pull her dress off her shoulders. He stood for a minute, and then went to the bathing room to run water in the tub. She could have a long soak, while he asked someone to bring food for her. Then, he'd come back and check on her although he wished he could stay until she fell asleep. He would have liked to lie on the bed next to her until she drifted off.

"Rob. Come here," she said, her voice thin and unsteady, before he could twist the handle of the water faucet. He straightened and swiftly turned, arrested by the soft urgency of her voice. Her heavy outer dress pooled at her feet where she stood. Light gleamed off the muscle of her arms, the soft slope of her throat, the indentation of her navel under her thin shift. She looked ashamed and uncertain. "I'm tired. I'm still scared. And I've been sweating in terror so I'm not very fresh. I know it's a lot to ask. You're worried about the people and the house, and my brother, and me wandering off like an idiot. But if I can't have your arms around me, I think I'm going to die."

In a heartbeat, Rob crossed the room, wrapping himself tightly around her.

CHAPTER 59

Old Col Rob shuffled slowly and patiently from bed to table to his chair; he had time for infirmity. The pain didn't trouble him much. He didn't mind being closed off from the world as long as he had his thoughts and frequent dispatches from the outside in regard to the results of his schemes and the consequences of his actions, both delicious and bothersome. It was like playing a wonderfully challenging game without the coarse and tedious interaction that the world demanded of a younger man.

There was a sharp knock on the door, and Rob entered. Whoever the boy's real father was, Rob had turned out to be a tall man, not stunted like one of those miners. Col Rob had never been able to worm the information out of his wife—speaking of challenges, she'd been a delightful source of them at times. Col Rob didn't think much of his son's coloring or looks. The boy always had a defiant expression when he should have been cowed, and behaved submissively when he should have been challenging. Col Rob snorted. Ah well, a small failure in a long list of accomplishments.

But wouldn't it be interesting to discover that the boy's father had been one of these horrid trogs? Had she perhaps been raped during a ride through the woods? He had always assumed the boy had been the product of an extra-marital transgression during one of her many trips south to Port Navio. But a trog . . . now, that was an interesting thought. Perhaps this could be used to their advantage. If they claimed mixed parentage on his part, they might be able to leverage a truce or establish an aboveground community of the creatures over which young Rob could preside. Pure physical power like theirs was not a commodity to be undervalued.

Col Rob painstakingly lowered himself into his chair by the fireplace. He pulled his heavy lap rug up over his aching hip joints and waited for Rob to assume his usual stance across from him. The boy always remained standing. Not a subtle tactic by any means, but understandable given his lifelong struggle for acceptance—no, approval—from Col Rob.

Comfortably seated, he studied Rob, now scrutinizing him for hints that his ancestry was subterranean. A heavy brow, but not even as pronounced as that low-intellect stableman who constantly flanked the boy. Now if that man Harro had been older, he'd be a likely candidate for Rob's true, blooded father. Dark coloring. Plenty of muscle to appeal to the sharp-mouthed harlot who had called herself wife to Col Rob. But, it was unlikely. The stableman Harro was only a dozen or so years older than young Rob, and certainly not old enough to be his father unless Col Rob's wife had been a seducer of children. Highly unlikely.

Certainly, Col Rob had appreciated certain of her unusual sexual proclivities in the early years of their relationship. He had enjoyed fighting her for dominance, though her eventual defeat and submission had spelled the downfall of their marriage. And he had so hoped for a worthy partner when choosing her. She had looked like a hellion, and he had not been disappointed at first. But she had had no staying power, and his interest in her eventually waned.

He pulled his thoughts from the past and gazed at Rob, who stood silently before him. Col Rob had thought that by precipitating the trog attack on the tent city, Rob would be forced to action. Col Rob still had hopes for the boy. He had wished his false son would evolve into manhood through battle, through strategy and skill acquired from experience. Scars made the man. Col Rob had plenty from his own father, who had them from his father before him. It was an honorable tradition. And it mattered not whether the archers Col Rob had sent to the mine entrance had survived their mission. He still had not received report back on that endeavor. But, the trog aggression had occurred, thereby sending him a sort of hearsay confirmation of his own success in evoking the attack.

"And what have you been doing this bright and delightful winter morning?" Col Rob asked the son who was not his son in a harsh and deliberately provoking manner. The boy was pale, but impassive, to Col Rob's amusement and surprising approval. To his credit, the boy mastered his expression. He remained in control, a definite improvement on all previous encounters. Before, Col Rob had always managed to elicit some kind of anger response. But the boy was stoic today. Perhaps he was evolving.

"The Masks are dead," Rob said flatly, expression remaining stonelike. Col Rob squinted at him. There was something not right in the inflection of his voice. He sounded unlike himself. Unemotional and distant. And, if possible, he seemed taller and darker.

"They lived to serve their purpose," Col Rob said. *Ahh, there was a response.* Just the smallest hint of one. A flicker of the eye darkening for an instant. It had turned to flint and sparked admirably.

"No one should have died this day," Rob said in a voice that was not his own. *This was not Rob.*

"Who are you?" Col Rob demanded abruptly, feeling a wave of suspicion and a small flicker of fear traverse his brittle spine. He wondered where his boy Charl had gotten himself. He could have used another in the room, someone who was in alignment with him against Rob. Or whoever this person was who had disguised himself as Rob.

"You are done meddling in the affairs of others," the man in the form of Rob said.

Col Rob frowned when he looked up at a blade that glinted in the firelight. He said to the stranger, "And that's not my son's dagger. Who are you? And how have you disguised yourself so well?" His old heart beat a little faster in his chest as he pondered the unexpected miscalculation of his moves and was briefly irritated that he would be leaving the game because of a trick, an exception to the rules. *Deception was a woman's game,* he nearly said out loud. Yet, how many times had he played the game himself?

Nevertheless, he tried to protest the unfairness of the trick by shouting out to his guards. But his voice deserted him in a wave of weakness. He looked down to see the blade push through his thick, finely-sewn robe and slice into his chest.

Not much resistance left in the old skin of this body, he thought in frustration. He would have liked to have seen some more of the seeds he'd sown lately come to grow and bear fruit, as sour and poisonous as it may have been to some. He would have liked to have seen the boy Charl one more time. The lad had such promise. Smart . . . quick . . . though not of his own flesh either. Col Rob had been unable to make any woman pregnant. That had been his curse. So many regrets. He would die alone instead of surrounded by sons. Or daughters who looked as beautiful as his dear adulteress of a wife.

Then Col Rob was unable to hold his head up on his neck. He leaned to the side and let out his last sigh.

CHAPTER 60

Standing over the old man's body, Guyse stepped back and withdrew the blade. He had used Rob's shape to gain access to the old man's chamber more easily. But now standing over the corpse slumped in its chair, Guyse wondered at the old man's uncanny perception that he was not his son.

That was for Ana.

Because of the old man's inability to leave the delegation alone, Ana had died. He'd had to dabble in the Masks' affairs and fix the outcome so that the trogs would attack. Why? Why had Col Rob done it? Had they been just pawns in a game to a bored old despot? Would Guyse ever learn why Ana had had to die?

And now, Guyse thought grimly, he would return underground and retrieve his daughter Mel. Or else never see the light of the sun again.

CHAPTER 61

Ott awoke belly-down under a highly uncomfortable blanket of debris and with a large knot on the back of his head. He sat up slowly and waited for the tremors in the ground to cease. Then he realized the ground was solid and that he was dizzy.

How fitting. Killed by a rock when I'd been trying to kill a trog with a rock . . . when I first met Mel.

He tried and failed to remember what had happened to pitch him under a pile of rubble. He sat grasping at the threads of his memory and trying to weave them together, trying put them together to create a reasonable . . . He lost his train of thought and leaned back. A stone dug into the small of his back. But if he didn't rest his head, he was probably going to throw up. Nausea made him think of bile, which was green . . . like agamite, which the trogs were protecting. Which meant he was in the mine, half-buried under yet another cave-in. Incapacitated by . . . what exactly had happened? He'd been picking at the great wall of rock ahead of him with his bare hands and there'd been some kind of blast, a wave of . . . sound?

He sat up a little quicker than was wise, and black spots swam in his vision. After blinking for a minute until his eyes cleared, he used his bloody hands to haul himself into a reasonable facsimile of a standing position. Then he wiped his hands on his dusty torso and squinted into the darkness.

He cursed. But it was a celebratory curse. Because the mine shaft was clear now. It wasn't walkable by any means, but he could see through it to the greenly-lit cavern ahead. A little crawling, a little wriggling, a little sloughing off of skin, and he'd be through to the cavern. He waited for the blood to recede from his brain and his eyes to clear from the rush of elation. Then he started forward.

It took him a good hour to make his way downward through the newly opened tunnel. But what was time in a place like this? Nothing. Time was absolutely nothing here. Maybe it was an hour. Maybe it was several minutes. He went heartbeat to heartbeat, handhold to handhold, nicked skin to the next sore spot. But he never considered staying still because stopping himself was the same thing as stopping time, he thought deliriously; he was time itself, and that was why he had to move forward.

When he reached the cavern, he tumbled in head first and landed hard on the floor, surprised that the latest cave-in had made his passage not at floor level but at chest level. He'd had more than his share of hard landings lately, so he got to his feet slowly to make certain he wouldn't be going down fast yet again. The cavern was empty, no people and no bodies anywhere. The place was surprisingly untouched by . . . whatever it was that had knocked him flat and made his head feel scrambled. But waking up and finding that the tunnel had opened up left him optimistic; the impossible task didn't seem so impossible anymore. What was lost might be regained. *Mel*. Frankly, it was impossible that he'd lost her. He felt strongly that she was there . . . he just couldn't see her. He picked his way across the uneven, boulder-covered floor to the opposite side where the trogs had been standing before. There was the entrance he meant to take.

He went through the opening in the rock and stood for a minute to let his eyes adjust. It wasn't too badly lit in here. Greenish, of course, but he was getting used to that now. Even his skin mixed with dust looked greenish. And with his new height thanks to Mel's healing—something burned in the lower part of his stomach just remembering lying in bed with her—he almost looked like a baby trog, he thought.

Don't be stupid. A baby trog?

Forty steps later, the smell hit him. Thirty more steps and he started to hear voices. Trog vocalizations. Grunts and hoarse rasping.

He'd come to the end of the tunnel. He paused, thinking the time was now or never. There was no turning back. Mel was not behind him. There was no reason to go back. So, he braced himself and stepped forward.

Less than a minute later, Ott was belly-down yet again, having taken another hard landing, possibly the worst yet, and ended up with two trogs on his back. His body was humming with . . . something . . . but there was no battle fury tinting his vision. They weren't pummeling him, just sitting on him, pinning him to the cave floor. He turned his head wishing whoever was talking and pleading with them like a scared child would shut up, then realized it was him babbling at them incessantly. So he stopped. There was no point. They didn't seem to understand him and they weren't speaking either, at least in any way he could discern with one eye and one ear pressed wetly into the dirt.

Then the pummeling began.

CHAPTER 62

Rob was just getting to the good part, his mouth on Jenny's. He'd found the perfect stroke of his tongue, the perfect rhythm. Jenny's face was flushed, shining, and gorgeous, her dark mass of hair tumbling over her shoulders on the pillow. Then the pounding on the door started.

"The door is solid. Made from local dried hardwood. Been there for a century or so. Ignore it," he told her, though she looked doubtful.

Then the shouting started. It couldn't be anything good. He cursed, thinking that word had come back about the delegation to the mine entrance. But they seemed to be saying Rob's father had been attacked in his bed chamber. That didn't sound plausible. The old man was on the top floor and surrounded by a veritable army of servants and sycophants; he had to be carried up and down the stairs to the great hall.

"Go on," Jenny said, giving him a shove that failed to move him away from her.

"No," he said. "You might be carried off by trogs again." But he got up and searched for his overshirt.

"I wasn't carried off by them before," she said. "Only by my own stupidity."

He gave her time to fix her hair and straighten her clothes. He pointed at her, though it was less of a command to her than a fervent wish that he could control everything in the entire living universe around him. "Stay there. I'm coming back." Then he went out.

A houseman stood looking pale and ill. "It's your father, Rob," he said. "He's been killed. Stabbed to death."

Rob frowned, shaking his head, not willing to believe it. "In his room?"

"Well, he weren't in the tents," the man said, not disrespectfully, just at a loss.

The houseman gestured for him to start walking as he talked, and Rob mourned the warm woman he was leaving behind more than he would ever mourn the old tyrant.

Col Rob was dead? The thought was shocking, certainly, especially the chilling idea that they had a killer moving among them in the house—*that* left Rob icy cold. But the news that the old man was dead was nothing but a longed for and inevitable end to a life full of misery-making and deceit.

Rob didn't wonder who had wanted to kill Col Rob, but rather which one of the old man's many victims had actually done it. And he felt relief. Maybe Rob was going to be damned to an after-life of eternal misery, but his overwhelming response to the news was relief that he hadn't been the one to kill his father after years of imagining it.

"Col Rob was discovered in his room, dead of a wound to his chest. He was sliced clear to his gut," the houseman told him. "The body was still warm when it was discovered. His usual boy Charl was sent away from the house some time ago."

"I did that," Rob admitted. "I sent him to the tents to tell people to come up here and take shelter in the great hall."

"Well, apparently, when the house maid went in to ready Col Rob's bed for sleeping, she discovered that he was dead."

They made it up the stairs, Rob on the houseman's heels. Stepping into the upper hallway outside Col Rob's chambers, they were confronted by a gathering of house servants and aides that the old man had kept close to him. They were murmuring and standing around trying to look scandalized and mournful. Very few of them were successful. Rob grimaced. He squared his shoulders and pushed his way through them with a feigned arrogance. He'd need to rid himself of most of them unless they could prove they were trustworthy and not hanging on just for the privilege or associated power. For now, he didn't trust a single one of them. They could all *take a walk in winter*, every one of them, for as much as he trusted them.

The doorway to his father's chambers was blocked by gawkers. Rob moved them aside, putting his hands on the closest shoulders and firmly pulling each obstacle out of the room. When they saw who was moving them they immediately bowed out, deferring to him in a manner that made him cringe even more. In short order, they cleared the room and shut the door behind them, and soon it was just Rob, alone with the old man's body.

Col Rob was slumped over in his usual seat by the fireplace, his lap blanket still tucked around his hips. His eyes were closed and his chin tucked serenely into the side of the tall-backed chair, as if he had simply fallen asleep in front of the warm fire, though the dark wounds down his chest and the blood that soaked into the blanket testified to the contrary. Rob stood in front of the old man and stared. After a minute passed, he realized that the old man would never call him to attention again. Or mock him. Or scorn him. Or, for the love of Lutra, though it hadn't happened in years, beat him again.

The door behind him abruptly opened, and Jenny walked in clothed in a robe, her eyes wide with horror and something else . . . pain. The hallway was empty behind her. She gestured feebly, "I asked all of them except for a few to go down to the great hall, where people need help. I think we're beyond help here." She stared at Rob, who was frozen where he stood in front of the body of the man who had been his father. For Rob, having her here in the old man's bed chamber was strange, even with the old man immobile in death. It seemed as though he should blink his eyes open and lash out with a disparaging comment.

Rob ran a hand over his face. Blood swam in his head. Everything was going downhill, a straight descent into the depths of hell. Jenny's small hand wound around his arm and pulled him a little away. It was just the sight of him—Col Rob. It seemed impossible that he was dead, though his skin was now turning grayer.

"I can't believe this," Rob managed to say to her as she led him around a dividing curtain out of sight of the body.

"It's all right," she said, making him take a seat in a solid wooden chair pushed up against the wall. "But horribly shocking." Her dark eyes, so close to his as she leaned toward him, made him feel a little better. He made an effort to pull himself together. The last thing he wanted was for the old man to be able to affect him in any manner, especially now when the man wasn't even alive. No. Col Rob would not manipulate, humiliate, or otherwise torture Rob again. Ever. Not Rob. And not the people Rob cared for.

A body suddenly loomed in the doorway, and Rob barely had time to grab for his dagger, which wasn't at the belt on his hip. Harro's face reared up on top of a black, mud-covered body.

"Gods above," Harro whispered hoarsely, "It's true then. He's dead." He looked with wild eyes at Rob.

"I didn't do it," Rob said.

"Where's your dagger?" Harro said with a glance at Rob's waist. Rob narrowed his eyes.

"I don't wear it in my room," he said sharply. Then he thought, *I gave it to Charl, my father's faithful companion, when I sent him away from the house. Yes, that looks innocent.*

Yet he knew that he was blameless in this matter. He also knew that as much as he had hated the old man and had wished a million times he were dead, Rob hadn't actually wanted him dead. Because that meant that the house and the mines were Rob's. And Rob didn't want them. He didn't want the heartache. He didn't want the responsibility for hundreds of people. He didn't want to condemn Jenny to a life in this frigid wasteland if she didn't want it. And above all, he didn't want her to leave him. He would do anything to prevent that, even if it meant failing to fill the shoes the rotted-souled tyrant had left behind.

He sat for a while with his head in his hands and his elbows on his knees. Then Jenny drew close and put her warm hand on his back. The touch of her hand sent heat through him, and disgusted with himself, he resisted the urge to pull her onto his lap and hold her close.

"Funeral pyre," she murmured. And he had the urge to make an inappropriate remark. He nearly laughed. He shook his head to clear the humor that was not true levity.

"Yes," he said. Harro rejoined them, as they turned their backs on the corpse of Rob's father. The stableman listened intently to his instructions. "We'll light the funeral pyre tomorrow night. These circumstances call for break with custom." Instead of waiting the usual two days' time to allow a viewing period, he meant. He didn't mean to imply any guilt on his part or suggest that any evidence needed to be destroyed. He would wait to meet with the other advisors and see what formal declaration they would make as part of the death ritual.

A houseman entered and interrupted them. "The advisors must come in and make their final viewing. They have been rousted from their beds and summoned."

"Please wait here for them. Give them what they require. And when they are finished, have the body prepared and taken to the wood shed for storage overnight," Rob said, his plea unnecessary. The man nodded, following his words as if they were commands. "Harro—" Rob frowned suddenly, focusing on the big man next to him, on his gore-covered clothing. "That's not mud."

Harro's face was stonelike. "No, it is not. And I have further news. The men have captured one of the trogs. They are housing him under guard in the old cellar."

Rob clenched his jaw. The cellar already housed bad memories for him. It was where his father had taken him for the most severe of his punishments. Harro, too, knew it, and he was watching Rob with carefully guarded eyes.

"Do you need to take food and rest?" Rob asked Harro, who shook his head. "Fine. Clean yourself up then, and supervise the prisoner until I can get there. I need to go down to the great hall first." *And find the boy Charl*, he thought. And tell him that Col Rob was dead. Charl was the one person who would mourn him honestly.

Jenny removed her hand from his back. "I'll go with you," she said, and Rob felt strangely buoyed. As if in the midst of this madness, things still had a chance of being all right again. Someday. Somehow. He didn't know how, but if he ever saw the slim chance of a path to getting there, he would take it.

CHAPTER 63

After stabbing Col Rob and leaving him with his life blood seeping into his lap rug, Guyse the shifter—now, assassin—left the big house and slipped through the trees down to the tent city. Silently, he made his way through the charred and muddied tents and was unmolested for his efforts. The slashed tent cloth flapped gusts of smoke all around him, and he used it to his advantage. No one saw him. No one was watching the hole now that the trogs had retreated. The withdrawal was considered a victory, and the people were no longer on guard, too exhausted to care, at least for now. Guyse made his way to the edge of the cavity and lowered himself down into the pitch black of the pit using his fingertips to find handholds in the frozen edges of dirt. Deeper and deeper he descended.

He shut down his sense of smell immediately before the fumes affected him, and filtered the poison out of his system before it became overwhelming. Hopefully Mel had had presence of mind to do the same, though she didn't seem to be skilled at that kind of thing.

What in the world had they been thinking, taking an untried novice—my daughter—along with them? False confidence born of intellectual arrogance. Guyse blamed his brother. Curse Ley'Albaer, the so-called seer, for failing his daughter, and cursed him again for dying.

Guyse's eyes adjusted to the dark while he crouched at the bottom of the pit, hoping that no trog stood sentry, hoping that they were just as foolish as the people aboveground in leaving the boundary between human and trog worlds unprotected and ignored. He looked around in the dark, noting two tunnels leading into the pit. Maybe an entrance and an exit. He scoured the ground, but found only footprints leading out. Not surprising. The trogs had used both tunnels for their rapid departure. Without hesitating any further, he chose the tunnel on the right. At fifty paces, he heard them. It was like approaching a barn full of cattle—stamping on the impacted dirt, hoarse lowing and rasping breaths, and the smell of beasts. He drew closer, following the brightening of the green glow of agamite. At the end of the tunnel, Guyse paused, and then stepped purposefully into the den.

To his surprise, many of the creatures were stooped low, resting on their haunches and holding their heads as if weak or ill. A few sprawled, leaning against the outward walls of the small cavern. The effect was that he towered over them. And they all saw him. Those who had been conversing with their language of hand gestures—surprisingly fluid, using their fingers in different combinations, as well as their wrists and occasionally forearms—paused to look at him warily. The closest to him tightened their grips on their weapons. But Guyse was unarmed except for the blade he had used to kill Col Rob, which remained sheathed at his waist. He halted, slowly raising his arms up to show that he didn't intend to draw his weapon.

Then, he shifted.

CHAPTER 64

Mel came back to consciousness when a hand gripped her bare shoulder. She hoped it was Ott waking her for breakfast. Why did it feel like days since she'd last seen him or felt him? Her mind struggled to anchor itself. She remembered the Keep. The attack on the Keep. Then, she thought it was blue-eyed Jenks with his warm hand on her shoulder when he'd retrieved her at Port Navio in the midst of the swirling crowd. Back before she'd learned that he was her father. She wondered foggily if any of them had made it out of the mineshaft alive. But as her mind sharpened and came back into focus, she shut down any more thoughts along those lines. She shook her head. She was in the frozen north. Trog attack.

The hand on her shoulder was small and strong. It was lean and smooth and made her think of the desert.

"I'd like to see the desert someday," Mel said without opening her eyes. The hand on her shoulder squeezed tighter, perhaps involuntarily. Mel tested her body gingerly by moving a foot, then an arm. "Why am I all wet, Rav?"

"Here, put this on," Rav said draping a blanket over Mel's bare back and drawing her off the strange wet platform she was lying on. She sat up, clutching the scratchy cloth to her naked shoulders and looked down. Soggy shredded clothing. Black, oily liquid. Bad smell. Drenched bed. Liquefied trog innards.

"I need a bath," Mel said, her teeth suddenly starting to chatter though the room was not cold. With Rav's help, she slid off the bed and the ruins of the corpse she had obliterated. "I need more than a bath," she amended. She wished she had a hundred brushes and a tub full of hot water and scrubbing herbs. She would never be able to get this stench off.

"Come away from this with me," Rav said gently guiding Mel out of the death-filled chamber and down a passageway. Mel shook so badly that her steps were jerky, thighs quivering, muscles variously clenching out of control.

They were back in Rav's room, and Mel hissed and drew back at the sight of the trog slumped on the floor.

"He won't hurt you. He's incapacitated," Rav said. She handed Mel a tunic to wear. The tone of her voice made Mel look again at the trog, and she recognized him as Rav's keeper, not Mel's attacker. She recognized him by the clothes he wore, a leather shirt, and also by the way Rav looked at him without fear and without shielding her body. He sat on the floor propped against the wall, his eyes rolled back in his head, arms hanging limp at his sides so the palms of his hands faced up. The skin of his palms in the exact center of each was a shockingly delicate and vulnerable-looking pink area the size of a coin.

"Is he dead? What did you do to him?" Mel asked, casting aside the scratchy blanket she held to herself and slipping the tunic on. It fell to her mid-thigh and was not as coarse as the blanket. It was far different from the last costume she had worn with Rav at the Keep, she thought with a sob. She fought between wanting to lie down on the bed and struggling to keep as far away from the creature as possible. She had the fleeting memory of the trog who had tried to take her looming over her, pinning her down, the thick hide of his neck stretched wide and dark above her face. Nausea swept over her when she remembered what she'd done to him. She had disassembled him to his most basic elements. She had liquefied him. Then full-body exhaustion won out and she sank down, grimy, on the sickbed that Rav had so recently occupied when she had lain bloated and sick with agamite.

"It was you, not me. I did not do a thing. I was sitting across the room when he fell to the floor. He fell like the mountain crumbling. You did this," Rav said, watching her carefully. "Whatever you did to that other one in there to turn him into water, you did this also."

Mel closed her eyes and kept her astonishment to herself. "Did you feel anything when it happened, Rav?"

"No, but you have already cleansed me. I don't have any of the green stone inside me anymore."

Mel suspected this was true, but she was surprised to hear Rav drawing the same conclusions and speaking them out loud. She remembered drawing the flecks of green toward her, inward, and changing them.

Moving them. Stirring them up to do her bidding. She just hadn't realized the magnitude of it. Fear and desperation had motivated her to be as powerful as she could. And maybe she'd gone a little too far.

"Stop looking at me like that," she said to Rav. "Whatever you're thinking, I'm not her." It was that Great Mother mythos that Rav had talked about earlier. The Great Mother coming to cleanse them all. Whatever that meant. Though Mel felt greatly soiled herself at the moment.

Rav gave a noncommittal shrug with her thin, brown shoulders. "*You* don't have to believe it for it to be true."

Mel sighed in frustration. Convincing Rav of anything different was going to be a difficult task. She'd just have to wait for time to prove her right. "Fine," she said. "And as soon as I can stand up, we're getting out of this place. You need to be aboveground where you can't be poisoned again." She left the thought unspoken. Mel didn't know how long the trogs were going to be in their weakened state, but they needed to move quickly. Otherwise, they'd be trapped again.

"Mel," Rav said and hesitated. "I want to take him with us." She gestured at the trog.

What? Mel looked at her, but said nothing, certain that her face was transparent anyway. The woman was clearly crazy. She frowned to herself. Rav was treating him like a human. More or less. Mel didn't know what to make of it. Maybe it was the only way Rav could allow herself to deal with her kidnapping and imprisonment. Or maybe she wanted revenge? Mel studied her. She didn't seem irrational. She didn't seem angry.

"How are we going to move him?" Mel said. Rav was kneeling by the trog, speaking to him calmly and quietly. He had opened his eyes, blinking rapidly. When Rav saw that he was able to see her, she switched to their hand signals. He gave a curt nod, and then Rav stood back.

"Don't try to help him," Rav said. "He's as big as a bull. If he falls, we will all go down." She observed him with an odd mixture of familiarity and distance. Mel watched her friend watch the trog. Take him above ground? In what world could this idea possibly have a good outcome? The creature took a few heaving breaths, increasing the loudness of the air passing in and out of his nostrils and open mouth. His gray lips hung open showing the pink insides of them. By insisting that he come with them, Rav was what . . . showing her loyalty to him? Bringing him as a hostage? He braced his arm against the cave wall and hauled himself upward with great effort, breathing hard and unsteadily. His eyes went in and out of focus. What in the world had she done to him with her blast of anger?

"This is not a good idea," Mel said under her breath, but she followed them into the passageway. After all, what choice did she have? They needed his help navigating out of the tunnels. And if they needed help getting past other trogs, he might be willing to assist them. However, she left as much room between them as she could. Judging by how the large creature was still weaving on his feet, he could go down at any moment.

They passed through branch after branch of tunnels, and Mel gave up trying to memorize them. Normally, she was good at direction and drawing mental maps, but down here with no sunlight and with the feeling they were at times climbing and at others descending, she had no idea if they had crossed over or under tunnels that they'd already taken. After a while, she wondered if she was even certain which direction was up. It all looked the same with the embedded flecks of agamite.

More than once, she thought she heard human voices. Women's voices, and more than one. Prisoners? she wondered sickly. Women who had been raped or impregnated? It made her ill to think she could not help them. She paused at one opening to a side tunnel and listened, but Rav's trog saw her and gestured rapidly to Rav.

"He says not to stop. Don't stop," Rav translated.

"How can we leave them?" Mel demanded, trying to keep from shouting. "They deserve to be saved."

Rav nodded. "Yes, they do. And they *will be* saved, as soon as we get out of here and get help. We cannot do this by ourselves," she said. Mel clenched her teeth, but forced herself to continue onward when the trog gestured once more and then walked on expecting them to follow. *At least her friend wasn't expecting her to stop and cleanse them all as the embodiment of the Great Mother*, she thought with a wry shake of her head.

A few junctions and criss-crossings of the tunnels later, Mel heard another human voice. There was a prolonged groan, distinctly human and male. Then the savory aroma hit her, and her heart threatened to pound out of her chest.

CHAPTER 65

Mel spun on her heel, stifling a yelp. The smell in the passageway was pure Ott. Essence of Ott. The scent of him filled her nose and trilled straight into her mind. She ignored Rav's shouts not to go after the voice and ran, stumbling blindly down the tunnels toward what she couldn't ignore. The savory smell that was forever imprinted in Mel's mind, in her heart. She had to go even if it meant she was condemned to a life below ground. Or a death below ground. Because without Ott, there was no life for her anywhere.

When she saw where the tunnel opened up ahead, she ran at full speed over the hard cave floor, her bare feet pounding on the dirt floor. His voice spurred her on. She stretched her pace until her body hurt, and her tunic chafed the tops of her thighs. She would not be too late for him; she would not allow it. She ran down the earthen tunnel until she burst out into a cavern full of trogs.

"What . . . what is this?" she shouted, outraged and confused, before she could stop herself. She was ready to act, to aid, to rescue, but was stymied by her incomprehension. It looked as though she'd stumbled into a gymnasium or training room. A dozen trogs were in a pile in the center of the room, wrestling and boxing, hand-to-hand combat without weapons. Their harsh grunts sounded when they struck blows, their fists contacting with flesh. What she had thought was a wrestling mat was moisture-darkened dirt. Sweat. Blood. She wasn't sure which. Another trog body rolled off to the side of the pile of wrestlers. Then she heard the voice again and realized it was coming from the bottom of the pile. Ott was being killed under there. Mel panicked, and then reached out, seeking a grip on the agamite to control the trogs.

Puppets, just like the other one. Should be easy, right? OK, then.

She *reached out* in her mind for the nearest trog, the one on the top of the pile. She waved her hand at him, trying to focus her efforts. With her mind, she gave the trog a small shove. Or rather, she gave the agamite inside of him a gust of repulsion to get him off the heap of bodies. With a shriek, he rose up in agony, his back twisting backward as his heavy hands and arms reached up to clutch at his head. His eyes were open and wet, glistening darkly. He fell back toward the side of the room where the other remains of bodies lay, and then he slumped down with them.

Easy, right?

Mel shuddered in revulsion, but she had no choice. Physically she was nothing to them, even with enhanced strength. She could only stand back and peel them off the pile one by one. Too slow. It was going too slowly. She snarled in frustration. Ott groaned again as a solid fist hit him.

"Too slow!" she said again aloud, irritated. Exhaling on a gust of air, she made a fist and then abruptly flicked her fingers outward, mimicking an explosion. Very carefully, she tried to take off just the top layer of writhing bodies; she was alarmed when the trogs burst off the pile as if they were leaves blowing in the wind. Several of them hit the walls of the cavern. A body flew directly toward her. She dropped to the floor but not in time to dodge the thick shoulder that collided with her forehead. She tried to shove the trog off her, so she could go to Ott, but she was pinned. After a struggle, she managed to drag herself out from under it, limb by limb, and then paused, panting and sweating. She rolled to her hands and knees and pulled herself up.

Ott lay on the floor, curled up on his side. He was beaten and bloodied, barefooted, and shirtless. Older bruises on his skin were painted with fresh blood. She turned him onto his back, and he did a full-body wince.

"Hello," she said as he opened his eyes and focused on her. He squinted at her, then slowly raised a finger and poked her twice on the cheekbone.

"Real?" he said. It was a whispered, pained gasp.

"Yes, I'm real," she said, unable to stop the corner of her mouth from lifting. His fingers traveled to the sore spot on her head where the airborne trog had just hit her.

She put her hands on the sides of his face and fished around inside him for agamite. He had quite a lot of it in him still—not as much as a trog— but still a large amount, maybe from breathing dust in the mine. Very gently, as if using one finger, she warmed the agamite up inside him, circulated it within him, and coaxed it to help heal him. He gasped and arched his back on the dirt floor.

"Ow," he said. But after a little while, he was able to sit up without help. He looked at her warmly while he was resting. She checked over his bruises gently, exploring tenderly with her fingertips.

"How did you get here?" she asked. She was leaning close enough in that she felt his breath on her shoulder when he answered.

"I came to rescue you," he said with badly faked nonchalance. She could feel his eyes on her and she smiled. Her body flushed, swamped with heat at his proximity. And she felt an honest surge of pleasure, something more than physical, something that took her entirely by surprise in this ghoulish setting. It was hard not to, seeing him safe. Well, relatively safe. Not being pummeled at least.

"Well, thank you."

"Who are *they*?" he asked, his green eyes suddenly locked on the passageway. She looked up.

"That's my friend Rav from the Keep and her . . . companion," she said. Ott frowned, looking suddenly a million years old. He abruptly wrenched himself upward to get on his feet. He pulled her up after him, eyeing Rav's trog as if it were going to jump him. Understandably.

"Is he important?" Ott said, suddenly focused, and Mel understood. Ott wanted to know if the trog could be used as leverage getting out of here and aboveground. If Rav's trog were high up in their warrior ranks, he'd be worth something in trade. At best, they might be able to exchange him for their own freedom. At worst, he could help them fight their way out. They were going to need all the muscle they could get.

Rav stared at them. Then she turned to the trog and gestured briefly. The trog said something back, and Rav translated. "He says he's a . . . " Rav frowned and turned back to the trog questioningly. He repeated the hand gestures that he'd done before. He widened his eyes at her and nodded back at them, goading her to relay what he had said.

"Are you sure?" she said aloud.

He chuffed and gestured again for her to tell them.

Rav said, "He says he's a . . . librarian."

EM Kaplan

CHAPTER 66

By shifting his shape back and forth from man to trog directly in front of the creatures, Guyse planned to sow more than the seeds of his survival. He depended on the hope that some of these creatures lived in envy of men aboveground. Because he didn't have trog attire and didn't speak their language, he'd had to wait until he was in front of them to shift. He needed the full impact with as little misunderstanding as possible. And if they saw how easy the transformation was for him, perhaps they could be tricked . . . *persuaded* into coming out into the open and seeing for themselves. At the very least, he just wanted to retrieve his daughter without causing a war. Though he didn't have much hope.

In an audience of fifty-odd trogs in various states of incapacity, he saw shock and envy on maybe a fifth of them. Ten. Of fifty. Damn him for not having a better plan. How on earth was he going to find Mel? As he stood in the middle of the room, a large hide-covered hand snaked out across the floor and shackled his ankle. His shoulders slumped in anticipation of the fight he had ahead of him. Then, he shifted once more—back into a trog—and stripped off his shirt, crouching for whatever attack came next.

But none came.

The hand around his ankle loosened its grip. Large, square-tipped fingers tugged the hem of his pants. Gently. A finger beckoned him to lower himself down to the floor to the trog's level. Maybe they were too fatigued or injured to take him on. Fine, he could get down on his hands and knees. But how was he going to communicate with them?

Use your senses, you fool. Do what you were trained to do. A voice in Guyse's mind told him what to do. It was a cranky voice that sounded suspiciously like his dead older brother. Guyse knew it couldn't possibly be his brother—he knew it was just himself—but it was damned good advice, so he listened to it. He was Mask-trained for godsake. Having chosen not to use the lessons he'd been taught as a young boy and as a young man, didn't mean that he hadn't learned them. And learned them well.

He slowly lowered himself to the floor and found himself face-to-face with a trog. He'd never been this close to one before. Close enough to see the fine wrinkles in the parched thick hide. He studied the wide, upturned nostrils, the clear eyes with startling thick lashes, and heavy brows.

This is what I look like right now.

He watched the trog's hands as they came together in a series of signals. It was a sequence of five, no six signs that the trog repeated over and over. After awhile, the gist of it came to Guyse. *You. Me. Go. Together. Aboveground.* As soon as he got it, Guyse nodded his assent and clasped the big man's hand in a sturdy grip. Two hands met. Bluish gray thick skin that matched and held together. Now he had eleven on his side. He stood.

"OK. Who else?" he tried to say, but his trog's vocal chords were damaged or simply malformed. No sounds came out that were recognizable as human speech, which explained the hand language. Well, what words could he use? He now knew one phrase. So, that was the one he used over and over as he stood in the center of this room of men from another race. Were they not men after all? Were they not at least as human as that snake Col Rob?

Guyse didn't know. He didn't care just so long as he was able to rescue his daughter.

In the end, he stood with nineteen trogs, who weakly raised themselves to accompany him. When he organized them loosely around himself, he shifted back to human form. Some of them were clearly discomfited by it, but he had to find Mel, and without his vocal chords, he wasn't sure how he was going to do it.

"Do you understand my words?" he asked them harshly. He received no sign of acknowledgment as he slowly turned in a circle looking at his newly formed guard. He circled twice before he caught a curt nod out of the corner of his eye. He turned on the trog who had admitted to understanding him.

"I'm here to retrieve my daughter," he said. "My offspring." The sole trog nodded again. Guyse continued, "She was captured in a cavern. Taken away from a group of us who came here to ask for peace."

The trog's eyes suddenly grew wide. Then he nodded again, more rapidly. Another of Guyse's newly formed group began signaling rapidly.

The trogs around him seemed to grow apprehensive. They conversed among themselves for a minute, arguing, and jostling each other aggressively, with probably as much force as a human man might strike another in anger. The trogs' punches and bumps seemed to punctuate their speech.

"Enough," Guyse cut them off. "Take me to her. This is part of our agreement. I will help you come aboveground, but only when we retrieve my daughter." The trog grunted, stared at him a long time, and then seemed to submit to his terms.

Guyse followed them as they shuffled single-file out of the room into one of the many tunnels that fed into it. Within minutes, they came to a set of rooms. He looked into them and cringed to see that they were sleeping quarters. They reeked of animals at close quarters—breath, sweat, and mating. Guyse seethed to think what might have happened to Mel. But the rooms were empty now.

The trogs stopped, confused, and consulted among themselves. Guyse was the first to smell the blood. He turned his head and sniffed. Trog blood, he recognized. It was gamey and greasy-smelling. But there was human blood, too. Not a lot of it. But then, Mel was not a big person. Guyse cursed and pointed down the tunnel from which the smell was emanating. "That way," he said.

CHAPTER 67

Ott was going to need an army to get out of this hell hole. He'd been at the bottom of a trog dogpile, and it wasn't fun. He had the cracked ribs to prove it. Actually, not anymore. He rubbed a tentative hand down his dirty, blood-covered side but felt only manageable aches and bruises since Mel had . . . done whatever it was that she did. It felt like she had taken his guts and stirred him up inside—in a not altogether unpleasant way. It kind of made his spine buck and his toes tingle.

But what he really needed right now was an army of strong fighters. What he wouldn't give to have Rob with him. And instead of one able-bodied trog, he had the equivalent of . . . well, a human. A trog librarian? Did they even have books? Well, the guy was an archivist of some sort, it turned out. Cave drawings or drawings on skins or some such thing. Ott shrugged internally. *Eh, to each his own.* And speaking of his own . . . he eyed Mel with admiration. Explosions. Healing. And, apparently, liquefaction, from what Rav was describing. Was there anything Mel couldn't do? She even made the sack cloth she was wearing look good. His eyes traveled the length of her slim legs.

"Look, Ott," she was saying. "I know you've been close to dead . . . more than once today, but can you stand up? We have to get moving."

"The faster we leave this place, the better," he agreed, bracing himself for the dizziness and inevitable room swirl when he stood. Good thing she was next to him, because he almost went down again. His hand on her shoulder helped balance him out. Plus, it gave him that warm feeling in the bottom of his stomach just touching her. Then his head cleared a little more and he looked at her. *Really* looked at her and noticed her clothes. Bruises on her legs and arms. Broken fingernails where she'd fought someone off. Red flooded his vision.

"Are you hurt?" he asked, trying to unclench his jaw while he searched her face, his fingers reaching for her hand. He braced himself to do damage if she had been hurt. Skulls would be crushed. But she was already scanning the exits.

"What?" she said, distractedly patting him on the lower back. She seemed ready to forge ahead. Maybe the momentum she felt wasn't something he should disturb. At some point, too, he would have to tell her that her parents were dead. He shoved the thought away for later, hoping for a better time and place to deliver the news.

"I said, how are you going to get us out of this mess?" he said, changing tack.

"Don't worry," she said, starting up again with that rhythmic, comforting patting. "I'll think of something." Her grime-covered face was knotted in concentration. He didn't know whether to be amused or insulted. He went with the one that took less energy because the rest of his effort was going toward simply remaining standing. And he kind of liked the patting. So, they shuffled their way toward Rav and her trog . . . trog scholar. They were in so much trouble.

Heavy footsteps came their way down the tunnel. A herd, he decided, based on the thudding and raspy breathing. For the rest of his dying days, Ott would never forget that wheezy sound.

"Lutra on a spit," Ott muttered to himself. Were they never going to catch a break? Probably not the direction they were headed. He turned, putting himself between Mel and the oncoming footsteps. He felt her warm hand on his arm. Not much good he was going to be able to do in the state he was in. No weapon. No armor. Nothing but exhaustion at this point. He wondered if he could at least give her a chance to run away. Though he didn't much want to think about where she could run.

More than a dozen trogs entered the room from an opposite tunnel, but they weren't in much better shape than Ott. A few of them limped. Then, all the tension went out of Ott as he saw Guyse in their midst.

"Mel. Thank God," the big man said, striding toward her. His furrowed brow pulled down deeper over his tightly closed eyes as he wrapped his arms around his daughter and held her close. Ott felt a weird pang of jealousy. Guyse pulled back from Mel and took her face between his two huge, paw-like hands. "Are you all right?" Guyse asked her.

Mel nodded her head. Ott didn't hear if she said anything. He was standing off to the side, petulantly wondering when she'd come back to stand by him. He was being a child about it. Maybe he'd feel less needy after a hot meal, a warm bed, and five solid days of sleep. If they got out of here alive.

"Mel," Guyse said. "Ana and Ley'Albaer are dead." Ott gaped at the man and his brusque delivery. It was cruel. She had already been through enough today. Ott had wanted to save her from the added shock and pain. Why had the man been so brutal about it? But straightforward, Ott realized. Like cutting away the dead part of a wound so it could begin to heal? And why hadn't Ott been brave enough to tell her himself? He should have been the one to hold her closely and comfort her.

"What? No," Mel said, and then shook her head in denial, her hair hanging in dirty hanks, her widened eyes standing out in the grime on her face. "No. You're wrong." Guyse gently held her shoulders and nodded.

"They died earlier. When you were taken."

Mel frowned, trying to understand. Then she abruptly covered her face with her hand. Ott shifted backward more so he was against the cold, rough cave wall, hanging back nearly out of sight. Mel's grief was palpable, a pain that he could almost taste and feel in his chest. He stood still except for his fingers, which he couldn't control. They moved restlessly against his palms because he wanted so badly to go to her, to let her collapse against him if need be, to carry her weight for her.

Guyse was whispering softly to her, describing the events in general terms. *Now*, the callous bastard was gentle. Ott heard his painting of the deaths of Mel's parents, and was surprised to remember very little of the details himself. Guyse lingered softly at the telling of Ana's death, and Ott knew suddenly that Guyse had loved her. That must have been hell, to have loved a woman who loved his brother.

Archers? Ott's mind suddenly fixated on the memory of them. Archers from Col Rob. It had to be him. "Col Rob is a dead man," Ott said under his breath. Not surprisingly, Guyse's Mask-trained ears heard him.

"Col Rob *is* a dead man," Guyse said, momentarily stunning all urges of vengeance out of Ott. "He died this evening in his bed chamber."

I have to get to Rob. He's going to need me, Ott immediately thought.

Then a sob broke from Mel's throat, and Ott found himself halfway to her before he realized it. Mel crossed the other half of the distance. He cradled her in his arms, wanting to wrap her up and to get her away from all of it. *This is where I'm meant to be*, he thought. Not the time, nor the place . . . but with her.

The trogs were shuffling their feet and looking restless. They were recovering from the earlier blast that had debilitated them. If these trogs were perking up, the other less-friendly ones would be, too. The tunnels would be rife with them. Ott's pulse ticked up a notch with the growing sense of urgency and the wish to leave. If they only knew how far below ground they were, maybe he could dig their way up and out. He eyed the ceiling, but it looked like solid rock. They were probably a stone's throw from the middle of the earth, for all he knew.

"What's your plan for getting out of here?" he asked Guyse over Mel's head. She, however, thought he was asking her. When she raised her face to him, he cringed, expecting her to rail at him or, even worse, to cry harder. Instead, she took a final deep breath in and set her shoulders, clearing her throat at the same time. *Well, OK, then.* Perhaps she had a plan.

"We walk out," she said.

CHAPTER 68

They stumbled through the catacombs, bodies littering their path. Mel saw their raggedy group fall into a natural order. Ott took the lead with Rav's trog beside him. Mel came next. Then Rav followed behind her, with Guyse on guard at the rear of the humans, his twenty or so ailing trogs limping behind.

Far too soon, the first trog came barreling down the tunnel at them. Mel barely saw it before it plowed into Rav's trog, knocking him back into Ott who, despite his ready stance, was thrown on his backside in the dust. Mel heard an inhuman snarl of rage and it was several more heartbeats before she could comprehend what she saw.

The trog who had attacked them never reached her. Ott was a blur, moving with an astonishing fluidity that Mel had seen only in animals. He leaped at the trog, wrapping his big hands around its thick gray throat. Ott's body tucked in mid-air and his feet landed on the trog's chest, from which he pushed off, at the same time wrenching and releasing its neck. The trog fell back, and Ott landed on his feet. Mel was fairly certain that only she and Guyse had the ability to see any of Ott's movements. And Guyse was behind them, partially blocked, focused on any attackers approaching from the rear. So, only she had witnessed Ott's sheer power and inhuman strength.

Mel swallowed and shuddered involuntarily. This was the man she'd held in her arms. He'd had his hands on her, all over her. The same hands that just snapped the neck of that creature. And it was stupid, she realized. Whatever he was . . . it was her fault because of whatever she had done to him by cleansing him. Now he was a killer. She took a breath. Yet, was she any better? Was she any less lethal? Would she do anything less to ensure his safety? She set her shoulders and tried to prepare herself for the next encounter. Ott stood ready, balanced on the balls of his feet. Rav's trog gestured for them to move, and they proceeded forward as a unit.

The next attack brought three trogs. Ott dropped one of them with a noise of snapping bones that made Mel's stomach clench. The other two trogs broke through their ranks. Guyse leaped forward to take one of them. The remaining beast went for Rav. With a hoarse shout, Mel clenched her hands and stirred up that trog from the inside until its eyes rolled back in its head and it sank to the floor. She had to be careful. Concentrating her movements so as to avoid stirring the agamite inside Ott, she turned toward Guyse, and with a gesture, flicked the trog off him so it crashed back against the tunnel wall, making a wet trail when it slid to the floor.

The others stared at it and then at Mel. She ran her hand over the lower part of her face, avoiding eye contact with them—especially with Ott. Hadn't she just given him the same shudder? When she finally braved a glance at him, he looked pale and somewhat aghast. She was a killer, an unnatural . . . manipulator of agamite. Some kind of magician. A spellbinder. Certainly not human. She felt like an abomination, as much a creature of children's tales as the ogres at her feet. She cringed, her stomach dropping, and a part of her shriveled with disgust and self-loathing. She was covered in dried gore and dirt and dressed in a cast-off filthy tunic; no amount of bathing was going to get her clean now. She tucked her chin down, and they moved on.

Their strategy worked fine for now, with Ott taking the first wave each time the trogs came at them. He didn't seem to be tiring. Mel cast a glance at his bare back, where the muscles bunched, tense and covered with streaks of dirt and blood. She wasn't close enough to touch him, but her hands were filthy anyway. She wouldn't have touched him with her soiled hands for the world. She'd done enough as it was. He seemed even taller than when they had left the house that morning. Every time she touched him with her so-called healing, she changed him, she thought queasily. She didn't want to change him. She wanted him as he was, but unharmed. No broken bones. No hidden wounds or punctures inside. She had wanted only to heal the damage. She wasn't sure she could go near him again with the amount of agamite sifting through his body.

They reached another dimly-lit cavern, but this one was crowded with trogs. With raspy snarls, the creatures leapt to their feet and charged at Ott. He crouched, ready to grapple the first of them with his bare hands even though there were too many by far; they were horribly outnumbered once again. Then Guyse barked a warning as they were attacked from the rear. The trogs who traveled with them were felled left and right, and Mel feared they all might be finished for sure. Yet she concentrated and held herself back from blasting them with a frantic wave. Now, more than ever, she needed her Mask-trained control and she struggled to keep her wits about her. She carefully repelled some of the trogs coming from the side, *pushing* them one-by-one, away from Rav. She couldn't panic now—anything she did to the trogs might affect Ott. Out of the corner of her eye, she saw him plow through the gray forms, lost suddenly in a sea of them. Then the creatures surrounded Rav and her. She tried holding them off in a tight radius, but they broke through.

Out of the ring around them, a trog lunged at Rav, grabbing her by the arm. Across the crowded chamber Rav's trog howled in rage, unable to protect her. But the trog who held Rav suddenly started and pulled back, his eyes opening white and wide in his gray, bristled face. He bellowed a hoarse cry that nearly blacked Mel's vision from its volume; it stilled and silenced the chamber. Another trog's hand gripped Ott by the throat, but that hand loosened at the shout, and Ott rubbed his freed, raw neck. As the commotion around them slowed, the trogs roughly hit those who still fought until eventually the room quieted—and all watched Rav and the trog who had her by the arm. Mel tensed, ready to strike him down to protect her friend if need be. But the trog leaned in, his thick lips curling, and took a deep breath near Rav's neck, *smelling her.*

Abruptly he dropped Rav's arm and started speaking to her in gestures. His huge paw-like hands with their yellowed nails flew, but Rav frowned and shook her head in confusion—he spoke too quickly for her. She looked for her trog, who was buried in the ranks of their attackers. He had been jostled and dismissed, pushed out of the way during the attack. He shoved his way back to Rav now and stood beside her.

Rav's trog and the other exchanged rapid hand movements while Rav watched, face tight in concentration as she tried to understand the interchange. Then suddenly the attacking trog fell back, a confounded expression on his gruesome face. He stared at Rav, and Mel caught how he looked at her belly. In Mel's ear, Guyse suddenly whispered, "Your friend carries a child by one of them?" Mel shook her head no. No child nestled in Rav's womb; could this other trog see the future? Had he seen what Mel had also seen? That there would be a human child one day? There was more to it than that, but she couldn't give even a shortened version here and now; she wasn't even sure what she had seen.

The trog speaking to Rav suddenly fell back a couple of steps. Then others followed his example. They stood at ease, watching her. Rav's eyes widened and she swallowed hard. Abruptly, a pathway was cleared between her and the doorway out of the cavern.

"Who's the Great Mother now, my friend?" Mel muttered under her breath. She could tell Rav was thinking the same thing. And she was horrified.

Mel stepped up behind her friend. Guyse fell in behind them. Then Ott wrenched himself away from the trogs whose hands were still lightly restraining him and came to stand with them. Together they stood in a tight grouping. And then, they walked out.

CHAPTER 69

Harro had been watching the pit, pacing the tent city like a dog that had fallen off a wagon and was waiting for his owner to return for him. The miners and their families were settling into the refugee camp in the great hall up at the house, displaced again, yet coping with typical northern stoicism. They didn't need his help up there. And frankly he felt so outside of himself thinking about Treyna he didn't know what to do.

He had tucked Treyna's possessions away in his room at the big house, a fine sensitive mess for a former stableman. Her things were wrapped in a bundle in a wooden trunk that he kept at the base of his bed. It was imbecilic. But once he had her things in his coarse hands, he couldn't throw them away. Even if she weren't coming back. He'd wandered around her shredded tent long enough to realize it now. He had not found her, though he had searched. Her body was not among the dead. She had been taken, whether alive or dead, by the trogs. Dead, he fervently hoped. But still, what if she weren't?

Survivors had hauled away the corpse of Jonas to the hastily-built pyre to prevent the trogs from taking more bodies for their grisly larder, so now the tent and surrounding ones were empty. Harro shuffled his feet carefully through the dirt, avoiding the worst patches of mud. He skirted the rest of the tents, the ruins of the half-constructed shelters, and the charred remains of the mess area where pots lay strewn on the ground. Pacing, keeping the motion of his feet moving forward though he walked in circles. The moon glinted above him, muted and silvered by clouds, reflecting in the shiny mud that was quickly freezing over.

What was there left for him now that Treyna was gone?

Harro was now almost certain his brother Haught had perished in the attack. He hoped Haught had died well. At the house, Harro had avoided his nephew Charl; there was nothing to do for the boy. And Lila, his brother Haught's wife, had come across Harro when he was still fresh from the battle, blackened with smoke and gore. The look on her face was one of pure horror, and she had shrunk back from him in the corridor outside the great hall, one pale, blue-veined hand raised to her mouth, her blue eyes wide in fear. A thousand thoughts might have crossed her mind at that point, but the one Harro recognized for certain was the repulsion. He'd never been able to win her good graces, even as the only brother of her husband. She was too fine a woman.

He toed an object in the mud distractedly, trying to see what it was. He nudged it this way and that in the mud, till he finally bent over and picked it up. The handle of a cooking fork. He pitched it aside and flung the thick mud off his fingers.

Col Rob was dead. Young Rob would take the reins of daily life at the house. He'd do fine with the support of the people, as long as those insidious advisors kept their power-hungry claws retracted. And the woman Jenny. She was small, but for sure there was something steely about her. Rob would do well to try to keep her beside him.

Harro did not even have an animal of his own: he'd had no more horses since he'd moved into the house. He'd given over care of the animals to his underlings. And they'd done well. His expertise was no longer necessary. He'd trained them well. And he was glad for them.

So, the question remained for Harro: *what was there left for him?*

He suddenly remembered the day he'd chosen the stables while his brother had been taken into the house. Haught and he had been together, inseparable their whole lives though they were as different as two boys could be. Their parents had been stablehands. They'd been raised with the animals, but his brother Haught had shown promise for indoor manners and matters of the mind. He was quick, clever, and handsome. One day, Harro had watched his brother enter the house, Col Rob's wiry arm over his shoulders, leading him away. Harro had watched for a moment longer, and then turned back to his chores, carrying feed for the animals. He couldn't have been more than seven or eight years old.

Harro had spent his life looking up the hill at the house, thinking about his brother. The fine clothes. The warm bedrooms. Hot baths whenever he liked. Hot meals at a moment's notice. True, Harro was a houseman of sorts now, but he'd never found his true place. Now, he had nothing. Not an animal of his own to handle. Nothing of his own, really. Not until

Treyna.

He looked at the pit again, then approached it indirectly, letting his steps take him first to the right, then a little to the left, then to the right again before he found himself at its edge peering downward into the blackness that might kill him. The odor was not as harsh as it had been during the fight. Either it went with the trogs when they had retreated, or he was getting used to it. He stood there quietly for a few minutes longer. Then, he slowly lowered himself so that he was sitting at the edge, dangling his legs into the pit, his rear pressing into the cold wet mud.

After a few more long minutes of the coldness sinking into the seat of his pants, he slid off the edge and descended into the pit.

CHAPTER 70

In the deserted camp the wind picked up, whistling through the shredded tents and making them flap frantically. Nobody stirred. No humans straggled to pick up their scattered and bespattered belongings. No trogs remained either, dead or alive. The moon flashed once between the clouds, and then the silver-laced clouds veiled it lightly. The first flakes of snow began to drift down, swirled by gusts of wind, falling downward to mix into the freezing mud.

Fingertips grasped upward, slipping through the debris. Small fingers, a woman's fingers, rose above the edge of the pit. A black top of a head appeared. Slick with sweat and melted snow. Black eyelids opened over bright white eyes that gleamed. Mel flexed her fingers, searching for a handhold. Below, her feet scrambled for purchase. Before she found it, strong hands shoved her upward over the edge of the pit, and out.

Next came Rav, half lifted, half pulled out by Mel. Then the others, one by one. As a group, they stood together at the edge of the pitch, catching their breath, hoarse rasping in the cold wind. They shivered, each one of them, trog's breath mixing with human as they stood in the dusting snow.

Part 7

Unmask

CHAPTER 71

Two days after they emerged from the pit, Ott lay in his room with his hand stretched out on the cold bed next to him wondering how long Mel had been gone and if she'd touched him or even looked at him while he'd slept. He had no memory of it, though he wished he could feel some kind of lingering sensation of her hand on his skin, some trail of residual warmth where she had run her fingers down his arm maybe or her hand on his messy hair. But nothing.

He was once again floundering . . . falling. He could walk perfectly well. Legs moved when he needed them to. His shoulders, arms, hips, hands, his whole body was functioning fine—better than ever—but his insides roiled in a black turmoil. Bits and pieces of his murderous rages were coming back to him, sickening him.

He and Mel had yet to talk about what had happened. They'd barely spoken at all. The first night, he'd left her and gone directly to find Rob to report what they had encountered underground, what they'd learned about the trogs, and to see how Rob was handling the death of his father. By the time Ott had gotten free for the night, Mel was asleep, so he'd washed up in the bathing room and slid under the blankets next to her. He'd fallen asleep almost instantly and when he woke up late the next morning, she was gone.

She was probably avoiding him, probably trying to find some other bed to sleep in for the night, the next, and all the others that followed in an interminable, neverending line of night times that he'd be spending alone till the end of his days. How could she not be thoroughly repulsed by him? He was a monster, just as bad as a trog. A slaughterer. An uncontrollable beast capable of going berserk with battle lust. The memory of the way it felt to snap a neck was imprinted on his hands, in his fingers. He pressed his head back into the pillow in disgust.

How can I blame her?

Maybe he could teach himself to control it better. And promise her that he'd never kill again. Or try not to.

Nice idea, you dunce. Now think about reality.

And what was reality now? Ott groaned to himself as he lay in bed and ran a hand up his belly to his aching chest. Nothing was predictable about him. Even his body. He was a hand taller than he had been a week ago and a hand again as broad through the shoulders. Thank Lutra he was somehow able to compensate for his body's changes as well or else he'd be stumbling and falling over his own feet like a newborn colt. At least he was spared that humiliation even if he had no control over the changes. Was he the same person as he was before? He couldn't say with any certainty that he wouldn't keep changing and stretch as tall as a giant . . . if such things as giants existed. And why not? It turned out that ogres were real, more or less, so why not giants or gnomes or elves or . . . or Masks.

He groaned again and pushed himself up out of bed, tired of feeling sorry for himself. He should pity Mel, if anyone. Her parents were dead, her poor choice of lover had turned out to be a mindless berserker, and she had a foot in two cultures, neither of which probably seemed like home at the moment. A squeeze of panic had Ott suddenly standing straight up.

Was she going to leave him? Was she going back to wherever it was that Masks came from?

He shoved his legs into his pants and jerked a shirt over his head. Oh, God. Or gods. Whichever would help him. He'd be happy to pray to any and all of them, the animal-guided deities of his people or the single god of so-called civilized people. He had to find Mel and convince her to stay with him. He didn't know what he was going to say. He didn't know what he could offer her. He didn't even have a house or a piece of land. He didn't even own the clothes on his back because he'd outgrown his in the last few days. Maybe he could just put his arms around her and just . . . and just . . . he didn't know what.

He lunged down the stairwell to the kitchen, feet pounding the stone steps. Nan looked up at him as he came in.

"Pants on fire again I see," she said with an indulgent smile at him. He grimaced and waved a hand at her as he jogged past the cookfires. He stopped at the door to grab an outer shirt and coat and to jam his feet into his boots. He was using borrowed boots because his own didn't fit anymore—they felt as if he were trying to wear his nephews' child-sized shoes. Nan followed after him, wiping her hands on the apron tied around her wide waist. "What is it this time, then? What's the terrible emergency?" she asked.

Bent over at the waist while he tugged at his boots, he muttered, "Usual idiocy."

"Don't hurt yourself," she advised. He did a double-take and saw she was pointing at his boots. "Most people use the bench so they don't fall over."

He stopped and, straightening, took a deep breath, standing with only one shoe on. "Nan," he said, "I'm a completely self-absorbed half-wit. I only ever think about myself. And when I realize I may have hurt someone, I try to fix it. Except, by the time I get to that point, some universal good luck happens and the person is no longer mad at me. How am I supposed to learn my lesson if no one ever stays mad at me? But this time . . . .this time, I think I've really fouled everything up. I'm an idiot, Nan. How am I going to fix it this time now that I actually have something to fix, now that the good Lady Lutra has left me on my own? Now what do I do?"

Nan, the sturdy, flour-dusted cook, smiled at him, half of her mouth quirking upward in the corner. She shook her head. "Gods, Ott. You're so damned attractive. If I were half my age, I'd make a play for you myself." Then she laughed, leaving him further bewildered. "Half my age and twice again as good looking."

He tugged a hand through his hair with frustration. "Can no one be mad at me?"

"Have you tried being a little less puppyish?" she said drily. She turned her back on him, but said over her shoulder, "I expect you're looking for Mel. She's out in the cellar with the trogs."

Ott froze as the cook's words sank it. Mel out with those animals? What was she thinking? If she wanted to gawk at them to satisfy her curiosity, she should have asked him to go with her to protect her. Without another word, he charged out the door, letting it slam behind him. Before it closed, he could hear Nan's laughter.

CHAPTER 72

Ott jogged across the snow-covered yard to the sheltered entrance of the original cellar doors. Fresh flakes had fallen during the night, but already a pathway had been tramped through the powder. He opened the cellar door, expecting to find it the way it had always been inside—dark, deserted, cold, and smelling of dirt—but was confronted with sharp changes. Lights flickered yellow, but the cellar walls glowed greenish, as if tainted by whatever glowed in the mines and underground. He did a mental forehead slap. It was the agamite, of course, flowing through the trogs and everything around them. The presence of the trogs activated it like the glowing bugs he saw in the warm nights down south.

Just inside the cellar doors, Ott was stopped by two guards. Or sentries. Or . . . he frowned. Houseboys? They were barely old enough to carry the spears by their sides. And they sat on chairs. Gods above, these two children wouldn't be able to do anything if the trogs tried to push them aside if they managed to break out of their cages . . . The smell hit him hard. It was an enclosed space with a lot of animal bodies. Ott looked ahead further and gaped at what he saw.

Trogs sitting casually at tables. Eating. Reclining on cots. Sleeping.

And Mel sitting among them. No, not sitting, *kneeling*. With a trog's hand on her head, on her beautiful gold-tipped hair. Touching her. Their hands on her. The one lying in the cot in front of her, looking at her.

Ott's vision flooded with red. His strangled exclamation drew all eyes toward him. A feral growl rumbled up from his throat, and he crouched ready to lunge at them. So help him, if they had harmed her in any way, he would go all beast on them in a way he'd never experienced yet. Lutra, he had to try to get a hold on himself. If he lost control again, he might lose her forever. He tried to take some deep breaths, but was pretty sure it looked like rabid panting through bared teeth.

But he was brought up short when he met Mel's eyes and saw the expression on her face. It was nothing short of beatific. Ecstatic. Gods above, she was beautiful. Her smooth skin and dark shining eyes. It halted him in his tracks.

"Mel?" he said haltingly.

She leaped to her feet and rushed toward him. The trog whose hand had been on her hair lay still, strapped to the cot where he lay. Passive.

"You came!" Mel said, taking his face in her hands, pulling him downward so she could raise her mouth to his. He bent toward her, confused, grateful, but mostly just . . . confused. The smell of her flooded his nose and filled his senses. The red in his vision abruptly faded as he closed his eyes and met her kiss, suddenly coming awake to the warmth of her lips on his, the soft moisture and intimacy of her mouth. She tasted like fruit, a flavor that made him fantasize about warmer climates . . . maybe the ocean, maybe just a warm bed.

She pulled away from him and smiled. "I didn't know if you'd come. I hoped you would, but I haven't . . . seen you really." A flutter of concern and unhappiness crossed her face, and then disappeared. It hurt him, that little moue of distress. He'd do anything to protect her from it if he could, especially if he were the one causing it. Thank Lutra, whatever higher power—or whatever base insecurity of his—had led him to the cellar, he was willing to take it. Blessing? Coincidence? His unfailing sheer dumb luck? Whatever it was, he was glad of it.

She took his hand and led him to the side of the chamber against the wall. "I haven't been able to find you these last two days," she said. He had trouble focusing on her words when she looked at him like that, so close he could feel the breath of her words stroking across his neck and chin. Her fingers wound themselves through his, stroking his palms and wrists like she was trying to get under his skin. Not close enough for him, as far as he was concerned. He freed a hand and wove it into the silky hair at the back of her neck, pulling her mouth back to his.

When she broke away, he let her lead him by the hand closer to the trogs, though it was against his every inclination. No, he'd rather a wall of granite separate them. The way it used to be before the monsters had erupted from the ground. And changed Ott into a monster himself.

She said breathlessly, "I'm so glad you're here. I've been speaking with the trogs using Bookman as an interpreter. I think I may be able to do something for them." He was distracted by the way her hair fell over her shoulder even though she was dressed in just a simple woven shirt. He liked the way she looked in it. Kind of like she carried warmth with her. He wished she had room for him to crawl inside of it with her.

He frowned, "Bookman?" He looked around. The girl Rav was there along with her trog. He felt a little sick when he thought of them together so much. He wondered how Rav's family would feel about it when the news of her rescue reached them.

"The trog who is Rav's companion," she said, gesturing at him.

"You call him Bookman?"

She shrugged. "It's as good a name as any at this point. Until we get to know him better. He's telling us a lot."

Ott didn't want to know him better. It gave him shivers to think that Mel had been conversing with him. They'd moved closer to the trog strapped onto the cot. The straps didn't look very tight, but the trog didn't look hostile. Downright docile, Ott thought, if he could believe the act. Which he didn't. He expected the trog to snap his restraints in an instant, grab Mel, and flee back down his hole. She moved to kneel again beside the reclining trog, but Ott put his hand out and stopped her.

"What are you doing?" He tried to keep the frantic cadence out of his voice but didn't think he was successful.

She said only, "Watch." Then she took the trog's coarse paw in hers, despite the low growl of protest that escaped Ott's throat. His skin crawled, and his hand itched to smack the trog off her. Gods above, she was kneeling again and putting the thing's hand back on her head. A voice in his head protested loudly, outraged. And then she smiled at Ott. And smiled at the trog, patting its side gently. Its filthy, reeking side.

What followed next was something Ott didn't quite comprehend. He felt, more than anything else, a weird gripping motion roll through him. Not as bad as down in the tunnels when the blocked mine shaft had been blown open and he'd been knocked unconscious. But it was a strange wave of something that made the walls tremble around him and forced him to loosen his stance to keep his balance as if the ground were shaking. And then it went through him, a strange, bit-by-bit kinking that unsettled his stomach and made his mouth water with nausea.

He swore and squeezed his eyes shut for a couple of long blinks. When he was able to look around, he was glad to see that no one was looking at him. He followed their gazes to the trog on the cot, who thankfully had not taken advantage of his disorientation and was lying peacefully, flushed and . . . pink-faced? Ott blinked and leaned forward. Holy gods. The trog had shrunk and turned paler . . . more human. And Mel had done it.

"How did you? . . . " he started to ask her. He froze when he looked at her, and his stomach clenched up. She was slumped over her knees on the floor, forehead against the edge of the cot. In two steps, he was there to take her up in his arms. Her head fell back from her neck lolling loosely. She was pale as the driven snow and covered with . . . soot? "Lutra, Mel, please tell me you're not hurt." A thousand things ran through his head, but they were too jumbled to make it out of his mouth.

She began to shake, a weightless flutter traveling through her body. Her eyes moved behind her lids, and her lashes rose up. She had such nice eyes. Kind of like a creamy batter for dark bread or a hot chocolate drink with warm milk swirled in it. He was never more glad to see them looking at him. She shook her head and greenish dust flew out of her hair. She sneezed.

"Did I do anything?" she asked, craning her head around, away from him and back at the trog, and he hated that her gaze had wandered off him. He was selfish and infantile in his jealousy.

"He looks different," Ott conceded, wanting her eyes back on him. Then they were. She stared at him with a sad smile that he didn't understand but felt guilty for all the same.

"The others are going to want it done, too," she said. "The ones who came up with us. Some of them want to be . . . "

"*Human*," Ott finished. "You can turn them into humans?"

"No," she said thoughtfully, letting herself relax in the cradle of his arms. He was selfishly glad she let him and no one else hold her. It was his job. "They *are* humans. Just contaminated by the agamite. For whatever reason, it's changed them. Maybe how it changes you. I don't know how. It's in their bodies, in their blood. I just . . . push it out."

He shook his head. "You can't do it again. You're exhausted."

She didn't say anything. He thought about adding a plea but didn't want to beg aloud in front of the trogs . . . people . . . whatever they were. It was bad enough that they were eyeing him holding her in his arms while she was so weakened. "I want to take you back to the house," he said.

"I want to stay here," she said weakly, trying to push her way out of his grasp. He held on tighter. "I need to stay and observe him. What if he changed back to his previous state over time? I need to know how he feels. What if he can speak now? That would be extraordinary." She wanted to stay and observe the trog . . . *man* on the cot to see if her treatment took? She had a feverish, almost obsessed light in her eye. Her mind was working quickly, Ott could see.

A spark had caught in her mind, and her natural Mask scholarship was taking over. He didn't care, as long as it kept her near him. As long as the trogs weren't going to injure her, and by the look of wonderment on the face of the man now lying in the cot, Ott figured her only danger from them was going to be exhaustion as they lined up to be cured by her.

"Please? At least rest for a while?" he said, trying to keep his voice level.

She looked at him suddenly. Intently. Then nodded at him. She gave over to him. Agreed with him. Allowed him to guide her. Sweet Lutra, he loved her. She leaned into him, and he thought his heart might beat out of his chest.

CHAPTER 73

Rob encountered Ott and Mel standing outside the great hall. The hallway was where throngs of displaced miners and their families were settling in, organizing themselves into a new too-tight camp. Their meager and muddied belongings lined the walls in fiercely-guarded heaps, but at least now the people were indoors. Rob was going to have to establish some rules immediately, he realized, before violence broke out. He looked around and signaled an older houseman to come closer. Instead, he received one gnarled finger, held up for him to wait. For the first time in days, maybe weeks, Rob had to suppress a grin. Very few dared make him wait now. The others, his father's old advisors, were genuflecting and generally making Rob feel queasy, the throng of sycophants making this man an uncut gem among them.

Rob looked back at Ott. *Gods, Ott's girl looked done in. Pale as frost.*

"What's the matter?" Rob asked immediately as he rounded on them. He gestured for them to go into a private chamber across the hall. He followed them, loosely draping his arm over Ott's shoulders, stopping himself inches away from doing the same to Ott's girl. He felt like he knew her better than he probably did, probably more than she would feel comfortable with. Rob already regarded her as an extension of Ott.

He closed the doors to the room behind them. The house staff had reserved the private room for his use, for hearing the troubles and complaints of his people in private. Col Rob had once used this chamber to decide the fate of others, to carry out his devious schemes, and to determine the punishments for Rob himself as a child. He cringed at the thought of his supposed importance and of the secrecy, but there was no helping it. People had issues that didn't need to be discussed in front of others. Damn him if he couldn't understand that. He would do what he could to protect the privacy of his people, each one of them. Especially in these terrible close quarters where they were trapped for what looked like the duration of the winter.

As if reading his mind, Ott said stiffly, muttering, "The bloody cold will be on us soon." Rob almost didn't hear him. Then he smiled grimly at his friend.

"There's no changing its course," Rob answered. Ott's girl was looking at him coolly. Suspicious, perhaps. She was very pretty, Rob thought in a detached way. Bright and sunny with a strange shine to her even though the room wasn't well-lit at this time of day. Good for Ott. It was rude of them to drop into the old customs in front of her, especially when it wasn't their habit to use it. Something about the room or the situation had inspired Ott to pledge his allegiance to Rob as if he were a lord, to invoke the old oath, the old custom. And damn, Rob realized, he supposed he was a lord now. They might as well have had a full court audience in formal dress. It was an old greeting, a ceremonial pleasantry between liege and subject, what passed for a reaffirmation of loyalty in these frozen parts.

"Then we had better prepare," she said, surprising them both into silence. She had completed the greeting. Rob watched mutely as Ott reached for her, tucked her into a strong one-armed embrace and pressed his mouth to her forehead.

Rob cleared his throat. "Apologies. Your pretty looks make me forget that you come from a community of scholars. I underestimated you. I'll try not to do it again, Mel." He used her name hesitantly, but marked how his inadvertent comment about her beauty made a pink flush creep up her neck into her face. For the second time that day, an unbidden smile came to Rob's face. He gave a half-shrug with one shoulder.

He gestured for them to sit and then was astounded when Ott told him what Mel had done to the trog in the old root cellar. She had cleansed the agamite out of it, but clearly at cost to her; she appeared exhausted.

"The trog was transformed into a human man? And you think maybe they were men to begin with?" Rob asked again when Ott was done speaking. "Is this what they want? To come aboveground and mix into our people?" A flicker of distrust made the hair on the back of his neck stand up.

"Some do," Mel confirmed. "Bookman can make up a roster of the ones in the cellar."

At Rob's raised eyebrow, Ott explained, though he had just recently learned it himself, "Rav's trog is calling himself Bookman. He's their storyholder, the teller of their history." Rob nodded, and gestured for Mel to continue.

"We have so much to learn about them. It might help us understand why they attack and what they want from people aboveground."

Rob didn't bother voicing his disgust and distrust of so-called trog motives. He was sure his doubt was written plainly on his face. And whatever Mel was thinking about her role here at the house in the future, he didn't think Ott would want her anywhere near them. If it were Jenny, he'd feel the same way. They could keep their filthy hands to themselves and at a good distance, too.

Mel continued, "Many of them distrust us. They want to remain aboveground, but in their unchanged state. We think it's a good idea. Their strength and endurance is phenomenal. They might be convinced to serve . . . as fighters aboveground," she said though she seemed uneasy at the prospect. Rob appreciated her astuteness. Clearly, it was a sore spot to recruit the trogs as their brutes to fight against their own brethren from below.

"Perhaps they might be convinced to protect at least their own kind who have been changed into humans," Rob suggested. Mel's face turned toward him and the full force of her concentration was trained on him. It was almost staggering, as if her eyes had spear-like points to them. Rob stood firmly, stolidly, almost as if he were being dressed down by his old man.

Gods above, she was not a force to be taken lightly.

He hid the tension in his jaw and the tightness in his chest until she broke the gaze and nodded. Then he took a gasping breath disguised as another clearing of his throat. Mel made him want to run to Jenny and bury his face in her neck and be wrapped up in her arms. Mel might be Ott's girl, but there was something about her that made Rob uneasy. She'd been a Mask, Colubrid swallow it, and that was *something*, no matter if she'd tossed the cowl aside or not. She was still one of them. She had their abilities.

"I've kept you too long," he said, softening his voice though it still felt rough-edged to him. "You need some rest, Mel." She nodded, glancing at Ott, but purposefully keeping her eyes away from Rob. Just as well to keep distance between them. He was finding himself trusting others too easily since the murder of his father. Not all of the snakes in the nest had been destroyed, that was certain. He had to remember that his world had not been cleared of enemies just because the old man was no longer there to torment him with his mind games. It was better to remember that he was on his own. Other than Jenny.

Ott led Mel out of the room as they promised to keep him abreast of the trog cleansing. Rob stayed in his private room, drafting a basic code of conduct for the people inside the great hall. It was nothing earth shattering. Just common courtesies set to paper with ink. Some other houseman could have done it, but they clearly had other things to deal with just now with all the new inhabitants lining the halls. Rob had no trouble taking care of it. The solace of his private room was a comfort. At least alone, he knew there was no one waiting behind him to take advantage of him or of the situation. Alone, he could let his guard down.

A knock at the door ended that, but he was more than pleased to see Jenny's sweet face peer into the room, scanning the shadows for him. She entered the room hesitantly, but he waved her over. "Come here," he said, then pulled her onto his lap when she was close enough. She smelled like the gentle floral soap she used to bathe the children. Her hands were rough from constant washing and plunging into water to wash some child's face or other with a washcloth. He stroked them between his own thinking he'd find her some *lanol* cream if he could. Jenny might like that. Maybe Nan in the kitchen would have some. Or that house girl Marget. He'd have to ask. Probably they even had some that had been made to smell nice.

"What are you thinking?" she asked. An innocent enough question, though her face flushed red when she looked at him. Her dark eyes glinted at him in recognition of what she saw on his face. He had wanted to tell her about the trog cleansing, but the blush on her cheeks made him kiss her instead. She had that telltale hint of mint on her tongue. She must have found the packet of mint gum that he had hidden in her pocket before she woke up that morning. He loved the taste of it on her breath, and it was several minutes before he remembered that he had something to tell her.

"Trogs," he said in his typical idiotic fashion, leaving her no time for recovery or even a small chance at comprehension. He was wrapping a strand of her curls around and around his finger. Her hands were all over his neck and in his own hair. She pulled back as if he had pinched her and stared at him, rapid breaths through open and swollen lips.

"All right," she said. She took a half-minute to compose herself, folded her hands in her lap primly, and sat with a straight spine in listener mode even though she was perched on his leg. "Go ahead."

He suppressed a chuckle at her indulgence of him. Thank Dovay. He was a lucky man. And it was the first time in his life he would admit to feeling lucky. Then he cleared his throat and told her about Mel and the cellar trog, that Mel could turn them into humans, and that she wanted to learn their history, their needs and wants. He tried to keep the bite out of his voice.

When he was finished, she said, furrowing her brow, "But this is good news, right? It means we have a way of communicating with them if some of them are staying here. I expect Mel will want to learn their language of gestures, and perhaps some of them would like to learn to speak ours. At least, the one who has been changed over. He should be able to speak." She had a look on her face that made him uneasy. He cursed silently. He knew what she was thinking now. She wanted to go with Mel and teach the trogs. Learn from them. Intermingle with them. It nauseated him.

"I thought you wanted to be in charge of giving the children their lessons. We have a lot of children to keep busy now," he said, thinking of the teeming masses packed in the great hall. The more occupied those people were during the winter months, the better off they all would be. In fact, he was thinking of setting them to work with some kind of indoor building project. A lot of them seemed good with hammers, as they'd proven with the construction of the tent city. But for now, he had to make them look desperate and needy to her—more in need of attention than the trogs, more deserving of her charity.

"An hour a day with the trogs won't take anything away from the children," she said. There was something steely in her voice that made him realize she'd already made up her mind. Things were moving too quickly for him. His father was dead. The Masks ambushed. The tent city attacked. But there was no time to stop and become emotional about it. Things pushed ahead. He had to fit himself to the pace of events rolling across them. But if there were one thing he could control, it would be keeping Jenny with him, keeping all of the closeness they'd forged in the last few days.

He wanted to protest, scrubbing a hand across his bristly face. He had just started to form the words when a sharp rap on the door brought him up short. He nearly roared with frustration, his fingers unintentionally tightening on Jenny's hip. Was he never again going to have an uninterrupted thought? Then he laughed sourly that this was the fate that Lady Lutra had apparently prepared for him . . . But, lucky. That's truly what he was. Maybe even more so than Ott, that lucky bastard. He loosened his grip on Jenny and stroked his fingers along the side of her dress. He would never curse his luck again because of her.

"Come in," he called in a relatively collected manner, and it was the wrinkled face of his new favorite aged houseman who looked in the doorway.

"Thank God you're here," the old man said, his eyes and mouth puckered with anxiety. Jenny slid from Rob's lap, but he grabbed her warm hand before she could move too far away.

"What's happened?" Rob asked, gesturing for him to come in.

"You're being taken before the council of advisors for murdering your father," he said bluntly, his sharp cheekbones working in distress. Jenny let out a sharp cry of anger. The old man continued, "I came here as soon as I heard. I wanted you to know it from me. They have cleared out a portion of the old cellar. They are constructing a jail cell. And they are going to hold you there."

Blood rushed through Rob's body into his head. He could barely hear the rest of what the old man was saying through the pounding in his ears. His vision narrowed and he thought he might pass out. He couldn't feel Jenny's warm hand in his anymore. The room was spinning away. He was going back to the cellar. The same dank dungeon where his father had strapped him to a post and whipped him countless times. The same dark place where he'd sat bleeding, passing in and out of awareness as his lash marks wept and ran to pus. The same hard-packed dirt floor where he had subsisted on water and bread, feverish, until Col Rob thought him sufficiently hardened. Col Rob was dead, but whatever sadistic lessons he had in mind for Rob were still in play. Even cold and lifeless with no beat in his heart, no pulse in his veins, the old man would not die.

CHAPTER 74

If it weren't for Ott, I would be dead, Mel realized.

A thousand terrible things might have come to pass. She could have been brutally abused by a trog underground, impregnated, and fated to die during childbirth. She could have been shot through with arrows in the mine like her parents. She stifled a sob when her thoughts drifted to them. She couldn't believe that she was never going to see them again. She wanted to turn back time, if only to ask them why they left her. Her father should have known. Was he not a seer? Why hadn't he seen that this would come to pass? She shoved the thoughts away before they overcame her with grief.

Even if she could turn back the hours, she could have died before then in the attack on the Keep. Without Ott, she could have been killed by that very first trog who took her from the carriage that day outside of Cillary. She could never have met him and could have returned to the Mask settlement never having met him. She could have lived out her entire life at the settlement. Without Ott, she could have died a slow death *just for lack of living a life*.

She and Ott had reached their room, and he closed the door behind them. The savory smell of him enveloped her as the door sealed the drafts of the hallway outside. They had food with them, so there were warm food smells, too. He had insisted on visiting the kitchen first, where he found something for them to eat. She was moving in an exhausted, dreamlike state. They brought the food with them to their room and now ate it quietly at the small table near the fireplace.

They sat across the table from each other eating silently, slowly, neither with much appetite, ingesting automatically. She wanted to say something to Ott, but words weren't forming in her mind; none could come out. She speculated in a detached manner that it was such a false, unnatural practice—saying everything a person was thinking and feeling instead of suppressing the emotion, mulling over it, analyzing what it meant in the greater context of her role as an observer, as an impartial outsider. As much as she wanted to be a normal woman in a marriage with the man she loved, this was all new to her.

She didn't want to be a Mask, but she didn't know how to be much else other than what her instinct told her. She knew Mask code of conduct. She knew what her mother would have done or said. And she realized with a start how much her mother must have loved Ley'Albaer. Passionate, romantic, unrequited love, perhaps her entire life.

Mel was bone-tired from removing the agamite from the trog in the cellar and from meeting with Rob. That had been nearly as exhausting as *pushing* agamite. In the private chamber earlier, she had tried to use Mask-taught skill to ascertain Rob's motives and goals. And failed. Instead, she ended up making him suspicious and wary of her. She never should have tried anything in her depleted state. Even her judgment was bad. She should have learned by now that the proximity of the trogs, and of Ott himself, made her self-control poor and her senses unpredictable. She was no good as a Mask.

I should know that by now.

But at least she had found a skill she was good at. Pushing the agamite. Controlling it. Manipulating it. Finally, she had purpose. She found her mind wandering back to the conversation she'd had with Jenks—Guyse, her natural father—back in his small cabin outside the Mask settlement, the day she'd run through the forest helplessly, out of control, thinking that she would never see Ott again. She and Jenks had talked about finding true purpose, finding what they each were meant for, if not for serving as Masks. Maybe serving the trogs who required her to manipulate their agamite was her real purpose.

Never mind the trogs' fascinating history. She would have to learn their signing language faster than she already was. She wanted to be able to converse directly with Bookman instead of using Rav, who was adjusting to the harsh northern climate as stoically as a native, as a partial interpreter. Maybe she could convince Bookman to let her inscribe their history . . .

Ott cleared his throat. She hadn't truly noticed till then that he was only picking at his food. At the rate he was increasing in size, he should have been inhaling the cured meat and smoked cheese. He abruptly pushed his chair away from the table, jostling their makeshift meal and cups with his long legs. No matter how it changed in scale, his body was still his body, familiar to her in a way imprinted on her mind, the feel of the skin on his belly, the smoothness of the side of his neck, but it was also new.

There was undeniably more of him. She felt stupid and dreamy, enjoying that there was more of him to love, but she was also sorry to have been the one who changed him. However the agamite had gotten into him—she would figure it out somehow, someday. But what she felt the most at fault for was that she, Mel, had been the one to stir it up inside him. It was entirely her fault that he'd gotten bigger. She had *changed* him when he hadn't needed to be changed.

He had expanded in her mind as well; he meant so much more to her now, and more every moment. He took over her thoughts just by being near her. A part of her focused entirely on him and nothing else. He consumed her attention and held onto her thoughts like an obsession. She tried to pretend indifference just to reach a state of affection tolerable enough that he wouldn't be afraid of her. She could easily overwhelm him with her need, with neediness enough to make him cringe away. Where was the balance in a normal relationship? She moved her eyes carefully away from him while he spoke.

"I won't hold you to it," he said. At her frown of confusion, he clarified for her, "The marriage. My proposal."

Surprise stunned her into a deeper silence as she scrabbled for words. The proposal had completely slipped her mind, but not for the reason he assumed. *He thought she didn't love him.*

It wasn't obvious to him? That was the real shock—that she had to reassure him of what she already knew and took for granted. One look at his face made it clear that her silence was a death sentence for him. Every second more she hesitated was another hellish eternity that he thought they had nothing between them. She took a breath, running a finger around the edge of her knife nervously, trying to find the correct words. She wanted to say out loud everything running through her mind though it nearly choked her to do so. Externalizing the interior narrative of her mind ran opposite everything she'd been taught and trained to do. But she was not a Mask, she told herself.

"I completely forgot about your proposal," she said. *Oh. Wrong thing to say.* He looked briefly like he was going to vomit, so she hurried on, "But only because I considered it done. I feel . . . I feel already joined with you, already married to you."

Now he was frowning, his wind-burned face showing first a total wash of color, then pallor, then flush again. She was glad he was sitting in a chair. Slumped, actually, like he was nursing a stomach pain. He looked completely overcome, twisted up with anxiety incongruous with his huge body, legs sprawled out under the table, enormous feet crossed at the ankles. She was startled into just beginning to comprehend the depth of his sensitivity, his insecurity.

How can I convince him otherwise? She didn't know, but she was willing to keep trying.

He said, "You never actually said yes, you know. I thought you might want to go . . . home. Wherever that is. Back to the Mask place. Now that your parents are gone. I'll help you get there, if you want to go."

He flinched when her eyes swam with tears. He was suddenly on his knees on the rug in front of her chair. She didn't bother to stop the moisture running down her face though it alarmed him. Tears were a normal reaction, she reassured herself, trying to stay objective and not fall apart completely. Then again, she couldn't stop them. She hadn't cried since she was a child. Now she was a wreck, an emotional eruption waiting to happen. The slightest thing could set her off. But she was not a Mask, so she allowed herself to cry and allowed herself to feel the warmth of Ott's arms wrapped around her as he knelt on the floor in front of her chair. He smelled so very, very good.

She said, with her mouth on his hair, "You don't understand. My home is wherever you are. Sometimes the need to be near you is so overwhelming, I'm afraid I might lose control of myself. All my life, I've been in control. I've hidden my feelings. I've suppressed my natural inclination to love, to feel, to express my emotions, whether they be joy or sadness, sorrow or pain. I don't know what's right, what's normal. I don't know what I'm supposed to do. Please, be patient with me while I learn. Because you make me want to learn, to discover what I was meant to do. I promise I will make it worth your while," she said.

He didn't move, so she thought he might not have understood her. She said it again, "My home is wherever you are," and his big arms tightened around her till she had trouble breathing. He eased up, but it didn't matter. She could never be stifled by him, by the scent of him on her skin, mingling in her hair, and on her clothes. She could carry the smell of him with her wherever she went and be reminded that she belonged to him, and likewise he belonged to her.

CHAPTER 75

Why now? Rob wondered as he sat in the dark on the cellar floor.

Why did fate strike him down now when he had so much to lose? Jenny. Her kids. Love . . . something he'd never felt for most of his own kin. But now, once again, the rug had been pulled out from under him. Just when he had begun to believe in something . . . even the smallest, most minute amount—brutal attacks, a small city of homeless citizens to worry about, and even Harro missing at the last report, threatened his sanity.

And where *was* Harro? Where had the stableman gone? Had he been ambushed? Dragged underground at the last? Charl had confirmed seeing him in the tent city when the trogs retreated. Rob himself had seen Harro in his own dead father's bedchamber, but Harro had since disappeared. Would he turn up before the harshest winds of winter blew or simply be assumed dead? Rob shook his head. Just another sign that things were falling apart around him.

So much for good luck—that nonsense was only for Ott. Rob had fooled himself into thinking things had been looking up. In fact, all that had changed was that he'd mistakenly thought he'd been granted a chance at a future with Jenny and that maybe she could be persuaded, over time, to love him. His bliss had clouded his mind and made him view everything through a glass the color of happiness . . . Happy?

He couldn't remember ever having been happy here in the big house. The only time and place he'd come close to contentment was out on the trail with Ott. Sleeping across the campfire from his friend, back to the ground, and stomach to the stars, his worries had been wrung into peaceful submission at the end of each day. Now, that was a feeling to recall in times of need.

Like now, he thought.

Or not, he corrected.

He frowned, trying to figure out what was wrong with him. The cold, hard-packed dirt floor of the cellar didn't bother him. It was oddly comforting in its familiarity. He'd been having flashbacks on and off the whole night long; memories of himself as a cold, scared boy tied to the lashing pole were bested by the warmth of the richer clothes he wore today. He should have felt as if he were trapped in a childhood nightmare. Except he was fully an adult now. Dressed warmly. Loved by someone.

He snorted, but the sound was drowned out by the shuffle of the trogs. He could hear them breathing. The trogs were in the cellar with him, on the opposite side of the cellar from him, but he could hear them and smell their gamey odor. Gods, did they sleep standing up? Did they have cloven feet? He couldn't see them. He knew they communicated with each other through hand signals. He wondered if being forced into darkness for the night drove them insane with frustration. He found himself wondering and wanting to ask them.

He listened carefully to them for a while but soon their sounds faded into nothing. They were sleeping.

Damn, the truth was odd. He didn't know what to make of it: he was content. He had been thrown in a dungeon, but he was actually as cheerful as a kid on the first warm day after a long winter indoors. Except the warmth was inside his chest. *In his heart and mind.* If this were love, and he were in a fool's state of bliss, he'd take it any day over the loneliness that paved the rest of his life up until now.

But his life before Jenny wasn't worth dwelling on. Now he was incapable of thinking beyond the minute, moments neither prior nor subsequent. Maybe that was the secret to Ott's infernal good luck. His unflagging, annoyingly buoyant optimism. Belief in the good of the common man. Brotherly—and sisterly and wifely and husbandly—love. A smile split Rob's face as he sat cross-legged in the dark on the floor of his cell.

CHAPTER 76

In late morning, the judgment council assembled. Marget the housemaid had secured a standing spot toward the back. The old advisors had chosen to use the great hall, as over-crowded as it was, and forced its temporary tenants to pile their belongings to one side of the room in a great, disheveled heap, evoking poorly-suppressed grumbling and a few rude hand gestures. As a conciliatory nod, the people were invited to stand witness to trial, and a good many people stayed to hear it. Bodies crushed against Marget, and someone grabbed a rough handful of her backside. She smacked the offending paw away without bothering to see who it was.

Minutes later, hundreds of eyes focused on the front of the room as burly guards, erstwhile stable hands, escorted in the young master Rob. Animal handlers turned into wardens. Miners turned into soldiers. People were falling out of the roles that had identified them their whole lives. Marget wondered what Lady Lutra had next in mind for them.

Rob was put in a chair toward the front of the room. Then the council members filed in. Old men, all of them, and dressed in their dark purples, reds, and goldenrod, necks stiff with ceremony and self-importance. More than a few observers' mouths puckered in disapproval. Most of them would take Rob over the whole council put together. *Any day, and that was Dovay's truth.* Even Marget was willing to bet her next turn in the soaking tub that the people around her would stand up for Rob, too.

The old men arranged themselves in the big chairs on the wooden dais. They took their time settling, speaking among themselves as if they didn't have so many eyes following them. Marget watched their sunken cheeks puff in and out like the bellows of fireplaces that spewed pointless words instead of smoke. Wispy hair near to falling out. They were a group of men patterned in the likeness of old Col Rob himself. Eventually a hush fell over the spectators, and then the silence swept over her in a wave until it caught hold of the whole room.

Marget craned her neck but didn't see handsome Ott anywhere. She was surprised he wasn't there standing by his friend. If anything could be said about Ott, other than his near-heart-stopping face and the casual way he had of trampling on a girl's heart, it was that he was unfailingly loyal to those who were fortunate enough to be loved by him. A very small set of people, from what Marget had observed, and she'd observed him for most of her life. She sighed.

At that moment, while she was on her toes, craning her neck for a better view, a hand shoved her in the small of her back. She was pushed off balance, which made her to jostle the person in front of her. When she turned back from shooting a dirty look at the person behind her, she was just in time to catch the glare from the person into whom she had inadvertently shoved herself.

"Sorry," Marget muttered and threaded her way out of the crowd toward the doorway. She'd had enough of the crowd, and it felt a little like the room was getting too hot for the crush of people in it. Made her feel a little dizzy and sick to her stomach. She made it to the entryway and spied Charl leaning against the wall.

Now, there was an attractive fellow. Blond. Taller than her by a head. Yet broad, too. He hadn't always been this way. No, this magical transformation had happened within the last couple years, probably when she hadn't been bothered to notice him. He was a good three years younger than her, so she'd been shocked to look at him lately and see nothing of the thin boy she'd often eaten dinner with in the kitchens. Before, she'd had eyes for no one but Ott.

Charl cast a glance her direction. His eyes were serious, and she felt a curious thrill run through her. He was refined and intellectual, and looking at her speculatively. Then she remembered . . . Charl was Col Rob's valet-in-training, his errand boy, his protégé. It was rumored that he had once defeated Col Rob at that dull table game they always played. The other housemaids found him cool and achingly unattainable.

Marget realized with a start that Charl had been for all intents and purposes raised by Col Rob. He was in attendance here in the great hall to see Rob found guilty and exiled—Rob wouldn't be killed for punishment. In these parts, a convict was forced to leave the region, to walk out with no belongings, in the dead of winter. Death, surely, but not considered execution by the council. It was called *taking a walk in winter*. An old-time practice that kept crime at a minimum and left the guilty to the merciless elements. It let the land do the killing so no one had actual blood on his hands.

In the coldest parts of winter, it was said that death came so quickly there was no pain. The worst time to serve out a punishment had to be in the earliest and latest parts of the season, when death was a slow and drawn-out business—when the bodies of the convicted were later discovered all the way down south, so very close to the port city before they had surrendered to exposure. During those times, the convicts sometimes chose to walk further north into the even colder, harsher cliffs, having admitted their guilt and accepted their crimes. They chose not to tempt themselves with hope by heading south. They knew what was in store for them and chose to accept it. *That's what I'd do, if it was me.*

Marget knew Charl was here to see Rob punished. Nonetheless, she approached him, unable to keep the long-studied flirtatiousness out of her glance as she leaned against the wall next to him, mimicking his posture. She'd often been told her eyes were her best feature, that they had great quantities of glitter and depth to them. Usually such compliments were punctuated with stolen kisses, but still, she was inclined to believe the flattery. She flicked a glance out of the corner of her eye at Charl, and found that he was watching her instead of the parade of ancient crusties in front of them.

"I'm sorry to hear about your father," she murmured, then was sorry that she mentioned it when Charl stiffened up. Word had spread through the great house that Charl's father Haught had been killed in a trog ambush at the mines, and that the Masks had also been killed. Marget had lost her own parents at a very young age, before she even knew them really. She didn't have memories of anyone other than the house staff who had taken her in. Nan in the kitchen. All of them were like family, so she didn't feel sorry for herself.

Before he could respond, the doors next to them burst open and Ott walked in. No, not really walked. He was kind of prowling, crouched low, ready to spring, much like a bear, Marget thought, although she'd never seen a bear attacking. The only one she'd ever come up close to had been a tired old thing in a traveling menagerie that she'd seen as a child. Marget's eyes fixed on Ott now in wonderment. She thought she heard a derisive snort from Charl, but she was amazed by the sight. After Ott came Mel, the woman who used to be a Mask but now was not. Then gasps rippled through the crowd, because flanking Ott and Mel were a dozen or so of the trogs, close enough to brush against her arm.

Charl reached out a thick arm and shoved Marget behind him protectively. As much as she appreciated the gesture, she found herself yet again being blocked from a good view. She leaned to the side just in time to see Ott and his entourage position themselves around the young master Rob. Like a king surrounded by his guard. It was thrilling to behold, momentous, like she was witnessing a change about which she would one day tell her children. She took a deep breath and she could feel the waves of . . . something . . . irritation . . . coming off Charl's back, off his skin where she was now gripping his arm trying to pull it away from where it obstructed her line of vision.

"Would you let me see?" she whispered fiercely into the back of his shirt. In a single, fluid move, he tucked her under his arm in front of him, so she was pressed with her back against his chest. He'd deemed it safe enough for her to stand in front of him. Then she realized belatedly that all the exciting things were now happening off to their right. Charl's body was still mostly between her and what interested her. She was annoyed. Though he felt nice. Until his fingers covered her mouth, effectively shushing her. She huffed, but found she didn't really mind his hand. It wasn't painful or constricting, just firm. And also, she wanted to hear what was being said, so she stopped squirming against him, although she found herself in an uncomfortable sweat from being a little too close to him. When she looked at him sideways, he was coolly observing the action ahead of them. She resolved to behave similarly and fixed her eyes on Ott and Rob.

"You have no proof against this man," Ott was shouting. It didn't sound at all like his voice to Marget. It had more of an outraged snarl to it. And gods, it was louder than she'd ever heard him speak. His voice penetrated right through the noise of the crowded hall. It didn't sound like the voice she knew, the voice that had at times made her sigh with longing when she was supposed to be fast asleep in the women's quarters.

"You will not proceed against him," Ott said, this time backing closer to Rob, putting himself between Rob and the house guards who had escorted him in. The trogs faced outward in a ring around them. And the woman Mel was standing amongst them looking icy-cold and inhuman,

Marget thought. There was something not right about that woman. Marget had seen her on the first day the Masks had arrived at the great house. And now two of the Masks were dead. She'd heard rumors that Ott had taken Mel to his bed, but it was hard to believe. Of all the women he could have had, this one was surely icy and distant. Something about the way light shimmered around her made Marget a little queasy. Did no one else see it? No wonder people hated Masks. They were deathlike without their strange garb.

The house guards looked at the council members for guidance and with great uncertainty. Each one of them shifted in his boots with clear indecision. Most of them had known Rob his whole life. Most were his age or younger. But one thing was for sure, if she had been in any of their shoes, she would not have hesitated a minute before poking her spear toward the old bastards judging them from their high and might chairs.

For a minute, it looked certain that there would be bloodshed. The collective breath of the room was drawn. Many of them lusted for it, she could sense, which made her want to inch toward the door. But those people—any of them with an ounce of self-preservation —knew that they didn't want to be trapped in the same room as a group of angry trogs and a man accused of being a usurper.

One of the councilmen had risen gingerly and was now returning shouts. "He will pay for his offenses upon this house," the old man rasped, his bony finger pointed in the air. The crowd reacted with simmering anger. Marget's heart pounded and she eyed the doorway again. She was a second from fleeing as fast and as far as she could. But, still, she couldn't tear her eyes away. And the warmth of Charl at her back bolstered her. He no longer restrained her, now it was more of . . . an embrace. She wasn't entirely sure how she felt about that.

Another old man had joined the first on his feet, their rich robes doubly imposing from their elevation on the dais. Marget wasn't too impressed. She could have knocked him over with her skirts. But then the first real jostling started in the crowd. Someone threw a shoe toward the front of the room, but the throw was bad, and Marget couldn't tell if it had been meant to hit the men on the stage or Rob and his followers. This was a bad place to be. She now was a hair's breadth away from springing through the door and pulling Charl with her. If there was going to be a brawl, people would press toward the door. She wanted to be the first ones out;

otherwise they might never make it out. If there was a stampede, they could be crushed.

Rob had risen to his feet now, and the old men panicked and gesticulated with a mixture of fear and anger toward the house guards to restrain him. Several other members of the judgment council stood up in outrage; they would not allow anyone to demonstrate such disrespectful behavior toward them. No one could, Marget realized, or else their poorly constructed facade of authority would crumble into dust.

When a house guard put a meaty hand on Rob's shoulder—whether to push him back down into his seat or to spin him for a face-first punch, they would never know—Ott pinned the guard to the floor. Marget gasped at the quickness of the attack. One minute Ott was in front of Rob and the very next, he had pounced on the guard, his face pressed against the terrified man's, a snarl distorting Ott's face.

More guards moved to help their fallen comrade, but the defensive positioning of the trogs halted them in their tracks. The presence of the trogs, however, was not enough to tamp down the anxiety of the crowd, and a surge from the back of the room traveled forward until the frantic front rows of onlookers were pushed toward the trogs. And though the trogs did nothing to threaten the crowd, several shrieks of dismay and fear came from the people. Hands flew forward to keep bodies away, but ended up flailing against trog skin.

Marget's fingers dug into Charl's arm. She hadn't noticed earlier, but his hand had slipped off her mouth and was now gripping her tightly across the front of her shoulders. Then the doors of the great hall banged open, and a cold wind buffeted Marget's skirts. The air traveled through the room, freezing each body in mid-action. Surprised faces turned toward the sound. A man stood in the doorway, and Marget recognized him as Guyse, the dark, glowering guard who had arrived with the Masks. His thick eyebrows were drawn down in a scowl. He had an air of the mystical about him, like a lightning ball surrounding his head. Marget's mouth dropped open. This man's anger had caused the rush of cold air, his frozen fury rushing into the hall ahead of him.

He addressed the council on the dais and the crowded room at once, though Marget wasn't sure how. His voice carried easily, as if he were standing next to her. Magic of some sort, it had to be. She had always been a firm believer in it. There was small evidence of it in everyday life, but this . . . this was an occurrence that she would never forget. It was confirmation of something she'd always wanted to believe. And she wanted to know more.

"This man," Guyse said as he pointed at Rob, "is innocent of this crime."

A high noise of protest came from the woman Mel. Marget looked at her curiously. Otherwise, the room had fallen astonishingly silent for the large number of people crammed in it.

A council member pushed his way to the front of the dais where some of them had stood grouped together, taking strength from numbers and elevation. With his wrinkled, clenched hands, he pushed the other robes aside and said irritably, "What do you know about it? And who are you to speak for him?"

Guyse paused and looked around. He met eyes with Mel, who had suddenly gone deathly pale. For a minute, Marget detected something soft and vulnerable in the woman. As tall and beautiful as she was, as steely and unapproachable as Marget found her, perhaps she was human under that façade. She was someone's daughter. She was Ott's mate. Marget considered her with a renewed curiosity. Just now, an errant ray of sun broke through the gray clouds visible in the high windows above and shined like a halo around the crown of her head.

Gods, she looked like a queen.

Guyse said, "I am the killer."

CHAPTER 77

Mel heard Guyse's words, but she couldn't comprehend them.

She had been prepared to help fight for Rob's freedom, to liberate him from imprisonment whether or not he had killed his father. She honestly didn't care. The old man, Col Rob, had been a horrible manipulator, and she had been suspicious of and repulsed by him at first glance. She didn't doubt he'd committed unspeakable acts against numerous people in the course of his lifetime. And she didn't need physical evidence—it had been etched in his face. Her mother had known it. Her father had known it. But what separated them from her was that they hadn't assigned guilt in that particular matter. No, they had been called into attendance by Col Rob to mediate a truce with the trogs. And in neglecting to acknowledge Col Rob's motives, her parents had gotten themselves murdered. Mel didn't care who had killed the man. All she cared was that justice had been done.

And that, she thought sourly, *was what disqualifies me from being a Mask.* As if she had any further doubt.

The room had fallen silent again. Guyse had confessed. He relayed the details of the murder with precision. So much so, in fact, that the guards were releasing Rob from his restraints.

Wait, wait, wait.

Guyse had murdered Col Rob? In his bedchamber. She heard his voice confessing to making the cut marks in the old man's gut. He told them how the old man had looked when he left him bleeding out into his lap rug. He described the dagger that he'd used. And then Guyse had said in a low voice, "I am the one you want. I killed him."

And Mel recalled that a sound had escaped her throat. She had been listening and paying attention and absorbing every little detail. Even though he stood there as Guyse, she could not help but think of him as Jenks. Twinkling blue eyes and a ready smile. Yes, he looked and acted like Guyse now. But he was her father. And he had taken a life.

And now her only living blood relative was going to be exiled. No one, not even a Mask, could survive their so-called walk in winter, their death-sentence of an exile.

She stifled a sob as Guyse let himself be led away by the same guards who had been restraining Rob. He was taken away without a glance in her direction. He had to know she was standing there, shell shocked and watching him. She knew because she could feel him—his even heartbeat, his lack of perspiration, his resolution.

Before the room began to empty, Mel found herself flanked on one side by Ott and Rob on the other. They led her out past the frozen faces of the house maid and an angry young man whose face looked as if justice had been denied. And Mel wasn't sure whether it had or not. All she felt was loss.

Within a few minutes, she found herself sitting in Ott's lap in the cradle of his embrace, numb to it. They were in Rob's private chamber where Jenny had been waiting for news of their failure or success at freeing Rob. Their initial embrace was so intimate that Mel had averted her eyes. Ott hadn't seemed to notice. He was holding her tightly like she might float away and he was kneading her fingers like she'd been out in the cold. And maybe she had. She couldn't feel a thing.

Guyse. Her last living blood relative. Her natural father. And she would never see him again. The reality of her parents' deaths compounded with Guyse's confession threatened to overwhelm her. She *was* adrift, in danger of losing her grip on herself and allowing her mind to sever itself from her body. The trogs were unimportant. Her friend Rav would be safe in the hands of the midwives here at the great house. Jenny and Rob had each other.

Ott's fingers pressed hers again and again. He squeezed her fingertips and released them. Pressed the blood back into them. Gradually, she felt the gentle insistence of his arms around her, pulling her back to him.

He said softly into the back of her neck, "I can't go into your mind and rescue you from the river of blackness. I can't do that like you did for me. All I can do is ask you to stay here with me." When she said nothing, he pressed her again, "Can you do that? Stay with me?"

He breathed again into the back of her neck and that familiar scent of him feathered itself through her hair and brushed up into her face, filling her nose, her mouth, going into her throat and down into herself, reminding her that he was part of her. He was the reason she knew she was more than just a Mask. He was her reason.

She twisted in his lap and put her arms around his neck. She put her cheek against his chest and held him as tightly as he held her.

He said, "Let's go home."

CHAPTER 78

As Mel and Ott trudged through the half-foot of snow that had fallen overnight, she realized what he was doing—distracting her from thinking about Guyse's departure from the big house. She knew that right about now, guards would be leading Guyse off the house's grounds. They would escort him a few miles away and leave him there to make the rest of the way on foot without food or water. Taking a walk in winter.

She and Ott were bundled up, pulling a light sled of supplies behind them. Just a few provisions—food for the day, water, blankets, and a little firewood. He said he didn't think there'd be anything left at his sister's former house, and the look on his face said he had his doubts the house itself would still be standing. The area was rife with looters, displaced miners and trogs, foraging for food and whatever wasn't nailed down.

It took them a couple hours to reach the little house, which was still there despite his earlier misgivings. A walk that would take normally less than an hour in clear weather now worked their legs until she started to feel fatigue in the muscles. Though her face was cold, she enjoyed the warmth of her heavy coat and hood. The gate was unlatched and braced back by a drift of snow. To Mel's eyes, the house looked empty, but unscathed, nearly the same as before. Ott, however, tsked as he inspected the railing on the front porch. He ran his hand over the door. She saw scratches, but they weren't bad, and at least the door was shut. He went in cautiously, checking for squatters, but the house was empty.

The kitchen had a broken window, and there were two more shattered in the back room, but the damage was minimal because the winds had been coming from the north and that wall was sheltered. The bulk of the winter was still ahead of them, so while the house would do for the night, it was still uninhabitable. Mel listened to the melodic rumble of Ott's voice as he said the best thing to do would be to board up the spaces, and then come back in the spring to repair it. She worked on starting a fire in the fireplace while he scouted around for planks that weren't too frozen to board up the windows.

In another hour's time, they had the three windows closed up enough that the heat stayed in the room. It was still drafty, but it would do for the night. The blankets had been long ago stripped from the beds, but they had brought some with them on the pull-sled, and Ott's favorite old chair was still there—it was probably too heavy for anyone to drag out and too bedraggled to capture anyone's attention. Ott shoved it close to the fire and sat down heavily, coaxing her to squeeze into it with him. The chair creaked when she sat. She didn't add much weight, but his bulk had increased substantially along with his height. The chair was a tight fit, but it was warm, and she savored being close to him.

For the first time in a long time, she allowed herself to seek him out, using her heightened sensitivity to try to read him. Just as she knew she would, she felt anxiety—that was ever-present in him, though few could ever guess it—but she also found hope and contentment in the solid rhythm of his heart, the sound of his breathing, and in his scent, that aromatic beacon that had entranced her from the beginning. He shifted her on his lap so he could spread out his shoulders better across the back of the chair. She laid the back of her head against his chest so they were both staring at the ceiling, her temple tucked against the side of his chin. For her, it was like sitting in a living, breathing chair, an embrace made of Ott.

"What do you think?" he said, lightly running a hand down her breastbone to her navel where he stretched his fingers out across her abdomen. Warmth curled across her midsection.

She stayed deliberately obtuse. She knew he was asking a bigger question than the one she pretended to hear. "About the house? Cozy. It's good for the warm seasons, but I think we should move back to the big house at wintertime." She was thinking ahead to next year, to the year after that, and more. His hand froze where it had been stroking her belly.

She half-expected another proposal of marriage, which he'd never repeated since that day. Maybe he never would. In some ways, she would be glad if he never did because it brought up the bittersweet memory of her parents and Guyse all in the sitting room, staring at him in amused surprise when he'd introduced himself to them. Instead, he said, "You *like* this house?"

She could feel him waiting very carefully for her answer. It mattered to him for some reason, so she thought about it before she spoke. "I like having our own place separate from them." They both knew what *them* meant—it was all of them at the other house, the trogs, Rob and Jenny, the tenants, the children, the household staff, other people, other eyes . . . no one to observe them, to force her to watch her behavior, to force either of them to please others. They could just . . . be themselves.

She twisted in his arms, feeling the immediate effect that her body had on his. She wedged a knee on either side of his hips and rose over him, stripping off her coat. His hands were on her hips slowly moving upward. She crossed her arms over her front, reaching for the bottom of her shirt.

"Don't," he said. "It's too cold in here."

She gave a wry smile, "Enjoy this. I don't need to feel the cold, remember?" And she lifted her many layers off at once and swept them off her arm. She rose above him again and shook out her hair, fanning her fingers through it. She used the flicker of the fireplace light behind her to weave through her hair, shifting it slightly so he could see the catch of gold in the strands. She used the light to catch the sides of her body, to accentuate the tapering down to her waist and the flare of her hips. She used the shadow to tuck the lines into the sides of her belly and the dip of her navel. She moved her blood and felt the push of it toward the surface of her body, to a flush on her breastbone, to other places that drew his eyes.

She watched his pupils dilate and his breathing become more rapid. He said an oath under his breath as he stared at her with open, unadulterated lust and admiration. Arousal overtook the usual expression of respect and love he wore when he looked at her. A look of fleeting panic crossed his face. He wriggled uncomfortably, and she saw him struggle to push her way, yet keep his hands where they were tightly gripping her hips.

"I can't control it," he said. "My . . . anger, the battle fury. It's happening right now. I'm starting to see the red in my vision. This is what happens. You have to get away from me or I might hurt you." But she partnered up with his desire and overruled him.

"No," she said. "It's not battle fury. It's passion. Let it go. You can't hurt me. I can be as strong as you." And when he froze again, she goaded him, "Do it."

She wouldn't let him shove her away. He struggled a minute longer to rein himself in and when he thought he was starting to get himself under control, she pushed him again. She arched above him, and he groaned, his body straining to get at her.

He panted. His eyes drank her in. With her hands on his shoulders, she leaned toward him and saw herself reflected in his eyes. She saw her eyes bright with unmitigated desire.

Almost quicker than she could follow, he lifted her off him and shifted them both in the chair so he loomed over her larger than the light behind him, larger than life, filling her vision and her mind. The chair groaned beneath them. He struggled with his balance, trying to hold his weight over her, and he swore as he fumbled. The chair creaked again and the back collapsed halfway to the floor. They froze, but only for a split second.

He kissed her roughly, his eyes unfocused and glazed over with what she now recognized as his fury. Pleasurable tension swept over her and turned off all thought. She felt only joy, happiness, and love. He leaned down again and, this time, pressed her lips gently, his eyes clear and catching firelight.

EPILOGUE

By the time spring arrived that year, the displaced people were more than ready to leave the big house and to return to their homes, although a few stayed to work on construction. Some had discovered they had skill in building and approached it with great enthusiasm. Col Rob's old suite was demolished and converted for other purposes—a study room for one, and they were changing the rooms on the opposite side of the hall into rooms for Rob and Jenny and the children; the mute girl Amber, the sole girl among the six of the children, already needed a place to get away from the boys.

Mel picked her way through the new spaces, avoiding debris, and tried to imagine what it would look like after it was complete. The amount of summer sunlight filtering down into the rooms was going to be wondrous. Seeing new things being built made her wonder if Cillary Keep would be restored one day. Would there ever be another season at the Keep?

She had met with Bookman and Rav earlier to continue working on their project recording what they knew of the history of the trogs. They'd only begun to delve into the stories that Bookman knew, and now that he could speak with his transformed human throat, it was going a lot quicker. Luckily. Because their baby, already late, was going to arrive any time and soon they wouldn't be able to work this quickly. The name Bookman had stuck with the poor man, though most people shortened it to Book. She still wasn't used to the way he looked now, with his pale skin and dark sweep of hair, but his eyes held the same intelligence as before and he had a solemn way of speaking that encouraged trust.

For now, Mel had other things on her mind. Earlier that morning, a trio of trogs had arrived at the doorstep of the great house. They were unarmed and non-threatening and they'd asked through hand signals to be taken in and converted into their human forms. As agreed by earlier decree, Rob let them enter.

Now trogs who wished to be cleansed were housed in the now-vacant great hall where Mel saw them daily. She had a partitioned corner of the room where she worked on them one at a time, cleansing them. The first two conversions had gone well, and they both had emerged from the treatment looking pale-skinned, tall, and striking, with throats that croaked in hoarse, hesitant voices. The third was more problematic.

At first, he seemed nervous and had gestured for the two others to go through the process before him. Now he was pacing the floor of the meeting room, its fine polished wood floor incongruous under his thick-hided feet. Mel was used to their odor now. She hardly even noticed it and suspected that it was on her clothes at the end of the day. Ott never complained.

But this trog in front now of her was clearly unsettled. "It's all right," she said soothingly. "The process won't injure you." At least, it wouldn't hurt. She still wasn't exactly sure if harm was something she'd care to quantify in changing a trog into a human. She still wasn't sure if it was the correct thing to do . . . the ones who wanted to be changed did it by choice. It wasn't a requirement of the trogs if they chose to live aboveground at the big house. All that Rob required was an oath of fealty, and that could be given in either form, human or trog. *Defend the house. Defend the people and their right to live.* That was all he required.

Mel speculated that the trog with her now was at odds about his identity. If he chose to transition to human form, would he still be himself? Trogs were nearly impossible for her to read, so she was guessing entirely. She stood still, and then patiently gestured for him to follow her behind the partition. She sat on the cot and patted the place next to her so he would sit. She'd stopped using a translator with the trogs, even the newly arrived trogs. Her signing repertoire was getting better, though she was far from fluent. Nonetheless, she began signing to him that he might lie down on the cot to make himself comfortable and to try to relax.

She carefully avoided standing as she shifted herself to a nearby chair. She didn't want to threaten him or make him feel submissive, though he was much larger than she was. When he was prone, she began telling him the basic ideas of what she would be doing, moving the agamite out of his body—gently—and what he might feel during the process. Some of the men, after they were able to speak a little, had reported feeling a little dizziness during the process. Some felt a heated flush throughout the body. Most felt the overwhelming urge to sleep after the process was complete, as Mel often felt herself. She still could attend to only a few of them per day and had to retire to her room to go to bed afterward. Ott always knew when she would be seeing a trog and came to check on her later.

"So when you're ready and if you feel comfortable with this," Mel began in her healer's voice, but the trog suddenly shot up into a sitting position and held up a giant hand telling her to stop. She waited, eyes wide in surprise, watching him. He rubbed his hand across his forehead in a very human gesture, and then peeked at her from under the hand.

She saw a glint of blue. *Blue?*

The eyes flashed blue, and then the lines of the trog's face wavered. The body shrank and grew shorter. More adjustments. The skin softened, and white hair feathered out from the top of the head. Then Jenks stood up from the cot in front of her.

Mel gave a gasp and flung herself at him, hugging him in a tight embrace. His body stiffened in surprise, and then he hugged her back. He chuckled and cleared his throat, which sounded raspy from lack of use.

"You might have been surprised had you looked inside me and found no agamite to push," he said, trying to lighten the mood.

She didn't care that he had cheated their system of justice using his Mask-given talents to shift and to hide among the trogs. All she cared was that she had been given one more chance to embrace someone of her blood, someone who had loved her mother and father as much as she had. She didn't know if she loved him by choice, or if biology and her nature required her to do so, but she did love him. And she knew that love itself is what she had in common with him, the ability to feel—and to feel deeply.

She couldn't speak, as overwhelmed as she was. He held her tightly and said softly, "So, you missed me." After she nodded, he said, "I know you have questions. You know I can't stay, but I can return again." She gathered herself enough to release him and step back just a small step. He smiled. She loved his sparkling blue eyes.

"I'm so glad you came," she said when she was finally able to say anything, to find the words to welcome her father.

His smile broadened. "The next time I come, I'll have a lot to tell you. I'm learning . . . so much." He shook his head in disbelief. "After all these years, I've become a scholar. And a scribe. I'll bring you notes," he promised. "I can write, though my hand is shakier when it's so big, but when I'm in that form, I hear so many different things. And I'll write it all down." He brushed her hair out of her eyes as they stood eye-to-eye.

"I have to go back," he said. And she nodded again, drinking him in through tear-blurred eyes. He kissed her on the forehead and hugged her one last time. Then he shifted. In trog form, he nodded. She turned around to watch him walk away and found Ott standing at the edge of the partition, his mouth slightly agape at what he'd seen.

Mel brushed away tears and waved her hand at his concerned look. She laughed, scrubbing a hand across her eyes. "You're always in the right place at the right time," she said. "How do you do that?"

She felt his gaze on her, though she wasn't ready to meet his eyes. She saw his feet come into view as she stared at the floor. The scent of him enveloped her. That heady, familiar scent would always intoxicate her. That unshakeable foundation of her being would keep her feet planted on the ground no matter what happened next.

Ott shrugged. He said with a smile, "I'm just lucky, I guess."

ABOUT THE AUTHOR

EM Kaplan has an MFA in Creative Writing from the University of Arizona. She lives in Illinois with her family and her dog.

If you liked UNMASKED, please leave a review on Amazon or Goodreads. Lots of reviews will lead to more stories about Mel and Ott. Thanks!

To see inspiration images for UNMASKED, go to: www.pinterest.com/meilaan/unmasked-the-novel

Visit EM Kaplan online:
www.JustTheEmWords.com
Facebook.com/emkaplan.author
twitter.com/meilaan

Email:
JustTheEmWords@gmail.com

Josie Tucker Mysteries by EM Kaplan:
The Bride Wore Dead
Dim Sum Dead (coming soon)

Made in the USA
Columbia, SC
19 November 2024